THE GREAT AWAK[ENING SERIES]

1740–1741

FIRE

BILL BRIGHT &

JACK CAVANAUGH

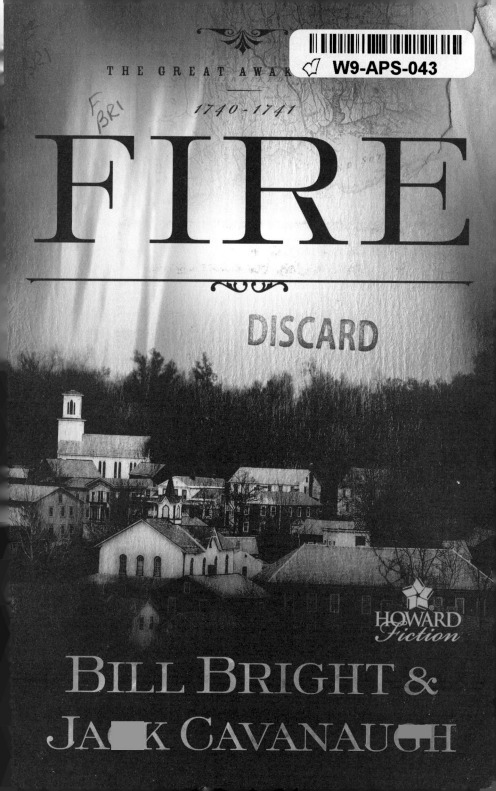

Our purpose at Howard Publishing is to:
- *Increase faith* in the hearts of growing Christians
- *Inspire holiness* in the lives of believers
- *Instill hope* in the hearts of struggling people everywhere

Because He's coming again!

Published by Howard Publishing Co., Inc.
3117 North Seventh Street, West Monroe, Louisiana 71291-2227
www.howardpublishing.com
www.thegreatawakenings.org

05 06 07 08 09 10 11 12 13 14 10 9 8 7 6 5 4 3 2 1

Edited by Ramona Cramer Tucker
Interior design by Tennille Paden
Cover design by Kirk DouPonce, www.DogEaredDesign.com

Library of Congress Cataloging-in-Publication Data

Bright, Bill
Fire / Bill Bright & Jack Cavanaugh.
p. cm. — (The great awakenings, 1740-1741)
ISBN 1-58229-459-3 (trade pbk.)
1. Clergy—Fiction. 2. Great Awakening—Fiction. 3. Connecticut—History—Colonial period, ca. 1600-1775—Fiction. I. Cavanaugh, Jack. II. Title.

PS3552.R4623F57 2005
813'.6—dc22

2005046114

Scripture quotations are taken from The Holy Bible, Authorized King James Version.

DEDICATION

To Jonathan Edwards, George Whitefield,

and all preachers, past and present,

who promote revival from the pulpit

ACKNOWLEDGMENTS

Our heartfelt thanks go to—

Helmut Teichert, for recognizing our mutual passion for national revival and our belief in the power of fiction. If not for Helmut, this book would not have been written, for he brought us together.

Freelance editor Ramona Cramer Tucker, managing editor Philis Boultinghouse, and the other staff at Howard Publishing for their continual encouragement and patience during what proved to be a long and personally difficult journey on this project.

And Steve Laube, loyal friend and agent.

CHAPTER 1

"This is a mistake."

From atop Fiedler's Knob, Josiah Rush surveyed home for the first time in seven years. The granite perch afforded him a sweeping view of the coastal town of Havenhill.

In the harbor below, a pair of merchant ships cozied up to each other. The smaller craft appeared bereft of activity, its masts and yardarms as bare as trees in midwinter. Next to it the larger ship, a snow, good for coastal and short-sea trade, had apparently set anchor a short time ago. Featureless sailors scurried about the rigging, fearlessly hauling in huge canvas sheets. A rowboat waddled its way toward the ship to inspect the recent arrival.

Josiah, throat parched and bone-weary, hitched up the worn leather haversack slung over his shoulder and knocked the mud from his shoes. He stank of five days' journey.

From here the postal road made a gradual descent into the town. Noticeably absent were the cherubim and flaming sword barring him from reentering his personal Eden.

"Would that I were so fortunate," Josiah murmured to himself. "Adam had a mere armed angel with which to contend. I have Eunice Parkhurst."

A familiar wind—moist, tangy, and smelling of spring—leaped the granite ledge. With it came memories of happier days—days of swimming and making sailboats, of flying kites and shooting marbles and exploring creeks.

Josiah winced, stung by nostalgia. He'd anticipated having these feelings, but he'd underestimated their strength. Tears of regret blurred his vision as his gaze jumped from landmark to landmark—First Church, the meetinghouse with its bell tower; the graveyard on the opposite side of the road; the village green; the schoolhouse; the gristmill; Bailey's Tavern.

Nabby's house.

Josiah's heart seized at the sight of the two-story yellow structure. His eyes panged with a seven-year hunger for just a glimpse of her as they searched the residence for movement, a door opening, the brush of a curtain.

If only his first glimpse of her could be from a distance . . . a trial run for his emotions. Maybe then he could keep himself from gawking or mumbling incoherently and generally making a fool of himself when he saw her face-to-face.

But the curtains of the yellow house were still. The doors remained shut. No movement except for two chickens pecking at the muddy ground between the house and the barn.

He would have no morsel of satisfaction today.

With a heavy sigh, Josiah lifted his eyes again to the wharf, the section of town most changed since he had seen it last. The new warehouses were twice the size of the old ones, a tribute to Philip's leadership. All that remained of the original structures was a portion of one wall, jagged, its bricks charred black with soot.

Why would they leave that portion of wall standing? A memorial to the three who died?

Josiah closed his eyes as the screams from that night echoed in his memory. Little girl screams . . .

Mary Usher—seven years old, round brown eyes, always barefoot, the edges of her dress dirty, clutching her straw doll. She was never without that straw doll. Molly, wasn't it?

Kathleen Usher, Mary's older sister by a year. Her face so covered with freckles that some of them merged into oddly shaped brown spots. The thing Josiah remembered most about Kathleen was that she got scolded every Sunday because she couldn't sit still during the sermon.

The third voice of the screaming trio of that horrible night belonged to an adult male, Reverend Parkhurst. He had been the spiritual leader of Havenhill, Josiah's mentor, and the father of Nabby, the only girl Josiah had ever loved.

The townspeople had found the three bodies huddled together. Reverend Parkhurst's arms had been wrapped around the Usher girls, attempting to shield them from the fire with his own body.

A fire Josiah had started . . .

All this pain—three lives lost; his own life ruined; and a town nearly destroyed—because of one senseless, drunken, muddleheaded night! The crazy part about the entire incident was that Josiah had never been drunk before that night, nor had he taken a drink since.

One night. One lousy night.

But lousy nights, no matter how bad, could not be undone. And Josiah could no more change the events of that night than he could take back a misspoken word. That night was history. The town's. His. They would forever be linked by tragedy.

What made him think he could ever convince the town to forgive him?

"This is a mistake," Josiah said again.

He stepped away from the ridge. The postal road offered him a choice. One way descended into Havenhill; the other way led back to Boston, where he wouldn't be reminded every day of his monumental sin.

"Having second thoughts?"

The voice startled him. Josiah swung around to see a man sitting tall on a horse.

"Philip! Back so soon from England?"

"The return winds were favorable."

For only the second time in seven years, Josiah gazed at his oldest and dearest friend. During their encounter in Boston a month ago, Josiah had found it difficult to believe this was the same Philip he'd grown up with. Even now it was hard to catch glimpses of the old Philip behind all the finery and polish.

This Philip appeared sophisticated, a gentleman sitting straight-backed on an exquisite horse. The last time Josiah had seen Philip on a horse, Philip's legs had flailed uncontrollably as he tried to stay atop Deacon Cranch's old field nag that had bolted into the cornfield. Josiah had nearly split his gut laughing, until Deacon Cranch got home and saw the path that had been plowed through his cornfield.

Could the horseman in front of him be this same Philip with his tailored green coat, white silk shirt and stockings, and impressive wig? From this distance Josiah couldn't be certain, but Philip's wig—pulled back and tied with a black ribbon—appeared to be made of human hair. Josiah had never known anyone wealthy enough to own a wig made of anything other than horsehair or yak hair.

"You look like you're having second thoughts," Philip said again.

"It's that obvious?"

Philip dismounted. He'd changed, and it was more than just the clothes. His demeanor, the way he carried himself, was different. Deliberate. Self-assured. Gone was the youthful slouch and impish smirk.

In the old days, they were inseparable. Philip, the prankster; Josiah, the philosopher; and Johnny Mott, the muscle. Oh, the pranks they pulled! And the unforgettable summer days of roughhousing, swimming, lying on the bank next to the water without a care in the world.

"Actually, your indecision is impressive," Philip said. "A sign of maturity. Only a fool would do what you're doing without reservations."

So solemn. So businesslike. As though an unfamiliar adult spirit had taken over the body of his friend.

"You were quite honest about the situation when you approached me in Boston," Josiah replied, matching Philip's tone. "I know it won't be easy, but it's something I want to do."

"Excellent!" Philip cried, allowing himself a smile.

"I want to thank you for standing up for me," Josiah said. "I know the only reason I'm being given this chance is because of you."

Philip's smile widened into one Josiah recognized. A shudder of joy passed through him at the sight of his old friend.

Philip leaned over and said quietly, "'A friend loveth at all times, and a brother is born for adversity.' Isn't that what the Good Book says? Besides, I think everyone deserves a second chance."

"That's all I'm asking."

Philip dismounted. Leading his horse, he inclined his head toward town. "Then let's greet your parishioners, Reverend Rush."

As they walked the postal road into Havenhill, Josiah brushed his nose repeatedly.

"Something wrong?" Philip asked.

Conscious now of what he was doing, Josiah lowered his hands. "It's nothing. Just something I picked up in Boston."

The tickling sensation grew worse. It was all Josiah could do to keep his hands away from his nose. If the pattern held, he knew what was coming next, and it wasn't a sneeze.

On cue, a wave of pleasure swept over him with nausea close on its heels.

Philip stopped and cocked his head in concern. "Are you sure you're all right?"

"It'll pass. I'm fine. Really."

Two years ago, when Josiah had first begun exhibiting these

symptoms, he'd mistaken them for signs of physical ailment. He knew better now. These physical manifestations weren't physical in nature at all. They were spiritual. He also knew what they indicated, and it wasn't good. It wasn't good at all.

As they reached the edge of town, the pain in Josiah's gut doubled him over. It was a sign of what awaited him ahead, not unlike Dante's warning at the gates of hell: "Abandon all hope, ye who enter here."

CHAPTER 2

Sailor George Mason emerged from the belly of the ship with one cask of rum on his shoulder and another under his arm. His head swam with sickness; his muscles felt like they were on fire. He hadn't felt this sick since his first full day at sea. He'd spent that entire day hanging over the railing, wishing he could die.

Now, having completed a voyage to the Caribbean Islands—or the Cribbey Islands, as the sailors called them—and having developed a leather stomach from eating Paddy's food, Mason had thought this kind of twisted-gut torture was a thing of the past. Another wave of nausea assured him otherwise. As he ascended the steps from the hold, his legs felt like cast-iron stumps.

"Step lively there!" Captain Coytmore ordered.

"Aye, Cap'n," Mason spat.

His reply was a reflex. Mason felt no affection or loyalty to his commander. The man was a sadist. Quick with the whip and without an ounce of compassion in him, Captain Coytmore earned every curse, every murderous thought, every bit of ill will the crew wished on him. If ill wishes had weight, the crew's thoughts about their captain would have capsized the ship on the first day out.

With a grunt Mason made the last step up and trudged across the deck. After lowering the two rum casks onto the unloading pallet, he turned back for another load . . . but not without stealing a glance of shoreline and home first.

On the day they had sailed, Mason hadn't cared if he never saw Havenhill again. Now it was all he could think about, and being a couple of hundred yards from shore without being allowed to disembark was torture.

The old salts had warned him it would be this way, just like they'd warned him about Coytmore. They had been right on both counts.

Mason's gaze lingered on the docks, hoping for a glimpse of Peggy Febiger, the woman he'd been courting before he left Havenhill.

The sting of the first mate's whip snatched his attention back to the task at hand.

"The cap'n said to step lively!" he shouted.

The burn of the whip, the nausea, the homesickness—it was almost too much for him. Mason fought his instincts to lash back. It would only land him in the brig and delay his return to shore. And for a man driven by the singular thought of getting off this ship, the thought of any delay was akin to spending avoidable time in purgatory within sight of heaven.

George Mason had a plan.

Get the cargo unloaded.

Get paid.

Get off this ship.

Simple. Direct. Doable. Throttling the first mate or tossing the captain overboard—while undoubtedly satisfying—would only hinder his plan.

Under the watchful eye of the first mate, Mason's next step was dutifully toward the hold. However, the second step strayed without warning. And the third step strayed even farther.

Again Mason felt the first mate's whip, but his flesh didn't register the sting, as though it was mute to pain. And his cast-iron legs no longer seemed able to balance his torso.

His collapse felt slow, as if the air had turned to water. The first mate's curses sounded distant. As his cheek pressed against the wooden planks of the deck, George Mason's last memory aboard ship was a sideways view of the docks of Havenhill.

Never had Josiah's gut ached with such unrelenting intensity. It was all he could do to walk upright. He did his best to hide the pain from Philip as they passed through town.

Through breaks between the buildings, Josiah could see the two ships in the harbor. There was some kind of ruckus on board the larger snow. A crowd had bunched around something on the deck. Before Josiah could see what it was, Gilbert's dry-goods store cut off his view.

"You've gotten fat," Philip said with a playful poke.

Josiah smirked. There was nothing like being ribbed by a friend. He'd missed it. While he'd had other friends at school, none of them ever became as close to him as Philip.

"At Harvard we call it the student body. According to campus lore, an inch of flab is added to your middle automatically upon matriculation."

"They feed you that well?"

"Actually, the food at the college is abysmal. It drives the men to the local taverns. Between tavern food and long hours of book study, the average graduate is ten pounds heavier than when he enrolled. However, I can't blame the taverns. I did this to myself."

"How so?"

"I don't want to tell you. You'll laugh."

"Try me."

Josiah evaluated Philip's expression. Already his friend was primed to laugh.

Josiah told him anyway. "I cook."

Philip didn't disappoint him. His laugh was so loud it caught the attention of everyone on the street.

Josiah laughed with him. "It gets worse." He held out his bare right arm.

Philip examined it. "What am I looking for?"

Josiah held out his left arm for comparison.

"Would you look at that!" Philip cried. "Your right arm has no hair on it!"

"It's called a baker's arm, from checking the temperature of an oven."

Philip guffawed. "Frankly, I'd expected there would be some changes in you after all this time, but I didn't expect to find that Harvard had turned you into a woman! Cooking. Baking. Did they teach you how to give birth too?"

Laughing with Philip lessened the pain in Josiah's gut, even more so as they approached the edge of town. He fortified himself with a deep breath.

The walk through town had been a gauntlet of disapproving glances from doorways, from behind panes of glass, and at times face-to-face from passing travelers. It was obvious he was the target of their glares. Josiah had expected it to be this way. Having Philip at his side had made the passage bearable.

"By the way," Philip said, "Johnny sends his apologies. He wanted to be here to greet you, but the *Nightingale* returned three days late, and he doesn't trust anyone else to oversee the unloading."

"Understandable," Josiah said, glancing in the direction of the harbor. Trees obstructed his view of the ship.

While Josiah, Johnny, and Philip had been a team during their school years, Johnny had been something of an addition. Josiah and Philip had been friends for years before Johnny moved to Havenhill, and Josiah's affections for him had never been as deep as they were for Philip.

The travelers came to the crossroads at Summit Street. Josiah slowed. Philip continued walking.

"I know I've been gone for seven years," Josiah said. "But isn't the old Gleason farm up this way?"

Philip gave a sly grin. "Change of plans. You're not moving into the Gleason place. This way."

Intrigued, Josiah followed his friend straight through the intersection. Philip had something up his sleeve and a smirk on his face.

"Well, are you going to tell me?" Josiah asked.

"You'll see soon enough."

"Get that laggard off my ship!" a harsh voice demanded.

George Mason could feel bodies close in around him like gathering storm clouds, blocking the sun. Someone had turned him over. He was on his back.

He couldn't see the captain, but there was no mistaking his voice. Mason had grown to loathe the sound of it.

"Goodwin, grab that man's legs. Tolliver, get his arms. Throw him in the hold or throw him overboard—it matters not to me. Just get him off my deck."

His senses rallying, George Mason opened his eyes just as the crowd of bystanders backed away. The sun hammered his eyes. Mason's arm rose to block it. He felt his legs being lifted while, at the same time, a pair of hands hooked under his arms, lifting him off the deck.

He struggled, afraid he was about to be thrown overboard. His struggle was ineffective. Whatever had struck him down had also drained him of his strength.

"Move it! Move it! Move it!" the captain shouted.

Mason's mind shouted in protest, but his mouth did a poor job expressing it. He managed barely a mumble.

"The rest of you! Get those casks on deck," Captain Coytmore ordered. "And the next sailor who feigns sickness will get a good taste of Mr. Whitlock's whip!"

George Mason, a fellow tar on the voyage until now, had been suddenly demoted to cargo status. He sensed the deck slipping beneath him as the crew unloaded him. The method of his unloading was soon to be seen.

"Hold!"

From months on ship, Mason thought he knew every voice on board. But this one was new to him. It was deep, and though the man uttered only a single word, it rang with authority. The men carrying Mason slowed to a stop.

"What's wrong with this man?"

Mason tried to open his eyes, battling the brightness of the sun and the sharp blue sky. A broad-shouldered silhouette of a man came into view.

"Answer me! What's wrong with this man?"

"Dunno, sir," Tolliver answered. "'e collapsed, jus' like that."

The silhouette hovered. "This man's sick. Where's the ship's physician?"

"Bes' we got is Paddy," Tolliver offered. "'e's the cook."

"The bloke's a laggard, nothing more, Mr. Mott," the captain insisted. "No need to concern yourself with the likes of him."

"What kind of a fool statement is that?" Mott said. "The man's obviously sick. Is he local?"

The captain didn't answer. Mason knew why. The captain didn't know the answer.

"Well, is he?" Mott shouted.

"Yes, sir," Tolliver answered for the captain.

"Then get him home. My carriage is on the dock. Summon a physician, then get back here and get this cargo unloaded."

"Yes, sir, Mr. Mott, sir," Tolliver said.

Mason felt himself on the move again. He tried to thank Mr. Mott, but his lips still weren't working. He blacked out just as they were lowering him over the side of the ship.

Philip's conspiratorial grin and refusal to tell Josiah where they were headed got him thinking about another time when a new preacher had arrived in Havenhill . . .

Josiah had been six years old when Reverend Nathaniel Parkhurst was called as pastor of First Church, Havenhill. The coming of the Parkhurst family had been a day of celebration. The whole town—it was smaller then—turned out. They assembled in front of the yellow two-story house that became the Parkhurst residence. Everyone brought a gift—prepared food dishes, quilts, flour, preserves, corn, and chickens. On behalf of the deacons, Elias Cranch presented the Parkhurst family with a hog. The day the Parkhursts arrived was like a holiday.

Josiah remembered it well. It was one of those events in his young life from which so many other events branched.

Within two months of Reverend Parkhurst's arrival, Josiah's father was killed in a skirmish with Indians over hunting rights. His mother died three months later from consumption. It was Reverend Parkhurst who arranged for Josiah to live with Deacon Elias Cranch, a widower who had no children.

Parkhurst and Cranch shared the yoke of Josiah's upbringing equally, assisted by an unofficial committee of mothers. As a result, Josiah grew up as the town's favorite son. Deacon Cranch taught him hard work. Reverend Parkhurst provided him with a moral compass and a daughter Josiah's age to fall in love with . . .

And now Josiah Rush was the newly arriving preacher.

While Josiah didn't expect a similar reception, Philip's behavior suggested that something was in the works. Given the circumstances, Josiah would welcome even the slightest encouragement.

"Have you guessed yet?" Philip asked.

They were certainly in familiar territory. This was where Josiah had grown up. From here he could see the oak that marked the turnoff to . . .

"You're kidding!" Josiah exclaimed, awestruck.

Philip grinned. "I bought it from Deacon Cranch's estate when he died."

"That was two years ago!"

"Something told me you'd be coming back someday."

"Philip . . . I don't know what to say!"

"We'll work out the terms after you get settled."

Josiah beamed. His arms flapped helplessly at his sides, needing to hug someone but not wanting to make a spectacle of himself.

"It's perfect!" he cried. "Now I really am coming home! Philip, thank you. I can't tell you how much this means to me. Not only the house but the chance to redeem myself with the town. A man couldn't have a better friend."

"My motives aren't entirely unselfish," Philip replied. "The town needs you right now. I orchestrated your calling, because you're the perfect man for the job. Now let's get you settled. The house has been vacant for nearly two months. It's going to need a little work." He cringed. "The last tenant was a clerk and his family. He didn't keep his books any neater than he kept the house."

Emotion blurred Josiah's eyes to the disrepair. He couldn't help himself. He threw his arms around his friend. "God bless you, Philip Clapp."

Josiah's sudden movement startled the horse.

Philip stiffened, looking embarrassed. "Yes, well, as I said before, a brother is born for adversity. Shall we continue on, or do you want to hug some more?"

Josiah released him.

They walked to the familiar turnoff and headed toward the old Cranch homestead. A short distance off the main road, they crested a small rise, and the saltbox structure came into view.

Both men stopped abruptly.

Josiah heard Philip's sharp intake of breath.

"Oh, Josiah, I'm sorry."

Josiah said nothing. He continued toward the house, though with less enthusiasm. He'd expected a surprise and that indeed is what awaited him.

The house in which he'd been raised dominated a clearing, as it had for decades. There was a modest barn behind it and a cornfield to one side.

"I guess the surprise is that it's standing at all," Josiah reflected.

The old house was intact, but the doors and windows were missing, and blood was splattered all over the exterior walls.

The source of the blood was not a mystery. Three lifeless chickens lay on the ground as a reminder of his sin.

Philip's fists clenched. "We'll find out who did this."

Josiah swallowed hard. "No. Don't mention it to anyone."

"But we can't have—"

"I knew my return would provoke hostile feelings. Responding with more hostile feelings will only do more harm than good."

"Josiah, I just can't stand by and let—"

"Please, Philip, respect my wishes in this."

They walked between the carcasses to the front door. Inside, on the wall, a squirrel had been nailed to the wall. Beneath it, in blood, were the words

BABY KILLER

That night, bundled in blankets and seated on the floor next to the blazing hearth of his doorless, windowless house, Josiah Rush wrote in his journal:

> *Arrived in Havenhill. Met by my good and faithful friend, Philip Clapp. Our reunion was a happy one. The man is a saint. On his own initiative, he secured the old Cranch homestead for me as a residence.*
>
> *I am eager to start my ministry here.*

CHAPTER 3

Two days separated Josiah from his arrival in Havenhill and the first Sabbath day. He spent them making his house habitable—installing windows and two doors, front and back.

Philip had arranged for the delivery of the items, along with two skilled servants to assist Josiah with the construction. Philip had sent his condolences that he couldn't lend a hand himself; he had pressing business to attend to. No one from the town came by or offered to help.

In a way, Josiah was grateful for the destructive work of his personal vandals. It forced him to acquaint himself with the house in ways he wouldn't have done otherwise.

He found it in excellent shape, a testimony to Elias Cranch. The one-story structure was as solid as the man who built it.

Set on a foundation of stone, the house had painted clapboard siding and a long, sloping, wooden-shingle roof upon which the fireplace chimney took prominent center place. The rear lean-to addition, which gave the house its saltbox shape, had been added when Josiah first came to live with Cranch. What had once been his bedroom had been divided into a pantry and cozy sitting area with table and chairs. In the morning, sunlight from the corner windows warmed the room. Here, Josiah placed his writing kit on a small table. He thought it would be the perfect place for his morning Bible reading and prayers.

On the afternoon of the second day, he sent Philip's servants home early. They protested that their master would not be pleased that they'd returned before the work was finished. Josiah assured them that he'd make certain Philip would be informed their return was at Josiah's request. All but one of the windows had been installed, and there was still some blood on the northern exterior.

Josiah wanted to be alone. He was feeling nervous about his first sermon and wanted to prepare. Finding his leather haversack, he extracted three worn pages and a piece of dried meat. He pulled a straight-backed chair close to the fire. His furniture consisted of a table and two chairs that had been in the house when he'd arrived. They were heavily scarred but sturdy.

Unaccustomed to the manual labor of the last two days, Josiah eased himself into one of the chairs. He groaned. His muscles ached, and his hands felt thick and sore. Still, it was a good kind of pain—the kind that signaled accomplishment.

Taking a bite from the strip of meat, Josiah surveyed his notes. The structure of the sermon, the sequence of logic, the underlying Scripture passage rose from the page readily. The gestation period for this particular sermon had been a long one. He'd labored over it for the five days that he'd walked from Boston to Havenhill. Tomorrow morning he would give birth to it. And, like all births, there was risk and uncertainty and an element of fear.

Unable to sit still, Josiah got up to pace. He chewed. He read. He formed and re-formed phrases in his mind. When the meat was gone, he tried some of the phrases aloud. Bouncing off his close quarters, his voice sounded strong. Confident. More confident than he felt.

After two hours of pacing, he had to get out of the house. The fire was too hot. The walls were too close. The approaching hour was too near. As he closed the newly installed door behind him, he told himself he wasn't running. He was thinking. Clearing his head. But his words were hollow, void of genuine conviction.

The night air wasn't so far removed from winter that it had forgotten how to slap a person's cheeks red. Josiah's step was brisk as he passed the oak and turned left onto High Street, going nowhere in particular.

His nose led him to Water Street, where he walked along the wharf, keeping to the shadows. He avoided contact with people. This was thinking time, not greeting and chatting time.

At Church Street he turned uptown and didn't slow until he reached the common. A heavy solemnity, thick as fog, blanketed him as he stood for a moment between the church and the graveyard, where Reverend Parkhurst and Kathleen and Mary Usher were buried.

Turning to the church, Josiah climbed the steps to the front door, mindful that he did so for the first time as the pastor. How many times had he and Philip and Johnny bolted down these steps on a sunny, warm day, eager to shed their Sunday clothes and jump into the river?

It was on these steps that he'd first held Nabby's hand on a sultry summer night while Reverend and Mrs. Parkhurst and Deacon Cranch had talked over church business. It had something to do with delivering food to a family in need, if he remembered correctly. At the time, Josiah's thoughts had focused solely on his own needs—the need to feel Nabby's hand in his.

Josiah normally considered Deacon Cranch's long-winded conversations a nuisance. However, on that particular night, the lengthy talk was a blessing. It had taken Josiah a good ten minutes to work up the courage to touch Nabby's hand. He had expected her to pull away, but she didn't. In fact, her hand sought his, as eager to be touched as his was to touch . . .

Josiah shook his head to clear it of the sweet memory. So much had changed since then.

Now his solitary footsteps echoed across the common. He reached for the door. It was locked.

Odd. Why would anyone lock a church door?

He tried again, thinking perhaps the door was simply swollen from the spring rains. But it wasn't. It was locked.

Josiah circled the building until he found a window that wasn't latched. Hoisting himself up, balancing his student-body bulge on the sill, he managed to swing one leg up and fall into the sanctuary. It was a rather clumsy and unceremonial entrance for the pastor of the church to make. He was glad no one was there to see it.

Breathing heavily from the exertion, his knee complaining because he'd banged it against the sill, Josiah waited for his eyes to adjust to darkness. Once he had his bearings, he made his way to the front of the church and stood behind Reverend Parkhurst's pulpit.

He didn't feel it was his pulpit yet. In fact, he was very much aware of the possibility that it might *never* be his pulpit. The next few months would determine that, wouldn't they?

A wave of uncertainty swept over him. He must have been out of his mind to agree to come back here. What was he thinking? Tomorrow this sanctuary would be filled with families coming to worship God, and who would they find in their pulpit? The arsonist who had killed their spiritual leader and nearly destroyed their town.

A repentant arsonist, yes. A humbled sinner, yes. A man who would willingly exchange places with the three who resided now in the graveyard if such a thing were possible. But was it enough?

Josiah sank to his knees, his hands slipping down the sides of the pulpit. He felt as though he were slipping into a morass reserved for those who didn't deserve to be forgiven . . . who for all of eternity would be linked to their sin.

"God, I know with certainty that You have forgiven me," he cried, "but the pains of the people I've injured press upon me with a fearful weight. How can I continue on if they refuse to forgive me? How can I minister to a people I have hurt so terribly?"

For an hour he lay at the foot of the pulpit, calling out to God for help.

Then, rising, he moved from pew to pew, praying for the people who would sit in them come morning.

The question had plagued Josiah ever since Philip approached him in Boston. What does one preach to a people after nearly burning down their town?

Matthew 6:14–15 came to mind: "For if ye forgive men their trespasses, your heavenly Father will also forgive you: But if ye forgive not men their trespasses, neither will your Father forgive your trespasses."

So did Matthew 18:21–22: "Then came Peter to him, and said, Lord, how oft shall my brother sin against me, and I forgive him? till seven times? Jesus saith unto him, I say not unto thee, Until seven times: but, Until seventy times seven."

But such topics seemed self-serving. Josiah wanted something that adequately reflected his remorse. He had considered the passage in Second Corinthians about the burden of excessive sorrow: "But if any have caused grief . . . sufficient to such a man is this punishment, which was inflicted of many. So that contrariwise ye ought rather to forgive him, and comfort him, lest perhaps such a one should be swallowed up with overmuch sorrow."

He had to say something about the fire, didn't he? About his heartfelt sorrow for the deaths? To enter the pulpit and preach as though it had never happened—say, for example, a stewardship sermon on the widow's mite—would be equally wrong, wouldn't it?

The week before his scheduled return, Josiah had finally felt led to an approach he thought suitable. He'd prayed over it and tested it for the five days of his journey from Boston to Havenhill. At the time, he had felt confident it was of God.

Now, on the morning he was to deliver the sermon, Josiah wasn't so sure.

He sat in the pastor's chair that was situated at a right angle to the congregation. Keeping his eyes forward, he heard rather than saw the congregation enter the church. They left their laughter at the door, exchanging it for whispers. Several times he heard his name but couldn't make out what was said about him. He gripped the wooden armrests and forced himself to pray.

A tickling sensation swept across his nose. It felt like a spider web. He brushed it away, trying to keep his mind on his prayer. Then a sweetness filled his mouth, followed by the familiar twisting in his gut. For two days the sensation had let up. Now it came on as strong as the day he'd entered town.

His breathing quickened, and he began to perspire just as it was time to begin the service.

As planned, the deacons took charge. The way Philip explained it to Josiah, the deacons saw this as their final act in the process that called him as pastor. It was appropriate that Philip would be the one to take the platform, since he had nearly single-handedly orchestrated Josiah's call against significant opposition. Josiah felt comfortable following his lead.

"Let the congregation's initial impression be your first sermon," Philip had suggested.

Josiah agreed, though it increased the pressure to deliver a good sermon.

From the platform, he fought the urge to look at his congregation as prayer was offered, the Scriptures were read, and they sang a hymn from the *Bay Psalm Book*. He didn't know why he couldn't look at the people's faces. Maybe he was afraid his face would give away the pain in his gut. Maybe it was because Reverend Parkhurst always kept his eyes straight forward during the singing. Josiah remembered his mentor sometimes singing and sometimes muttering silent prayers or fussing with his sermon notes.

As the congregation sang, Josiah did his fair share of fussing, working himself into a panic over the sermon topic. At one point he began flipping through the Bible frantically, trying to piece together a sermon he'd preached in Boston on the evils of the sluggard.

Then the singing ended, and Philip offered a prayer.

The time for the sermon arrived.

Josiah remained sitting.

Philip returned to the deacon's pew, and still Josiah sat.

The congregation stirred. A cough was heard. Throats were cleared.

And still he sat, paralyzed by the pain in his gut. Invisible hands squeezed his throat. His heart hammered in a chest that felt like it was made of brick.

From the front row, Philip leaned forward. "Pastor . . ."

Josiah stood. He didn't know how he did it, he just did. Turning stiffly toward the congregation, he stood awkwardly in Reverend Parkhurst's pulpit. He kept his head down, careful not to look at the congregation, fearful that he would be distracted and forget what he intended to say.

"The life of Sa—" he croaked. Bowing his head, closing his eyes, Josiah cleared his throat and began again. "The life of Saul of Tarsus is the story of a man redeemed."

Instinctively, he lifted his head. His mind on the sermon, he momentarily forgot the warning he'd just given himself. By the time he realized what he'd done, it was too late.

Seven deacons met his gaze. They all wore the same dour expression, as though someone had handed it out at the door.

Johnny Mott sat among them. Josiah hadn't seen Johnny in seven years. He'd aged. His face, weathered and lined, appeared more like forty years of age instead of twenty-six. His shoulders were still as wide as Josiah remembered them. They took up the space of two men, forcing the deacons on either side of him to sit at an angle.

"Um," Josiah said, trying to recover, "redemption is a prominent theme throughout Scripture. In fact, it . . . has come to symbolize the essence of Christianity."

He blinked as sweat trickled into his eyes and blurred his notes. He wiped the sweat away with his hand.

"The first references to redemption in the Bible have to do with property, as money was exchanged to purchase back a piece of property previously owned.

"Later the term was used to describe our salvation in Christ. Think of it as a ransom. Christ redeemed our sinful lives through an exchange; His sinless life paid the debt of our sin. But there is a third aspect of redemption in the Bible. One that has to do with relationships. It is this third aspect that is our topic today."

Josiah settled into the preaching task. He had found that the first few minutes behind a pulpit were always unnerving, but once he got going, he would begin to feel more comfortable, more confident. He felt that confidence now, that flow of thought and expression. Enough to risk eye contact with his congregation.

Nabby.

Hers was the first face he saw.

It was nearly his undoing.

In a word, she was stunning. She sat erect, her hands folded in her lap, adorned in a blue and white dress trimmed tastefully with white lace. The brim of a straw hat highlighted the coal black hair that hung in perfect curls to her shoulders.

But the dress, the hat, the curls were little more than a frame for her eyes—glistening blue orbs that flashed playfully when they met his gaze, then darted away.

Josiah not only lost his place in the sermon, he lost his place in time. In that instant he was in a hundred places at once—every place he had ever been when he'd looked into those eyes.

His reverie lasted but a moment or two, but it was enough for the deacons to crane their necks to see who or what had distracted the preacher.

Nor was the object of his distraction lost on Mrs. Parkhurst. Seated beside Nabby, her back ramrod straight, she scowled disapprovingly.

"Our t . . . topic," Josiah stammered, "is Paul . . . actually Saul at first, then later, Paul . . . and redemption . . ." It was no use. His thoughts had scattered like papers in the March wind.

The Emerson girls tittered at his distress, earning glares from their father.

Josiah tried again. "The apostle's life is a story of redemption. Three . . . incidents in his life in particular demonstrate our point."

By now he'd stared at his notes long enough that, gratefully, they began to look familiar to him again. He took a deep breath, silently berating himself for allowing himself to be distracted.

"We find the first in the book of Acts, chapter eight, verse one," he announced with authority. "The incident is the stoning of Stephen, shortly after he had preached the gospel message to the collected Sanhedrin. The uproar was such that they took him out and stoned him. We read, 'And Saul was consenting unto his death.'

"Stephen's martyrdom launched a wave of intense persecution against the early believers. The Bible records that this man, Saul, went from house to house, dragging Christians, men and women alike, to prison. His intent was to destroy the fledgling church."

Josiah took another bracing breath. "The second incident in our study of redemption is a familiar one indeed. In Acts chapter nine, verse three, we read the following account of Saul, who is on his way to a neighboring city to arrest more Christians: 'And as he journeyed, he came near Damascus: and suddenly there shined round about him a light from heaven: And he fell to the earth, and heard a voice saying unto him, Saul, Saul, why persecutest thou me?'

"This, of course, is the turning point for Saul of Tarsus, when he encounters Christ and is converted.

"The third incident of his redemptive life occurs in the same chapter, beginning with verse twenty-six:

> "And when Saul was come to Jerusalem, he assayed to join himself to the disciples: but they were all afraid of him, and believed not that he was a disciple. But Barnabas took him, and brought him to the apostles, and declared unto them how he had seen the Lord in the way, and that he had spoken to him, and how he had preached boldly at Damascus in the name of Jesus. And he was with them coming in and going out at Jerusalem."

Josiah dared a glance at his congregation. But he carefully avoided looking in Nabby's direction, lest he be distracted again.

"Three incidents," he said. "The first, Saul at his worst. Then, Saul's salvation encounter with the Lord Jesus. And finally, Saul returning to Jerusalem, 'coming in and going out' with the very Christians he once persecuted."

Josiah paused for effect. "I wonder what it was like for them to be coming in and going out with a murderer in their midst. That's not too strong a statement, is it? He was a murderer—or at least an accomplice to murder. The fact that he'd been converted on the road to Damascus didn't change the fact that he was the reason many of their number were still in prison. The fact that Saul was now preaching Christ did not bring Stephen back from the dead. I wonder . . . What was it like for the Christians of Jerusalem to go in and come out of their city with a murderer?"

The sanctuary was as quiet as a tomb.

Until now Josiah had not seen Judith Usher, the mother of the two girls who had died in the fire. But his remarks had prompted glances that pointed him to her. She sat in the back of the church with her son, Edward—her only surviving child—next to her. *How the boy had grown*, Josiah thought. He had been only five at the time of his sisters' deaths.

His eyes lingered on Judith Usher. Her head was bowed. She didn't look at him. Josiah couldn't blame her.

"And I wonder," he continued, "what Saul said to Stephen's mother. Surely at some point in his comings and goings in Jerusalem, he encountered her, didn't he? What did he say to her? What does a man say to a woman when he is responsible for the death of that woman's child?"

Again Josiah paused. This time it was not for effect, but to manage his rising tide of emotions.

"Personally, I wish his encounter had been recorded. It's a selfish wish, I know. But I'm certain his words would be better than anything I can think to say.

"However, I can reflect on how Saul must have felt and what he must have thought in anticipation of such an encounter. This is something for which, to my shame, I am uniquely qualified.

"No amount of sorrow can raise the dead. No words are adequate to the occasion. The only recourse a man in this position has is to hope that his life and actions will—in time—be sufficient to prove the change that God has wrought in the man's heart. In short, the belief in redemption is such a man's only hope—that a life once worthless has been restored to value.

"Redemption implies satisfaction on both sides of the transaction. In a property sale, money is paid, and both seller and buyer are satisfied. In salvation, mankind is redeemed and both the Law Giver and the transgressor are satisfied. Can we hope for anything less when relationships are redeemed?"

Abandoning his notes so that he could speak completely from his heart, as God was leading him, Josiah stepped to the side of the pulpit. He presented himself to his congregation.

"My hope, my prayer for us as pastor and people, rests on the promise of God's ability to redeem our situation—to take something that has lost its value and make it valuable again, to everyone's satisfaction.

"I do not believe that my hope is in vain. For it does not rest on my ability or on your ability, but on *God's* ability.

"God will not erase the pain of the past. That would be too easy. Instead, God does what others would deem impossible. He uses yesterday's pain to build a better tomorrow.

"Do you think it coincidence that God would choose Paul to convey to all mankind one of the greatest promises of hope in all Scripture? I quote: 'And we know that all things work together for good to them that love God, to them who are the called according to his purpose.'"

CHAPTER 4

Following the second service of the Sabbath, Josiah watched helplessly as Nabby disappeared out the door on her mother's arm. He was hoping to talk to her, but James Dunmore, one of the deacons, cornered him about what he called the sad state of repair work being done to the church. For ten minutes Dunmore elaborated on floorboards that were warped and needed replacing, a roof that leaked and caused water damage to walls, and windows that were swollen shut and wouldn't open or close. From his impassioned tone, a person would get the impression that at any given moment, simultaneous sneezes would bring the entire building down.

Waiting in queue behind Dunmore was an equally impassioned Mary Bollman, who railed for several minutes over young people's lack of respect for their elders. Then Ezra Lee complained that the west side of the sanctuary was too cold. Betsy Walker complained that the east side of the sanctuary—the side with the morning sun—was too hot. Then George Carr complained that there were too many complainers in the church and that people didn't spend enough time rejoicing in their salvation. Of course, he had several suggestions of how the pastor could make the people more joyful.

When the last naysayers had left, Philip asked with a grin, "Do you feel like a pastor yet?"

It was just the two of them as they closed the last door of the building and wandered into the sun and onto the village green. Josiah walked with his Bible tucked under his arm. With a wave of his hand, Philip signaled the driver of his open coach to wait.

"Both sermons were good," Philip said. "Especially the first one. Stephen's mother. Interesting observation. I think it hit home."

They walked in stride onto the grassy expanse around which the town was built. Josiah was beginning to feel the effects from the combined exertion and nervous tension of two sermons. He felt tired, but he was also pleased with the way the morning had gone. The pain in his gut had not gone away, but he'd found that, when preaching, he could pretty much ignore it.

"The people were guarded, but that's to be expected," Philip continued.

"Guarded." An understatement, Josiah mused. But it was certainly an improvement over nailing dead animals to his walls and stealing his doors and windows.

"Is Johnny going to join us?" Josiah asked.

"He usually gives Widow Delor a ride to and from church. After that . . . well, I really can't tell you what Johnny does with his Sunday afternoons."

"It's just that I've been home since Thursday and have yet to talk to him."

Philip stared down at the grass and didn't reply.

The Buckman family walked by. Philip and Josiah waved. No pleasantries were exchanged, this being the Sabbath. Everyone passed from location to location only out of necessity and then in solemn reverence and dignity.

"Is George Buckman still the smithy?"

Philip nodded. "Only one in town." He turned and hailed his coachman with an uplifted hand. "Can I give you a ride home?"

Josiah shook his head. "I think I'll just wander the streets for a while. Show my face. Give people something to gossip about, that sort of thing."

The coach arrived and Philip climbed in. "Anybody in particular?"

Josiah grinned sheepishly. "Oh, I don't know. Thought I might wander over to the Parkhursts and give Eunice a chance to throw me out."

He meant it as a jest, but Philip wasn't smiling.

"Do you really think that's a good idea?" Philip asked, anxiety creasing his brow.

"I can't avoid her forever," Josiah replied.

"Her—Eunice or Abigail?"

Josiah was the only one to call her Nabby.

When he didn't answer, Philip sat back in his seat and stared into the distance. His disapproval was obvious. "I just hate to see you complicate such a promising start on your first Sabbath as the preacher."

Josiah's ire rose, but he tried not to let it show. "I fail to see how a visit to the Parkhursts will scuttle any progress that might have been made today."

Philip appeared to mull over Josiah's statement for a moment. Then he blurted out, "You fail to see it—"

Silence enveloped both men.

A questioning expression overtook Philip's countenance. "Unless you don't know."

"Unless I don't know what?" Josiah asked, puzzled.

"About Abigail."

"What about Abigail?"

Philip studied him carefully. "About Abigail and Johnny . . ."

The two names linked by the most common of conjunctions fashioned an effective harpoon, piercing Josiah's romantic dreams with a single mortal blow. He didn't need to hear any more.

Philip completed his sentence anyway. "The wedding is planned for next spring. I'm certain they'll be asking you, as the new pastor, to perform the service."

Josiah steadied himself with a hand on the wheel of the coach. "No . . . I didn't know," he said softly.

"Johnny couldn't be happier. It's really quite funny. He keeps saying, 'Now I know there is a God.'" Philip laughed.

Josiah half-chuckled, and that was hard.

"Well, that explains it," Philip concluded merrily. "If you didn't know, of course, you'd see no reason why you shouldn't make a call on Abigail. But now that you know, I didn't think you'd do something like that to Johnny. You're too good of a friend for that."

"Yeah," Josiah muttered. "I wouldn't want to do anything to come between Nab—I mean, Abigail—and Johnny."

"Well, I must be off. Sure I can't give you a ride?"

"No. I think I'll just wander around here for a while. Thanks, anyway."

Josiah stepped back, expecting Philip to order his driver to proceed. When the carriage didn't move, Josiah looked up into the face of a grinning Philip Clapp.

"What a day this is!" he said enthusiastically. "You, the pastor of First Church. Johnny and I deacons and selectmen. Not too shabby for Parkhurst's boys, wouldn't you say?"

"He always told us we were the sons he never had," Josiah replied.

That night a blaze broke out on the wharf. It was the first one on the docks in seven years. A section of one warehouse suffered significant damage, and a shipment of fur pelts was ruined by the smoke and flames and water. Fortunately, Johnny Mott happened to be passing by and saw the flames. He managed to muster enough men in time to put the fire out before it spread to the other warehouses.

The cause of the fire was suspicious.

CHAPTER 5

Hearing of Nabby's impending marriage to Johnny Mott devastated me. So much so, I found it impossible to pen an entry in my journal last night. Even now, a day later, my hand shakes as I write.

For one thing, I'm angry at myself over how deeply I'm affected by the news. I told myself repeatedly that I wasn't returning to Havenhill for Nabby. And until yesterday, I succeeded in convincing myself of the truth of that statement. However, upon hearing the news, my emotions reveal me for the fraud that I am. I can't say for certain that had I known Nabby was promised in marriage to another, my decision to return would have been different. But I know I would not have returned so readily.

Then there was the suddenness of the news. A bolt of lightning could not have struck more quickly or with greater pain.

The news is not without its perplexing aspects—Johnny Mott? The two were never close. Even now I am unable to picture them together.

Abigail Parkhurst and Johnny Mott?

Inconceivable!

I will forever remember yesterday's Sabbath day as one that began with promise and ended in twin tragedies. First, the news concerning Nabby; then, later, the fire at the dock. Thank God the damage to

property was limited. As for the damage to me, time will tell.

This morning Philip and Deacon Dunmore stopped by to inform me of the fire, though I'd smelled the burnt wood in the air the moment I stepped outside. It became obvious to me that Philip and Dunmore's visit was not solely to deliver news. While their inquiry into my evening activities was discreet, their distress was obvious when I informed them I was home alone at the time of the fire. Considering the fact that the fire was obviously set and my past history with the town, I can't blame them for having their suspicions.

On Wednesday morning as Josiah was praying, he thought he heard a light tapping on his door. When he opened it to check, he found a skinny little girl wearing a mobcap and holding a paper in her hand. She didn't look up at him.

"Reverend Rush—" She held out the folded paper, still without looking at him.

"Thank you. And what is your name?" He took what was offered him.

The instant the paper left the girl's fingers, she was off and running.

Josiah called after her. "Should you wait for a response? Who's this from?"

But the girl wasn't listening. Her feet were a blur beneath a swishing dress.

Standing on the threshold, Josiah unfolded the paper. The penmanship was very feminine.

The Mason family needs a visit.
Goodwife Parkhurst

Josiah looked up at the rapidly retreating servant. He couldn't help but smile at the thought that Eunice Parkhurst was still very much the center of church activity. How many times in the past had she directed the activity of her husband, the pastor?

Grabbing his hat and coat, Josiah set off at a brisk pace to make his first pastoral visit.

From what Josiah could remember, the Masons lived on the fringe of town, geographically, socially, and spiritually. He could remember only one time when the family had attended a church service—a Christmas Sunday many years ago.

Josiah had gone to school with Jabez, the oldest of the Mason boys. Jabez was a year younger than Josiah. Josiah remembered him as a thick-headed, surly boy who got into a number of scrapes. If Josiah remembered right, Jabez had a sister and brother who were much younger.

As Josiah approached the house, he walked a heavily rutted road that threatened to turn an ankle with every step. The fields on either side were littered with trash. Even from a distance, the house appeared to be in disrepair. The wood was weathered black, and the roof sagged.

Josiah heard anguished female wailing coming from within as he avoided a broken and splintered step. It took two knocks—the second attempt louder than the first—to get a response.

Heavy stomping, shouting, and a string of curses preceded the opening of the door. "I told you I'd kill you if you ever—"

The threat went unfinished.

Josiah thought he recognized Jabez behind the thick bush of facial hair. The man's clothes were threadbare and soiled. Despite the morning chill, the man was barefoot. In his right hand, he gripped an ax.

"You! I heard they was lettin' you back in town. We got no use for the likes of you."

Jabez looked as mean as Josiah remembered him, only bigger. The ax might also have enhanced the man's stature, Josiah thought. That, and the fact that he felt woefully inadequate to the situation. He couldn't recall any of the Harvard lectures instructing him on the subject of pastoral visits to ax-wielding homesteaders.

Josiah cleared his throat. "It's come to my attention that your family might need a pastoral visit."

"It's come to your attention, has it?" Jabez mocked. A step forward closed the distance between them.

"Um . . . yes . . . yes, it has."

"Someone been talkin' about us? Who?"

Josiah took a step back. Not a big step, but enough of one that he felt a bit safer. But only a bit. "It's not so much that they've been talking about you, but that they're concerned for you."

Behind Jabez the wailing rose to a crescendo. Turning and shaking the ax in the direction of the noise, he shouted at the woman to shut up.

"I'll give you real money to cart her off!" he told Josiah.

"Your wife?" Josiah asked.

"Wife? Nah, that's my sister, Phoebe."

Josiah leaned to one side to look past the brawny Jabez, but the room was too dark for him to see anything inside.

"I'd be willing to talk to her. Maybe I can help," Josiah suggested.

"Would be a waste of time. She's just wailin' 'cause John slapped her face."

"Her husband? He hit her?"

"She deserved it," Jabez announced matter of factly.

"You're the one what deserves a good poke in the eye and more, Jabez Mason!" his sister shouted behind him.

Jabez swung around, raising the ax. "You shut your mouth, Phoebe! We got company!"

Alarmed, Josiah placed a restraining hand on Jabez's raised arm.

Jabez shrugged it off, then lowered the ax. "I swear, someday she's gonna push a man too far!"

When Jabez let the ax fall to his side, Josiah breathed easier. He was grateful his first pastoral visit wasn't going to be bloody.

"Back here." Jabez motioned for Josiah to follow. "You can talk to my younger brother. He's probably what them old hens in town are jawin' about. Took sick aboard ship."

"The snow in the harbor?"

"That be the one. Just got back from the Cribbey Islands. Georgie's first trip. Musta caught whatever he's got down there."

As Josiah removed his hat and stepped across the threshold, the wooden floor moaned. *A warning?* He couldn't help but wonder.

When Josiah started to close the door, Jabez told him to leave it open.

Even with the open door, the interior of the house was fairly dark. A heavy, rancid odor dominated the room. Jabez kicked clothes and jars and farm tools out of his way as he made a path.

In the corner, two women came into view. They sat on a broken-down sofa that leaned to one side. The younger woman was twice the size of the older woman who was comforting her. When Josiah reached them, he noted that the two shared a family resemblance—tangled brown hair and mournful eyes.

"Ma, this here's Josiah Rush. You remember him, don't ya?"

"Mrs. Mason." Josiah gave a nod.

"The fire starter?" she asked.

Jabez chuckled. "Aya. That be him. We finally got us a preacher as bad as the rest of us. I kinda like it."

Josiah locked eyes with Phoebe. Her face was tear stained and flushed. She glared at him with murderous eyes, though Josiah didn't know what he'd done to deserve her wrath.

"This way," Jabez said to Josiah.

"Keep an eye on him!" Mrs. Mason called after them.

Josiah didn't know if she was warning Jabez about him, or him about Jabez.

If the word *squalor* in the dictionary had a picture next to it, it would have been a picture of the Mason home. The deeper they went into the house, the darker and grimier it got. They passed one room that had its door knocked cockeyed, its lower hinge busted. Broken tools, soiled clothing, and trash were thrown everywhere—on the floor, on tables, hanging out of open drawers. Josiah brushed aside cobwebs at the same time Jabez kicked a chicken carcass out of his way.

"Hey, Georgie! Ya got company!" Jabez announced before he disappeared into a black hole of a room.

Josiah, two steps behind, slipped in some kind of grease. When he made a grab for the doorjamb to steady himself, he touched something as grimy as what he'd slipped on.

In the far corner of the room, the figure of a man lay on a cot. The only light in the room was a single candle near his head. The man's arm was draped over his forehead.

"It's the new parson," Jabez called to his brother. "I went to school with him."

"Georgie, I'm Reverend Rush," Josiah said quietly.

"George," the young man insisted in a weak voice. "I hate being called Georgie."

"That's why I do it, right, Georgie?" Jabez teased. He righted a small wooden barrel that smelled of rum. "You can sit here, Parson. I'll leave you two to talk."

The wailing in the front room started again. Jabez swore. He could be heard shouting at his sister all the way down the hallway.

Josiah tested the barrel. When he was confident it would hold his weight, he straddled it. "You're a sailor," he said, getting situated.

"Jabez told you that?"

"That, and your canvas breeches."

Josiah leaned forward, his forearms on his legs. It was his first good look at George Mason in the dim light. A deadly intuition caught in Josiah's throat. The man on the cot was covered—face, hands, and forearms—with white-capped pustular pimples.

"They're even on the bottom of my feet," George explained. "Inside my mouth too." He squirmed on the cot, trying to get comfortable.

"The worst part is the pain in my back."

Trying not to show his alarm, Josiah asked, "Have you seen a doctor?"

"Nah. They brought me here from the ship. We was unloadin' the cargo. I was feelin' real tiredlike. The next thing I knowed, I was layin' on the deck."

"Any of the other sailors sick?"

George shrugged. "Don't know of any." His face twisted with concern. "Are you really a parson? I stayed away from the really bad places in Port Royal, I swear I did. Didn't do nothin' with any of them women there, so this can't be that kind of disease, can it? I mean, some of the other guys, they did, and one of them sleeps in the hammock right next to mine. I couldn't get one of them diseases just by sleepin' next to him, could I?"

"No, this isn't that kind of disease," Josiah said.

"You know what it is, don't you? Ma don't believe me that I didn't do anything with them women at Port Royal. But if you tell her it ain't like that, maybe she'll believe you."

"I'll tell her," Josiah promised.

He stood, a little too quickly, and knocked over the barrel.

"You goin' already? I sure would appreciate it if you could stay and talk awhile. I ain't had someone to talk to . . . hey, could you stop by the Febiger farm and tell Peggy why I ain't come to see her yet? She's gotta be plenty mad at me with the ship bein' in for days now and I ain't gone a courtin', especially after bein' gone so long."

"I'll . . . I'll get word to her." Josiah backed out of the room. "And I'll get a doctor here to see you. You just rest."

"You'll come see me again, won't you?" It was a plaintive plea.

"Of course I will," Josiah replied strongly, hearing the fear in the man's voice. "And before I leave, I'll pray for you."

He kneeled by George Mason's bedside. Placing a hand on the sick man's arm, Josiah prayed to the Great Physician for mercy and healing.

Smallpox. Dr. Wolcott confirmed it.

Several other members of the Nightingale are exhibiting early symptoms—fever, fatigue, back pain, vomiting—and all of them are highly contagious.

We traced their movements. The wharf. High town. The common. Outlying farms. There is no quarter of the city in which they have not been.

Josiah sat back and stared at what he'd just written in his journal. The page was illuminated only by a flickering candle flame. Night had closed in around him after a long day.

"God help us," he prayed.

CHAPTER 6

Two weeks after Josiah visited George Mason, the funerals began. Infants and the elderly were the first to die. Two, sometimes three times a day, the church bell would toll, and Josiah would don his mourning cloak to lead parents, a widow, or a widower in a solemn procession to the church graveyard, where they would stand in silence among a growing cluster of freshly dug graves.

He'd once heard an elderly minister boast a collection of "no less than fifty-seven mourning rings" given to him by families of deceased church members. At this rate, Josiah figured he'd have that many black-enameled rings his first year of ministry.

And gloves too.

Though they were customary, the gloves disturbed him. It was obvious the townspeople were using them to remind him of his probationary status. Never had Josiah seen or heard of a minister receiving gloves of such poor quality.

It was customary for people of standing to be given gloves worth twelve shillings. White lamb's wool gloves were a sign of honor and respect. Gloves for friends and family sold for five schillings. Gloves for underbearers and gravediggers sold for two shillings.

If the gloves presented to Josiah cost two shillings, the person buying them had been robbed. Philip had attended three of the funerals.

Each time the family had presented him with white lamb's wool gloves.

Give it time, Josiah counseled himself. But he also found himself consciously hiding his gloved hands at funerals.

The sun wasn't bright enough, the sky wasn't blue enough, and the spring breeze wasn't fresh enough to lift the black mood that covered the town.

Josiah himself, who under normal circumstances was invigorated by nature's colors and scents, strode the streets oblivious to them all. Since the outbreak of smallpox, he'd made it a custom to rise early and walk to Dr. Wolcott's house, where the two of them would pray for the sick, name by name, from a list that was growing alarmingly long.

For his part, Wolcott was giving Josiah a chance to prove himself, having come to Havenhill the year after the fire. Josiah appreciated having one house he could visit without the dark cloud of his past preceding him.

This morning one of the additions to the list was twelve-year-old Edward Usher, the brother of the two girls who had died in the warehouse fire. Having lost her husband in a freak warehouse accident days before Edward's birth, the boy was all Judith Usher had left.

Josiah made his way to the Ushers' house, grim of heart. The mounting number of deaths had taken their toll on everyone in Havenhill, including Josiah. But he also felt like an eyewitness to human suffering—someone whose hands were tied behind his back. He could speak comfort, counsel the grief-stricken, hand off the dead to God, and pray for the living. But he couldn't prevent even a single death. And now the reaper's icy claw rested upon Edward Usher.

Helpless as he felt, Josiah couldn't stay away. As long as Edward was still breathing, Josiah could intercede for the boy in prayer and trust God to be merciful.

The Usher house was a narrow, forest green, two-story structure in need of repair on the edge of town. As Josiah approached it, he worried about how he'd be received, since he'd not had a chance to speak to Judith Usher since returning to Havenhill. He hoped this visit would serve a double purpose. He would pray for Edward, but he also hoped he would have a chance to say to Judith Usher what he imagined the apostle Paul had said to the martyr Stephen's mother.

Josiah's heart lodged firmly in his throat as he knocked on the front door. He heard steps, then the door swung open.

"Nabby!"

From the look on her face, she was as surprised to see him as he was to see her.

"What are you doing here?" she cried.

Josiah had anticipated this question for months. He had given it careful thought and had even crafted a little speech for just this occasion. Only now, caught off guard, he couldn't remember it.

"I'm here because I . . . I . . . didn't . . . what I mean to say is that while you figured into my decision to return—naturally, considering our past, how could you not figure into it? Only at the time, I didn't know that you and Johnny Mott—"

She raised an eyebrow.

This wasn't coming out well. He tried again. "Of course, that's between you and Johnny, though I can't say that I'm not surprised, considering . . . anyway, when I made the decision to return to Havenhill, I made it clear that you were not the sole reason behind my—"

She interrupted him. "Josiah, why are you *here*?" She pointed at the spot on which they were standing. "Why have you come to Judith Usher's house?"

"Oh! Here, *here*. Not here as in Havenhill here." Josiah felt his face redden.

Abigail crossed her arms, waiting for his answer.

She looked tired. But even so, Josiah hadn't been this close to her or this alone with her—if you could call standing in front of a house on a public street alone—for seven years. Just looking at her stunned him senseless and brought back so many memories.

There was so much he wanted to say. So many questions he wanted to ask. All of which depended upon a functioning mouth that seemed to have broken. But his eyes were working exceedingly well, and they couldn't take in enough of her fast enough.

"Nabby," he began.

"*Abigail,*" she corrected him. "Considering the fact that I'm promised in marriage to another man, it hardly seems appropriate for the town minister to use an intimate form of address."

She was right. Of course, she was right. But it would be painful. Calling her anything other than Nabby was just another reminder that he'd lost her.

With forced effort, Josiah assumed the role of town minister in posture and tone. Speaking dispassionately, he said, "I learned that Edward Usher has fallen ill. I've come to pay a pastoral visit."

"Do you think that's wise?"

Why did everyone keep asking him that? First Philip. Now Nab . . . Abigail. Every time he turned around, someone was questioning the wisdom of his decisions.

"I'm his pastor," Josiah said testily.

"Be that as it may, considering . . ."

"I'm here in a professional capacity, making a sick call," he snapped. "Are you going to deny me entrance?"

Abigail reacted in anger. Her lips pursed in a familiar way. He saw the spark in her eyes as she took a step backward. "I'll announce your presence, *Reverend* Rush."

"Thank you," he replied curtly.

"You may keep your thanks to yourself." She turned her back on him.

He followed her into the house and was closing the door when he heard another familiar voice.

"Abigail, who was at the—? What are *you* doing here?" Eunice Parkhurst appeared like a ship emerging from a fog, armed and ready for battle. She'd always been a sturdy woman with a hearty soul, a true reflection of her colonial ancestors who had faced all manner of hardships and survived. Her face was long. A thin line of a mouth—curved downward at the moment—was set beneath a prominent nose.

"Why does everyone keep asking me that question?" Josiah asked.

"I thought you had better sense than this!" Eunice barked. "You shouldn't be here!"

For the second time in as many minutes, Josiah was confused as to which "here" they were talking about—the Usher house or Havenhill. Maybe it didn't matter. From the look on Eunice Parkhurst's face, her reply would be the same to either location.

"I've come to pay a pastoral call on Edward Usher," Josiah said.

"Haven't you hurt this family enough?" Eunice cried.

She loomed over him. She'd always been a formidable presence, Josiah thought, but no more so than now.

"I heard Edward had taken sick with smallpox and thought I'd—" he began to explain.

"He's being cared for," Eunice interrupted. "Judith is distraught, as you might expect. Right now, the last thing she needs is *you*."

Abigail had stepped aside. Eunice had taken up position as the first line of defense and wasn't about to budge. Josiah would have to push her aside physically to get any farther into the house.

He tried reasoning. "Eunice, despite what has happened in the past, I'm the pastor of First Church now. Please let me do my job."

Her eyes narrowed in anger. "The church may have called you as the minister of the church," she said frostily, "but for some of us, you will never be our pastor."

Her eyes were hard, unblinking; they moved side to side, challenging him.

Josiah knew it was no use. He backed down. "Please inform Goodwife Usher that I was here."

"I'll do nothing of the kind. It will only upset her."

Josiah sighed. He looked past Eunice to Abigail. Her eyes were downcast.

"May God bless you both and this house," Josiah said quietly.

And then he left.

CHAPTER 7

After his visit to the Usher house, Josiah took out his frustration chopping vegetables, spices, and venison for a pot of stew. This activity followed a rigorous session with an ax that had doubled the size of his woodpile and ripped the shoulder seam of his shirt.

By necessity, the wood chopping came first. Normally, it would have made sense to put the stew on, then chop the wood. But after his encounter with the fiery, immovable Eunice Parkhurst, had Josiah immediately taken knife to vegetable in his fury, he might have lost a finger or two. This way, though he would eat late, by the time the stew was simmering, he would have exhausted his anger and still retained all his fingers.

As he stirred the stew, his stomach growled, goaded to readiness by the aroma. It was the first real cooking he'd done since his arrival, having survived to this point on foods he could eat while walking, like samp and hoecakes.

Tasting the broth, he decided it needed something. Returning to the cutting board, he chopped some dried parsley, balanced it on the edge of the knife, and turned to add it to the stew.

Just then someone knocked at his door.

Josiah's hackles rose. It was probably Eunice Parkhurst's servant with another message, telling him someone needed a visit. The servant had been appearing at his door regularly, and he was getting tired of Eunice Parkhurst's telling him who to visit and who not to visit.

Josiah felt a fresh flush of anger. He slammed the knife on the cutting board, sending bits of parsley flying everywhere. He shook his head in dismay. A simple knock at the door had undone a woodpile's worth of catharsis.

His hand on the latch, Josiah reined back his emotions. The servant girl didn't deserve the anger that rightfully belonged to Eunice Parkhurst. The girl was already frightened of him as it was.

Forcing a smile, Josiah answered the door.

"Did we come at a bad time?"

Two women stood side by side in the orange twilight.

"Grace and Mercy!"

The younger woman smiled. "When you say our names like that, Reverend, it sounds like a benediction."

She carried a basket on her arm. This was obviously a social visit.

"You walked all the way out here? Come in!" He backed up to let them in.

The women exchanged glances. From the exchange, Josiah gathered that this moment had apparently been a point of discussion between them—and one that had not been resolved. Standing on the porch stoop, they craned their necks to see inside, curious and fearful of what might await them inside a bachelor's house.

"Of course, you're welcome," Josiah said. "Unless you feel uncomfortable." He had a thought. "If you feel it would be more appropriate, I could leave the door open."

Mercy put a toe on the threshold. "I guess it wouldn't hurt, sister, would it . . . if the door were open?"

With an all-knowing smirk, Grace said, "You know as well as I, Sister, that the gossips will start wagging their tongues as soon as they learn we came out here!"

"Then let's give them something to talk about!" Mercy said cheerily. She took one step inside and smiled as proudly as any of the Pilgrims who landed on Plymouth Rock.

Grace shook her head, clucked, and stepped inside too.

Clutching the basket on her arm, Mercy Litchfield happily surveyed the room. Josiah remembered her from their school days together as a silly little girl, four years younger than he, who giggled a lot. Now a twenty-two-year-old woman, she was a couple of inches over five feet tall. She'd gained weight since Josiah had last seen her—her cheeks and bosom and hips were rounder now. But she still had the same fair skin and happy disposition, despite having been knocked about by hardship.

Josiah heard about the tragedy three years after he left Havenhill. News from home reported that Mercy had married a sailor named Jonathan Litchfield and that soon afterward his ship had gone down on a run to Africa, making the newlywed a widow.

Grace Smythe's husband had also been a sailor on that ship. Soon after their husbands' departure, Mercy had moved in with Grace while the men were at sea. Mercy was afraid to live alone, and Grace welcomed the company.

The two women lived together amiably and became close friends. They received the news of their husbands' deaths at the same time. After that, they were inseparable. They were known around town as "the sisters."

"Oh Grace, I fear we may have misjudged the man!" Mercy cried, her nose lifted slightly.

"Misjudged me?" Josiah said, startled. "In what way?"

"That aroma! It's heavenly!"

Josiah watched the two women with amusement. Both had their noses in the air, and their gazes followed the scent to the fireplace.

Grace, ten years older than Mercy, was painfully thin. Time had weathered and scored her skin. While Mercy appeared playful and happy, Grace had a more cautious approach to her—very much the attitude of an older sister.

"I'd offer you some stew, but I'm afraid it won't be ready for a while," Josiah apologized.

Mercy snatched a wooden spoon from the table and hurried to the pot. Stirring the stew, she inspected its contents and took a taste.

Grace, meanwhile, ambled over to the cutting board and examined the chopped parsley, some of it having scattered on the floor.

"Very tasty!" Mercy cried. "Very tasty, indeed. But it needs a touch of parsley."

"Here's some," Grace said, pushing some with her toe.

Josiah grinned sheepishly. "An accident. I was just about to add some parsley when you knocked."

"Imagine that!" Mercy exclaimed. "A man who cooks! Can you cook anything else? Or is your culinary ability limited to stew?"

Before Josiah could answer, Grace said, "Why would he need to cook at all? He's a minister. Everyone knows that ministers always eat at someone else's table."

Mercy looked horrified. "Grace! That's rude!"

Josiah laughed. "Actually, I like to cook. Fish. Oysters. I have an eel recipe that I'm partial to—stuffed with nutmeg and cloves, cooked in wine, garnished with lemons."

It was evident from her frown that Grace didn't believe him. "Now he's poking fun at us!"

"I've cooked duck, ham, chicken, and beef. I make creams and custards, but I'm particularly fond of baking—buns, fruit pastries, pies."

The women stared at him, unsure whether to believe him or not. So he pulled up his right sleeve and held out his arm as proof.

Mercy examined it. She looked up at him, convinced. "Are your pies as good as your stew?"

Josiah smiled. "Better."

Mercy sighed. "Sister, it seems we walked all this way for nothing."

"What do you mean?" Josiah asked.

She pulled back the covering on the basket and took from it a loaf of bread and a fabric bag of pudding.

"Pumpkin bread!" Josiah cried with enthusiasm. "My favorite! I can smell the cinnamon."

"I suppose you make your own preserves too," Grace stated flatly.

"No. That's something I've never done."

Grace nodded to Mercy, a signal. With a smile Mercy pulled a jar of preserves from the basket.

"Apricot," she announced.

"Bless you, ladies!" Josiah said, taking the jar from her. "You've made your pastor a very happy man."

Mercy smiled triumphantly. Even the sardonic Grace allowed herself a grin.

Josiah picked up the pudding. "Let me steam this, and we'll eat it now. And we can slice the bread too."

"We brought those for you!" Mercy protested.

Josiah chuckled. "Food always tastes better when it's shared with friends."

"Friends? Is that what we are?" Grace said, looking a bit confused. "I've never been friends with a parson."

"We can stay awhile, can't we?" Mercy begged.

Grace shrugged her approval. "As the saying goes, 'I came in season—in pudding time.'"

While Josiah hung the pudding to steam over the pot of stew, Mercy pulled out a chair and sat.

Josiah turned back and almost ran into Grace.

She pulled at the threads of his shirt, torn at the shoulder. "I suppose you sew as well as a seamstress."

Josiah grinned. He liked this woman.

"Can't sew a stitch," he confessed.

Mercy jumped up from the table. "We can take it with us! It'll be good as new by tomorrow afternoon!"

That night, after sharing the bread and pudding with Grace and Mercy, Josiah stood in his doorway until he could no longer see the sisters. He'd offered to walk them back to town, but Grace wouldn't hear of it.

"We've given the old biddies enough to talk about for one night," she insisted.

Josiah had given them a taste of his stew to take home with them and his shirt, having changed while the pudding steamed.

Once they were out of sight, he closed the door and began to clear the table. Several minutes passed before he realized he was still smiling. For the first time since returning to Havenhill, he felt happy.

But it was more than just emotion. Since returning to Havenhill, this was the first time his gut felt no pain.

It had hit hard when he first entered the town, and since then it gnawed away at him like a low-grade fever. Most of the time, he could ignore it. Sometimes it flared. But for the last couple of hours, talking with Mercy and Grace, he realized now that he hadn't been ignoring it. It had gone away completely!

Setting down a bowl he'd just picked up, Josiah went to the door and stepped outside. He knew he couldn't see Mercy and Grace, but he looked just the same.

Then, under the twinkling lights of the stars, he prayed that God would bless the sisters.

CHAPTER 8

As soon as he heard the news, Josiah rushed over to the Parkhurst house. There were a few times in his life when he wished he owned a horse. This was one of them.

The servant girl—the same one who delivered messages to him from Eunice Parkhurst, telling him who in the town needed a visit from the pastor—responded to his insistent pounding on the front door.

Why hadn't she sent word to him?

He'd worried the question like some men worry a coin, mindlessly flipping it over and over in their hands.

Why hadn't Eunice sent word?

He could come up with no good answer. The woman was quick enough to inform him of every other person in the town who needed a pastoral visit, why not her own daughter? Why did he have to hear the news from Dr. Wolcott?

The more the question flip-flopped in his mind, the angrier he got, so that by the time he reached the door, he was simmering.

The servant girl appeared surprised to see him. She didn't say the words aloud, but the question was in her eyes: *What are you doing here?*

"Inform your mistress that Reverend Rush has come to pay a pastoral visit to Nab . . . to Abigail," he said, irritated by the delay that etiquette was imposing on him. It was all he could do to keep himself from rushing up the stairs unannounced.

The servant girl stared at him with wide, frightened eyes. She made no move to announce him.

"Well?" Josiah shouted. "Have your feet grown roots? Be on your way!"

The girl's lower lip trembled. She teared up. The door closed, and Josiah heard sobbing and the sound of feet scurrying away.

He felt bad about making the girl cry. But at the moment, he was not himself.

While he waited, he paced. The village green stretched peacefully in front of the house, just as it had every day for years. Lush. Green. Springlike. Birds chirped merrily in the trees. This, too, irritated Josiah. Nabby was ill. She could die. All the springtime goodness seemed to fly in the face of her peril.

It didn't matter that the view from this porch had been a constant through the years, ever since Reverend Parkhurst had bought the house from the brother of Samuel Fiedler, the founder of Havenhill. It was the same view as on the day Reverend Parkhurst died. The same view when Josiah said good-bye to Nabby and moved to Boston. So why would the view change now simply because Nabby lay in bed . . . sick and within an arm's reach of the grave? People died every day, and still the sun rose, the birds made their nests, couples fell in love, some got married, babies were born. Josiah was fully aware of the cycle, only not until now, when someone he cared for deeply was close to death, did he feel irritated by it.

The front door latch clicked. Josiah swung around, fully expecting to do battle with Eunice Parkhurst. This time he was ready for her. This time she wasn't going to stop him.

But it wasn't Eunice who blocked him from the door. This time the obstacle was more substantial in both height and width.

"Johnny!"

Mott stepped onto the porch and closed the door behind him. His intent was clear. Josiah would not be walking through this doorway today.

Josiah felt dwarfed by Mott's physical presence. He'd forgotten how intimidating Johnny's size could be face-to-face. Since his return to Havenhill, Josiah had seen Johnny only in church, and then Josiah had looked down on him from an elevated platform.

This close, Johnny Mott's head was huge. He had a flat nose that, as boys, they'd always attributed to the fact that Johnny had been a fighter. A bully. He still had the massive shoulders and arms of a fighter.

Josiah extended his hand. "It's good to see you, Johnny."

Mott stared at Josiah's hand for a long moment before gripping it. His handshake held no warmth. "Can I do something for you, Reverend?"

Despite the circumstances, Josiah couldn't help but grin at hearing a boyhood buddy call him "Reverend."

"Well, for one thing," Josiah said lightly, "you can tell me how . . . um, how Abigail is doing. Dr. Wolcott said she'd taken ill."

Mott nodded grimly. "She's got the pox."

This wasn't news to Josiah, but that didn't make hearing the news any easier. Deaths in the town were increasing at a steady rate. From here Josiah would leave to lead a funeral procession for a thirty-two-year-old mother of five children. After that, he'd watch as an eleven-year-old girl was put in the ground. The realization that Nabby could be next haunted his thoughts.

"I've come to see her," Josiah said softly. "To . . . to pray for her."

Mott studied him with the appraising eye of a merchant. It was a side of Mott Josiah had never seen. But then, for the last seven years, Johnny Mott had been supervising Philip's enterprises on the wharf. It was just surprising to Josiah how well Johnny wore the mantle of authority.

Of course, it was represented authority. Everyone knew that. The real power lay with Philip. But from what Josiah had heard, everyone also knew that on the docks when Johnny spoke, he spoke with Philip's voice. But what about here on Eunice Parkhurst's porch? Whose voice would come out of Johnny's mouth here?

"Abigail's resting," Mott said. "She's not receiving visitors."

"I'm not a visitor, Johnny. As a deacon of the church, you know that. I'm here in a professional capacity."

Mott's eyes restricted. "Are you?"

"What do you mean by that?"

"I mean, Abigail Parkhurst has consented to be my wife, and you would do well to remember that."

It's not that simple, Josiah thought. *Not when your friend is promised to marry the woman you've loved all your life.* However, he said, "I assure you, I'm here as Abigail Parkhurst's pastor, nothing more."

It was evident Mott didn't believe him.

Josiah didn't blame him. There wasn't enough sincerity in his voice to convince himself.

Mott leveled a hefty index finger at Josiah. "I'm going to tell you this only once. Stay away from Abigail."

Then the Parkhursts' door shut with authority, and Josiah was left standing alone on the porch.

"Philip, we have to do something! We can't just stand by and do nothing while people are dying!"

Josiah had stewed over his encounter with Johnny Mott through two funerals and the bulk of an afternoon as he walked and prayed along a path that ultimately led him to Philip's house.

It was a huge red brick structure with pillars and gardens. A shiny black coach, hitched and ready, awaited service when Josiah arrived, indicating this would not be a leisurely meeting. But then, Josiah's arrival had been unexpected.

"You mean while Abigail Parkhurst is dying," Philip clarified as a servant helped him on with his coat. "Johnny told me you'd stopped by to see her. He was angrier than I've seen him in a long time."

"It was a pastoral visit!" Josiah cried. "What kind of minister would I be if I neglected the ill? The fact that Nabby and I have a past has nothing to do with it."

Philip had moved to a mirror where he adjusted the coat. He met Josiah's gaze in the reflection with skepticism.

"Besides," Josiah continued, "I'm tired of being greeted by, 'What are you doing here?' every time I show up on someone's doorstep."

"Then show some common sense in your choices," Philip snapped. "If everyone's saying the same thing—as you insist they are—doesn't that tell you something? Whether it's right or not is beside the point. It's not wise."

Josiah lowered his gaze. "I just didn't expect it from Johnny. I thought we were friends."

Philip adjusted his white wig, then turned to Josiah. "What do you expect? You're a threat to him."

Josiah laughed. "Yeah, I can be real intimidating sometimes, especially to man-mountains."

"Sarcasm, Reverend Rush?"

"We're talking about Johnny Mott! We used to be friends! 'Never leave a jibe unspoken,' remember that?"

"And now your friend is promised in marriage to your old girlfriend! He knows how you feel about her, and how she used to feel about you. With you being back in town, he's afraid Abigail's feelings for you might be rekindled."

Josiah couldn't argue with that. "Why doesn't he just tell me how he feels? He didn't have to threaten me. Besides, we have a bigger problem."

Philip's servant handed him his hat.

"You're a minister," Philip said. "What can you do about smallpox other than what you're already doing?" He walked to the door.

Josiah followed him. "There was an outbreak in Boston while I was there. There are some doctors who advocate a more aggressive approach to battling the disease, instead of relying on this black powder made of toads and charcoal."

Philip pivoted sharply. It was clear Josiah had caught his attention.

"Inoculation," Philip guessed.

"It's becoming increasingly popular."

"And controversial." Philip climbed into the carriage. "Have you talked this over with Dr. Wolcott?"

"He's against it," Josiah said plainly.

Philip shrugged and settled into his seat. "Well, there you have it."

Josiah grabbed the side of the carriage. "But it could save lives!"

"From what I understand, it doesn't work on those who already have smallpox."

Josiah caught the implication. "This isn't about Abigail!" he shouted. "This is about saving the town!"

The horse jumped. Philip jerked back as the carriage bolted forward, nearly knocking Josiah over. The driver quickly reined the horse back, but not before casting a frown at Josiah over his shoulder.

For the second time that day, Josiah fell under the evaluating gaze of a boyhood friend.

"What do you propose?" Philip asked.

"A town meeting. Bring a doctor from Boston who's done the procedure. Let him describe the procedure."

"Do you have a doctor in mind?"

"Dr. John McCullough."

"And you think he'll agree to this?"

"There's only one way to find out."

Philip was silent for a minute. Then he said quietly, "It's been my experience that the town responds positively to strong leadership. Following the fire, the town floundered, a ship without a rudder. Johnny and I stepped forward and presented a course of action. Not everyone embraced it, but enough people did so that we were able to move forward. Time and perseverance have proved us right. If you want to establish yourself and win the approval of the town, be a leader."

Josiah nodded. He took a step back.

"There's a horse in the carriage house if you need one," Philip offered.

"Thanks. I suppose you're off to meet some pretty young maiden. An heiress, perhaps?"

Philip laughed. "Would that I were so fortunate. No, I get to spend the evening with some very old, very round, very pompous English investors."

"Thanks for hearing me out."

"A friend loveth at all times."

A word to the driver and the crack of a whip later, and Philip was gone.

CHAPTER 9

Josiah accepted Philip's offer of a horse and made plans for a trip to Boston.

On the morning he was to leave, he heard a knock at his door. It was the little Parkhurst servant with another message for him.

Widow Delor needs a visit.
Goodwife Parkhurst

"Has Widow Delor the pox?" Josiah asked the girl.

"No, sir."

The girl ran away. Since the day at the Parkhurst house, she was scared of him.

Josiah looked at the note. Widow Delor was a lonely middle-aged woman who was known to fabricate or exaggerate illness to get attention. She was like molasses—once you made contact with her, you were stuck for a good two or three hours while she rattled on about trifling topics.

Folding the note, Josiah slipped it into his pocket. He mounted the horse and set out for Boston, making a mental note to visit Widow Delor upon his return.

The journey to Boston went without incident. The sun has removed the last of winter's mud, and the roads were in tolerable

shape. I found Dr. McCullough more than eager to assist me in my cause. He repeatedly remarked how he wished more clergy were willing to embrace medical advances. After making a few hasty preparations, we were on our way.

The return trip passed quickly with company to pass the time. For the most part, Dr. McCullough is a pleasant enough sort, though his manner is sometimes abrasive. He has an opinion on everything and is quick to argue that his opinion is the only conclusion a reasonable man can come to. After spending several days listening to his judgment on everything from King George to potatoes—he referred constantly to his journal for facts and details—I look forward to the completion of our journey, when hopefully I will be able to enjoy some peace and quiet.

We arrived in Havenhill late tonight. I've put him up in my back room. Tomorrow I'll introduce him to Philip and arrange for a town meeting.

Very early the next morning, Josiah woke to pounding on his front door. While persistent, it wasn't the heavy pounding of a male fist. But the noise was enough to also wake Dr. McCullough.

They exchanged half-awake glances—a knowing exchange of two men whose professions often woke them at odd hours.

Josiah opened the door to find Eunice Parkhurst's servant girl, fist raised, in tears.

"Reverend Rush, come quick!" she cried. "Please come quick!"

That was all she was able to get out before she collapsed on his doorstep in tears.

Josiah knelt beside her, doing his best to comfort her. But after several attempts, all he managed to get from her was that Eunice Parkhurst had sent her and had told her not to return "*under any circumstances*" without Reverend Rush.

"Do you know what it is?" McCullough asked with a frown of concern.

A dreaded intuition leaped up inside Josiah. "Her daughter," he said softly, stunned by the sound of his own words.

"The pox?"

"Yes."

"I'll get the horses."

Josiah didn't wait for the horses. Jumping into his breeches, shirt, and shoes, he took off down the road. Running past the servant girl, he gave her instructions to wait for the doctor and show him the way to the house.

By the time he reached the oak at the junction of the main road, his lungs were burning. He didn't care. He urged his legs to move faster.

His mind leaped ahead of him to the two-story yellow house. He saw himself bounding up the front porch steps and throwing open the door. And then he saw the stricken faces of the servants, confirming his worst fear: Nabby was dead.

Another mental leap and he was standing beside her graveside, unable to comprehend a world without her. First her father, then Deacon Cranch, his mentor, and now his only love!

At last he realized just how much Abigail Parkhurst had figured into his decision to return to Havenhill. Yes, he wanted to redeem himself. But more than that, he wanted to reconcile with Nabby. He wanted to hear her say she forgave him for killing her father—that she knew it was an accident. He wanted her to look at him again with those doe eyes that stirred his insides to love and romance, banishing forever the horrific, pained expression that haunted his dreams. The expression that had twisted her face when she'd learned that *Josiah* was the one responsible for the fire.

But if she was dead . . . *No!* He refused to give in to the thought. He pushed it out of his mind. But it didn't go far. It lingered in a side room, like a guest who'd come calling and waited patiently to be received.

Josiah's throat was raw by the time the Parkhurst house came into view. His legs moved by instinct, unable to respond to his repeated commands to move faster.

He reached the front of the residence, his imagined scenario playing itself out. He leaped up the steps, taking two at a time, landing on the porch with a loud *thud*. His fist flew to the door. He pounded on it but didn't wait for an answer. Throwing the door open, he barged inside, startling a servant carrying a pitcher. Her hand flew to her bosom. She stifled a scream.

The servant, a middle-aged African woman who had served the Parkhursts for years, was the aberration from Josiah's imagined scenario. It was her eyes. Startled, not grief-stricken.

The second aberration followed quickly after the first in the form of Eunice Parkhurst. Appearing suddenly, she cried, "What is all the commotion?" Clenched fists rested on her ample hips.

The disturbance was standing in the middle of her parlor, struggling to catch his breath.

"What is the *meaning* of this, bursting into my house?" she shouted angrily. "And where have you been?"

"Nab . . . Nab . . . Nabby," Josiah fought to say between gasps. "How . . . is . . . she?"

"ABIGAIL," Eunice said with emphasis, "is none of your concern, or hasn't that been made clear to you yet? Where have you been?"

Josiah doubled over, hands to knees. "You . . . sent . . . your . . . servant. I . . . thought . . ."

Before Eunice could answer, her servant and Dr. McCullough burst through the front door.

"Mercy sakes alive!" Eunice shouted. "Who are you?"

Josiah's breath was returning. He straightened himself. "This is Dr . . . John McCullough."

McCullough appeared flummoxed at Eunice's anger.

"It's not what we thought," Josiah explained.

"The girl has improved?" McCullough asked.

"Josiah Rush!" Eunice thundered. "You went to Boston to get a doctor for Abigail without consulting me?"

Apparently her repeated, "Where have you been?" question was rhetorical, Josiah thought. Eunice Parkhurst knew exactly where he'd been.

"We don't need a Boston doctor coming into our town and treating Dr. Wolcott's patients," she continued. "Jeremiah Wolcott has been treating this family and the residents of Havenhill for over twenty years. It is insulting to him and unprofessional for you to bring in another doctor to treat his patients without consulting him."

"Eunice, I—"

He couldn't get an explanation out. She didn't let him.

"Frankly, Josiah, I don't know what's gotten into you!"

"I'm only trying to—"

"While you were on a fool's errand in Boston, meddling in matters for which you are not qualified, your work here—the work for which you were *called* as pastor—has gone undone. And, quite frankly, many of us in the church are beginning to think that we made a mistake when—"

"I was gone for only a short time," Josiah interrupted, defending himself. "And for reasons that will soon be made—"

"Widow Delor is dead," Eunice said flatly.

The news cut Josiah short.

"She died a frightened woman, refusing to be comforted by her son and friends. Her fears were of a spiritual nature. She wanted to talk to her minister, but you weren't here, were you? You were playing doctor in Boston."

Josiah's arms hung limp at his sides. "I . . . I . . . didn't know that she was—"

Eunice's eyes narrowed further. "You knew enough. Why do you think I send my servant all the way out to your place? Do you think I have nothing better to do than to sit around and think up places to send the new minister?"

"Well, yes, that's exactly what I have been thinking," Josiah couldn't help but mutter to himself.

"You've been away for seven years," she continued. "How can you know the spiritual state of your congregation within just a few weeks? I thought I could be of assistance to you."

Dr. McCullough backed away, his head hung, as Eunice Parkhurst scolded Josiah. The servant girl hid her face behind her hand. Josiah thought he saw her smirk. Evidently she was entertained by her master's tongue-lashing of the minister.

"I'll go visit Widow Delor's son," Josiah said weakly, "and make arrangements for—"

"The woman's already in the ground," Eunice stated coldly. "And Peter Delor has made it clear he wants nothing to do with you or the church."

Horrible didn't even come close to describing how Josiah felt.

"His mother has been praying for her son's salvation for years," Eunice continued, "but whenever she brought up the topic, he'd walk away. Until recently. 'At least he doesn't walk away now,' she told me."

Josiah didn't think he could feel any worse. He was wrong.

"Widow Delor was excited that you had been called to the church. She thought that her son would talk to a young pastor."

"But he never got the chance, did he, *Reverend* Rush?"

With those final words of condemnation, Eunice Parkhurst turned her back and ascended the staircase of her home.

CHAPTER 10

Josiah expected a greater attendance at the town meeting, especially since Philip and the other selectmen had called it. The meeting was held at the church, as usual.

The solemnity of the gathering didn't come as a surprise, considering the nature of the meeting. Nearly every person in Havenhill had been touched by a smallpox-related death. From the platform, Josiah looked out over a sea of stern and worried faces.

While the majority of those in attendance were church members, about a third were not. Eunice Parkhurst sat in her pew, with Johnny Mott beside her. The sisters—Grace and Mercy—were there. Mercy smiled encouragingly at Josiah. Dr. Wolcott was also there. He wasn't smiling.

Philip began the meeting by narrating Josiah's appearance at his house, his concern over the smallpox deaths, and his proposal that the townspeople be inoculated.

Josiah stood and introduced Dr. McCullough, who described the outbreak of smallpox in Boston and the inoculation procedure. The doctor gave testimony to the number of lives saved by inoculation. But he was also quick to admit that his numbers were based solely on his own observations as recorded in his journal and not the result of a scientific hospital study.

As McCullough spoke, Josiah studied the people's faces, attempting to read their reactions. To his surprise, they appeared almost bored. He thought Dr. McCullough—though his arrogance sparkled in a few places—was making a competent, evenhanded presentation of the benefits of inoculation. He didn't oversell it; neither did he downplay the risks. Yet the reaction of the townspeople bordered on nonchalance!

When McCullough was finished, Philip called for questions. Josiah sat forward in his seat. The nature of the questions would give him a better idea where the people stood.

No one raised a hand.

Philip asked again if there were any questions for Dr. McCullough.

Johnny Mott raised his hand.

Philip called on him.

Mott stood. "I make a motion we thank Dr. McCullough for coming all this way to instruct us on inoculation, and that we add a vote of confidence to Dr. Jeremiah Wolcott for the way he has conducted himself during this time of crisis."

Someone seconded the motion.

Philip called for discussion.

Nobody raised a hand.

Josiah could not believe what he was seeing, or not seeing. He stood.

Philip recognized him.

"I'm not sure everyone realizes the purpose of this meeting," Josiah said as calmly as he could. "This is not simply an informational meeting. Dr. McCullough has come prepared to inoculate as many people in the town who wish to be inoculated against smallpox. The purpose of this meeting was, hopefully, to endorse a town-wide inoculation effort. It's our best hope of combating this disease that is ravaging our town!"

The people stared at him blankly.

"Therefore, as your pastor, I make a motion that we take advantage of Dr. McCullough's presence and that we, as a town, vote to inoculate as many people as possible."

Philip shook his head. "You're out of order. There is already a motion on the floor. In order to entertain your motion, we would have to vote down the motion on the floor, after which time you can reintroduce your motion."

"Then I speak against the motion," Josiah insisted. "Let's vote it down so we can get a real motion on the floor. And I want everyone to know that I have nothing against Dr. Wolcott. I think he is a wonderful doctor, and we're blessed to have him here. However, as you probably all know, he isn't convinced that inoculations work."

"They're dangerous," Wolcott claimed. "People have died from them. As a physician I cannot in good conscience purposefully infect a person with the smallpox virus and pretend that's a good thing."

McCullough was on his feet. "The introduction of the virus in the host—"

Philip held up a hand. "Please, Doctors. This is not a debate. If either of you has something to say, identify yourself, I'll call on you, and then address your remarks to the chair. At the moment, Reverend Rush still has the floor."

"I've said what I have to say," Josiah concluded. "As your pastor I believe inoculation is our best chance of defeating this smallpox epidemic."

"What about prayer?" Deacon Dunmore shouted. "You'd think the pastor would believe in prayer as a weapon against evil."

"Mr. Dunmore, please raise your hand," Philip warned.

"I *do* believe in prayer," Josiah replied." However, I also believe God has given us the capacity to fight disease through scientific methods. As Christians we should use both."

"Josiah, address your comments to the chair," Philip ordered.

Josiah threw up his hands in frustration. "I'm done. However, I would like to hear what you have to say about all this—you being a community leader, a selectman, and a deacon."

"Unfortunately," Philip said, "as chairman, by the rules of order, I am prohibited from issuing an opinion."

"Rules be hanged, Philip!" someone shouted. "Tell us what to do!"

Laughter rippled across the room. However, there was enough general consent to the comment that Philip shrugged. "Very well."

Josiah took his seat. It was obvious the town wasn't ready to listen to him, but that didn't matter. All that mattered was that the town realized that inoculation gave them a chance of defeating the smallpox epidemic. It didn't matter who convinced them of it.

Philip cleared his throat. "I've given the matter a great deal of thought and prayer."

He did not look at Josiah. In fact, it appeared to Josiah that Philip was intentionally *not* looking his direction. Josiah's heart sank.

"And while I wish inoculation provided the benefits Dr. McCullough claims it provides, I've heard of too many horror stories and read of too many deaths associated with it. I believe our best course of action in the present crisis is to pray and trust the wisdom of Dr. Jeremiah Wolcott, the man God has sent us to be our physician. However, having said that, I would add that anyone wishing to be inoculated would be free to accept Dr. McCullough's services without recrimination. However, the town as a whole will not embrace his methods."

The meeting ended quickly after that.

Josiah couldn't believe what had just happened. The one man he'd expected to back him had done just the opposite.

The people began filing out of the building. Several people gathered around Eunice Parkhurst and, from the way it looked to Josiah, congratulated her. She smiled and accepted their comments.

Josiah stood and shouted over the din, "I, for one, will be inoculated. Anyone wishing to follow my example, please stay for a short time for instruction from Dr. McCullough."

Five minutes later McCullough and Josiah were the only two left in the building.

CHAPTER 11

With the word *fool* ringing in his ears, Josiah led Dr. McCullough back to his house.

"That was, without doubt, one of the strangest meetings regarding smallpox inoculation I have ever attended," Dr. McCullough said, sounding puzzled. "The topic normally generates no small amount of impassioned debate. I don't recall ever being at a meeting of this kind where no one had any questions."

"It was a waste of your time, Doctor," Josiah replied. "For that, I apologize. The matter was decided before the meeting began."

"But the people didn't have the facts of inoculation before the meeting."

"They didn't need the facts. They weren't voting on inoculation. They were voting on me."

McCullough stared hard at Josiah. "Does this have something to do with that Delor woman?"

"More specifically with Eunice Parkhurst," Josiah clarified. "She is a force in this community."

"But she didn't say anything during the meeting."

"Being a woman, she wouldn't have had the opportunity, would she? Her being a woman and all. But rest assured, I'm certain she did plenty of talking before the meeting ever convened."

McCullough nodded knowingly. "Are you going to survive this?"

Josiah laughed nervously. "The vote or the inoculation?"

A short while later, McCullough was ready for the inoculation.

"Hold out your left arm," the doctor said.

Josiah did as he was instructed.

With a lance, Dr. McCullough cut an incision about a quarter of an inch in length, just deep enough for blood to appear. He then inserted a piece of string the length of the incision.

"The string has been infected with the smallpox disease," he explained.

Josiah nodded confidently, though he was feeling a little lightheaded. *Just nerves,* he told himself.

Dr. McCullough bandaged Josiah's arm.

"Go about your business," McCullough explained. "Your body will react to the disease soon enough. When it does, climb in bed and let it run its course. Eat nothing but bread, milk, pudding, and rice."

"I'll ride back with you to Boston," Josiah said.

McCullough smiled. "I doubt you'll be in any condition to travel within a day or so."

"Then I want to apologize again for dragging you all the way down here."

"If you ever find yourself in need of a new position, look me up in Boston. I'll recommend you to local churches. We can use men with your vision."

Josiah thanked him.

Eunice Parkhurst sat in her rocker by the fireplace. Her bedcovers were turned down. The door was closed. Her Bible on her lap, she stared vacantly across the room.

As was her nightly routine, she'd tried to read a chapter from the

Psalms. But tonight there was no room in her mind for King David's words. Her head was already packed with thoughts of the day's events, which circulated continuously for her review.

She found no joy in them.

Stirring herself back to the present, she ran her wrinkled hands across the cool pages. With a sigh, she closed the book. The corners of loose pages protruded from the back. Lifting the back cover, she retrieved the pages. Holding them in a trembling hand, she stared at her husband's handwriting.

A single tear tracked down her cheek.

After McCullough left for Boston, Josiah began to think about the doctor's offer. He began to wonder if McCullough expected to see him soon.

Soon afterward, though, Josiah didn't give it another thought. He didn't give anything much thought. He was too busy moaning and suffering from headaches, backaches, knee aches, and gagging fever.

For three weeks he lay on his bed, certain he was poised on the edge between this life and the next.

No one other than Dr. Wolcott visited Reverend Josiah Rush when he was ill from the smallpox. During his visits, the doctor was outwardly kind, but Josiah could tell by his cool manner that he still held a grudge against Josiah for publicly challenging his medical assessment of inoculations. Josiah feared the friendship he and Wolcott had forged from their early morning prayer meetings had suffered permanent damage.

After the third week of fever, Josiah finally climbed out of bed. Out of necessity, he wandered outside and came upon a slip of paper that had been wedged between planks of the clapboard siding of his house.

He carried it with him, unread, back to bed. Exhausted from the journey just outside his door, he collapsed onto the bed. The note slipped from his hand onto the floor as he, once again, succumbed to the healing power of sleep.

Days later, Josiah found and unfolded the note. Since it was from an anonymous source—and anonymous notes are usually by nature unkind—he fully expected it to be a message of hate. Or perhaps it would gloat over his pain for subjecting himself needlessly to the smallpox disease.

However, when he actually steeled himself to read it, he discovered something completely unexpected:

It took courage for you to return to Havenhill. Greater courage still to do what you did to try to save lives during this plague. I want you to know that someone is praying for you.

Tears welled in Josiah's eyes. It had been years since he'd seen Nabby's handwriting, but he felt certain this came from her hand. The penmanship was feminine, with a boyish quality to it. She had always been a better reader than writer.

He stared at the note again, carefully going over every word and letter separately. Just knowing that her hand had touched this paper and formed these words made his heart swell with happiness.

She'd probably had the servant girl deliver it, instructing her to be careful not to be seen and swearing the girl to secrecy. Given the town climate and her relationship to Mott, she couldn't be too careful.

The note sent Josiah's spirit soaring. It meant Nabby was feeling better and that, despite her arrangement with Johnny Mott, she still had feelings for him.

Josiah clutched the note in his hand as he curled up on his bed, his head and belly throbbing. A few minutes ago, he wouldn't have cared had he lived or died. Now he had reason to live again. And reason's name was Abigail Parkhurst.

CHAPTER 12

Having survived the smallpox inoculation, I will never again in good conscience recommend inoculation to others as lightly as I have in the past. Clearly, it is only for the strong and healthy and should be administered only after considerable thought and prayer. It is no small thing to introduce a dose of death into one's body.

However, the ordeal has not changed my opinion regarding inoculations. While I would not wish suffering upon others, it was minor compared to the suffering that accompanies the actual disease, which ends so often in death.

That said, good news awaited me upon my return to my pastoral duties. Three people for whom I have been praying night and day, even in the midst of my own illness, have survived the full onslaught of the disease:

Abigail Parkhurst, who has only a few pockmarks on her face.

Edward Usher—how grateful I am that God has spared Judith of sorrow upon sorrow!

And George Mason, though the illness was particularly unkind to him, having scarred his face considerably.

For George Mason, the illness was only part of his suffering. The story, as I heard it, was that as soon as he was well, he went calling on a young lady friend for whom he has deep affections. This was the first time he'd seen her and she him since his return from the Caribbean Islands. One look at his scarred face, and she informed him she could never love a man so disfigured.

My heart went out to him. I am not unacquainted with the crushing pain of a woman's rejection.

From there he went to Bailey's Tavern, where he got drunk on ale. Another tavern patron, unaware of what had just transpired, apparently made a few unkind comments about his face. George, already reeling from romantic rejection, took exception to the comments. A fight ensued, and George was arrested.

I go to the jail to see him this afternoon and pray that God will give me the words to console him, guide him, and strengthen him.

Havenhill's public jail was a substantial brick structure, where men awaited trial in general court alongside debtors, runaway slaves, and occasionally the mentally ill.

The jail keeper, an unassuming jolly man whose shirt was tucked half in and half out of his breeches, showed Josiah to the cell that held the now sober George Mason.

"Guess this won't be the last I'll see of you, is it, Parson?" the jailer said. He'd been jabbering from the moment Josiah met him. "Old sin nature and all that, you know. Lately we've been havin' as many church members in here as nonchurch members. More, sometimes. That old sin nature's a hard habit to kick, ain't it?"

Josiah stepped inside a ten-by-ten-foot cell, thanking the man who locked him in. He stood on straw that looked like it hadn't been changed in weeks.

Six men shared the cell. Some of them wore handcuffs; others, leg irons. George was fitted with both.

George looked up. Seeing Josiah, he gave a slight smile of recognition, as though he knew that Josiah would get around to visiting him sooner or later. As Josiah had promised, he had come to see George several times at the Mason house while he was ill.

"I'm surprised to see you here, George," Josiah said. "You don't strike me as the tavern-brawler type."

George hung his head. "No excuses, Reverend. I got drunk. I got angry. I fought. It felt good."

"Will that be your defense to the judge?"

George shrugged. "What defense? I'll take my punishment—stripes, prob'ly—and go on my way."

"Go on your way?"

"The *Nightingale*'s sailin' in a couple of days."

Josiah crossed his arms. "You told me you hated sailing. That it was the worst experience of your life."

George grinned sadly. "Turns out comin' home was worse."

"You've had a rough time of it."

"You heard about Peggy?"

Josiah nodded.

"Can't say I'm surprised. I always thought she was too beautiful for me . . . that I was lucky to have her . . . know what I mean? Can't really blame her for not wantin' to look at this for the rest of her life." He motioned to his face with both hands, a necessity since they were locked together.

"For a relationship to last," Josiah said, "it has to be rooted in something more substantial than appearances, George."

"Aya? Well, Peggy is a simple girl. You know what I'm sayin'? Gettin' dressed up and paradin' around all pretty-like makes her think she's better than she is. I don't mean royalty or anything like that, but better than a cooper's daughter. One of Peg's sisters told her I looked good on her arm, and after that she became friendly to me."

"There are other women, George. I know you don't want to hear that now, but running off to sea isn't the answer."

"What else is there? I'm not a farmer. I've known that since I was four years old. I hate the farm. My father? He was kin to dirt. Ploughin', hayin', thrashin'. It made him feel alive."

"What makes *you* feel alive, George?"

"Peggy used to," George said with a laugh. "I don't know . . . maybe I'll find whatever it is in some other port."

"It may not be something you find in a location."

"What do you mean?"

"You may find what you're looking for in here." Josiah patted his chest. "Yours is a spiritual problem, George."

"You sound just like a preacher."

One of the prisoners—a young, scrawny man who'd been in jail a long time if the length of his unkempt beard was any indication—laughed at George's comment. Every prisoner without exception was listening to the conversation, not caring that it was rude. It was entertaining, and that was enough.

George paid no attention to them, so neither did Josiah. He grinned at George's comment. "Maybe so, but that doesn't make what I'm saying any less true."

"You know, it wasn't all bad," George said, gazing at the ceiling, "those days on ship, I mean. The first days were rough—getting used to sharin' quarters with rats and cockroaches and maggots . . . and then there was the vermin."

Josiah laughed.

"And learnin' the difference between stem and stern, starboard and larboard; the difference between backin' and reefin' and furlin' the sails—that was kinda interestin'. How to tell a splice from a hitch from a knot—that took me almost the whole voyage to learn. Learnin' to read the sky—now that's a whole different story. I took to that easily—squalls, tempests, scuds . . . and at night, the constellations . . ." George's eyes were alight with fascination.

"Have you considered studying navigation?" Josiah asked.

"I'd go to sea in a heartbeat if I could do that," George replied.

"Maybe I can put in a good word for you. You probably don't know it, but I have some connections with the *Nightingale*."

Suddenly, George's smile faded. He glanced at Josiah, then averted his eyes quickly.

Is he unable—or unwilling—to look me in the eyes? Josiah wondered.

"Thanks, anyway," George muttered. "But I'll just work things out on my own."

"But I can help you!" Josiah insisted. "I know Philip Clapp, who owns the *Nightingale*, and also Johnny Mott, who oversees loading and unloading . . ."

"I know who Mott is," George said.

"All I'm saying is that they were my two best friends in school."

"Yeah." George sniffed. "I heard somethin' about that, but thanks just the same."

Josiah was puzzled. George's whole demeanor had changed. The prisoner repositioned himself at an angle away from Josiah and stared at the patch of sky through the window high up the cell wall.

"Help me out here, George," Josiah said. "Why don't you want me to put in a good word for you?"

George shook his head. "You seem like a nice-enough sort. Let's just leave it at that."

"As opposed to Philip Clapp or Johnny Mott?"

"I didn't say that," George insisted.

"Don't you like them?"

"Can't say as I know them."

"Well, then? What?"

George sniffed and rubbed his nose with a forefinger. He glanced anxiously around the cell and lowered his voice to a whisper. "I've seen things . . . heard things. And then there's Coytmore. He's the captain. He's their man."

"Is Coytmore a bad captain?"

"Worse than bad. None worse than Coytmore on the high seas, from what I hear. And that's sayin' a lot. None of the sailors want to sail with him."

"Maybe I could speak to . . ."

"Don't say nothin'!" George shouted, so loud everyone in the cell looked at him. "Just don't say anything. Understand? You'll only make it worse, if that's possible."

"George—," Josiah tried.

"Look, I know you've been gone awhile and all, and sometimes people change or aren't who you think they are. All I know is that there's some bad stuff goin' on with those ships. Either your friends are blind, or they're behind it." He raised his hands. "Just forget what I said. You know, business is business, and I'm just a common tar. I've said too much already."

CHAPTER 13

I find myself pondering George Mason's observation—there's evil here. It's an astute observation of a "common tar." I sensed the evil the day I walked into town. George confirmed it. What does the Bible say about such things?

> *One witness shall not rise up against a man for any iniquity, or for any sin, in any sin that he sinneth: at the mouth of two witnesses, or at the mouth of three witnesses, shall the matter be established.*
> *—Deuteronomy 19:15*

George Mason is the second witness.

One wouldn't know this was a town of iniquity by its appearance. The town is thriving. Never has it been more prosperous. Yet the people are discontent, suspicious, secretive, generally unhappy, and quick to take offense. They find no joy in worship and no satisfaction in service to the Lord.

I pray for them. Yet I believe I should be doing more. Unfortunately, I fear I am the last person to whom they will listen.

My recent association with Dr. McCullough has given me an idea. He recorded daily his medical observations and drew conclusions regarding the disease of smallpox, formulating a diagnosis and method of treatment. I will begin using my journal in a similar manner.

Only, instead of logging medical observations, I'll compile a record of spiritual observations. Then, after examining the symptoms, I will attempt to diagnose the spiritual malady that is affecting this town and arrive at some method of treatment.

"Havenhill isn't what it once was," Mercy said.

Josiah looked up from the bowl in which he was creaming the butter. He hadn't prompted her in any way for an assessment of the town. She'd just offered it.

"That's stating the obvious, isn't it?" Grace asked from the corner. She sat in a rocker and knitted.

"I was speaking *spiritually*," Mercy defended herself. "Of course the buildings and leadership have changed. But we as a town are not as spiritual as we once were."

Grace seemed to think on that for a couple of stitches. "I'm not sure that's true. When we're young, we tend to think our elders are wise. Then, when we grow up, we learn they're human and fallible. We think they've changed, when, in truth, they were that way all along."

"I understand what you're saying," Mercy replied. "But that's not what I mean. There's something different about this town . . . I don't know." She looked down at the floor. "Maybe this is too harsh . . . but I feel there is something evil here."

The third witness, Josiah thought.

He continued folding the butter while Mercy assembled the other ingredients—two eggs, sugar, rose water, cream, currants, and flour.

For several weeks now the sisters had been coming over to Josiah's house every Wednesday evening. As Grace predicted, after their first visit, the gossips had gone to work, prompting an investigation by the deacons.

Josiah had gotten wind of it. He had suggested to Mercy and Grace that, for the sake of their reputations, they should probably suspend their Wednesday evening activities. But Grace had a better idea.

On the night the three-deacon delegation—led by Philip—arrived at Josiah's house, there was a complete dinner waiting for them. Josiah and Mercy explained, with edible examples, that on Wednesday evenings they exchanged food recipes, nothing more.

Following the dinner, it was reported that one deacon found the evening most sinful. "The most sinful and finest feast I've ever eaten" were his exact words. Furthermore, they reported that even if there were any romantic inclinations, Grace Smythe—an upstanding member of the church—was present as chaperone.

Philip told Josiah confidentially that the deacons' report had not placated everyone in the church. Although Philip didn't identify Eunice Parkhurst directly, the inference was clear enough. One of the phrases that kept coming up was that the pastor should "abstain even from the appearance of evil."

"These are the same ingredients I use when I make Queen's Cake." Mercy pouted. "Why does yours taste so much better than mine?"

"That's why you're here, isn't it?" Josiah said in jest. "To learn from the master baker?"

Mercy picked up an egg, threatening to throw it at him. Grace lowered her knitting into her lap, amusement on her face.

Josiah clucked his tongue. "Resorting to violence—the actions of the truly desperate."

"Throw it!" Grace urged.

Josiah calmly set his spoon to one side. Then, with a quickness that caught Mercy off guard, he grabbed her wrist, the one holding the egg. As she squealed and struggled to get free, he turned her wrist so the egg was pointed at her.

Grace, still in the rocker, laughed at the struggle.

Unable to control the egg any longer, Mercy tried transferring it to her other hand. Without releasing her wrist, Josiah moved to intercept the transfer with his other hand.

Mercy's free hand, Josiah's free hand, and the egg all met in a violent collision. Josiah jumped back as egg yolk and white slid down Mercy's arm and dripped from her elbow onto the floor.

"Look what you did!" Mercy cried, laughing.

"I'm not the one who threatened to use an egg as a weapon!" Josiah said with a huge grin.

"Children! Look at the mess you've made!" Grace chided from the corner. "If you can't play nice, I'm not going to let you play at all!"

Josiah handed Mercy a towel. She used it to wipe egg from her arm, then knelt down to clean the floor. As she was scrubbing, something evidently distracted her. She reached to a shelf beneath the table and pulled out a book.

"Grace," she called, "look what I found!" She held up the book so Grace could see the cover.

Seeing what she had, Josiah tried to grab the book from her. Mercy kept it out of his reach.

Grace clapped her hands together and howled.

"*The Compleat Housewife*?" Mercy smirked.

Josiah reached unsuccessfully for the book again. "I've learned a lot from that book!"

Grace and Mercy were laughing so hard by now that tears flowed.

"Oh, we're perfectly aware that it's a good book." Mercy wiped tears away. "We're just a little surprised that *you* have a copy." She read from the cover. "*The Accomplished Gentlewoman's Companion.*"

"Gentlewoman Josiah," Grace said. "Has a nice ring to it."

"What else am I supposed to do?" Josiah claimed. "It's not like anyone's written *The Compleat Bachelor Parson.*"

Mercy flipped the pages. "Recipes . . . instructions for painting rooms . . . remedies for a variety of ailments . . . oh, here's a good section: removing mildew."

"A constant problem for bachelor parsons everywhere," Grace added. "We really do have to talk about our mutual mildew problem someday, Reverend Rush. Possibly you can pass along a few tips you've received at Harvard on the matter."

Josiah reached for the book again. This time Mercy made no attempt to keep it from him.

"This has all been fun, but we're here to bake a Queen's Cake," he insisted. He put the book back where Mercy had found it.

Both women attempted to dry their eyes.

"The secret to Queen's Cake," Josiah said, "is not the ingredients, but the oven temperature."

Mercy was still laughing as she followed him to the oven, which was built into the side of the fireplace.

Josiah ignored her levity, though he loved the way her eyes sparkled blue when she was happy.

"Heat the oven with riven—finely split wood," he instructed. "Then test it. A baker worth his salt can discern the temperature of an oven to within a few degrees by how long he can hold his arm inside."

Rolling up his shirt sleeve, Josiah demonstrated. He stuck his arm into the oven up to his elbow. After several moments, his lower lip curled. After a few more moments, he bit it. A few moments longer, and he extracted it. "It's ready."

"Where did you learn to do that?" Mercy asked.

"I lodged with a baker in Boston for a year. I paid for my lodging by assisting him early mornings, long before the sun came up."

Following Josiah's instructions, Mercy mixed the rest of the ingredients in the bowl in which Josiah had creamed the butter. Then they poured the mixture in greased pans and put them in the oven.

Josiah looked forward to Wednesdays.

While they waited for the cake to bake, they sat and talked. Sometimes about Josiah's sermon on the previous Sabbath, and sometimes about passages of Scripture Grace and Mercy read at home.

Tonight Josiah returned to something that was said earlier. "Grace, you said it's obvious Havenhill isn't what it once was. That's the first time I've heard anyone admit it."

"It's no secret," Grace replied, knitting needles flashing.

"Why haven't the leaders done something about it?"

"Maybe that's why you were brought back," Mercy said.

"Do you think so?" Josiah asked.

"No." Grace's answer was as immediate as it was definite.

Josiah cocked his head. "Why do you say that? If I wasn't brought back to make things better, why was I brought back?"

The knitting needles froze as Grace studied him. "Trust me. They have their reasons."

Her ominous tone prickled the hairs on the back of his neck. He wanted to ask her to whom she was referring but was hesitant to press. He didn't know Grace well enough yet to know whether her comment had merit, or if it was groundless conspiracy gossip. And he didn't want to lose one of the few friends he seemed to have in town. So he decided to steer the discussion back to where they had started.

"If it's no secret that the town is not what it once was—spiritually or otherwise—why don't they talk about it?"

"Facial wart," Grace muttered.

"I beg your pardon?"

"Facial wart. People who have facial warts are fully aware that they have blemishes everyone can see. Yet, when they look in the mirror in the morning, do they stare at the warts? No. They cream their cheeks, groom their hair, adjust their caps—all with complete disregard to the warts. They don't want to look at the warts because they make them feel ugly . . . so they don't."

Josiah gave this some thought.

Grace continued. "For a people who are proud of their spiritual heritage, resident evil is an unsightly wart. They ignore it. And they find it rude and take offense at anyone who calls attention to it."

Josiah liked the woman's candor. He decided to test it. "If what you're saying is true, then that makes me . . ."

"Oh, you're the town's wart," Grace said readily. "No doubt about that."

"Then why bring me back? Doesn't that call attention to the wart?"

Grace lowered her needles. "That is a puzzle, isn't it?"

CHAPTER 14

"Exactly what happened seven years ago?" Mercy asked. She dropped her eyes. "That is, if you don't mind telling me. I can be a little forward at times, asking things that aren't any of my business."

Half of the Queen's Cake remained on the table between them. Grace slumped in the corner rocker. She was asleep, her knitting resting on her lap. The fire danced behind Mercy. She and Josiah spoke in hushed voices so they wouldn't wake Grace.

He sighed. "That night has haunted me a thousand times."

"Then don't relive it again on my account," Mercy said.

Josiah smiled at her. Her compassion was refreshing. "Nobody has asked me to recount that night with such obvious concern for me. I want to tell you."

Mercy laid one hand on top of the other on the table and leaned forward to listen.

Josiah couldn't ever remember being able to talk to another woman so freely. With Nabby the romance kept getting in the way. Talking with Mercy was different. Easier. He didn't have this overriding fear that at any moment he was going to make a fool of himself.

His mind went back to that night. "It was a celebration. The day before, I'd received a letter from a Philadelphia physician, informing me that he would sponsor me in a medical internship. He was an old friend of Deacon Cranch. Reverend Parkhurst had written a recommendation on my behalf."

"You were going to be the first physician the town of Havenhill ever produced," Mercy said.

Josiah chuckled. "You remember that?"

"Everyone was talking about it."

"Aya." Josiah sighed again. "Everyone was so proud."

"You had reason to celebrate," Mercy insisted.

"I was just glad I wasn't going to have to work at the docks for the rest of my life. Philip, Johnny, and I got jobs there after school let out. Long, tedious, mindless hours. Our supervisor kept threatening to fire us and replace us with pack mules, because mules were more intelligent and didn't bray as much."

Mercy laughed. She had an easy, delightful laugh.

Josiah's tone turned serious. "I don't know where he got it, but Philip managed to get his hands on some rum. Johnny brought a bottle of hard cider. We thought we'd celebrate my upcoming departure."

He chuckled at the irony of it. "Well, the departure took place on schedule, but the circumstances surrounding it changed. Johnny was the accomplished drinker among us. He'd gotten drunk before. Philip was acquainted with hard liquor but had never gotten drunk. As for me, Deacon Cranch never allowed strong drink in his house. Both his grandfather and father had ruined their businesses and families because of their weakness to liquor, so he would have none of it and saw to it that neither did I. Had I ever come home with alcohol on my breath, he would have thrashed me within an inch of my life."

"What was different about that night?" Mercy asked.

Josiah grinned with shame. "I was feeling my oats. I was on the threshold of a whole new life and thought myself man enough to make my own decisions. Famous last words, wouldn't you say?"

Mercy smiled sympathetically.

Josiah continued, "We went to the docks and climbed in a window that happened to be left unlatched. Philip brought some candles with him, and we found a comfortable spot. We drank and laughed and had a great time. I remember tearing up a couple of times at the thought of how much I was going to miss Philip and Johnny and the Parkhursts."

"You mean Abigail," Mercy clarified.

Josiah grinned. There was no use denying it. Everyone in town back then knew how he felt for Abigail.

"But also Reverend Parkhurst," Josiah added. "He and Deacon Cranch had raised me. I used to think that I didn't have a mother, but I had two fathers to make up for it. Eunice was the closest thing I had to a mother. Did you know that she counseled me to be a doctor?"

Mercy shook her head.

"It was following a church service. Reverend Parkhurst preached on how all of creation naturally praised God, except for man. Man was the only holdout. Anyway, during that church service, I remember feeling that I wanted to spend the rest of my life communicating God's truth to people and pointing them toward God."

"God was calling you into the ministry."

"Ironic, isn't it? I wanted to talk over what I was feeling with Reverend Parkhurst following the service, but he wasn't available. One of the deacons had pulled him away on some business. Eunice noticed that I was troubled about something. She sat me down and we talked. I told her what I was feeling. She said that, while my desire to serve God was admirable, He had evidently gifted me to become a physician and that God needed devout laymen too. This was before Reverend Parkhurst wrote the letter of recommendation for me for the medical internship. Looking back, I think she preferred for her daughter to marry a promising young physician rather than a struggling young pastor."

"And now you're her pastor," Mercy said.

"God certainly has a sense of humor, doesn't He?" Josiah grinned, then straightened his back. "How did we get so far off-track?"

"You were telling me how much you were going to miss everyone."

"Aya. It was one of those times in life when you stand on the edge of your future. You think you know what lies ahead, but then everything changes . . . Well, we drank, we laughed, and we drank some more—too much. At one point Philip and Johnny got up to . . . well, to go do what has to be done when you consume a lot of liquids. I barely remember watching them stumble through the dark warehouse. After that I passed out. But I must have knocked over a candle, because the next thing I knew, there were flames all around me, and Philip and Johnny were half dragging me, half helping me to my feet."

Josiah stared solemnly at his hands. "We managed to climb out the window. And that's when we heard the screaming—the girls . . . and then Reverend Parkhurst . . . There are no words to describe how horrific it is to be aware that someone needs help, and that under ordinary circumstances, you might be able to help them, but that you're so drunk, you have no control over your limbs. It was like I was a rag doll. My mind kept yelling at my arms and legs to move, only they couldn't because they were full of stuffing."

The fire popped and crackled.

Mercy looked over at Grace, who hadn't moved. "Of course, you realize God has forgiven you," she said softly.

"Aya."

"Regardless of whether or not the townspeople ever forgive you."

Josiah stared at his hands. The next thing he knew, one of Mercy's hands covered them.

"Some of us already have forgiven you," she said.

Her hand was warm, but not nearly as warm as the expressed thought. It was a balm to his tortured soul. Who would have thought that the silly little girl he barely knew in school would one day minister comfort to his soul?

He looked up at her. "May I tell you something?"

Their eyes met and held.

When Mercy blushed and averted her eyes, Josiah was afraid he'd given her the wrong idea. So he went on hurriedly, "It's related to something we spoke of earlier—about evil in the town."

Now Mercy appeared embarrassed for being embarrassed. "Certainly . . . I guess . . ."

Josiah hesitated. Now that he'd started, he wasn't sure he should continue. "Well, for one thing, I just wanted you to know how much I enjoy you and Grace coming over. How much I like our time together—the three of us—cooking and having fun."

She raised an eyebrow. "And how is that related to evil in the town?"

He had said that, hadn't he? Now he wished he hadn't. But he had, and now he had to explain it to her. How could he begin? He studied her eyes. They were innocent, and there was no condemnation in them. He could confide in those eyes.

He took a deep breath. "While I've been away, God has been working in my life. Not just academically and in preparation for a pulpit ministry, but spiritually."

"That's evident in your preaching," Mercy offered.

"It is?" *That is encouraging,* Josiah thought. "Anyway, in Boston, while I was ministering there, God—"

He'd walked to the edge. Should he take one more step and take the plunge? He'd never told another soul what he was about to tell Mercy Litchfield. He'd wanted to tell someone, but he'd never felt comfortable bringing the subject up. Until now.

"God . . . ?" Mercy prompted him.

He examined her eyes again. Yes, this was a pure soul sitting across from him. He was certain of it. He took the plunge. "God gave me a gift."

She didn't laugh. Didn't mock him. Didn't blink or sit back repulsed or in disbelief. Mercy's reaction was as though God handed out gifts every day.

"It's a spiritual gift," he continued, "with physical manifestations."

He waited for a response.

She waited for more information.

Josiah continued, "God has given me the gift of discerning spirits. I can sense the spirit of a person or situation."

Mercy leaned forward. "You said it had physical manifestations."

"A joyous spirit buoys me. I can feel a person's joy or peace. Do you understand what I'm saying? I know what righteousness feels like."

"And sin," Mercy said.

The memory of the pain of recent days hit him. His chin quivered. His eyes glazed with tears. "Yes. I know what sin feels like."

Tears also filled Mercy's eyes. "That explains it. When you preach."

"Aya?"

"You look like you're in pain."

Josiah nodded. "I am."

"How horrible and wonderful it must be for you."

Josiah grinned weakly. "That pretty much describes ministry."

"What does it feel like? Sin, I mean. How do you sense it?"

"Actually, it's a progression of feelings. It begins with a tickling sensation across my nose and cheek, like a spider web, only moist and cold."

Mercy shuddered. "How awful!"

"It gets my attention—possibly so I don't get confused over what comes next."

"Which is?"

Josiah wanted to tell her, but he found it embarrassing describing the sensation to a lady. "I'd always associated evil with a loss of joy, a draining sensation . . . like draining the life from someone. It's just the opposite. As soon as I feel the brush against my cheek and nose, a pleasurable sensation sweeps over me. Cravings stir inside of me that I can't begin to describe other than as a rush of appetites. I feel more alive than I've ever felt before, but in an aggressive, domineering way. I get this incredible urge to compete, argue, buy, eat, sing, romance a beautiful lady, outwrestle a strong man, and be adored and worshiped by thousands and thousands of people. But it doesn't last. I feel all of that in an instant, and then—"

"Pain," Mercy said. "Like a child who eats too many sweets and ends up with a bellyache."

"Exactly! Only the pain is deeper. There's a hollowness to it, an ache that cannot be relieved. Sometimes the pain is sharp. Over a period of time, it lessens, but it's unrelenting."

Mercy turned and stared toward the wall, as if in thought.

"What?" Josiah asked.

She opened her mouth, then hesitated.

"Go ahead," Josiah urged. "Tell me what you're thinking."

"It's not my place."

"Please," he begged. "Tell me."

She took a breath. "Some people might interpret what you've told me as nothing more than a nervous stomach. You pick up on someone else's anxiety and take it upon yourself."

Josiah nodded. "At first that's what I thought it was. Until God showed me otherwise."

Mercy appeared eager to hear the details, so Josiah told her.

"I was in a Charlestown tavern, dining with a friend. I've never met a man who could pick up languages so easily. He helped me with Greek and Hebrew; I helped him with rhetoric. He was an upstanding man. Married. Six-month-old child. Everyone expected him to be teaching languages at Harvard within a couple of years.

"He arrived late. We shook hands. That's when I felt it. The brush of a web, the thrill, the pain. All in a quick succession and sharper than I'd ever experienced.

"I did my best to disguise it. We ate. We talked about college and upcoming exams. He spoke glowingly about his wife, had me laughing over the changes a child brings to a household, and excitedly told me about a discussion he'd had with the dean about his future with the college. A pleasant evening. Good conversation. Had it not been for the discomfort in my gut.

"I wanted to say something. To ask him if something was troubling him. From all appearances he was happy and cheerful, and we'd been laughing so much, it seemed foolish just to blurt out my suspicions.

Besides, I told myself it wasn't my place. I wasn't his conscience or his spiritual advisor."

"But the feeling persisted," Mercy said.

"Aya. We were having coffee. He was stirring his when I just couldn't hold back any longer."

"What did you say?"

"I said, 'I know this is going to sound crazy, but something's terribly wrong in your life.'"

"And what did he say?"

"At first nothing. He just stirred his coffee. But then his hand began to shake so violently that the spoon clanged against the cup and coffee spilled over. 'You couldn't have known,' he said. 'There's no way you could know.'"

Josiah paused to take a breath.

"He'd just started up with a woman, his wife's best friend. He'd just come from being with her. After praying with him, the feeling lifted."

For a time Mercy and Josiah sat in silence. Then she exclaimed, "How awful that you suffer so!"

"I pray for relief, but not for release from the gift."

"And the only way that will happen . . ."

". . . is for the townspeople to return to God," Josiah concluded.

Mercy reached across the table and put her hand on Josiah's arm. "Thank you for sharing that with me. I know better now how to pray for you."

A stirring in the corner made Mercy retract her hand quickly.

Grace stretched and eyed them. "What time is it?" she asked through a yawn.

As he did every Wednesday night, Josiah watched Grace and Mercy as they walked to the main road. Tonight Grace turned suddenly and hurried back, leaving Mercy standing in the road.

She rushed past Josiah into the house, saying, "Forgot my shawl" as she passed him.

Josiah followed her into the house.

She was waiting for him. Grabbing him by the wrist, she glared at him with clear, no-nonsense eyes. "All that talk about pain and spiritual suffering? It had better be the truth. Because if I find out that you've been weaving a story as a lure to snag Mercy, believe me, I'll show you pain!"

The next moment she was gone. Josiah could hear her calling to Mercy, "It was by the rocker, right where I left it!"

CHAPTER 15

After nearly a summer of journal entries, I am beginning to see patterns in my study of Havenhill's spiritual condition. There are definite, identifiable symptoms. I am close to formulating a progression of symptoms for what I am calling Soul Sickness.

Meanwhile, events at the church are simmering. While there are no open hostilities, at every turn animosity underlies attitudes and comments. The situation is dry tinder. All it will take is a single spark to set it off.

I still have yet to speak to Nabby. It seems the whole town is shielding her from me: Every time I approach her at church or on the street, someone intercepts me or whisks her away. She still manages, however, to deliver notes anonymously to me. They appear at the house and sometimes on the pulpit before I preach. The message is usually the same with little variation in expression. She's praying for me. I take great comfort in that thought.

A sliver of August moon shimmered on the water. The docks were dark and silent, except for the slapping of the tide against pillars below.

Strange.

As Josiah walked Water Street, he peered between the rows of warehouses. There should be all manner of noise to direct him to the scene of the emergency.

Thirty minutes ago he'd been asleep. A male voice shouting for him, accompanied by the rapping of knuckles against wood, had awakened him.

There'd been a fight at the docks, he was told by a sailor, if his baggy canvas breeches were any indication. Josiah didn't recognize him. He was still a boy. He said his older brother had been stabbed and was near death and was calling for a preacher.

"You gotta come," the boy pleaded. "Mick's real scared of dyin'."

Josiah told the boy to wait outside for him while he dressed, but when he stepped out of his door, the boy was gone. So Josiah had hurried to the docks. But once there, he saw no signs of any altercation, nor any signs of life.

A prank probably, Josiah decided, but he had to be sure. He wasn't far from Bailey's Tavern. Maybe someone there would know something. Maybe they would know a sailor named Mick who had a little brother.

Just as Josiah turned in the direction of the tavern, a movement at the far end of the warehouse caught his eye. When he looked, it was gone, but he'd seen enough to know it was too big to be an animal. It was tall, like a man, and big. Yet now there was nothing but moonlight reflecting on water and wood.

Josiah was certain he'd seen something. There was no doubt in his mind that a shadow had passed between him and the silvery reflection.

"Who's there?" Josiah called.

His voice bounced between warehouse walls.

"This is Reverend Rush. Is anyone there?"

If they knew he was a minister, maybe they'd realize he was no threat to them.

Josiah stepped between the warehouses toward the open end of the dock. Between him and the water, the passage was like a tunnel. Darkness engulfed him. Out of necessity, his steps were cautious.

A Bible passage came to mind—"*Yea, though I walk through the valley of the shadow of death . . .*" The valley of concealed death—isn't that how he'd translated the Hebrew?

"Thou art with me," Josiah said, completing the psalmist's sentence.

The passageway narrowed in places where barrels and crates were stacked against the walls. It was the perfect haunt for a predator, coiled and ready to leap at an unsuspecting passerby.

"Hello? Reverend Rush here," Josiah shouted again, hoping to ward off any predators with sound.

He slowed to half steps.

The docks and the town were eerily silent. Only shadows and moonlight surrounded him.

His heart beat with greater confidence when he reached the end of the warehouse canyon. The dock opened up to him, stretching both left and right.

He heard, then smelled it, even before he saw it.

Fire!

Huge tongues of it licked the side of a warehouse to the right. Smoke rose starward into the night, like some ancient sacrifice to the god of fear and chaos.

Josiah ran toward it, looking for something with which to battle the flames—a blanket, a bucket, *anything.*

The fire had a significant start on the warehouse and was greedily consuming more.

"Fire!" he shouted. "Fire on the docks! Fire!"

As he ran toward the blaze, his mind raced. He'd yet to find anything with which to battle the blaze. And the closer he got to it, the more he realized there was little he could do alone. Should he try? Or should he run for help? But if he ran for help, how much greater would the fire be by the time he returned?

He was close now. The blaze had grown with incredible speed. He was helpless before it. He should have run for help in the first place. Now he'd wasted too much time.

He had to get to Bailey's Tavern. He turned and began to run.

One step. Two.

A hand shot out from the shadows. It yanked Josiah through a warehouse door with such force that he was lifted off his feet.

"What are you doing here?"

The voice was familiar. Feeling as though the wind had been ripped from his lungs, Josiah sputtered, "Joh . . . Joh . . . Johnny?"

Holding a fistful of Josiah's clothing, an angry Johnny Mott glared at him. "I asked you what you were doing here!"

"F . . . f . . . fire!" Josiah managed.

Still seething, Johnny released him. "This way."

Still unable to catch enough breath to speak, Josiah motioned helplessly in the direction of the fire.

With an impatience that bordered on rage, Johnny Mott grabbed Josiah and dragged him the length of the warehouse. At the far end, he opened a door, looked out, then pulled his head back quickly.

On the other side of the door, men shouted, raising the fire alarm. A moment later their voices became inaudible. Johnny stuck his head out the door, proclaimed that the coast was clear, then pulled Josiah through the door behind him, flinging him outside.

Josiah stumbled and went down.

Johnny towered over him. "Go home!" he hissed.

Sprawled on the ground, bewildered, Josiah looked up. "Johnny—"

"I'm not going to tell you again, Josiah. Go home! And don't let anyone see you!"

The warehouse door slammed shut.

Josiah heard shouts and the thunder of a herd of feet. He scrambled behind a stack of crates.

A dozen or so men ran in the direction of the fire. When they were past him, Josiah stepped out onto Water Street. The flames of the fire arched over the warehouse.

He stared at the flames for a moment, then at the closed door through which Johnny Mott had disappeared. As he made his way home, by way of back streets, he encountered no one.

CHAPTER 16

As expected, Josiah received another visit.

"We lost half of the warehouse before the fire could be contained," Philip said.

As Philip spoke, the eyes of a selectman and a deacon studied Josiah from beneath furrowed brows.

Josiah lifted his chin. "I didn't start the fire."

"Ask him where he was last night at the time of the fire," the selectman demanded. He was a tall man, with big ears. Josiah hadn't met him before.

Philip frowned. "I thought we agreed I'd ask the questions, Fitch."

"Ask him!" Fitch insisted.

Josiah took a step toward Fitch and looked him in the eyes. "On my honor, as a man of God, I did not start that fire." For extra measure, Josiah held the man's gaze, but Fitch didn't back down.

Philip stepped between them. "We did what we came to do. Fitch, you and Gleason go on ahead. I'll catch up with you."

Fitch left, but he clearly didn't believe Josiah.

A few moments later, Josiah and Philip were alone.

Philip stared at the floor. "Josiah, I need you to be completely honest with me."

"You don't believe me!" Josiah cried.

"Johnny said he saw you on the dock last night, just as the fire broke out."

"I'd been called to an emergency!"

Josiah told him about being roused in the middle of the night and about his search for a wounded man.

"And you've never seen this sailor before?" Philip asked.

"No."

Philip stroked his chin in thought.

"I didn't start that fire last night!" Josiah insisted.

"Johnny thinks you did," Philip countered. "He helped you escape unseen to protect you."

"He told you that?"

Philip nodded.

"I saw someone just before the fire broke out," Josiah said.

"Did you recognize him?"

"He was just a shadow, and I only caught a glimpse, but it looked like a big man."

"What are you saying?"

"I don't know."

"Josiah, we've never hidden anything from each other before. We're never going to reestablish the friendship we once had if we keep things from each other."

He was right, of course. "It's just that I haven't been around Johnny for years. And since I've been back, because of the situation with Abigail, I've not had a chance to spend much time with him. You know him. Do you think . . . is it possible . . . he was down there . . ."

"Are you telling me you think Johnny Mott started the fire last night?"

"That's what I'm asking you. Is it conceivable?"

Philip grinned widely. "Not likely."

"I don't under—"

"Johnny's warehouse is the one that went up in flames," Philip explained. "We own it jointly."

It didn't make sense for Johnny Mott to burn down his own warehouse. Still, Josiah knew what he saw, and he wasn't as confident as Philip that Johnny wasn't behind the blaze. But why would a man burn down his own warehouse? And, even more disturbing, why would he lure Josiah to the docks to cast suspicion upon him?

Of course, there was the obvious motive—jealousy. Philip himself had said that when it came to Abigail, Johnny viewed him as a threat. But if that were the case, why did Johnny drag him through the warehouse so he could escape undetected? And why tell only Philip that he was in the vicinity of the fire? Why not tell the entire town?

So many things didn't make sense, which only added to Josiah's impression that a seething cauldron of secret activity lurked just beneath the surface.

Such were the questions plaguing Josiah the next day when he strolled by the millinery shop on New London Street. Glancing inside while passing, he saw Nabby framed within a windowpane—a perfect portrait of feminine beauty. She appeared to be alone.

Josiah watched shamelessly as she examined a velvet handbag, her slender fingers caressing the fabric and testing the drawstring. Whether by movement or shadow or simply by seeing him out of the corner of her eye, she must have sensed she was being watched. She glanced out the window.

Josiah smiled.

Abigail returned his smile and lowered her gaze coyly. Her cheeks colored.

For a man who needed so little encouragement, her smile was a mugging. He couldn't have prevented himself from being dragged into the millinery shop had he wanted to. He didn't want to. Bounding up the steps, Josiah burst into the shop.

"What are you doing?" Nabby exclaimed, evidently shocked by his eager advance. She glanced nervously in the direction of the back room.

It was hardly the greeting he had hoped for. He halted and searched for a reason to be in the shop. "My shirt cuff needs sewing."

"You're not wearing cuffs."

Josiah looked at his sleeves. She was right. He wasn't wearing cuffs. "Well, then, I came in to shop for a new greatcoat."

Again she peered toward the doorway that led to the back of the shop. "You shouldn't be here," she whispered.

Josiah shrugged innocently. "In a town this size, we're bound to have occasional innocent encounters. It's inevitable."

"I know that look in your eye, Josiah Rush. There's nothing innocent about it. You should leave."

Was he being that obvious? He couldn't help it. This was the first time he'd been this close to Nabby since his return to Havenhill. And now he was alone with her . . . at least for the moment.

His heart stuttered. She looked incredible, even if the smallpox had left its marks—one on her forehead between her eyes, another beside her right eye at the temple, and still another on her jaw close to her chin. But she wore the marks well. Only someone who had spent hours studying every inch of her face would notice.

Josiah's cheeks hurt from grinning so hard. He felt giddy. Not exactly something a man wants to admit, but that's how he felt. And he didn't want the feeling to end. Just being this near to Nabby was intoxicating. His eyes eagerly registered the bounce of her hair when she turned her head and the sleek white curve of her neck.

"You're staring!" Abigail hissed, turning away from him.

"Aya," he agreed, without making any effort to look away.

"Please leave," Abigail pleaded, her voice quivering.

"I miss you," Josiah whispered.

He knew it was wrong to tell her this, him being a minister and her promised to another man, but he couldn't help himself. The words formed and would not be denied life.

She refused to look at him. She searched for and found a handkerchief. The soft sound of weeping followed.

A wave of anguish swept over him. This wasn't what he'd intended. He had wanted to see sparkles of joy in her eyes, not tears.

"Nabby," he began softly.

"*Abigail,*" she corrected sharply.

"Please," he pleaded. "This was not my intention. Must our encounters always be painful?"

She turned on him suddenly. "Yes, they must. How can they be anything other than painful? You seem to forget . . ."

"Don't say that I forget you're promised to another man! It haunts me every minute of every day. What I don't understand is, why? Why Johnny Mott?"

Abigail's gaze was cool. "He's kind to me."

"Kind. Johnny Mott?"

"What do you mean by that?"

"The word *kind* and Johnny's name haven't exactly been synonymous lately."

Abigail's brow furrowed. "Why? What happened?"

The front door of the shop opened. A short woman dressed in black put one foot inside, saw Abigail and Josiah standing close to each other alone in the shop, and froze. "Oh!" Her eyes widened with surprise and delight.

"Goodwife Hibbard!" Abigail greeted her. "How nice to—"

Before Abigail could say another word, the woman closed the door and hurried away.

"That's just great!" Abigail said. "Within the hour everyone in town will know that you and I were caught alone in the millinery shop."

"But we're just standing here," he reasoned.

Abigail gave him one of those men-can-be-so-dumb looks. "Not by the time Goodwife Hibbard gets done telling it."

Josiah stared helplessly at the closed door. Through the windowpane he could see Goodwife Hibbard bustling across the street at nearly a run, hailing two women he didn't recognize.

"I didn't mean to—"

"Yes, you did!" Abigail snapped. "You knew better than to come in here."

"I know," Josiah agreed lamely. "But once I saw you, I couldn't . . . I had to . . ."

"Josiah Rush, you are just going to have to accept the fact that it's over between us."

"Is that what you want, Abigail? Do you want it to be over between us?"

Tears filled her eyes. "That's not fair."

"What isn't fair is that just because of one night seven years ago, you feel you're condemned to marry a man you don't love!"

Abigail was weeping openly now. "What makes you think I don't love Johnny?"

"Because you still have feelings for me. Don't try to deny it. I can see it in your eyes."

Abigail turned her back on him. "I think you should leave."

"The store? Or the town?"

The instant he said the words, he regretted them.

Abigail swiveled to face him, disbelief and pain marring her beautiful face.

"I'm sorry," Josiah said. "I shouldn't have said that. I didn't come in here to hurt you. I'll leave."

He turned to go, then remembered something. "I hope you'll continue sending me the notes and prayers of encouragement. I can't begin to tell you how much they've meant to me."

She stared at him blankly.

Just then the curtain separating the showroom from the back room parted. A middle-aged woman stepped through it, carrying a bolt of cloth. Behind the storekeeper was Judith Usher, the mother of the two girls who had died in the fire.

The storekeeper began midsentence, picking up the conversation with Abigail as though she'd never left. ". . . buried deeper than I thought it was. The color isn't what I'd remembered. However the pattern—" She stopped midstride and midsentence when she saw Josiah. Looking quickly toward the weeping Abigail, the woman began to scowl.

Judith rushed past the storekeeper to Abigail's side, pulling her away, talking to her in whispers.

The shopkeeper gave Josiah a territorial glare of warning, like a lioness protecting her turf. "Are you buying today, Reverend Rush?" she growled.

"Well, I had hoped to." His eyes scanned the shelves, landing on the first male product he saw. "Aya. There it is! I came to purchase . . ."

The storekeeper followed his gaze. "A beaver hat?" she asked skeptically.

"Aya!" Josiah said a little too enthusiastically. "I've always wanted a hat made of beaver fur."

The shopkeeper took the hat from the shelf and Josiah tried it on.

He looked ridiculous in it. Nevertheless, he bought the hat and insisted on wearing it as he left the shop.

CHAPTER 17

On the following Wednesday, Josiah waited for Grace and Mercy to arrive. The usual hour came and went. An hour passed, then another. Josiah grew concerned. Finally, he could wait no longer. But just as he stepped out the door, he spied Grace approaching the house.

Alone.

"I'm not staying," she snapped. She handed him a bundle of envelopes tied with a string and a book.

"I was getting concerned," Josiah said, taking what she offered without knowing their purpose. "Is Mercy all right?"

"Mercy is not feeling well. She wanted you to have these. The letters are from her cousin in Northampton. Return the book at your leisure." Grace turned to leave.

Josiah called after her.

Grace kept walking.

"I'll come with you," he offered, hurrying to join her. "I'll pray with her. It's not the smallpox, is it?"

"It's not the pox," Grace tossed back curtly.

"Thank God for that," Josiah said, relieved. The smallpox epidemic had appeared to have run its course. For Mercy to have come down with it now would have been doubly tragic.

Josiah now fell in step with Grace. But the next instant, he realized he was walking alone.

"Mercy is in no condition to receive visitors," she said.

"I'm not expecting to be entertained. This is a pastoral call."

"She's in no condition for pastoral calls."

Grace stood, hands on her hips, looking like the proverbial unmovable object.

"All right," Josiah conceded. "Tell her I'll visit her tomorrow. I'll put on a pot of soup tonight and bring her some. Does she like—"

Grace interrupted. "Are you always this thickheaded?"

"What are you talking about?"

"Then let me spell it out for you. Mercy is in no condition to receive a call from YOU."

Josiah closed the distance between them. In a soft voice, he said, "Grace, have I done something to offend Mercy?"

Grace rolled her eyes in disbelief. She pressed past him, continuing on her way.

Josiah was left standing alone on the road. Perplexed, he held the bundle of letters and a book more tightly.

Grace turned around long enough to give him one final glare—the kind that could curdle milk. "Let's just say Mercy isn't partial to beaver-skin hats."

I'm afraid I've made a royal mess of things with Nabby and Mercy. My attempts to make amends have fared no better.

First, I went to the Parkhurst house. Not unexpectedly, my request to speak to Abigail was rebuffed with a bushel basket of unkind words from Eunice, who repeatedly emphasized her disappointment in me.

Then, despite Grace's warning, I made a similar attempt to see Mercy and was likewise thwarted by a passionate guardian who would not permit me a hearing.

Lord, what am I to do? You know my heart. I wish neither woman sorrow, yet I seem to dispense strong doses of it at every turn. I enjoy Mercy's company immensely, but my heart belongs to Abigail.

Lord, how well I remember Reverend Parkhurst's sermon describing how You chose Rebecca for Isaac. Since that day I have known that Abigail is my Rebecca and that in Your good time and in Your own way, You will make it possible for us to be united as man and wife—despite my clumsy social skills, which I am certain are a grievance to You. Almighty God, give me the desire of my heart in spite of myself.

Regarding the condition of the town, the patterns I indicated earlier are being confirmed every day. The symptoms reveal a disease that is unmistakably spiritual, affecting the judgment, emotion, and general disposition of those infected. (It affects their eternal state as well, but that portion of the study is for God alone to evaluate.)

After months of observation and collection of data, I am more convinced than ever that Havenhill is suffering an epidemic of Soul Sickness that is just as deadly—nay, deadlier—than smallpox. Two reasons lead me to this conclusion:

One, smallpox attacks the body, while Soul Sickness attacks a person's eternal soul.

Two, while the infection of smallpox is evident to all, the infection of Soul Sickness is more insidious. Those infected with Soul Sickness often go about their daily business oblivious to the symptoms and seriousness of the disease and the effect it has on their lives and relationships.

Symptoms of Soul Sickness are everywhere. Since my return to Havenhill, I have had occasion to observe and provide counsel in situations involving discord and belligerence, intolerance, immorality, corruption, and profanity. Men are out of control. Women are vain and immodest. Young people are conceited and self-absorbed. Parents provoke their children to anger. Fits of rage occur daily, while acts of selfish ambition, dissensions, and factions are everywhere present.

Given the infection and the resulting climate of the townspeople, is it any wonder they have lost their first love and that they no longer find joy in worship or peace with God?

Lord, how my heart aches for them. As a mother's heart aches for her fevered child, so my heart aches for those You have entrusted to my care.

The scope of my study includes a comparison of Havenhill residents I knew seven years ago and presently; conversations with people regarding the lives of their relatives, their children, and themselves; and a lifetime of memories of people I've met and observed.

While any definitive study will take years to complete, I believe I have gathered enough material to hypothesize that there are six distinct stages of Soul Sickness.

1. *Insensitivity. In this initial stage, there is a cooling of spiritual zeal. Worship becomes routine. Bible reading and prayer are neglected. The things of this world take on greater importance than the things of God's kingdom. God is thought to be distant, and thus is no longer feared. Men's spirits become calloused.*

2. *Initial pain. Those infected become increasingly dissatisfied with life. Things that once were pleasurable become ordinary, even despised. There is no satisfaction in work. Family members are taken for granted or ignored. Food and drink lose their ability to cheer. There is a general feeling of anxiety about life.*

3. *Increased pain. Depression sets in, as does bitterness and resentment. Dissatisfaction turns to anger. Those infected are*

quick to blame others and quick to find fault. There is a loss of sleep and a loss of appetite. At this stage, relationships cause more pain than joy. People are defensive and quick to anger.

4. *Uncharacteristic behavior patterns emerge. There is a noticeable change in personality. There are premeditated acts of revenge and hate that never would have been associated with the person previously. Camaraderie and wicked joy is found in promoting acts of party spirit. (At this stage, Christians often realize that what they are doing is wrong, but they find themselves unable to stop.) The cycle of guilt starts.*

5. *Increase in destructive behavior. Shameful, hurtful, divisive acts are rationalized as being justified. The infected persons are blinded to the consequences of their actions. A prideful martyr spirit grows to such extent that the persons infected not only believe they are justified in their sinful acts, they take pride in their sin.*

6. *The spirit dies. At this stage, all guilt is gone. A person sins without fear of impunity. Corruption, immorality, blasphemy, rage, drunkenness, orgies, factions, and idolatry are accepted and at times embraced as part of being human. Acts of sin are viewed as empowering. Violence is enjoyed. Self-destructive behavior results. The person lives as an antichrist.*

Unlike other diseases, there seems to be no common pattern of time associated with Soul Sickness. The worst cases move from stage to stage with frightening speed. More commonly, cases take years to progress through the stages, often stalling at a stage for a period of time. The inevitable end of Soul Sickness is self-destruction or such behavior that forces society to restrain or destroy the infected person to protect itself. In many cases, the infected person dies miserably, disillusioned with life.

Josiah sat back. The realization of what he'd written sat heavy on his chest.

Dipping his pen, he leaned forward to finish.

Because Soul Sickness is by nature a spiritual disease, the cure must also be spiritual. While many succeed in alleviating the symptoms temporarily with entertaining diversions, unless the root cause of the disease is treated, the symptoms will return and the disease will progress. Spiritual renewal and cleansing alone can cure this disease and purify the soul. And such renewal and cleansing will only come from God and through prayer.

Placing his pen on the table, Josiah rubbed weary eyes, satisfied with what he'd written. But if his role in the smallpox incident was any indication, knowing the nature of the disease and possessing the cure were not enough if the people wouldn't listen to him. Somehow he had to find a way to reason with them, to help them see their need, and then to lead them to God, the Source of all healing power.

But how?

Mercy's bound letters and the book she'd loaned him sat on the edge of his desk. Josiah had intended on taking a look at them tonight before retiring, but his eyes were tired and his back ached.

Blowing out the candle, he stumbled to his bed in the dark and fell into a fitful sleep.

CHAPTER 18

The string tying Mercy's letters lay undone. The letters themselves lay unfolded and tossed one on top of the other on Josiah's desk. Morning stretched elongated squares of sunlight across them.

With a hand covering his mouth, Josiah stared at the letters with glistening eyes. So overcome with emotion was he, it was a wonder he didn't burst at the seams!

Contained in these letters was the answer he'd been looking for, longing for, praying for! He couldn't believe it! Yet, here it was—the cure to Soul Sickness! He was certain of it!

With a yelp, he stood, knocking his chair backward.

"Thank you, God! Thank you!" he shouted at the ceiling.

So dark had been the pit of despair he'd uncovered during his study of spiritual disease that he'd almost despaired of ever finding a cure. But now it had found him! Flying to him on the wings of Mercy.

He laughed at the thought.

Mercy didn't exactly have wings, but she had a cousin who wrote letters to her. And what letters! Wondrous letters! The letters that were currently bathed in morning light on Josiah's desk.

A promise of brighter days?

Havenhill's rainbow?

"And thank you, Lord, for Mercy!" Josiah shouted. "And for her cousin, Esther Garrick of Hadley! God bless them both!"

His energy needing an outlet, Josiah walked in a circle—then again, never wandering too far from the source of his joy.

Righting his chair, he sat and picked up the top letter to read it again. Then he stood, unable to contain the energies that surged within.

He paced as he read, scanning over the first paragraphs that were largely family matters, reports of illnesses, and comments about the weather.

His concentration quickened when he found the paragraph he was looking for—

Mercy dear, I can't tell you how exciting it is to see the meetinghouse overflowing with souls seeking a fresh outpouring of the Spirit of God! Since the revival began, hundreds of hearts have been melted, including several of the deacons of our church. Some of them wept openly during the preaching of the sermon and cried out to God, pleading with Him to save them and heal their families. Hadley hasn't been the same since the revival began. Oh, Mercy, for the first time in years, people are happy!

Josiah picked up another letter.

I wish you could have been here, Mercy. Reverend Edwards—you would like him. He's a very stately and controlled preacher—preached last Sabbath at our church. His topic was, "The Lord Our Righteousness." During the sermon one young girl became so distressed, she sank to her knees. She cried out to God with such heartfelt desire that ripples of conviction seemed to emanate from her, melting one stony heart after another.

And another letter, dated a week later.

A great moving of the Spirit of God is felt not only in Hadley and Northampton, but in the surrounding regions—Suffield, Sunderland,

Deerfield, Hatfield, Long Meadow, Coventry, East Windsor, Lebanon, Durham, Stratford, Ripton, Guilford, Tolland, Bolton, Groton, and Woodbury. O Mercy, the entire countryside is aflame with the Spirit!

Josiah lowered the letter. "And Havenhill, Lord? Will You add Havenhill to this list of towns?"

Still another letter—

Dear Mercy, events of late are astounding. I can scarcely believe them myself. There have been some unbelievable transformations among people who, until now, have been of the most deplorable nature. They come to the meetinghouse with a thoughtless and vain spirit, scarcely conducting themselves with common decency, only to be suddenly and overwhelmingly convicted of their sin. I've seen women gripping the pillars of the church as though they were slipping into a pit of condemnation, crying out for God to save them. And He does, Mercy! Oh, He does! Having immersed themselves in the cleansing power of God's Holy Spirit, they find peace of heart and mind for the first time in—well, in some cases, decades!

Another letter—

I traveled with Hank Ury and his wife—you remember Martha, don't you? She's the one who uses earwax for lip balm. Regardless, I traveled with the Urys to Enfield where we heard Reverend Edwards preach "Their Foot Shall Slide in Due Time." It was a powerful sermon, dear. Reverend Edwards said, "It is nothing but God's mere pleasure that keeps you from being this moment swallowed up in everlasting destruction." And then he told them how God had granted them an extraordinary opportunity, for He had thrown open the door of mercy to cry with a loud voice to sinners. O Mercy, dear, many are daily coming from the east, west, north, and south. They come in miserable condition and leave with their hearts filled with love to Him who has loved them!

Josiah's chest heaved with excitement. Clutching the letters, he shouted, "Bless your heart, Mercy Litchfield! Bless your heart!"

Not only had Mercy loaned Josiah her cousin's letters, but also a book—one that bore a now familiar name on the spine. In his excitement over the reports in the letters, Josiah nearly passed it over, so eager was he to tell someone about the wondrous events that were occurring to the north of them.

However, out of curiosity, he lifted the book's cover and read the title page:

A Faithful
NARRATIVE
of the
Surprising Work of God
in the
CONVERSION
of
Many hundred souls in Northampton,
and the neighboring towns and
villages of New Hampshire in
New England
In a LETTER to the Rev. Dr. Benjamin
Colman of Boston.
Written by the Rev. Mr. Edwards, Minister of
Northampton, on Nov. 6, 1736
And Published,
With a large PREFACE,
by Dr. Watts and Dr. Guyse.
LONDON

Intrigued, Josiah began to read. The accounts as recorded by Reverend Edwards captivated him:

> I was surprised with relation to a young woman, who had been one of the greatest company keepers in the whole town. When she came to me, I had never heard that she was become in any wise serious, but by the conversation I then had with her, it appeared to me that what she gave an account of was a glorious work of God's infinite power and sovereign grace; and that God had given her a new heart, truly broken and sanctified. I could not then doubt of it and have seen much in my acquaintance with her since to confirm it.

On another page—

> Presently upon this, a great and earnest concern about the great things of religion and the eternal world became universal in all parts of the town, and among persons of all degrees, and all ages. The noise amongst the dry bones waxed louder and louder; all other talk but about spiritual and eternal things was soon thrown by; all the conversation, in all companies and upon all occasions, was upon these things only, unless so much as was necessary for people carrying on their ordinary secular business. Other discourse than of the things of religion would scarcely be tolerated in any company. The minds of people were wonderfully taken off from the world. It was treated amongst us as a thing of very little consequence. They seemed to follow their worldly business, more as a part of their duty, than from any disposition they had to it; the temptation now seemed to lie on that hand, to neglect worldly affairs too much, and to spend too much time in the immediate exercise of religion.

And still another page—

> There was scarcely a single person in the town, old or young, left unconcerned about the great things of the eternal world. Those who were wont to be the vainest and loosest, and those who had been disposed to think and speak lightly of vital and experimental religion, were now generally subject to great awakenings. And the work of conversion was carried on in a most astonishing manner, and increased more and more; souls did as it were come by flocks to Jesus Christ. From day to day for many months together, might be seen evident instances of sinners brought out of darkness into marvelous light, and delivered out of an horrible pit, and from the miry clay, and set upon a rock, with a new song of praise to God in their mouths.

In his excitement, Josiah began reading faster than his mind could comprehend, with the exception of the names of the towns. They stood out as though emblazoned with stars in the night sky—

> In the month of March, the people in SOUTH-HADLEY begun to be seized with deep concern about the things of religion; which very soon became universal. . . . About the same time, it began to break forth in the west part of SUFFIELD (where it also has been very great), and soon spread into all parts of the town. It appeared at SUNDERLAND, and soon overspread the town: and I believe was, for a season, not less remarkable than it was here. About the same time, it began to appear in a part of DEERFIELD, called Green River, and afterwards filled the town, and there has been a glorious work there. It began also to be manifest, in the south part of HATFIELD, in a place called the Hill, and the whole town, in the second week in April, seemed to be seized, as it were at once, with concern about the things of religion; and the work of God has been great there. There has been also a very general awakening at WEST-SPRINGFIELD, and LONG MEADOW; and in ENFIELD.

"And Havenhill, dear Lord, and Havenhill!" Josiah murmured, his flesh prickling with emotion.

The wondrous events of God as recorded by Reverend Edwards began to cascade into an avalanche of God's grace and mercy—

> About the same time that this appeared at Enfield, the Reverend. Mr. Bull, of Westfield, informed me that there had been a great alteration there, and that more had been done in one week than in seven years before.
>
> This seems to have been a very extraordinary dispensation of providence; God has in many respects gone out of, and much beyond, His usual and ordinary way.
>
> The work in this town, and others about us, has been extraordinary on account of the universality of it, affecting all sorts, sober and vicious, high and low, rich and poor, wise and unwise.
>
> These awakenings, when they have first seized on persons, have had two effects; one was that they have brought them immediately to quit their sinful practices; and the looser sort have been brought to forsake and dread their former vices and extravagances.
>
> When once the Spirit of God began to be so wonderfully poured out in a general way through the town, people had soon

> done with their old quarrels, back-bitings, and intermeddling with other men's matters.
>
> The tavern was soon left empty, and persons kept very much at home; none went abroad unless on necessary business, or on some religious account, and every day seemed in many respects like a Sabbath day.
>
> It has put the people on earnest application to the means of salvation, reading, prayer, meditation, the ordinances of God's house, and private conference; their cry was, What shall we do to be saved? The place of resort was now altered, it was no longer the tavern, but the minister's house that was thronged far more than ever the tavern had been wont to be.
>
> Conversion is a great and glorious work of God's power, at once changing the heart, and infusing life into the dead soul.

Josiah could contain himself no longer. Snatching up the letters and the book, he bolted for the door and was running on the main road before he realized he'd left his front door open and a pot of stew over the fire.

He dismissed the thought of retracing his steps. Eternal matters were at hand. He'd found the cure to Havenhill's Soul Sickness. The cares and concerns of this world faded into inconsequential nothingness in comparison.

CHAPTER 19

A long-faced house servant and a field hand with a black beard glared angrily at Josiah as he excitedly read to Philip a passage from Reverend Edwards's book.

Josiah's exuberant approach to the house had raised such a clamor that several of the servants took it for an alarm. They thought Indians were attacking. The field hand came running with a pitchfork. The house servant appeared with a flintlock, which he now gripped testily.

Philip, initially alarmed, was now amused. He looked on with a wry smile at his excited friend.

"Here it is," Josiah cried, finding his place in the book. He read:

> "While God was so remarkably present amongst us by His Spirit, there was no book so delightful as the Bible; especially the Book of Psalms, the Prophecy of Isaiah, and the New Testament. Some, by reason of their love of God's Word, at times have been wonderfully delighted and affected at the sight of a Bible; and then, also, there was no time so prized as the Lord's day, and no place in this world so desired as God's house. Our converts then remarkably appeared united in dear affection to one another, and many have expressed much of that spirit of love which they felt toward all mankind; and particularly to those who had been least friendly to them. Never, I believe, was so much done in confessing injuries, and making up differences, as the last year."

Josiah looked up. "So what do you think?"

Philip regarded him a moment. "It sounds like a preacher's dream."

"Don't you see, Philip? This is what we've been praying for . . . what Havenhill so desperately needs! Revival! A town-wide conversion! This is the cure for the town's Soul Sickness!"

"Soul Sickness?" Philip's eyebrows arched.

Josiah shuffled his feet in a nervous manner. In his excitement he was getting ahead of himself. "A term I coined to describe the spiritual condition of the townspeople. You see, Philip, after much observation and prayer, I've come to the conclusion that the town is suffering from a spiritual disease. And because the disease is spiritual, so must the cure be spiritual. And this is the cure!" He poked the page with his finger for emphasis. "Spiritual renewal! Revival! A fresh movement of the Spirit!"

Philip crossed his arms. With a nod, he signaled to his armed servants that they were no longer needed. He put on his business face. "If I understand you correctly, Havenhill is suffering from an invisible epidemic of a spiritual nature."

"Correct! It manifests itself outwardly in people's attitudes and behavior."

"And you think this fellow—" Philip pointed to the book.

"Edwards. Jonathan Edwards. He's a pastor in Northampton."

"This Edwards fellow has found a cure for it."

"Exactly! God has been using his preaching in an unprecedented way as a vehicle for His Spirit to effect salvation and spiritual renewal in dozens of towns in Connecticut."

"And you're proposing . . ."

"We invite him to preach in Havenhill."

"To bring the cure, so to speak, that the town desperately needs."

"What do you think?" Josiah asked.

Philip took a deep breath. "Well . . . to be honest? For one thing, it sounds a lot like the recent smallpox inoculation incident. And we all know how that turned out."

The reminder of Josiah's earlier failure punctured his enthusiasm. He could feel his hopes deflating.

"The action you're proposing in this case is similar, isn't it?" Philip asked. "You propose to bring in an outsider in an attempt to introduce a cure nobody wants. Only in this case, it's to introduce a cure to a disease that nobody knows they have."

"But that's the insidious nature of the disease, Philip!" Josiah cried. "People suffer its effects, yet, for the most part, are completely unaware of the root cause of their problems. They shrug it off as human nature or a personality quirk or justify their action as someone else's fault. In reality, their hearts are infected by sin!"

"Ah, sin! Well, see, that's the problem, isn't it?" Philip reasoned. "These are good people you're talking about. God-fearing people, for the most part. Do you really think it wise to call them out publicly as backsliders and sinners?"

On the defensive now, Josiah's mind scrambled for a way to make Philip understand. Maybe he'd sprung it on Philip too suddenly. *After all,* Josiah thought, *the study of Soul Sickness had occupied my time for months.* Maybe it was asking too much for Philip to grasp the magnitude of it all in just a couple of minutes.

Josiah closed the book. In a calmer voice, he said, "Maybe you're right. But I'd still like to travel to Northampton and see this phenomenon myself. For all I know, this"—he hefted the book—"is an exaggeration of the incident."

Philip nodded agreement. "After the inoculation fiasco, I think it wise that we not rush into anything. Go hear the man preach, gather your impressions, then we'll talk some more."

Josiah smiled, making every attempt to disguise his disappointment.

"Meanwhile," Philip said heartily, "it's fortuitous that you chose this time to stop by."

"How so?"

Philip ambled farther into the house. Josiah followed. The sites along the short journey—oil paintings of English nobility, exquisitely designed French furniture, and Belgian tapestries—reminded him of Philip's success.

"I just received news from England," Philip said with excitement. He walked to a fireplace mantle, where he picked up a letter. He turned to Josiah with a roguish grin. "It's from Anne."

"Anne Myles?"

Josiah set the book down on a small table. It was instantly forgotten.

"Remember the day you arrived in Havenhill?" Philip said, bursting at the seams. "I was returning from England . . ."

"And from that grin on your face, I'm guessing it wasn't all business."

"I met with Anne's guardian."

"You old dog! Why didn't you tell me?"

"Frankly, I wasn't sure how it was all going to work out. But now . . ." Philip held the letter up in triumph.

"He's given you and Anne his permission!" Josiah cried.

Philip's face flushed. "Aya."

"Congratulations! I mean it, Philip! That's the best news I've heard in a long time!"

Josiah's arm raised in a long, sweeping handshake, and the two men hand-wrestled congratulatory joy. With his free hand, Josiah slapped Philip on the arm.

"You're bringing her here, aren't you?" Josiah asked, suddenly concerned that the good news might have a thorn in it.

"Aya." Philip beamed. "Anne will be returning to Havenhill."

"That's great news, Philip! Great news! How long has it been?"

"Seven years," Philip said.

"Of course!"

In the joy of the moment, Josiah had suffered a momentary memory lapse. Of course it had been seven years. Anne Myles had returned to England just two months before the fire that had so altered Josiah's life.

Philip had taken her departure hard. Anne Myles had been his Nabby. While Josiah mooned over Abigail Parkhurst, Philip pined over Anne. Her father was a lawyer representing merchant interests in the Colonies. In the course of his duties, he made frequent trips to England.

Often he left Anne behind, for months at a time, to stay with the Parkhursts. Her mother had died when she was young.

Two months before Josiah's life was altered forever, so was Anne Myles's life. While in England, her father was killed in an accident when he lost control of his carriage. Anne returned to England to be raised by her uncle.

They all felt her loss. Anne and Abigail were friends. Josiah and Philip were friends. And when Anne sailed for England, it just wasn't the same anymore.

"You've been in touch with her all this time?" Josiah asked.

"Aya."

"And you never gave up on her."

Philip beamed.

"A fall wedding? Spring?"

"Spring, most likely."

Josiah couldn't stop grinning. This was just like Philip. He kept after something until he got what he wanted, including a wife.

"Two out of three," Philip said. "Two out of three."

"I don't follow."

"Johnny and Abigail. Now Anne and me. When are you going to take the plunge, old friend? You ought to try it. The water's fine."

The comment might well have been a fist. It hit Josiah hard in the gut, knocking the wind out of him and wiping the grin from his face.

Philip was still all smiles, seemingly unaware of what he'd said.

"Yeah, well . . ." Josiah's wit failed him. Turning his back on Philip to hide his pain, he retrieved the book he'd brought with him. "I'll . . . I'll put together an itinerary of my trip to Northampton," he said weakly. "It shouldn't be more than a week or two."

The two men walked to the front door.

"A word of advice?" Philip said.

Josiah turned to face him.

"Patience. These are good people. Give them a chance to do the right thing, and they'll do it. But they're a stubborn lot. Force them into something, and they'll dig in their heels and bray like donkeys until you're all too tired to do anything."

"I'll keep that in mind." Josiah reached the door. "And again, congratulations. It'll be good to see Anne again. Is she still as pretty as she was when we were in school?"

"More ravishing than ever."

Josiah manufactured a smile.

Josiah found Eunice Parkhurst's servant dancing impatiently on his doorstep when he arrived home. She'd apparently been told to wait for him, for when she saw him coming, she ran to him and, without a word, shoved a note at him. The next instant she was stirring up the dust in the road as she hurried home

Standing in the middle of the road, Josiah unfolded the piece of paper.

Mason family needs a visit.
Goodwife Parkhurst

It was the first note from Eunice since Goodwife Delor's death. Was this her way of giving him a chance to redeem himself?

Turning back to the main road, Josiah set out for the Mason house.

CHAPTER 20

The door to the Masons' house stood ajar as Josiah approached it. The familiar sound of a woman's wailing came from inside. When he'd first met Phoebe, the day of the smallpox outbreak, she was wailing. On every visit of Josiah's since then, the woman was either crying or shouting. She was the noisiest woman Josiah had ever known.

Standing on the doorstep, he announced himself, timing his call with the break in Phoebe's wailing when she took a breath.

"Jabez?"

He waited. No one answered. Phoebe let loose another wail . . . more of a shriek this time.

Again Josiah waited for her to take a breath.

"Ma Mason?"

He waited. Phoebe let loose again.

It was dark inside the house, just as it had been during his previous visits. Josiah looked around outside the house, hoping to find Jabez working. But from the state of disrepair of the house and the land, it didn't appear his chances were favorable to find Jabez working.

After a third failed attempt at announcing himself, Josiah cautiously pushed open the door and called again. He stepped inside.

When his eyes adjusted to the dimly lit interior, he found the room as he remembered it—strewn with garbage and clothing and broken furniture. In the corner, huddled in their usual place on the slumping couch, were Phoebe and her mother.

"Mrs. Mason," Josiah said, approaching them, "I got word—"

Ma Mason whirled with a ferocity he never would have thought her capable of. He could have sworn her eyes spit fire. Beside her, Phoebe became suddenly and eerily silent.

The back of Josiah's neck prickled, as though he was confronting a couple of wolves in their den.

"Is . . . is . . . J. . . Jabez," Josiah stammered, taking a cautionary step backward.

"Went to the docks to kill your friend," Ma Mason said with a tone of righteous satisfaction.

"What?" Josiah cried. "Johnny? Jabez went to kill Johnny? Why?"

"He killed my boy." Ma Mason rose from the sofa and advanced on him. Now not only did she *look* like a wolf, she *moved* like one.

"Killed . . . I don't understand . . ." But then, in the next instant, he did understand. "George? No—George is dead?"

At the sound of her brother's name, Phoebe took to wailing again.

Ma Mason continued to advance.

Josiah retreated, stumbling over an old boot. "I've got to stop him!" he cried.

"If you knows what's good for you, you'll stay out of it," Ma Mason warned. "An eye for an eye. A tooth for a tooth. Isn't that what the Good Book says?"

Why was it that people who couldn't quote any other verse of the Bible could quote that one?

Josiah turned toward the door, yet without taking his eye off Ma Mason. "I'll . . . I'll come back later, when you're more—"

Josiah didn't finish the sentence. The next moment he was out the door and running toward the docks.

Not until Josiah was halfway to the docks did he realize he didn't know exactly where to find Jabez or Johnny. But then, if a fight were to break out, it would pretty much call attention to itself, wouldn't it?

As he ran he considered going first to Philip's place to enlist the aid of his pitchfork-wielding servant, then decided against it. The time lost could be the difference between life and death.

Johnny's or Jabez's? he wondered.

In all the years Josiah had known Johnny, if there was one fact that stood out about Johnny, it was that he'd always been able to take care of himself. Besides, Jabez was invading Johnny's realm. Surely, dock workers and sailors would come to Johnny's aid, wouldn't they?

But then, who knew what havoc a half-crazed, vengeance-driven man like Jabez could unleash?

Which made Josiah think of George. Could it be true? Was he dead? And while Josiah didn't think for a minute that Johnny had killed him, what had led the Masons to believe he had?

"I've seen things. Heard things."

Isn't that what George had told him?

"All I know is that there's some bad stuff goin' on with those ships. Either your friends are blind, or they're behind it."

Reaching Summit and High Streets, Josiah pulled up long enough to catch his breath. Below him was the harbor, the docks, and Philip and Johnny's warehouses.

Everything looked peaceful.

Was terror lurking in the shadows? Or had it already struck? The thought entered Josiah's mind: *Stillness is a trait peace and death share.*

When Josiah reached the waterfront, he found the docks relatively quiet. Nobody could tell him where to find Johnny Mott. Nobody had seen him all day. All they could tell him was that a man with a heavy black beard was also looking for Johnny.

Josiah half-walked, half-ran down Water Street, past one warehouse after another, praying for a glimpse of something—a sign, a clue, *anything.*

Everything was still. Too still.

The midday sun glared off the massive sides of the warehouses, reducing the shadows between them to thin black slivers. It wasn't a great time for lurkers. That worked to his advantage, didn't it?

But the sun also worked against him. Overheated and drenched, Josiah blinked salty sweat out of his eyes. Tired from running and drained by the sun's rays, Josiah's strength had been severely tapped. Even if he were to come across Jabez, Josiah didn't know how much of a fight he could manage to restrain the man, if it came to that.

Josiah reached the end of the warehouses. This was maddening. Just like the other night when . . .

The memory stopped him dead in his tracks.

The other night. He had encountered Johnny in one of the warehouses. It was just a hunch, but what if Johnny had not been at just any warehouse? What if he had an office or a workbench in that warehouse? It was possible, wasn't it? There had to be a place where they kept the paperwork. And since the docks were Johnny's domain . . .

Josiah doubled back, hoping he could remember which warehouse it was. At the time it was dark, but surely he could remember the building Johnny had thrown him out of.

This one!

He found the door and tried it.

It was locked.

But then Johnny had dragged him the length of the warehouse. Possibly the office was at the far end.

Josiah quickened his step. He sensed that every second was precious.

Halfway down the walkway, he heard something other than the pounding of his own shoes. He heard voices. Shouting.

Jabez!

Josiah broke into a run.

Crashing into the room—it wasn't hard to know which room once Josiah reached the door—he found pretty much what he expected to find. Only the combatants were reversed.

Jabez lay on the floor, his ax out of reach. Johnny was on top of him with a fist poised to make its imprint on the black-bearded man's face. Both men were red-faced, furious, and shouting simultaneously.

Josiah's entrance got Johnny's attention, momentarily staying the imminent pummeling.

"What are you doing here?" Johnny shouted.

Out of breath, it took a moment before Josiah could respond. "Rescuing you," he said weakly.

"Turn around and walk out the door," Johnny ordered. "This doesn't concern you."

When it came to a fistfight, or a physical fight of any kind, of the three men, Josiah Rush was definitely the least likely to survive. Nevertheless, he took a good step inside the room and closed the door behind him.

"Get out of here!" Johnny shouted.

"Yeah, Preacher," Jabez said. "You'd better leave."

Ironic, Josiah thought. At least that was something on which the two combatants agreed.

Instead, he folded his arms. "I'm not going anywhere."

Then, seeing the ax on the floor, he bent over and picked it up. He hefted it several times to get a feel for it.

"The way I see it," he said, "one of you is going to knock the other one out. At the moment, the odds seem to favor Johnny, since his arm is cocked and his fist is aimed squarely at your face, Jabez. It's been a few years, but I've seen Johnny's punch. It can stagger a good-sized bull. Chances look pretty good he's going to knock you into next Tuesday. The instant he does that, the blunt end of this ax is going to collide with the back of his head."

Johnny shot Josiah a glance of disbelief.

"Oh, I'll do it," Josiah promised him. "But even with a good swing, with a head as thick as yours, I doubt I'll do any real damage. Just enough to accomplish my purpose. Once you two are snuggled up next to each other on the floor, I'll get the jailor to slap irons on both of you and cart you off to separate cells where we can sort all this out."

"You wouldn't," Johnny said.

Josiah hefted the ax in preparation to swing it. "The way I see it, if I don't, someone isn't going to leave this room alive." He chuckled. "Of course, with the headache you're both going to have, I imagine there'll be times you'd welcome the relief from pain death would bring. But you'll get over it."

Johnny chewed his lower lip, as if weighing whether Josiah would follow through with his threat.

Jabez saw Johnny's indecision as an opportunity to squirm free. He slid to one side and took a hefty slap at Johnny's arm. He'd have had better luck trying to fell an oak with a single slap.

Johnny retaliated by pressing down harder against his chest. Jabez grimaced and groaned that he couldn't breathe. Josiah raised the ax.

Confident that he had Jabez under control, Johnny turned his attention back to Josiah. "All I know is that I was working away, and this lunatic burst into my office and tried to kill me with that ax!"

"His name is Jabez Mason," Josiah replied wryly. "We went to school together."

Johnny looked down at his attacker, trying to see something familiar behind the dense black foliage that covered the man's face.

"And, of course, Jabez, you already know Johnny here." Josiah tried to keep the tone light.

It was clear that neither man on the floor thought him particularly funny.

"He killed my brother!" Jabez wheezed with as much voice as he could muster, considering there was a mountain on his chest.

"I ain't killed no one!" Johnny shouted.

For Josiah, this was the tough part. In the rush to keep Jabez from killing Johnny, his mind hadn't been given sufficient time to register that George Mason was indeed dead.

"His brother is George Mason," Josiah explained. "He's a crew member onboard the *Nightingale.*"

The expression on Johnny's face confirmed George's death. "That was your brother?" Johnny said to Jabez.

Jabez's only reply was an undisguised glare of hatred.

"It was an accident," Johnny said to Josiah, making no attempt to convince the man beneath him, who obviously was beyond convincing.

"Liar!" Jabez shouted. "Twarn't no accident! I could round me up a dozen sailors that'll say differently! Georgie was beat to death!"

Johnny turned his head.

"Is that true?" Josiah asked Johnny.

"Look at 'im!" Jabez shouted. "'Course it's true!"

Taking a deep breath, Johnny said to no one in particular, "It was a disciplinary problem that got out of control."

"Your cap'n ordered Georgie killed! It's not the first time he's killed one of his sailors, neither! He killed another one in the Cribby Islands. George tol' me so hisself."

Josiah eyed Johnny, hoping he would deny Jabez's account. He didn't.

"Johnny . . . ," Josiah prompted him.

"Sometimes a heavy hand is required to maintain order onboard a ship," Johnny said solemnly.

Josiah cringed. "But, Johnny! Beating a man to death?"

"At *his* orders!" Jabez shouted. "They're *his* ships! He hires the captains!"

"That's not true!" Johnny said quickly. Emphatically. "I have no say over the captains."

"Liar!" Jabez shouted. "Everyone knows they're his ships!"

And Philip's, Josiah thought. But he thought it best not to say anything, lest Jabez take his vendetta to Philip's house. Josiah studied

Johnny. The look on his old friend's face was one of helplessness. He was speaking the truth.

"Jabez, go home," Josiah ordered.

"I'm not goin' anywheres until I kill Johnny Mott."

"Think, man! What is the likelihood of that happening? You're flat on your back, like a bug about to be squished."

Jabez blinked several times as Josiah's description of the situation registered. He made one last effort to wriggle from beneath Johnny and evidently realized that what Josiah had said was true. "A'right," he said. "Get this ox offa me."

Josiah nodded at his friend.

At first Johnny appeared reluctant to relinquish his advantage. Then, cautiously, he got up and stepped back.

Grasping his chest and gasping for breath, Jabez managed to get to his feet. On weak knees he stumbled toward the door. "You know I'll be back," he told Johnny. He meant it too. There was murder in his eyes.

Johnny's stance signaled that he'd be ready.

"No, you won't," Josiah said.

Jabez turned on him. "You callin' me a liar?"

"No, I'm saying that your business with Johnny is done."

"It's not done until I kill him. Georgie deserves that much."

"Then here—" Josiah handed Jabez the ax.

"What!? Josiah! What are you doing?" Johnny's hand flew up to defend himself.

Jabez grinned wickedly at his good fortune. He gripped the ax with familiarity.

"But you'll have to kill us both," Josiah added. He stood in front of Johnny. "And you'll have to kill me first."

Jabez gripped the ax. He locked eyes with Josiah. "You're no match for me. I can take you."

"I have no intention of fighting you." Josiah stretched his arms out. "You'll have to murder me."

Jabez blinked at the word *murder*.

"That's right. Murder. Because I'll offer no defense."

Jabez hesitated.

"But I don't think you'll kill me," Josiah pressed, "because you're not a murderer."

Jabez stared at him. He sniffed. Then, with a murderous cry, he swung the ax at Josiah's head with all his might.

The ax blade arched high, barely giving Josiah's mouth time to drop open.

Johnny shoved Josiah aside, stepped forward, and caught the ax handle below the blade just as it was starting its downward arch.

The deadly edge stopped midair, as abruptly as it would had it imbedded itself in a sturdy tree. Johnny was that strong. With ease he pulled the ax out of Jabez's hands and, in one continuous stroke, swung the handle, cracking Jabez in the jaw and knocking him senseless to the floor.

By now Josiah's jaw had dropped open. Speechless, he stared at his fallen attacker.

"That was dumb," Johnny said to Josiah.

Josiah didn't disagree with him.

"But thanks," Johnny added. "What you did took courage. It was dumb. But it took courage."

"Aya," Josiah said.

It was all he could say as the reality of what had almost happened caught up with him.

CHAPTER 21

The day after Josiah nearly got himself killed while trying to prevent Johnny Mott's murder, he rode out of town on the postal road.

Meanwhile, Jabez Mason was nursing a sore jaw in jail while the story of Josiah's heroics circulated around town. To Josiah's relief, Johnny Mott had conveniently left out the part of the story where Josiah handed the ax back to Jabez. According to Johnny, Josiah had stepped between them, a scuffle ensued, and Jabez was knocked out.

Johnny's generous rendering of the account hadn't stopped Josiah from pressing him about George Mason's death.

"Were you aware of Captain Coytmore's barbaric punishments?"

"Yes."

"Had other men died from similar beatings?"

"Yes."

"Will Coytmore be called to account for George Mason's death?"

"Probably not."

"Why not?"

"It's not up to me. Ask Philip."

"Were you aware of Coytmore's character when you hired him?"

"I don't hire captains."

"Who does?"

"Philip."

"But certainly you—"

"I'm done talking with you."

"But—"

"Talk to Philip."

"Johnny—"

"Talk to Philip."

Josiah had gone directly from the docks to Philip's house.

When he had asked Philip about Coytmore, Philip appeared genuinely distressed over the captain's actions and George Mason's death. However, Philip insisted the employment of Coytmore was a concession to his financial backers and that, while he would investigate the incident, he doubted anything would come of it.

It was generally conceded by all men of business that a merchant captain's authority over the men aboard his ship went unquestioned. Life at sea was dangerous and unforgiving. Captains did whatever was necessary to deliver the goods entrusted to them. At times their actions may have appeared cruel to the uninitiated, but to those who daily risked their lives at sea, such stern measures were necessary for survival.

Philip's explanation had been less than satisfying, but what could he do about it? Josiah ached every time he thought of George Mason. He remembered the first time he met the man. Newly returned from the Cribbey Islands, George was lying on a cot covered with pox. Josiah also remembered George sitting in jail, telling him how much he hated the sea, yet how he felt he had little choice but to return to the ship.

George deserved better.

The thought that plagued Josiah most was that he didn't know if George was faring any better in the next life. The one time Josiah broached the subject of George's spiritual condition, George had chuckled and accused him of acting like a preacher, then had changed the subject.

George had been spiritually aware, though, hadn't he? He had confirmed the fact that there was evil in the town. Was he also aware of the sin in his own heart?

Josiah had lain awake most of the night, regretting that he hadn't pressed the matter with George Mason when he had the chance.

He had thought he'd have more chances.

Then, this morning, before setting out for Northampton, Josiah had found another anonymous note stuffed under a slat outside his door.

I heard of your courageous act, and I can't say that
I'm surprised. Hopefully now the townspeople will
look on you in a different light, as I do.
I pray for you nightly.

His heart warmed, Josiah had decided to stop by the Parkhurst house on his way out of town. He could thank Eunice for informing him of the Masons' need for a visit. After all, that resulted in a life saved, didn't it? And he could tell them of his spiritual quest to Northampton. He could ask them to pray for his success. Surely no one would object to his stopping by to request prayer for his travel, could they?

However, when he reached the center of town, he urged his horse on rather than stopping at the Parkhurst house. Every imagined scenario that had flashed in his mind regarding the visit ended up with Nabby rushing into his arms and expressing her undying love and admiration for his recent heroics. Who did he think he was fooling? He couldn't even convince himself the call was of a spiritual nature.

Besides, for the first time since returning to Havenhill, he was in Johnny Mott's good graces. He'd be a fool to jeopardize that so quickly.

He did, however, stop at Mercy and Grace's house to return the letters to Mercy and ask her if she wanted him to deliver a letter to her cousin in Hadley.

At the door, Grace informed him rather curtly that Mercy was still in no condition to entertain visitors.

Had they not heard of his heroics?

Thinking of no humble way to ask, Josiah offered his prayers for Mercy and left it at that.

As the horse he was riding ascended Fiedler's Knob, the pain that had been building in Josiah's gut eased and then eventually vanished. The feeling of relief was so incredible, Josiah felt almost giddy. It was a promising start to his journey.

Josiah met up with the Connecticut River just below Hartford. Philip had offered him passage by ship up the river to Hartford, but it would have meant a week's delay while the ship was outfitted. Josiah was anxious to get underway.

That wasn't the only reason he declined. With the George Mason incident still fresh in his mind, Josiah wasn't eager to submit himself to the authority of a ship's captain.

Josiah's hopes rose as he made his way through Hartford. He had never been to the city. The only thing he knew about it was that the *Fundamental Orders* had been adopted here in 1639, a document that established a government of rule by the consent of the people. The idea of government by local representation was a deeply cherished tradition among the colonists—one that England seemed eager to challenge as the Colonies grew larger and wealthier. England's tight-fisted rule over the Colonies was a subject of increasing conversation at taverns and meetinghouses.

From Hartford, Josiah followed the course of the Connecticut north through Windsor and Longmeadow.

The road into Northampton descended more gradually than did the road into Havenhill. Josiah swayed side to side atop his mount, enjoying the breeze that wafted up the slope from the river.

The wind was more than just moist air. Healing and refreshment rode its waves, washing over Josiah like a balm. Revival lived here. He could feel it.

At first he told himself he was imagining it—that the good feeling was nothing but the result of getting away from the pressures and responsibilities of Havenhill. Then he passed a man laboring under a heavy sack. Josiah greeted him and received silence and a stony glare in return. The inhospitable greeting came as no surprise, for as the man approached, a gnawing ache wormed into Josiah's belly, the kind he was accustomed to feeling in Havenhill. It grew stronger the closer the man came, then dissipated as soon as he passed.

The momentary nudge of the familiar convinced Josiah there was something different about this place.

Dusk had overtaken the town when Josiah arrived. He asked a lamplighter for directions to Reverend Edwards's house and soon found a modest structure with cheerful light coming from the windows.

His knock was answered by a bright-faced child holding a calico cupboard cloth. Josiah began to introduce himself when a pleasant woman appeared, wearing a mobcap and modest attire. The most striking thing about her was her smile. He began again. "Forgive the intrusion. I'm Reverend Josiah Rush from Havenhill. And I've—"

"Come to see my husband," the woman said, smiling.

Behind the woman and child at the door, five, six, or maybe seven other children of various ages bustled about, preparing the supper table.

Josiah paused. "However, if I've come at a bad time . . ."

"Reverend Edwards is out riding. I expect him home at any moment. Please come in." Mrs. Edwards opened the door and stepped back to let Josiah in. The child with the cupboard cloth—a little girl with shoulder-length curls—moved with her.

Removing his hat, Josiah repeated, "If my timing is inconvenient—"

"Nonsense," Mrs. Edwards insisted. "You'll dine with us tonight and tell us all about Havenhill."

When she closed the door, Josiah found himself the object of furtive glances. The children were not impolite—simply curious.

The woman whispered something that sent the little girl scurrying on an errand.

"Let me take your coat," Mrs. Edwards said.

Just then the door opened and a tall, thin man entered.

"You're late!" Mrs. Edwards called. Then, with a smile, "And I can see why. It's been a productive ride, hasn't it?"

Josiah's first thought was that the man had been attacked by moths. His coat was splattered with patches of white.

Leaving Josiah with one arm still inside his coat, Mrs. Edwards attended her husband. She began unpinning what Josiah now recognized as white scraps of paper.

Edwards stood still, his arms outstretched like a scarecrow as she worked.

"Ideas come to him as he rides," Mrs. Edwards explained as she worked. "He writes them down and pins them to his cloak."

"Sarah harvests them and arranges them for future reference," Edwards said, pivoting so she could reach two notes near his right hip.

They moved with an intimacy that comes only from years of marital communion.

When the last note was lifted, Edwards let his hands fall to his sides, and Sarah hurried off with the notes, carrying them as though they were of great value, which made Josiah all the more eager to know what was written on them. What slivers of inspiration had Jonathan Edwards not trusted to his memory for safekeeping?

"I'm Reverend Edwards," the tall man said. "How may I be of service to you?"

CHAPTER 22

After a meal of boiled mutton, turnips, and bread—during which Josiah joyfully shared a trencher with his curly-headed greeter—the men took a walk while Sarah Edwards marshaled the troops to clean up and prepare for their hour of nightly instruction.

"Every Christian family ought to be as a little church," Edwards explained to Josiah. "Consecrated to Christ and wholly influenced and governed by His rules. Family education and order are some of the chief means of grace. If these fail, all other means are likely to prove ineffectual." He turned to Josiah. "Do you come from a large family, Reverend Rush?"

"I'm an orphan," Josiah replied. "A godly widower raised me."

"And now? Do you have a family?"

Josiah thought of Nabby. "God has not yet seen fit to give me a wife."

Edwards said, "I was raised in a large family. The fifth of eleven children."

Josiah's eyebrows raised.

Edwards grinned at his reaction, waited a beat, then added, "The only boy."

Josiah laughed. From the practiced delivery, Edwards meant for him to laugh. Josiah found the Northampton preacher to be deliberate and articulate, with a qualified intensity about him. Josiah felt comfortable with him.

They walked under a spangled sky. Edwards looked up at it as he would gaze upon an old friend. "It was John Locke who impressed upon me that knowledge comes through the senses. Since then I've come to believe that we can know God's grace through nature."

He strode casually, giving each thought a time to breathe on its own before supporting it with another thought. His manner reminded Josiah of classical Greek teachers who taught as they walked.

"I used to walk in my father's pasture," Edwards continued. "And as I walked, I would look up at the sky and clouds. There came to my mind so sweet a sense of the glorious majesty of the grace of God that I didn't know how to express it. I seemed to see them both in conjunction—majesty and meekness together. It was a sweet, gentle, and holy majesty, and also a majestic meekness. An awful sweetness; a high and great and holy gentleness.

"Back in those days, I used to be uncommonly terrified of thunder and was struck with terror when I saw a thunderstorm rising. Now, on the contrary, it makes me rejoice. I feel God, so to speak, at the first appearance of a thunderstorm. I often fix myself to view the clouds and see the lightnings play and hear the majestic and awful voice of God's thunder, which is oftentimes exceedingly entertaining, leading me to sweet contemplations of our great and glorious God. At such times, it always seemed natural to me to sing or chant my meditations or to speak of my thoughts in soliloquies with a singing voice."

Josiah felt a kinship, a feeling of brotherhood, linking them. "I'm often reminded of the Scripture passage myself: 'Now unto the King eternal, immortal, invisible, the only wise God . . .'"

Edwards finished it, "'. . . be honor and glory for ever and ever. Amen.'" He looked at Josiah with a sparkle in his eyes. "Do you walk often, Reverend Rush?"

Josiah smiled. "*Solvitur ambulando.*"

Edwards nodded and translated, "The solution comes through walking. I like it. From your studies?"

"Harvard."

Edwards screwed up his face. "I'll try not to hold that against you. I'm a Yale man."

As they walked into a pasture, the sky appeared like a vast dark blue canvas, splattered with specks of shimmering light.

"Walking with you reminds me of a time when I lived in New York," Edwards added. "I used to walk the banks of the Hudson with a friend by the name of John Smith. Those were sweet hours. We often lost track of time conversing on the things of God, especially when our conversation turned to the advancement of Christ's kingdom in the world and the glorious things that God would accomplish for His church in the latter days." He sighed heavily. "My heart was knit to John with great affection."

Sadness tinged that last sentence. Josiah sensed there was an unspoken strain associated with the relationship.

"So, Reverend Rush," Edwards said with renewed enthusiasm, "why has God brought you to Northampton?"

The question surprised Josiah, which was odd since he'd traveled all this way to answer this question. Yet now, for some reason, his mind was a jumble. His words bunched in the back of his throat, none of them wanting to be the first to come out. Was it that he just didn't know where to begin?

The length of silence grew embarrassing. Edwards glanced over at Josiah to see if anything was wrong.

Finally Josiah blurted, "Havenhill is infected with a spiritual disease."

Edwards leveled an evaluating gaze, as though weighing the words and the manner of the speaker. "And upon what are you basing your conclusion?"

It was a good response. Josiah liked it. Most ministers he knew would be quick with a response. Too quick. Eager to establish themselves—at least in their own minds—as a spiritual sage.

Taking a deep breath, beginning with the smallpox epidemic and Dr. McCullough's diary, which was the inspiration for his study, Josiah described his observations and the resulting list of symptoms he'd recorded regarding Soul Sickness.

Edwards listened without interruption as they walked.

After relating how he unexpectedly came upon private correspondence relating to the revival events at Hadley and other towns and of Edwards's own narrative of spiritual renewal, Josiah concluded by saying, "And that's what brought me here. I came to seek your counsel and to invite you to preach at First Church, Havenhill."

They came to a row of stately trees, timeless black sentinels against the night sky. Bent slightly by a gentle wind, they appeared to be leaning over to hear what the two men were discussing. With a motion of his hand, Edwards indicated a change in direction, down a narrow footpath that would lead them past the trees and back to the house.

"Have you considered publishing your observations and conclusions?" Edwards asked.

"I hadn't given it any thought," Josiah said. But he had to admit, the suggestion was attractive to him.

"Did you bring a copy with you?"

"I brought my journal."

With a tilt of his head, Edwards seemed to dismiss the idea of reading Josiah's study. After all, it would be impolite for a man to ask to read another man's journal.

"I'd be pleased to have you read it," Josiah offered. "I would greatly welcome your thoughts."

Edwards nodded. "As for your presence here, it appears as though you are following the same course of action that you pursued with the smallpox epidemic. You are enlisting someone from outside the town to bring a cure to the town.

"With the smallpox, you sought a doctor who agreed with you regarding both the disease and the method of treatment. I assume you have a local physician in Havenhill. What was his reaction to this outside medical authority?"

Josiah grinned sheepishly. "He speaks to me only when it can't be avoided."

Edwards didn't appear surprised to hear this. "With the Soul Sickness, however, you are the town's spiritual physician. So, the question is naturally raised, why seek outside assistance? You have identified the disease. You believe you know the cure. Why not administer it yourself?"

As the direction of Edwards's thoughts became apparent, dread and terror enveloped Josiah. He had been hoping to avoid this part of the story.

Must the whole world know what happened on that dreadful night seven years ago? His sin was a dog hounding him every place he went. It seemed that since that night, his life's duty was to inform the world personally, one person at a time, of his moral failings and resulting guilt.

"I'm the last person to whom they'll listen," he said rather bluntly.

Edwards stopped. His brow furled with concern. "Now, that's a statement that requires an explanation."

Starting with the events the night of the fire, Josiah related the night of his shame and his resulting exile, his time of soul-searching and spiritual study in Boston, and Philip's hand in bringing him home.

"Do you regret your decision to return to Havenhill?" Edwards asked.

"I've questioned the wisdom of it at times," Josiah replied. "My presence there is a daily reminder to many people of their personal loss and pain."

"It is also a daily reminder of God's redemptive grace," Edwards said. "A lesser man would have gone to a town where no one knew his past. Now, tell me more about the smallpox inoculation. Having received an inoculation yourself, do you still advise others to be inoculated? Sarah and I have had no small number of discussions on this topic."

The sudden shift in conversation back to smallpox caught Josiah by surprise. At the same time, it pleased him that Edwards didn't dwell on his past sin. But that was how it should be, shouldn't it?

God had dealt with it.

Forgiven it.

And forgotten it.

"*As far as the east is from the west, so far hath he removed our transgressions from us.*" Isn't that what the psalmist wrote? So why couldn't the people he most cared for do the same?

He'd hurt them.

He knew that.

He'd killed their loved ones, and nothing could bring them back.

He knew that, too.

At the same time, Josiah knew if he admitted that the people of Havenhill had a right to their pain and were justified in hating him for the rest of their lives, it also meant that a sin existed that was greater than God's grace. That Jesus's death on the cross covered most sins, but not the really big ones.

But the Bible taught that no sin was greater than God's grace, and that once God had forgiven a sin, He forgot it too.

Now, if only the people of Havenhill would do the same . . .

"Inoculation," Edwards prompted again, when Josiah didn't respond. "Would you recommend it?"

Josiah turned to his host. If for nothing other than this moment, the trip had been worth it.

Still, he couldn't help but wonder if Edwards's interest in inoculation wasn't a polite way of declining his invitation to preach in Havenhill. He'd acknowledged Josiah's request but had never given an answer.

Josiah wondered if he should ask again or if that would be impolite.

The logical side of him answered, "The science of inoculation makes sense." But then the side that remembered three weeks of agony in bed added, "The act itself, however, is another matter altogether . . . one that should be approached only after due consideration."

CHAPTER 23

Sarah Edwards insisted that Josiah lodge with them for the night. He watched with interest as the antics of the younger members of the household slowed from a beehive of activity to the quiet he was accustomed to.

He sat with Edwards and his wife beside the fire. Using a soft voice in consideration for his sleeping children, Edwards regaled Josiah with one personal account after another of persons and events associated with the Connecticut Valley revival, stories that were either too personal or lengthy to record in his narrative.

Josiah sat in rapt attention, mentally fitting various Havenhill residents with the stories, trying them on for size to see how they fit. He liked what he envisioned.

After a time, Sarah interrupted her husband—who, it was apparent, could go on re-creating revival incidents well into the daylight hours—to inquire about Josiah and Havenhill.

Actually, it was Edwards who related the incident of the fire to her, re-creating the story in amazingly accurate detail. He spoke matter-of-factly about the events themselves, then grew animated as he cited it as a wondrous example of God's redeeming grace and Josiah's courage in returning to Havenhill.

The way Edwards told it, Josiah almost felt like a hero. It was certainly the first time he'd ever felt that way over the matter.

It was possible Edwards noticed Josiah's chest puffing, for the reverend hastened to add a final comment about how God is able to take a despicable wretch of a man and reform him into a God-fearing servant.

Josiah nodded to indicate the point was well taken. God alone deserved the praise for the change in Josiah's life.

Sarah Edwards showed particular interest in his relationship to Eunice Parkhurst and Abigail. "To have such a beautiful relationship so horribly scorched by the fire," was the way she put it. When Sarah told him she'd pray for Abigail's and his eventual union, Josiah realized he'd omitted an important detail: that Abigail Parkhurst was promised to another man. After Sarah had offered her prayers, it seemed awkward to tell her that fact. So Josiah thanked her and left it at that.

Sarah seemed to thrive on their discussion, while her husband began nodding off in his chair. After twice waking him with a comment, she touched her husband's arm lovingly and suggested he say a prayer for Josiah before they retire.

Following the prayer, Josiah was shown to a room that was already warm from four sleeping bodies. Sarah had made up a narrow trundle bed for him in the corner with flaxen sheets, a feather pillow, and an embroidered coverlet. She bid him good night.

Josiah lay on his back, staring at the dark beams of the ceiling. Accustomed to the silence that comes from sleeping alone, it took him awhile to get used to the sounds of the children. Then the weight of sleep settled upon him. He succumbed to it while debating whether he should resurrect his preaching invitation and present it to Edwards again in the morning.

As it turned out, Josiah didn't have to.

"I have prayed about your gracious invitation to preach and discussed it with my wife," Edwards said.

The house was once again alive with activity as children of various ages got dressed and did their morning chores. Edwards leaned back in his chair. His Bible was open on the table in front of him, having just yielded up a lesson from the book of First Samuel.

The passage Edwards had read aloud depicted the prophet Samuel confronting an errant King Saul. The prophet informed the king that he'd acted foolishly, and because he had not kept the Lord's command, the Lord would appoint a new leader, a man after God's own heart.

Edwards had read the passage with great solemnity, as though it were he who had been the one to deliver the unfavorable news to the king.

He spoke with a similar tone now. "As much as I would like to accept your invitation, I'm afraid I'm going to have to decline it."

Josiah's disappointment was great, but he tried not to show it. Managing to produce a weak smile, he said, "I understand, and let me say—"

"I'm not finished," Edwards said.

Duly chastened, Josiah waited for the rest.

"After having meditated and prayed regarding the situation at Havenhill, Sarah and I were jointly impressed that you are correct in your conclusion that God's Spirit alone can save the town. And we covenant with you to pray to that end."

Josiah could guess what was coming next. With his position as pastor, God had given him charge of Havenhill. If it took the rest of his life, it was his duty to minister to them and be a living example of God's grace and forgiveness. Josiah wouldn't be surprised if this admonition was followed by an historical anecdote in which some struggling saint exemplified the great men and women of the faith who were extolled in Hebrews chapter eleven, who collectively never lived to see the fruit of their labor.

"And Sarah and I also agree . . ."

Here it comes.

". . . that you are the last person they will listen to, and that the situation calls for an objective voice. For a man of God who can stand between a pastor and his people and reunite you much as he might do with a man and his wife."

Josiah didn't know what to think, or how to respond. If this is what Edwards believed, why would he turn down the . . . ?

Edwards continued, "I am confident that I am not the man whom you are seeking. But you will find that man in Philadelphia."

"Philadelphia," Josiah said, stunned.

"He's preaching there now. From the reports I've received, he has the blessing of heaven attending him wherever he goes."

"How will I find him?"

"You must go to Philadelphia."

Josiah was hoping for more than that, but Edwards had no more information other than Josiah would find his preacher in Philadelphia.

"One thing more." Edwards leaned forward and spoke in a confidential tone. "God has also impressed upon me to relay to you a message."

Josiah leaned forward to receive it.

"Beware the river gods," Edwards said.

"River gods?"

"Those who control the commerce. Those who channel profits into their own pockets at the expense of the farmers and the townspeople."

"The merchants."

"Those who control the financing, the marketing, and the distribution of Havenhill's produce. They are ministers of fear, covetousness, and pride. Wicked and debauched men who serve mammon, not the Lord God."

Like Havenhill, Northampton depended for its economic livelihood on shipping along the Connecticut River.

"You must lead your people to ask God to transform Havenhill's marketplace with values that promote the common good above private gain."

Josiah smiled. "Remember I told you about Philip Clapp? The one who made it possible for me to return to Havenhill? He's the leading merchant in town. A good man. More importantly, a friend. I can count on him."

Edwards sat back in his chair, thoughtful, almost bewildered, as though he didn't understand. After a few moments, he said, "I have delivered the message. That is enough. What you do from here, you must do acting on faith. God will make all things plain in His time."

For the last several moments of conversation, the noise of the activity around them had faded so far into the background that Josiah had not been aware of it. With the conversation coming to an end, he was once again aware that he was in a house with eleven children.

Josiah pushed back his chair. "I want to thank you for your hospitality. But if I'm going to ride to Philadelphia, I'd better get started now."

CHAPTER 24

With his back to Northampton, Josiah couldn't shake the feeling that he'd failed, at least partially. He'd left Havenhill for the purpose of meeting the author of the book on revival in the Connecticut Valley, and he'd done that. With great joy, he might add. But he'd also left with the hopes of getting Edwards to preach in Havenhill.

Josiah left Northampton with fond memories of hearing Edwards recount intimate details of the revival and with a renewed zeal to replicate those stories in Havenhill. The time alone with Edwards and the lovely Sarah was worth the trip, not to mention the relief from the constant belly thrum he endured daily at Havenhill.

However, feelings aside, he still had a problem. He had told Philip that he would bring the great revival preacher himself back to Havenhill. Having failed to accomplish that, he now found himself on a road to Philadelphia to hear a preacher he'd never heard of. A voice inside his head told him to stop wasting time and return to Havenhill and tend to his responsibilities. It was the voice of Eunice Parkhurst. A couple of times he almost listened to her.

Then the strangest thing happened.

A half day out of Philadelphia, he fell in with another couple traveling to the city—a farmer and his wife. Loud and cheerful in a child-like manner, they, too, were on their way to hear the revival preacher that Edwards had said had the blessing of heaven attending him.

"You've heard him preach before?" Josiah asked.

"Nah. Heard a lot about him, though," said the farmer.

"Tell 'im 'bout the boy," his wife said, nudging her husband in the ribs with an elbow.

The farmer reacted to the nudge but ignored her. He had his own story to tell. "Was out in the field when I heard he was gonna be preachin' today in the city. Dropt my tool and ran right into the house the moment I heard, didn't I, Ebbie? I dropt what I was doin' and runned inside."

Ebbie nodded. "He dropt his tool straightway."

"Got my wife, got my horse, and we set out straightway. I said to her, 'We're gonna hear that preacher Whitefield, 'cause Lord knows we may not get another chance.' That's exactly what I said, ain't it, Ebbie?"

"That's what he said, exactly," Ebbie replied. "Tell 'im about the boy."

"And we ain't stopped all day, neither. I jus' hope we ain't late."

"Tell 'im about the boy, Henry."

Henry pulled a handkerchief from his pocket and wiped his brow. He was a middle-aged man with an already healthy deposit of wrinkles on his face, no doubt from long hours in the sun. They walked at a brisk clip, one that was getting harder to maintain. When Josiah came upon them, they were riding double. Now neither of them rode, giving the horse a rest.

"Tell 'im about the boy!" Ebbie cried.

Henry shooed her with his handkerchief, as he would a fly.

Josiah waited politely for Henry to honor his wife's wishes. Henry didn't seem in any hurry. It seemed he was delaying for no other reason than to irritate Ebbie.

Finally, Ebbie said, "In Jersey there was this boy—"

"Hush, woman!" Henry shouted.

Ebbie hushed, but not without a scowl of protest.

Henry sniffed. "The way we done heard it, in Jersey there was this boy . . . He was wailin' and carryin' on somethin' awful. It was as though his little heart would burst from the cryin'."

"There's no need to make it bigger than what it already is," Ebbie scolded. "Jus' tell the story."

Henry turned on her. "Will you let me tell it?"

The couple exchanged glares that had no doubt been honed to perfection over many years of practice.

"As I was sayin'," Henry said, "in Jersey, there was this boy . . ."

Ebbie rolled her eyes.

". . . and he was cryin'. Well, Mr. Whitefield broke off his preachin', right there and then. He had the boy handed up to him in the wagon in which he was standin' to preach. And then he said, so that everyone could hear, that all the old professors of all the universities in the world—"

"You're gettin' carried away again," Ebbie said.

Henry ignored her. ". . . would not cry after Christ. But that this boy would preach to them. That out of this boy's mouth, God was declarin' His greatness and announcin' His praise."

"Declarin' His *sovereignty*," Ebbie corrected him.

"I told it the way I heard it," Henry replied.

"You told it wrong. He said God was declarin' His sovereignty and perfectin' His praise."

"*Soverntу* ain't no word."

"Is too. It's in the Bible."

"Well, you're jus' gonna have to show me, 'cause I'm tellin' ya, there ain't no word *soverntу*. But you can't show me, can you? You know why? 'Cause it ain't a word."

It wasn't long after hearing the story of the Jersey boy that traffic along the road began to thicken. They were close to the city now. But unless Philadelphia was twice the size of London, the amount of traffic on the road for the middle of the week was remarkable.

Conversations soon revealed that most everyone was traveling to Philadelphia for one reason. To hear George Whitefield preach.

There was an excitement among them, despite the occasional domestic squabble. Josiah had never seen anything like it. Nor had he been a part of something this exciting. The anticipation seemed to build with each new encounter.

By the time they were crossing the Delaware River, had a boy with two loaves and fishes joined them and told them that Jesus Himself would be preaching on the hillside, Josiah didn't think the crowd would be any more excited.

Standing in the city of Philadelphia at the edge of the crowd, Josiah marveled at the articulate speech of the speaker.

The preacher stood at the top of the courthouse steps, at the corner of Market Street and Second Street. He was younger than Josiah expected—probably in his midtwenties. Josiah's age.

What struck Josiah most about the man was that he was not your typical preacher. Whitefield moved vigorously across the top step, eyes flashing, hurling gospel truths like thunderbolts.

The intersection was packed with all those who had come to hear him, extending in four directions down each of the streets. Josiah had already heard enough to be praying blessings upon Jonathan Edwards for directing him to Philadelphia.

"His enunciation is flawless," a voice said.

Josiah turned to the man standing next to him. He was portly and bespectacled. A genial sort by his appearance.

"You've heard him preach before," Josiah stated.

"London, and on several occasions here," said the man, obviously fascinated by the speaker. "Have you noticed? Every accent, every emphasis, every modulation of his voice is perfectly tuned and well placed. Even without interest in the subject, one could not help but be pleased with the discourse. The actor David Garrick once remarked of the preacher Whitefield that he could make an audience weep or tremble simply by the utterance of the word 'Oh.'"

From what Josiah had heard, the actor's comment was not overstated. At present, Whitefield was describing the need in Georgia for an orphanage. The colony had been founded by debtors, prisoners, and idlers who were sadly lacking in the industrial habits necessary to establish a thriving colony. As a result, children were born who could not be provided for. Whitefield presented their case to the hearers and asked them to do what they could to support the building of an orphanage.

The man beside Josiah tightly folded his arms as Whitefield's men were sent among the crowd to collect an offering as Whitefield continued to address the need.

"We disagree on this," the bespectacled man told Josiah. "I do not disapprove of Mr. Whitefield's intentions, but of his proposal itself. Georgia is destitute of the necessary materials and workmen to build such a facility, whereas here in Philadelphia we have both materials and workers. Why not build the house here and bring the children to it? I told him as much myself. But he is most resolute on doing it his way."

The man's arms folded tighter across his chest.

Josiah dug in his pocket for a couple of silver dollars.

As one of the collectors came by, Josiah deposited his coins. To his surprise, the man next to him surrendered a fistful of coppers.

Whitefield continued making his plea.

"Having conversed with him personally," Josiah said, "would you vouch for the man's character? You see, I am a minister myself, and I'm considering inviting him to preach in my town."

Before answering, the man studied Josiah. "From where do you hail?"

"Havenhill."

"Ah, Connecticut! To answer your question, there are those who suppose that Mr. Whitefield would apply these offerings to his own coffers. But having been associated with him on several business endeavors—"

"Of what kind?"

"Publishing. Mr. Whitefield has employed me on occasion to print his sermons. And having done business with the man, I can assure you that his conduct is that of an honest man."

"That's good to hear."

"That is not to say the man is without his enemies and detractors. But it's hard for them to argue with the results of his preaching. It is wonderful to see the change made in the manner of our inhabitants. From being thoughtless or indifferent about religion, the town appears to be growing religious. One cannot walk through Philadelphia in the evening without hearing the strains of psalms sung in homes on every street."

Josiah couldn't have received a better report. This was exactly what he was seeking for his own town.

Another offering taker came by. Grumbling, the man next to him produced four silver dollars and handed them over.

On the courthouse steps, Whitefield preached with increasing fervency. A reverent stillness covered the crowd.

"How many do you suppose are gathered here?" asked the man. In his hands were a pencil and a pad of paper. These tools were not strangers in this man's hands.

Josiah looked around. Estimating crowd size had never been a skill he'd had to practice as a preacher.

"Better yet, how many do you suppose Mr. Whitefield could preach to in the open air?" The man began to walk backward down Market Street. "How far can we go until we can no longer hear him?" A boyish curiosity framed the man's face.

Josiah joined him.

They walked the cobbled street toward the river, stopping occasionally to determine if Whitefield's voice could still be heard.

"Can you make out what he is saying?"

If Josiah nodded that he could, the man would take a few more steps. "Now? Can you still hear him now?"

Josiah listened, then nodded again.

This continued until they reached Front Street, where normal traffic obscured Whitefield's words.

"Now imagine a semicircle, of which our distance from the speaker is the radius. Then fill it with auditors, say"—he thought for a moment—"allowing two square feet per person. Given these figures, how many people might Mr. Whitefield be able to preach to in an open field?"

The man scribbled on his pad of paper, and Josiah gladly let him do the figuring.

The man looked up in triumph. "According to my computations, Mr. Whitefield might well be heard by more than thirty thousand persons, which reconciles the newspaper accounts I've read that reportedly have him preaching to twenty-five thousand people in the fields."

Having concluded their experiment, the two men returned to the edge of the crowd. Whitefield was praying. Following the prayer, another offering taker meandered by, giving the hearers one last chance to contribute to the orphanage.

With a grunt that would have made a bull moose proud, the man thrust a hand into his pocket and emptied it, handing five pistoles in gold to the taker of the offering.

Turning to Josiah, he said, "I have been pleased that you helped me with my little experiment. May I return the favor by providing an introduction to Mr. Whitefield?"

"I would be most grateful!" Josiah cried, scarcely able to conceal his good fortune.

The man took a step, then swung back around. "It occurs to me that if I am to provide this introduction, it might be helpful if I knew your name."

With a grin, Josiah introduced himself.

"Pleased to make your acquaintance, Reverend Rush," said the man. "And I am Benjamin Franklin, at your service."

CHAPTER 25

Despite Benjamin Franklin's knowledge of the streets and alleys of Philadelphia, with the flow of the departing crowd working against them, the hoped-for introduction to George Whitefield never happened.

Franklin was apologetic. He sent an apprentice to inquire into Whitefield's schedule and to present Franklin's compliments, requesting a meeting at the evangelist's earliest convenience. Meanwhile, after apologizing for the scanty nature of his accommodations, the printer entertained Josiah with tea and an endless stream of stories, anecdotes, and observations regarding human nature, all of which kept Josiah thoroughly amused.

Eventually, the conversation returned to Whitefield.

"There are some in our city who propose erecting a building for Mr. Whitefield so that the occasional inclemency of the weather might not prohibit him from preaching. They've received sufficient sums to procure the ground and erect a building one hundred feet long and seventy feet abroad, about the size of Westminster Hall. The work is already underway."

"And Mr. Whitefield is agreeable to this?" Josiah asked.

A pleased smile spread across Franklin's face. "You say you have never heard Mr. Whitefield preach before?"

"Today was the first time."

Franklin nodded. "You are an astute judge of character, Reverend Rush. At first Mr. Whitefield sought to preach in churches in the Colonies. He was granted invitations by some. However, his dramatic style curried no small amount of disfavor among some of the more staid congregations, forcing Mr. Whitefield into the fields and streets, to which he is so excellently suited. He has let it be known he prefers preaching in the open."

"And the building? Will it still be built?"

"Its use will be vested in trustees for the use of any preacher who might desire to address the people of Philadelphia. It will not accommodate any particular sect, but the inhabitants in general, so that if the Mufti of Constantinople himself were to send a missionary to preach Mohammedanism to us, he would find a ready pulpit."

Josiah sipped his tea.

Franklin studied Josiah. "You disapprove, Reverend Rush?"

"I'm your guest, Mr. Franklin. It would be impolite—"

"Speak freely, son."

Josiah couldn't help but think that Franklin knew what he was going to say even before he said it. Still, Josiah spoke his mind. "It's just that I find it odd that a good Christian man such as yourself would grant a pagan speaker a pulpit so that he might teach that which is contrary to the doctrines of Christ."

Franklin let loose with a huge laugh. "I see I must take back my earlier comment on your being an astute judge of character. When it comes to matters of the faith, I fear I am something of a renegade. While I applaud Mr. Whitefield's preaching for its positive effects on the morals of our citizens, and while I genuinely like and admire the man—after all, we both come from modest beginnings; we both have something of an entrepreneurial spirit and have struck out on our own; and we both came to Philadelphia as outsiders, only to be adopted by the city—that is where our similarities end."

"But you publish and distribute his sermons."

"Business, my son. I print and distribute books and newspapers of popular interest. And Mr. Whitefield generates a lot of interest. Personally, I find Mr. Whitefield's teaching antirationalistic and enthusiastic. And while he has on several occasions prayed for my conversion, I fear he has not had the satisfaction of believing that his prayers have been answered. Ours is a mere civil friendship, sincere on both sides."

"If it's all the same to you, Mr. Franklin," Josiah said, "I will join Mr. Whitefield in praying for your salvation."

At that point the door opened and Franklin's apprentice appeared. The apologetic slant of his eyes indicated the news wasn't good. Whitefield had left the city. He was heading for Boston.

Early the next morning—after spending an entertaining evening listening to Dr. Franklin describe his inauspicious arrival in Philadelphia as a young man—Josiah set off for Boston.

He was feeling desperate. Already he'd extended his trip in an attempt to enlist a revival preacher for Havenhill. And, despite being impressed with George Whitefield's preaching—more than impressed, actually; listening to Mr. Whitefield preach was like listening to a man who had come directly from God's throne room with a message from the Almighty Himself—Josiah felt uneasy about delaying his return to Havenhill further.

There were those in the church who had grumbled about his trip to Boston earlier to get Dr. McCullough, claiming he'd flown off on a fool's errand. Then there were those who thought the preacher should never be gone if it meant being gone on a Sabbath day. It didn't take much imagination to conjure up the conversations that were taking place in Havenhill right now over his absence, especially considering that his absence from his duties was extending beyond his stated itinerary. The words *irresponsible* and *neglect of duty* were most certainly among the comments.

A feeling of fatalism had figured in Josiah's decision to continue on to Boston. By now those in Havenhill who would crucify him for being gone longer than he'd anticipated would already have the timber and nails ready for his return. What difference would a few more days make? So, with a surly attitude, Josiah had mounted his horse.

But within the hour, his heart had become exuberant and his mind convinced he'd made the right decision.

The change had come not long after he fell in with a group of nearly a dozen travelers. The way they were laughing and carrying on with one another, he thought they were a traveling troop of some sort. Then he found out something startling: none of them had met before this morning. And yet they were acting as though they'd known one another for years.

Slowing his horse to match the travelers' pace, Josiah soon learned that the one thing the travelers had in common was that they had all attended Mr. Whitefield's outdoor service, the same one he'd attended. And they had all come away from it changed. The effect was astonishing.

It was different from the warm afterglow that a small group of friends might feel after attending the theater or a musical production. This was deeper. It was as though the hearts of this band of strangers had been knit together. And it was more than just newfound friendships—it went deeper than that too—more like blood kin, more like family.

They spoke openly of intimate matters of the heart. They listened without judgment. They shared emotions as others would share a loaf of bread, feeding off the same joy or heartbreak or passion. They stopped frequently and dropped to their knees to pray over some confessed wrongdoing or ill-spoken word; for a sick relative or a wayward child; or for wisdom in a business decision. They could barely get fifty paces without finding a reason to kneel and pray.

Naturally, they were interested in Josiah's impression of the sermon and the revivalist. With upturned faces, they listened with intensity, drinking in his tale as though it were a fountain for parched travelers. When he told them of his mission, in their eagerness to pray for its success, they fairly pulled him to the ground. Surrounded on every side, a dozen or more hands descended upon him. Josiah felt their weight pressing down on his back and shoulders and head as these fellow sojourners—Josiah didn't even know most of their names, having picked up but a few in casual conversation—took turns beseeching God and the angels of heaven to intercede for him, his church, and all the residents of Havenhill. Their voices cracked with emotion as they prayed; tears fell freely.

Josiah was struck by the realization that he was kneeling in the dirt on a public thoroughfare somewhere between Philadelphia and Boston, surrounded by people he'd never met before today, their hands pressing down upon him. What an odd sight they must be. Yet he didn't care. He soaked up their encouragement, their support, their prayers.

For Josiah the most difficult part of the journey to Boston came when he reached his destination and bid farewell to those he'd journeyed with. He had five open invitations to dinner and three offers for lodging. More importantly, he had a fresh vision of the power of the Holy Spirit. If God could form a community out of twelve strangers, imagine the possibilities of what He could do among a people who had lived and worked together for decades!

But the residents of Havenhill would have to let Him. Josiah knew enough about God to know that He would never force a person to change against his will. But then, that's where Mr. Whitefield came in. If Josiah could get Mr. Whitefield to come to Havenhill, to state the case for Christ and a renewed spirit the way he had done in Philadelphia, Josiah was certain stony hearts would melt and beat once again with Christian love.

Which made the success of his task in Boston all that much more imperative. Josiah was convinced George Whitefield was the key. One way or another, Josiah had to get the evangelist to agree to preach in Havenhill.

CHAPTER 26

Josiah's three days in Boston were the most frustrating days of his life. Having spent seven years in the city, he figured that it would be easier to approach Whitefield here than it had been in Philadelphia, where the crowd was so great.

It had been Josiah's observation that the people of Boston—who were the wealthiest among the Colonies—were remarkable in their external observance of the Sabbath. Men had a high regard for religion, but it was appearance only. Religion was fashionable in Boston.

Infants brought for baptism were wrapped in the finest apparel. So many pains were taken to dress them that one would think they were being presented to the altar of society rather than to God.

Given such a religious climate, Josiah expected Mr. Whitefield's outdoor, charismatic style to be greeted by the Bostonians with detached amusement.

He couldn't have been more wrong.

So great were the crowds at the Old North Church in Boston that Governor Belcher was forced to make emergency plans for an immediate relocation of the service to the commons, where according to newspaper reports, twenty-three thousand people gathered to hear the evangelist preach.

Josiah never got within shouting distance of the preacher.

FIRE

It was with a strange mix of emotions that Josiah turned south toward Havenhill. On the one hand, he was never more certain that he knew exactly what the people needed. They needed God, pure and simple. They needed a fresh outpouring of the Holy Spirit to rekindle the love they had once had for the things of God.

The maddening element was that not only did Josiah know the cure for their Soul Sickness, he knew who could deliver the cure. Only, after repeated attempts, he had failed to secure the antidote, as it were.

So close.

So close.

Taking the postal road—the same road he took when he had returned to Havenhill seven months ago—he walked the horse. Not that the horse needed the rest. Josiah walked because he needed to think.

Solvitur ambulando.

The solution comes through walking.

By the time Josiah reached Dedham, he'd come to a decision. It would mean adding several more days to his journey and further stoking the anger of his congregation, but the thought of facing their wrath paled in comparison to the thought of returning to a sick town without a cure.

So at Dedham, Josiah doubled back into the heart of Massachusetts and set his sights once again on Northampton.

The New England fall festival of color, an annual event sponsored by nature, was off to a resplendent start as Josiah rode into Northampton, this time from the east.

By now his speech was well rehearsed. It was detailed without sounding pedantic. Passionate, but not whiny. Persuasive, but not pushy.

At one point he'd considered winning Sarah Edwards to his side first so she could help persuade her husband to preach in Havenhill. But that approach seemed underhanded and deceptive. Josiah decided he'd use it only as a last resort.

As Josiah rode into town, his thoughts were distracted by its peacefulness, the afterglow of revival. He prayed that—God willing—he'd be able to stroll through Havenhill and sense the same feeling.

But that would never happen until they recovered from this epidemic of Soul Sickness. Somehow Josiah had to convince Jonathan Edwards to preach in Havenhill.

Reaching the Edwardses' house, Josiah dismounted. As he approached the door, he wondered if he'd be greeted once again by the little curly-headed hostess.

He knocked.

Moments later the door opened.

"Why, Reverend Rush! We were just praying for you!" A surprised Sarah Edwards smiled warmly and invited him into her house.

Josiah thanked her. He dismissed the thought that her greeting was disingenuous. While he hadn't known her long, he knew her well enough that if she said they'd just been praying for him, they had indeed been doing just that.

With one foot inside and one still out, Josiah looked past his hostess.

What he saw made him stop so suddenly that he appeared to have walked into an invisible wall.

Seated in front of the fire were Jonathan Edwards and George Whitefield.

CHAPTER 27

At the sight of George Whitefield stretching his legs in front of Jonathan Edwards's fire, Josiah needed several moments to chase down and gather his wits. They had scattered in all directions, like birds chased from a tree.

If his host noticed Josiah's dumbfounded orientation, he didn't acknowledge it. The taller man moved with long strides toward him, his hand extended in greeting. Then, having gripped Josiah's limp limb—for he had yet to chase down the last of his wits—Edwards pulled him into the room for introductions.

Whitefield stood and faced them.

"Mr. Whitefield here was just telling us how he wished he could have met you," Edwards said.

"And it seems God has seen fit to honor that wish," the evangelist said, offering his hand.

"Th . . . the . . . ," Josiah stammered. He cleared his throat and tried again. "Indeed, sir. The pleasure is mine."

How ordinary the man appears, Josiah thought. Had he passed Whitefield on the road as a stranger, he would not have taken notice of him. But having seen him preach on Philadelphia's courthouse steps and then again at Boston Common, for some reason Josiah expected more. When he thought about it, that seemed ridiculous. After all, did he really expect the man to be bathed in a heavenly sheen?

Of the three men, Whitefield was shortest. He had a good-natured glint in his eyes, and the corners of his mouth had an impish upward tilt to them. Again, Josiah was struck by the preacher's youth. They were about the same age. And yet, look how much God had used Whitefield—first in England, now in the Colonies. A feeling of shame at having not accomplished nearly so much for God settled over Josiah.

"Mr. Edwards was just telling me you traveled to Philadelphia, intending to meet me," Whitefield said. His voice inflection was clear and had a familiar ring, though it seemed surprising to hear it so soft-spoken, instead of charging like wild horses over the heads of so many thousands of people.

Josiah nodded. "Yes, sir, that was my intent."

Sarah brought a third chair and situated it between the ones Edwards and Whitefield had been sitting in. As the three men sat, Josiah couldn't help but realize the blessedness of his position, with Jonathan Edwards on his left and George Whitefield on his right.

"And again at Boston," Josiah said.

"You were in Boston?" Whitefield exclaimed. Then, to Edwards, "God blessed us with crowds in Boston beyond our expectations. And the people of Boston were dear to my soul. They were greatly affected by the Word and were very liberal to my dear orphans."

"Over twenty thousand at one meeting," Josiah added.

Edwards's eyes lit up at the numbers. "It seems there are a few names left in Sardis who have not defiled their garments."

"Indeed," Whitefield replied. "It was our prayer that the Lord would grant to the remnant that is still there . . . that their number would take root and bear fruit and fill the land!"

A shudder of pleasure and expectation shook Josiah. He was seated at a spiritual oasis between two men of God—men who understood the spiritual needs of the Colonies and who shared his heartfelt desire to lead the nation back to God, her first love. Now he knew exactly how Peter felt on the Mount of Transfiguration. He wanted to pitch his tent here and stay awhile.

"Which brings us to you, Mr. Rush," Whitefield said. "Mr. Edwards has been telling me how impressed he is with the depth of your spirit, and about the scientific study you have done on the nature of sin. I believe you have compared it to a physical ailment?"

Josiah's head was swimming. As best he could, he described his observations and conclusions regarding Soul Sickness, and of his desire to introduce a cure to the town.

Whitefield listened with interest.

It was at this point in the story, Josiah realized, where Edwards had asked him why he didn't provide the cure himself. All of a sudden Josiah felt uneasy. Had Edwards also told Whitefield about the fire and the three deaths? Would Whitefield be as understanding?

Edwards seemed to sense his discomfort. "Having sought my advice on the matter, I suggested to him that you might be the exact prescription his town needs."

Josiah wanted to hug the older preacher.

"That is," Edwards concluded, "after you preach here in Northampton."

Whitefield laughed, and Josiah got the impression this was the first time the question of Whitefield's preaching here had been addressed.

"You hardly need me in Northampton," Whitefield cried. "You forget. I've read your *Faithful Narrative*. God has already established a strong voice in this wilderness. It was your record of the acts of God here in the Colonies that has been my inspiration for England."

"I would warn you that the Colonies as a whole will present a special challenge," Edwards said. "We who have dwelt in a land that has been distinguished with Light and have long enjoyed the gospel and have been glutted with it are, I fear, more hardened than most. A fresh voice is needed. My invitation stands."

Whitefield paused. He appeared taken aback by the fact that it was Jonathan Edwards who was making the request. Finally, Whitefield said, "I am your humble servant."

Edwards smiled. "You are an answer to our prayers."

Whitefield turned to Josiah. "And if after having met me, you still want me to preach in Havenhill, I would be pleased to do so."

Maybe it was the anxiety that had been building inside him day after day; maybe it was the weariness of road travel. Whatever the reason, emotion rushed to Josiah's eyes. "Sir, you are an answer to my prayers."

"Your perseverance on behalf of your people is a testimony of your love for them," Whitefield replied. "I count it a privilege to preach in the pulpit of a man of your character."

After a meal of pot roast with onion and carrots, and a plum pudding, the men resumed their discussion of the spiritual needs of the Colonies while Sarah and the children cleaned up and prepared for afternoon lessons.

"You may have been wondering how it was that you were a topic of conversation before you arrived," Edwards said to Josiah.

Until now, the thought had not entered Josiah's mind, so surprised had he been when he arrived to see that George Whitefield had preceded him to Northampton. But now that Edwards brought it up, it was rather curious that they would be talking about him just as he arrived.

Edwards solemnly produced a broadsheet and handed it to Josiah. Josiah noticed a distasteful expression on Whitefield's face.

"There are similar handbills being distributed up and down the Connecticut River," Edwards said.

"And in Boston," Whitefield added. "I saw identical broadsheets posted along the quay."

At first glance, the relevance of the broadsheet made no sense to Josiah. It was an announcement for a slave auction. He was about to hand it back to Edwards and to ask him how this concerned him when a single word near the bottom of the broadsheet leaped out at him.

Havenhill.

The slave auction was to be held at Havenhill.

"This must be a misprint," Josiah murmured.

Whitefield and Edwards exchanged glances.

Josiah stared dumbly at the broadsheet. "It has to be a misprint," he insisted. "There's no other way to explain it. The people of Havenhill would never . . ."

Whitefield inched close to him and pointed to a name at the very bottom of the page.

Josiah read it aloud: "'Lord Percival Bellamont.' I've never heard of him."

Whitefield slumped back in his chair. "Wish to God, neither had I. It was his name on the broadsheet that arrested my attention. Many a godly man in England has done battle against the wicked and immoral business tactics of Lord Bellamont, including Dr. Isaac Watts, who had a hand in publishing Edwards's *Faithful Narrative*."

Josiah knew of Isaac Watts for his wonderful hymns.

"Bellamont is at the heart of the controversial money measure currently being debated," Edwards added. "As I'm sure you've heard, wealthy merchants are pressing for the establishment of a Silver Bank, which would restrict the amount of cash in circulation to the silver supply."

Josiah nodded. He'd heard of the attempt.

"Meanwhile, farmers and smaller merchants are calling for a Land Bank, whereby landholders would be given notes of legal tender for their land as security."

"Which makes sense, considering the fact that a farmer's wealth is in his land," Josiah stated.

"Yet the merchants argue—and they have a point—," Edwards said, "that the farmer would not be able to survive, were it not for the risk merchants take to distribute their produce and lumber and goods abroad, and that with the cash they receive in return, farmers are able to pay their taxes."

"Which is an appealing argument to the Crown and Parliament," Whitefield added. "However, the problem is not that one side is right and the other is wrong. It's that there are unscrupulous men who see the debate as an opportunity for personal financial gain."

Josiah made the connection. "Lord Bellamont."

"His name has become a byword in England for ruthlessness and disreputable business tactics," Whitefield explained. "He has made a vast fortune importing rum. Recently, however, he has given public notice that he plans to expand his financial empire by investing aggressively in the slavery business."

Which explains the broadsheet, Josiah thought. But how was Havenhill involved?

"Remember when I warned you about the river gods?" Edwards asked.

Josiah nodded. He remembered.

"Lord Bellamont has made several unsuccessful attempts to get a toehold in the Connecticut River Valley. He came offering easy credit to landowners, with attractive repayment plans."

"He ensnares landowners and other merchants by appealing to their desire to own things they haven't earned," Whitefield added.

"Men who live day-to-day in economic uncertainty buy their wives and daughters velvet hoods, red cloaks, and silk garments," Edwards said. "The result is that they're caught up in a web of extravagance and economic dependence."

"What happened?" Josiah asked.

"God happened. That was the same time the Holy Spirit swept through this region, and people's hearts were turned away from greed and self. However, not until many of them had mortgaged their lands to Bellamont. So a few godly businessmen stepped in and rescued those who were in debt to Bellamont and forced him out of the region."

An uneasiness began to settle over Josiah.

Whitefield pointed at the broadsheet. He said, "At present, a hundred and fifty ships transport forty-five thousand slaves every year to America. Only thirty-five percent of the slaves are sold in New England, with the bulk going to the middle and Southern Colonies. Bellamont not only wants a piece of this lucrative trade, he wants to expand it by increasing the number of slaves sold to New England Colonies."

"That's why he was here in the Connecticut River Valley," Edwards said. "He was looking for an available port so he could turn it into the slave capital of the North."

Josiah looked at the broadsheet in his hands. The word *Havenhill* burned on the parchment. Had Lord Bellamont found his slave capital? But how?

CHAPTER 28

Josiah spent a fitful night in the same bed he'd slept in previously when he stayed with the Edwards family. As the night hours dragged on, all he could think of was the slave-auction broadsheet. Philip had to know about it, didn't he? And how many others knew about it? Was the whole town in on it?

Twice Josiah threw back the coverlet, thinking that he couldn't wait until morning. He had to get back to Havenhill. And twice he pulled the coverlet back over him. Leaving now would be rude to his hosts. Besides, there were still some details he needed to settle with Whitefield to arrange for his coming to Havenhill.

Josiah tossed to one side.

Maybe he should withdraw the invitation. Somehow inviting an evangelist to the slave capital of New England just didn't seem proper. Of course, Josiah didn't know it was the slave capital of New England when he made the invitation. But Whitefield knew, didn't he? Or at least he suspected. He acknowledged seeing the broadsheets in Boston. He was probably eager to preach in the slave capital of New England. What evangelist wouldn't be? It was like preaching in Nineveh, or Sodom and Gomorrah.

With a grunt, Josiah turned his face to the wall.

Come morning, Whitefield saw Josiah off. Sarah Edwards made apologies for her husband.

"He was ailing when I arrived," Whitefield said of their host. "Strong of spirit, though, as is his wife. A sweeter couple I have not yet seen."

Josiah smiled. He noticed that Whitefield was taken by Sarah Edwards. A couple of times, he caught the evangelist following her with his eyes. Not in a wicked way. More like admiration.

"I find the woman attractive in a godly way, wouldn't you agree?" Whitefield said, as though reading Josiah's mind. "She is adorned with a meek and quiet spirit; she talks solidly of the things of God and seems to be such a helpmeet for her husband. Are you married, Mr. Rush?"

"No," Josiah said somewhat forlornly. Truth was, he readily identified with Whitefield's comments regarding Sarah Edwards. She'd made the same impression on him.

Referring again to their hostess, Whitefield said, "She has caused me to renew my prayers, which for some months I have put up to God, that He would be pleased to send me a daughter of Abraham to be my wife." In all seriousness, he continued, "I desire to have no choice of my own. God knows my circumstances. He knows I desire to marry in and for Him alone. And just as He chose Rebecca for Isaac, I believe that someday He will choose a helpmeet for me, so that together we may carry on this great work that has been committed to my charge."

Whether preaching or speaking of love, the man was passionate. Josiah admired that in him. He shared the feeling. As Whitefield was speaking, Josiah's thoughts turned to Nabby. God would make a way for them. He knew this in his heart.

"You have someone special, do you?" Whitefield said, grinning, as he studied Josiah. "I can see it on your face."

"A helpmeet," Josiah said.

"Do you marry soon?"

Color rose in Josiah's face. "In God's good time," he replied.

Whitefield nodded knowingly.

After concluding their business, the two men prayed that God would prepare the way for Whitefield's arrival in Havenhill.

After Josiah had mounted his horse, Whitefield said, "I have often said from the pulpit that the reason why congregations have been so dead is because they have dead men preaching to them. How can dead men beget living children?" He paused, then added, "But after meeting Mr. Edwards, and now you, I have hope that God has great things in store for the American Colonies, because the American churches are led by such passionate and godly men."

The return journey from Northampton to Havenhill went without incident. By the grace of God, having accomplished what he had set out to do—though it had taken considerably longer than he'd anticipated—Josiah felt good about the trip.

Yet, at the same time, the slave auction broadsheet was never far from his mind. There had to be an explanation. Some sort of error. A mistake. Philip would explain it away. He might even laugh that Josiah would have made such an issue of it.

At least that's what Josiah told himself on the road between Northampton and Havenhill. But Josiah couldn't even convince himself. No amount of imagined explanations relieved the knot of worry in the pit of his stomach.

At last he reached Fiedler's Knob. With a weary groan, he climbed down from the horse and stood on the edge of the precipice overlooking the town, just as he had done seven months earlier.

He was a different Josiah now.

He knew better what awaited him.

At least he thought he did. In some ways he thought he knew less about the town than when he'd left. But of this he was certain. God knew exactly what was happening in the town. Nothing was hidden from Him. He knew the intentions behind the remarks. The unspoken thoughts. The secrets hidden so deeply within that people wouldn't admit them, even to themselves.

God knew what was going on in Havenhill. And whatever it was, the first step in fixing it was for the townspeople to put their spiritual house in order. Once that was done, all other issues could be resolved. Until that was done, nothing would be resolved.

Getting down on his knees, Josiah prayed over the town.

"Lord, you have entrusted this town into my hands. Why, I cannot say. For, of all men, I am the least able to effect the change that is necessary among this people. Nevertheless, You have seen fit to put me at this place and at this time. So I pray for them. Lord, as You have done in Northampton and Hadley and Philadelphia and Boston, send Your Spirit to bring this town to their knees so that they might rise anew as blessed and righteous saints of the Almighty God. So that everyone who hears the name of Havenhill will be filled with a living hope that no sin is too grievous that it cannot be forgiven and no person so lost that he cannot be saved."

Rising from his knees, Josiah made his way down the postal road into Havenhill. With each step it felt as though he were being immersed in a warm, nauseating bath.

CHAPTER 29

It was late afternoon. Josiah encountered no one directly as he passed the common, though he was subject to several distant stares which, when he waved an acknowledgment, were quickly averted.

He found a note waiting for him when he reached his house. From its curled edges and general blanched appearance, it had been pinned to his door for several days at least.

See me IMMEDIATELY upon your return.

Goodwife Parkhurst

"And so it begins," Josiah said with a sigh.

He noticed another note, folded and wedged under the clapboard siding.

Be strong and of good courage. I'm praying for you.

The handwriting was the same as before; and as all the notes before this one had been, it was unsigned.

Josiah's shoulders slumped. He was road-weary and dusty; his feet and legs were cramped; and he was hungry. The last thing he wanted to do was deal with a disgruntled former pastor's wife. But Eunice Parkhurst's capital letters and triple underlining trumped his discomfort.

Taking time only to water the horse, he set out on foot, returning the way he'd just come. As he walked, he worked up his resolve to withstand the bucket of abuse Eunice would surely pour over his head. The thought that he might also see Nabby and possibly get a chance to speak to her was the silver lining in this otherwise grim scenario.

As he mounted the steps to the Parkhursts' front door, his toes felt gritty and his hair oily. Normally he would never make a pastoral call in this unkempt condition. However, this time he hoped the road dirt would testify on his behalf that he took Eunice Parkhurst's sense of urgency seriously. He knocked on the door.

"Look at you!" Eunice cried in disgust. She covered her mouth and nose with a handkerchief. "You could at least have had the decency to clean up before calling! In all my days, Reverend Parkhurst never, NEVER would have called on a parishioner in your condition!"

"My apologies," Josiah said, feeling filthier now than when he entered the room. "Your note . . . there was an urgency to it. Three underlines." He fumbled for the note in his pocket.

Eunice turned her head in disgust. She was dressed in a modest, pale blue, cotton dress with a lappet cap covering her hair, which she always wore up. As usual, she was neat and clean. The room looked like it always did. Tidy and clean. The furniture was dusted and clean. The floors were polished and clean.

The only dirty thing in the room was Josiah.

Dispensing with her handkerchief, Eunice opened a drawer and retrieved a fan, which she worked furiously.

"My apologies," Josiah said. "I'll return when I'm more presentable."

"Stay where you're at!" Eunice ordered. "I have something to say to you."

Her eyes were as hard as marbles, and from the way she was approaching him, she appeared to have more than one thing on her mind.

"Just what were you thinking, riding off like that without telling anyone?" she shouted.

He opened his mouth to protest, then closed it. Philip knew where he'd gone. Grace and Mercy knew where he'd gone. By her comment that he didn't tell anyone, what Eunice really meant was that he didn't tell *her*.

"You're a pastor! People depend upon you! In all my years, I've never heard of a minister showing complete disregard for his congregation the way you have! We've been sheep without a shepherd. How do you think that makes us feel?"

Josiah thought the biblical analogy was a nice touch. He made no attempt to answer her. He knew Eunice well enough to know that once she built up a good steam, there was no stopping her. She had to get it out. Even then there would be no reasoning with her. No explanation would satisfy her. No fact would convince her. An apology may soothe her somewhat, but not always.

As Eunice began to list in detail every person in town who, because of his irresponsibility, suffered unduly without their pastor by their side, Josiah slipped a finger into his pocket and felt the other note, the folded one.

Be strong and of good courage. I'm praying for you.

The diversion buoyed his spirits.

For a moment.

Just then the front door slammed open.

"There you are! I got word you were back in town!" a male voice announced.

Johnny Mott's frame filled the door. Not until he stepped inside did Josiah see that Abigail was with him.

"Where have you been?" Mott shouted.

The absurdity of this scene struck Josiah. When he was in town, everybody wished he'd leave; when he was gone, they all complained he wasn't in town.

"What are you grinning about?" Mott cried. "You laughing at me?"

"Most assuredly not," Josiah said, losing the grin.

Eunice narrowed her eyes further. "I'm not done with him, Johnny. You can have him when I'm finished."

Josiah risked looking at Nabby. She had backed against a wall, her hands folded in front of her—in prayer?—to stay out of the line of fire. She looked stunning.

Demure. Sweet. Her pale skin shimmered. Her lips were soft and sensuous.

Suddenly his view was blocked by the massive chest of Johnny Mott. "Where do you get off spreading rumors that I had George Mason killed because he found out I was keeping two different sets of ledgers?"

"What?" Josiah asked.

"I'm not finished with him!" Eunice insisted, elbowing her way between Josiah and Johnny.

"I never stole nothing from anybody, and you know it!" Johnny shouted, poking a beefy finger over Eunice's head.

"Johnny, believe me, I never—," Josiah tried.

The door slammed open again.

Deacon Dunmore stormed in, his face as purple as strained beets. "There you are!" he shouted at Josiah.

Those three words seemed to be the town's rallying cry.

"Where were you last Tuesday?"

"Tuesday? I was in—"

"When the deacons call a meeting to talk to the pastor, it's customary for the pastor to attend!"

"You know I had nothing to do with George Mason's death!" Johnny Mott shouted.

"Goodwife Hibbard had an awful bout with her rheumatism, but when her daughter sent word to her pastor—," Eunice said over the top of Johnny's words.

"Good, I want to talk with the deacons," Josiah told Deacon Dunmore. "I've invited an evangelist to—"

"An evangelist?" Dunmore shouted. "We can't get one preacher to do his job! And now you want us to pay for another one?"

Josiah was outnumbered and overwhelmed. He surrendered to the onslaught. After a while, Eunice grew faint, and Abigail helped her upstairs. Deacon Dunmore announced there would be another meeting of the deacons, and this time Josiah had better have the good sense to attend. Then the still-irritated deacon left.

Johnny turned to follow Deacon Dunmore.

Josiah had seen his childhood friend angry like this before. Johnny looked like he wanted to hit someone, and if he didn't walk away, there was no telling how much longer he could fight the urge.

Josiah had to risk it. He caught Johnny by the arm. "I have to talk to you and Philip," he said in a low voice.

"Philip's in Boston."

"When will he be back?"

Josiah could tell that Johnny was straining to hold back the emotion, to keep his pent-up violence from bursting out all over Josiah. For the second time, Johnny turned to leave. And, for the second time, Josiah stopped him.

"I've seen the broadsheets," Josiah said.

"What are you talking about?"

"Boston. Up and down the Connecticut Valley. The broadsheets announcing the slave auction."

Johnny's eyes darted away from Josiah's. "I don't know what you're talking about."

Johnny was a bad liar. He always had been.

"Is it true?" Josiah asked.

Johnny Mott turned away again; this time there was no stopping him. Josiah watched his friend, who appeared ready to explode. Halfway down the street, Johnny did. With a roar, he punched a small tree. There was a crack. Birds scattered. A few moments later, Josiah lost sight of him.

Josiah stood alone in the doorway of the Parkhurst house. It was quiet.

Shutting the door, he turned toward home.

As he rounded the side of the house, he saw Abigail out back. She was feeding the chickens, scattering seed from a small burlap bag.

Josiah glanced around. No one else was in sight. Eunice was upstairs lying down. Johnny had just left and was unlikely to return anytime soon.

He couldn't help but wonder if Abigail had come to the same realization and picked this particular time to feed the chickens, knowing that he'd see her.

This was the first time in a long time that Josiah could gaze at Nabby without fear that someone might notice. Maybe that was why she had never looked more beautiful. Her hips were wider now than they were when she was in school, and her bosom fuller, giving her a mature figure. Her hair was tucked up beneath a mobcap, revealing a satiny, white neck. Josiah had always loved the curve of her neck.

She appeared not to know he was there. Or was she just acting coy?

Josiah shuffled his feet to announce his presence.

She started slightly. Her head swung his direction.

Their eyes met.

Soft azure orbs swallowed him whole.

She looked away. "You shouldn't be here."

"I saw you standing there and couldn't help myself. You know I've never been able to control myself when it comes to you."

Her cheeks reddened. "Don't say things like that!" she snapped. There were teeth to her response.

Josiah didn't care. He was tired of pretending. Tired of being cautious. Tired of waiting.

Yet, despite his feelings, he reined in his impatience. He was afraid that if he went too far, she'd fly away like a frightened bird. And he didn't know when he'd get another chance like this one.

He searched for some common ground and found it in his pocket. Her note. He pulled it out. "I want to thank you for these." He fingered the folded piece of paper.

"What is that? I don't know what you're talking about."

Josiah smiled. She wanted to remain anonymous. That made sense. If she didn't admit to sending the notes, she wouldn't feel as though she was doing something behind Johnny's back.

"I understand," he said. "Still, they've meant a lot to me."

He expected her to smile and that would be that. Message delivered and understood. It would be their secret.

Instead, she walked over to him and took the note from his hands, unfolded it, and read it. "Who sent you this?"

Now she was toying with him, he thought.

He'd go along with it. "A friend," he explained with a smile.

"Do you know who?"

She wasn't toying with him! She was serious. Still, he didn't believe her. He didn't want to believe her.

"That's your handwriting," he insisted.

She shook her head and handed the note back to him. "No, it isn't."

The moment she disclaimed any connection with the note, it now felt strange in his hand.

"It seems like Reverend Rush has a secret admirer," Abigail said in an adolescent tone.

"You really haven't—"

"I'd better get inside and check on Mother." Abigail began to walk toward the house. She turned abruptly and walked backward a few steps, just long enough to add, "Really, Josiah, you have a knack for setting the town's teeth on edge, don't you?"

CHAPTER 30

Had he been wrong all this time?

Seated at his writing table beside the window, Josiah stared at the note in his hand.

Be strong and of good courage. I'm praying for you.

He could have sworn it was Nabby's handwriting. But if it was, she couldn't have conjured up such a surprised expression when she read the note. Or denied that she'd written it. But if Nabby wasn't the one leaving him notes, who was?

And what was the rumor Johnny was so upset about? Josiah had never told anyone Johnny had George Mason killed. What reason would he have for fabricating such a rumor? And where did Johnny get the idea he was behind it?

Jabez, George's brother, was a likely candidate. He'd been angry enough to try to kill Johnny. But a rumor? Jabez was more of an ax kind of guy. And why attempt to divert suspicion to Josiah?

Josiah squeezed his eyes shut. His head hurt.

And what was Deacon Dunmore's gripe? What Tuesday meeting? Josiah knew nothing of a Tuesday meeting. How could he? On Tuesday he was on the road between Northampton and Havenhill. Why would anyone set up a meeting, knowing he was out of town? It didn't add up.

And what about Johnny's reaction when the slave auction broadsheet was mentioned? If Josiah had read Johnny correctly, his old friend knew about the auction but seemed surprised that Josiah knew about it.

His head swam as he remembered standing in Eunice Parkhurst's entryway. For a while there, with all the accusations flying at him, Josiah felt like a lone target for a band of archers. How could so many people get so angry with him while he was out of town?

Eunice he understood. He'd anticipated her wrath. And, sure enough, she didn't disappoint him. Nor had he heard the last from her, he was certain. He could count on a second round.

And then there was this note. He stared at it again, as though if he stared long enough, it would identify its author. After a time he set it down on the table. It was a mystery that would have to wait.

Opening his journal, he reached for a quill pen. His hand hovered over the pen, then withdrew. His writing, too, would have to wait. His mind was in too much of a jumble.

Other things required his immediate attention.

The first order of business was to make something to eat. Something simple that didn't take long. Eggs . . . possibly throw in a slab of bacon and some potatoes.

The second order of business was to clean up. He could barely stand himself.

In the morning he would begin preparations for the arrival of George Whitefield. He'd stop by the sisters' house. He wanted Mercy to know an evangelist was coming to town and to ask her if she'd heard of George Whitefield.

Then he'd get to the bottom of the slave-auction broadsheet. But that would have to wait for Philip's return from Boston.

Josiah didn't have to wait long.

Word reached him the next day that Philip had returned from Boston. Josiah had spent the morning working his way down Eunice

Parkhurst's list of people who had needed the services of a pastor while he'd been away. For the most part, their needs had been greatly exaggerated. A deacon or close friend could have filled in adequately, and in most cases did.

His last call took the longest. Goodwife Hibbard. When he called on her, she greeted him by telling him she wasn't speaking to him. Then she proceeded to tell him she was disappointed in him for abandoning her in her time of need and that he was a poor excuse for a minister, though she liked his preaching. For two hours nonstop, she bent his ear, frequently mentioning that she wasn't speaking to him.

It wasn't until early afternoon that Josiah had a chance to ride out to Philip's place.

Philip wasn't in. A servant told Josiah that he would be busy all day. Josiah asked if Philip would be home that evening. The servant would neither confirm nor deny his master's schedule.

Was the servant protecting Philip? Josiah wondered.

Leaving the horse he'd borrowed from Philip, Josiah walked back to town.

He reached the sisters' house just as they were leaving. Mercy smiled at him sweetly and asked about his trip—if he had made it to Hadley. Grace did not smile. Her responses were terse.

Josiah had caught them on a mission of mercy. They were taking a container of soup and a fresh loaf of bread to Goodwife Hibbard, who had been feeling a bit weak lately. Did Josiah wish to join them?

He begged off, wishing them well.

Returning to his house, he spent the remainder of the afternoon preparing for Sunday's sermons. He made little progress. He found it difficult to keep his mind on the text. Several times he caught himself staring blankly into the distance and formulating what he would say to Philip when he saw him.

That night Josiah took the slave-auction broadsheet he'd picked up and packed away in Boston. From a distance, Philip's two-story house appeared as a ghostly apparition, bathed in the silvery light of a full moon. The front windows were dark. However, as Josiah got closer, he could see a light inside the house, glowing like the last ember of a fire.

The servant with the long face answered the door. When Josiah requested to see Philip, he replied, "Master Clapp is entertaining and cannot be disturbed."

"This will only take a minute."

The long face drew even longer as the servant bent forward, as though speaking to a child. "I'm certain if you return in the morning, the master will see you then."

Philip's laughter came from the back of the house.

"If you'll just announce me," Josiah said, trying to be patient, "I'm sure your master will want to see me now."

"I'm sorry, sir." Long-face started to close the door.

"Fine." The broadsheet in one hand, Josiah used the other to push his way past the servant into the house. "I'll announce myself."

Long-face made an attempt to grab Josiah by the arm, but Josiah shook him off.

Striding toward the light, Josiah heard more voices and feminine laughter.

Before Long-face could catch up with him, Josiah managed to make it into the room. His momentum carried him into the brightly lit dining area, a cavernous room colorfully decorated with tapestries, ornate trim, and a crystal chandelier.

At his abrupt entrance, the four people at the dining table stared at him and fell silent.

Josiah instantly wished he'd listened to Long-face.

"Well!" Philip rose out of his chair. "An unexpected entrance, but not unwelcomed. Come in, Josiah. I'm sure you know everyone."

He did. All too well.

Seated around the table was a party of four. Abigail Parkhurst, Johnny Mott, Philip, and . . .

"You remember Anne, don't you?" Philip said with an unrestrained smile.

An elegant figure set aside her napkin and stood. Dressed in red silk, Anne Myles was more ravishing than Josiah remembered. She moved as royalty, extending a hand to Josiah. "You look well," she said, her eyes sparkling.

Josiah accepted the offer of her slender fingers. He'd never felt so underdressed and uncultured as he did greeting this woman. Meeting her gaze, he caught just a hint of the awkward, boy-crazy Anne from their school days.

He positioned the slave-auction broadsheet behind his back.

"Well!" Philip exclaimed. "Look at us! We're all here. Reunited once again!"

It was a good attempt to move past an awkward situation. It didn't work. Everyone smiled, but behind the smiles, everyone—including Josiah himself—was wishing he wasn't in the room.

Johnny Mott stared at the dead pheasant on his plate. Abigail took great pains to look anywhere but at Josiah. Anne smiled indulgently.

Philip addressed the long-faced servant who stood at the edge of the room, looking for some way to fish Josiah out of the water without wading in after him.

"Foster, bring another table setting for Reverend Rush," Philip said. "He'll be joining us."

"No . . . no, um, that's not necessary. I can't stay."

If ever truth was spoken, it was spoken now. It would have killed Josiah to stay and watch Johnny and Abigail act as a couple—one of two couples in the room—with Josiah playing the role of odd man out. He backed his way toward the door.

"Are you sure you won't stay?" Anne asked. "It's no trouble, really."

She seemed sincere enough. But Josiah couldn't tell if she meant it or was just being polite.

"That's very kind," he said, still moving backwards. "But I dropped by for just a moment. I didn't know—" He made a helpless gesture at the dinner table. "My business can wait."

Anne got up and walked toward him. She hooked his arm, stopping his retreat. Was she really not aware he was dying here?

She tilted her head toward him intimately and spoke softly, although Josiah knew the others could still hear. "When it's convenient for you, Philip and I want to talk to you about officiating at our wedding service. We're looking at an April date."

"Certainly. I'll be glad to talk to you . . . anytime . . . just send word. I'm free most anytime. Except Sunday mornings, of course. I tend to be busy Sunday mornings." It was a bad attempt at humor. Josiah knew he was rambling, but he couldn't help himself. He stared at her arm as though it were a snake wrapped around his arm.

"My uncle Percival plans to sail over for the wedding," she said happily.

"That's good!" Josiah replied too eagerly.

"He's my guardian."

"I look forward to meeting him."

Philip stepped forward and disengaged Anne from Josiah. The instant he was free, he resumed his retreat.

Philip said to him, "You may not realize what an honor it is for her uncle to attend. He's a member of the House of Commons."

"Is he?" Josiah said. "Yes, that is an honor! A member of the House of Commons. Here in Havenhill! That doesn't happen every day, does it?"

He was one step away from the door. One more step and he could disappear and try to forget that this night ever happened.

Anne turned to Philip. "Has Havenhill ever entertained a member of the House of Commons?"

Philip thought a moment. "No, I believe Lord Bellamont will be the first."

Josiah froze. "Lord Bellamont is your uncle?"

Anne smiled sweetly. "Yes! Have you heard of him?"

CHAPTER 31

"Last night was a little awkward, wasn't it?" Philip said. "Foster tried to warn you. We would have invited you—Anne wanted to—but I talked her out of it. I told her you probably wouldn't feel comfortable being the only unattached person in attendance. But then, no harm done. Everyone survived. Anne looked striking, though, wouldn't you agree? That's the first time you've seen her since she returned from England, isn't it?"

Josiah's face burned at the remembrance. It was going to take him more than a day to recover from his previous night's embarrassment. "Anne has developed into quite a lady," he admitted.

Philip grinned. "Yes, she has, hasn't she? Now, what is it that has you storming my house like some medieval crusader? It isn't more of this spiritual epidemic nonsense, is it?"

They stood opposite each other in Philip's sitting room. Josiah had interrupted Philip's shaving, though it was almost noon. He'd entered the room wiping his face. Bits of soap that he'd missed flecked his face.

Josiah could no longer wait to discuss the matter at hand. He slapped the slave-auction broadsheet down on the small, polished table situated between two chairs.

From the startled look on Philip's face, it was clear he didn't have to read the broadsheet to know what it was.

"Tell me this is a printing error," Josiah insisted.

"You were in Boston?"

"Yes. But I hear they're also posted up and down the Connecticut River Valley."

"What were you doing in Boston? You said you were going to Northampton."

"I went to Northampton. Then I went to Philadelphia, and—"

"Philadelphia?" Philip cried. "No wonder you were gone so long! You realize, don't you, that I had to quell a storm over your absence. Half the people were calling for your resignation. The other half thought you'd run off and we'd never see you again."

"I told you what I was doing!"

"You told me you were going to Northampton to drag some preacher back down here. You said nothing about Philadelphia and Boston and who knows where else. So, did you get him? The Northampton preacher. Is he coming?"

"No, his health isn't good and—"

"All that time and you came back empty-handed? What are we going to tell the deacons? Some of them are calling for your head."

"Reverend George Whitefield has agreed to come and preach."

"Whitefield. A different preacher?"

"He's why I went to Philadelphia. Edwards recommended him."

"And Boston?"

Sheepishly, Josiah said, "I wasn't able to connect with him in Philadelphia. That's why I went to Boston."

"He'd better be good, that's all I have to say. In fact, he'd better be better than good, considering how much time you took to track him down."

"Which brings us back to this broadsheet," Josiah said. "Is it true, or isn't it?"

For the first time, Philip really looked down at the broadsheet. He flopped into a chair beside it and dabbed at his face with the towel. "I don't know why they're putting them up so early. The auction isn't until spring."

Josiah lowered himself into a chair. "So it's true."

Philip took a while to answer. When he did, he merely said, "A concession."

"To Lord Bellamont."

Philip stared at Josiah. "Aya. It's a one-time auction. Bellamont owes a favor to a wealthy English merchant, who owes a favor to . . . well, it's complicated. But Bellamont needed a location to unload the cargo."

"Cargo. You're talking about human beings."

"Call them what you will. Slaving is a legitimate business—and a very lucrative one in the middle and Southern Colonies."

"Philip! Do you hear yourself? Do you really want to turn Havenhill into a slave port?"

"I told you, it's a one-time proposition!" Philip cried, leaning forward with his forearms on his legs. "These are powerful men we're dealing with, Josiah! We'll be doing them a favor. They'll owe us! When the time is right, we'll call in the favor. This could be big for Havenhill!"

Philip was so earnest that Josiah wondered how much more there was to the deal that Philip wasn't saying.

"Beware the river gods," Josiah murmured, remembering Jonathan Edwards's warning.

"What was that? I didn't catch what you said."

"Is Anne part of the deal? You hand over Havenhill in exchange for a wife?"

Philip's face revealed that Josiah had gone too far. A mask of pure hatred had slipped over it.

"I'm sorry," Josiah said quickly. "That was meanspirited. I shouldn't have said it."

Philip stood. A portion of the hatred dissipated, but not all of it. "What do you plan to do?"

Josiah picked up the broadsheet and also stood. "The townspeople are going to find out. I'm surprised they don't know already."

"Some of them do."

Josiah walked toward the door.

"Don't fight me on this, Josiah. You'll lose."

Had Josiah not heard Philip utter those words, he never would have guessed they had come from his friend's mouth. The voice was hard. Cold. Deadly.

Josiah's response was to turn his back on it.

"Wait!" Philip exclaimed, sounding like Philip again. He caught up with Josiah. "You owe me. Remember, I was the one who made it possible for you to come home. And how many times have I interceded for you with the deacons and church members? You ride away and don't come back for weeks, and we never hear from you."

Josiah pivoted to face his friend. "Do you want me to resign?"

"No! That's the point! I want us to work together! That's why I went to Boston to get you! Who better to lead this town than us? Me in financial matters, and you in spiritual matters."

"The two belong to different worlds and have different values. Can they ever see eye to eye?"

"Sure they can! Church members have to live in this world, don't they? Listen, I have a proposal. A deal. Just listen to it. Will you at least just listen?"

Josiah wasn't anxious to hear about any deal if it had anything to do with Lord Bellamont. He still didn't think Philip was being completely honest with him about Bellamont's plans.

Philip took Josiah's hesitation for a willingness to listen and launched right into the deal. "All right. You're not exactly basking in the good graces of the church right now. There are some who are furious with your disappearing act. A number of the deacons—a majority if I know my deacons, and I think I do—are ready to call for your resignation."

The worm in Josiah's gut squirmed, sending a flash of nausea to his head, as if to confirm what Philip had just said. "Go on."

"I can smooth things over with them. Tell them you came and talked to me before running off to all points north."

"I did come talk to you!"

"Exactly! But given the current attitude of the church, what do you think your chances are of getting them to welcome your visiting preacher? It wouldn't surprise me if they insisted you withdraw the invitation altogether."

That was unthinkable. After all Josiah had gone through to get Whitefield to come to Havenhill, he couldn't bear to think of sending word to the evangelist that he'd have to withdraw the invitation.

Philip could make that happen. One word from him, and Whitefield would never preach in Havenhill. While Philip was presenting the idea from the position that he could bring it about, the opposite side of that same coin meant he could just as easily prevent it.

The consequences were dire. If anything, since his return, Josiah was more convinced than ever that the town was in the deadly grip of Soul Sickness. He could see it in their attitudes, their speech, their actions. More than ever, they needed revival. They needed what George Whitefield could deliver.

"And in return," Josiah said, "you want me to promote the selling of slaves in Havenhill."

"No," Philip replied.

"No?"

"I know you too well, Josiah. If you agreed to promote the slave auction, I wouldn't believe you. You'd never be able to violate your conscience that way."

"Then what do you want?"

"Your silence."

Josiah said nothing.

"I'm not asking you to promote the auction," Philip explained. "All I'm asking is that you don't oppose it publicly. Leave it to me to persuade the town that this is in their best interests. It's something I can do with conviction, because I believe it is in the best interests of the town."

Josiah weighed his options: Refuse the deal, and Whitefield would not come. There would be no revival, the people would continue to suffer the effects of Soul Sickness, and in all likelihood, Josiah would be forced out of the pastorate and possibly out of town.

All Philip wanted in return was for Josiah to not speak out against the slave auction.

"Agreed," Josiah said at last.

CHAPTER 32

My reasoning is this . . .

Hunched over his journal, Josiah scratched furiously to get his thoughts down. He was afraid that if he didn't pen them fast enough, he would suddenly realize he'd acted irrationally and had just made a pact with the devil.

Agreeing to Philip's deal ensures that George Whitefield will preach in Havenhill. This is the key to victory. If we get only half the results I witnessed in Boston and Philadelphia, this town will be turned upside down.

It was foolish for Philip to suggest such a deal. He underestimates the power of the Holy Spirit to effect change by the transformation of people's minds. He didn't witness the things I witnessed in Northampton and Philadelphia and Boston. He didn't read the revival record in Jonathan Edwards's Faithful Narrative. He didn't take into account the fluidity of revival . . . the way it spreads from town to town.

I am convinced that once God's healing Spirit has been loosed among us, my voice will not be needed to speak in opposition to the slavery auction. The people themselves will rise up with a single voice and stand against it. For a revived town would never

permit such an evil to take place in their midst.
I won't have to stop it. The town will.

Two days later Philip kept his part of the deal. At an emergency deacons' meeting, he stood up for Josiah and played the role of pastoral advocate to perfection.

The meeting began with the deacons' stepping all over themselves in their eagerness to give voice to the multitude of complaints church members had with Josiah's performance as pastor of the church. While the complaints reportedly came from various quarters, it was evident they originated from a central source.

Eunice Parkhurst.

As a woman she was unable to confront him from a position of authority. So she orchestrated the deacons to do it for her. Each deacon spoke with the resolve of a crusader who was giving voice to the downtrodden and helpless.

The meeting began with a band of men passionate for justice. Each speaker fed off the emotion of the previous speaker until the room was charged with intensity. Josiah was beginning to think the only way this meeting was going to end was with bloodshed. And he knew who would supply the blood.

Philip sat in a corner, legs crossed, listening stoically as one accuser after another grew red in the face and jabbed an angry forefinger at Josiah. Philip said nothing to contradict them. He nodded with each speaker.

Finally, when the deacons began to repeat themselves, Philip stood and, with a single comment, deflated their primary piece of evidence against Josiah. "Pastor Rush's recent trip was undertaken with my full knowledge and consent. He went to Northampton with the express purpose of bringing much needed revival to our church."

Having shouldered responsibility for the trip, Philip let the deacons know that if they were going to go after Josiah, they'd have to go after him too.

"Furthermore, the length of the trip—while it proved a temporary hardship for some here in Havenhill—was an unforeseen necessity, and when you learn why the trip took the time it did, I'm sure you'll agree with me that the benefits will outweigh any immediate inconvenience. In fact, I'm also certain you'll agree with me that the extended length of the trip is a testimony to Reverend Rush's determination to go literally the extra mile for the good of our town."

Josiah watched with a mixture of bewilderment and amazement.

First of all, bewilderment. Why hadn't Philip told the deacons sooner that he'd given his consent for the trip? A lot of the anger could have been avoided, had he done so.

However, that question was quickly forgotten in Josiah's amazement at how readily the deacons acquiesced to Philip. Josiah could have spoken the exact same words, and they wouldn't have listened to him! In fact, he was certain that nothing he could have said would have appeased them. Yet with a few words, Philip had them exchanging a hangman's noose for a medal of service.

"The result of which, we are proud to announce," Philip continued, "is that due to our pastor's diligence, we have succeeded in extending an invitation to one of the greatest preachers of our age—Reverend George Whitefield."

A couple of the deacons gasped. They'd heard of Whitefield and of the crowds associated with him and were soon talking excitedly about their pastor's coup in obtaining such a sought-after preacher to come to their small town.

A short time later the deacons, eager to spread the news, departed from the meeting.

Feeling like a man who had escaped execution, Josiah, too, headed for the door. But he wasn't able to leave before Philip pigeonholed him.

"See what can happen when we work together?"

The following Sabbath, the church was abuzz. Two things created the stir. It was the first Sabbath since Anne Myles had returned to Havenhill. She arrived like royalty on the arm of a smiling Prince Philip of Clapp.

The second item of conversation among the church members was the news that George Whitefield was coming to Havenhill. Their excitement was contagious.

In preparation for revival services, Josiah preached from Hosea: "Break up your fallow ground: for it is time to seek the LORD, till he come and rain righteousness upon you."

What Josiah expected to be the most difficult Sabbath of his tenure at the church turned out to be the best day of his brief pastorate.

Everyone was excited. Many thanked him profusely for going the extra mile to secure such a noteworthy man of God as George Whitefield. The phrase "extra mile" was repeated often. The deacons were evidently quoting Philip directly in their reports.

Even Eunice Parkhurst appeared happy at the news. While she never told Josiah directly she was pleased about the scheduled revival services, he saw her in animated discussion with other women and heard the evangelist's name mentioned often.

Josiah counted Eunice Parkhurst's lack of condemnation as a victory. However, she still didn't listen to him when he preached. As she had every Sabbath since he'd arrived, whenever the preaching began, she would pull pages she'd tucked into the back of her Bible and read them. They looked like a letter. When the sermon was finished, she would slip the pages back into her Bible.

Besides being curious as to what it was she was reading, Josiah wondered if she would do the same thing when Whitefield preached. From the pulpit, her reading was a distraction. Josiah hoped she would be more courteous to their guest evangelist. For himself, he could think of worse things she could do to distract him, so he considered himself fortunate that all she did was read when he preached.

Following the service, there was the usual queue waiting to talk to the pastor. Deacon Dunmore had a long list of repairs he insisted needed to be completed before the revival services. And several others had to tell Josiah in great detail some of the things they'd heard about the revival, both good and bad, from relatives in other towns.

After sitting and listening to Reverend Rush preach for an hour, it seemed many in the congregation were now bursting to do the talking while he was forced to listen. In a way it seemed only fair, and normally Josiah didn't mind it. However, on this particular Sunday, he was distracted.

Glancing up while Deacon Dunmore explained in detail why the front steps creaked and what needed to be done about it, Josiah noticed Johnny Mott propped against a wall watching him. Johnny just watched. He didn't join the queue; he didn't wander away. His attention was focused completely on Josiah.

While person after person took their turns with the pastor, Johnny stood there looking on. His jaw worked back and forth, as though something was stuck between his teeth.

Finally, after the queue vanished, Josiah took the direct approach. He went to Johnny. He didn't say anything. He just walked up to him.

"Over here," Johnny said, pulling him aside.

When they were out of earshot of any straggling worshippers, Johnny squared his shoulders and stared down at Josiah.

The fact that Josiah had known this man since school days did nothing to lessen the effect this staredown had on him. There was no other way to put it—the man was intimidating.

"Philip told me about your deal," Johnny said.

And now he's sent his enforcer to remind me of it? Josiah wondered. Or was Johnny here on his own to gloat?

The big man grabbed Josiah's arm with his huge paw and squeezed.

His eyes bored into Josiah. "You don't fool me. I know what your plan is."

Josiah met his gaze. Now was not the time to waver.

Then the strangest thing happened.

Johnny Mott's eyes became glassy.

Tears? Tears in Johnny Mott's eyes? Josiah didn't think it possible.

"No matter what happens," Johnny whispered, "no matter what is said, no matter what is done . . . stay strong."

Before Josiah could recover from his shock, Johnny Mott released him and was gone.

CHAPTER 33

To prepare for the upcoming revival services, Josiah thought it best to consecrate the site. To do this, once a day he would walk around the building seven times, praying that God would sanctify it and use it to His glory.

After circling the church, Josiah would go inside and kneel behind the pulpit and spend an hour praying that God would sanctify the pulpit and prepare the heart of the messenger who would stand behind it.

His daily ritual caught the town's attention. Before long an audience waited on the common, watching him as he circled the church. After several days of this, he invited them to join him as he walked and prayed.

No one accepted his invitation. It was amazing how many different excuses they came up with. However, the excuses didn't stop them from watching him.

Undaunted, Josiah continued this daily practice. He carried out the ritual for two weeks while Whitefield preached in Northampton and the surrounding towns. Reports of the enthusiasm with which he was received were encouraging.

Mercy's cousin wrote daily of the events, and Mercy would then deliver the letter to Josiah for him to read. She usually did so alone. They would talk of Hadley and her cousin, the upcoming revival services, and things of a general nature around town.

To Josiah she seemed like the old Mercy. Happy. Pleasant. A good conversationalist—at least until Josiah ventured into restricted waters.

Mercy's comments became short and cryptic whenever Josiah inquired after Grace. Apparently, Grace did not approve of Mercy's visits. It was a subject of contention between them. And once, when Josiah suggested the sisters resume their Wednesday-night cooking visits, Mercy grew suddenly sullen. That conversation ended so abruptly that Josiah vowed never to make that mistake again.

But he missed their Wednesday evenings. How he wished women didn't always insist on seeing romantic intentions where none were intended. It always complicated what was merely friendship. He felt comfortable with Mercy. He liked her and enjoyed their conversations and the time they spent together. He admired her Bible knowledge and the depth of her spirituality. She was the one person in town who understood that side of him. Why spoil it with romance? It didn't make sense. Both Mercy and Grace knew how he felt about Abigail.

With about an hour's worth of sunlight left, Josiah approached the church. Normally he did his consecration prayers shortly after noon. Today at that time he had been consoling an anxious father-to-be while his wife gave birth to twins.

He'd been awakened shortly after 5 a.m. with the news that Mary Pemberton was in labor. He had dressed and then hurried to the Pembertons' house on the outskirts of town. Isaac, Mary's husband, was nearly beside himself. He squealed himself with each scream that came from the bedroom. Of the two, Mary was the stronger one.

For ten hours Josiah paced with Isaac, offering prayers and consolations.

Several times Isaac broke down and cried. "What'll I do if she dies?" he moaned. "What'll I do?"

Josiah assured him that God was watching over Mary, that she would survive the birth.

"But what'll I do if she dies?" Isaac shouted. "Who will take care of me? She can't do this to me! She can't!"

With Isaac everything was about himself. Josiah had hoped that becoming a father would make a man of him. That he would learn to take care of Mary, who would depend on him now, and the baby. Just when Josiah thought he was making some progress with Isaac, shortly before noon Isaac asked whether Josiah thought Mary could take a break birthing their baby long enough to fix him dinner.

Now, walking across the common that was striped with late-afternoon shadows, Josiah muttered a prayer for Mary. With twins and Isaac, she now had three babies to care for.

For the past several days when he'd arrived to pray at the church, an audience was waiting for him. When he didn't show up at the usual time, they must have grown tired and gone home.

Josiah wanted to join them. Weary from trying to grow a boy into manhood in one afternoon, he was looking forward to a quiet evening at home, dinner, propping his feet up, and possibly doing a little reading before bedtime.

Having reached the church, he did a quick mental calculation and decided it would probably be dark by the time he circled the building seven times.

He'd do fourteen laps tomorrow. Today he'd do the pulpit prayer and then head home.

Mounting the steps, he opened the front door. It was unlocked. Keeping the church door unlocked was one of the first things he'd insisted upon when he arrived as pastor. He remembered the first time he tried to enter the church and found the door locked. Why would anyone lock the door to a church? To him it was an admission of failure—that the sin outside was stronger than the God inside. And as long as he was pastor, the door to the church would remain unlocked.

He pulled open the door.

"Oh!"

The startled voice came from inside the church.

It took Josiah's eyes a moment to adjust. At first he couldn't make out who it was. All he heard was a rustle of a woman's petticoat.

Then he saw who it was. "Mercy!"

She was nearly to the door. Because he was still standing in the doorway blocking her escape, she turned sideways to squeeze past him.

"I was just praying," she apologized.

"Don't let me interrupt you," Josiah said.

"No, I was . . . I was all prayed out anyway." She eased into the doorway.

"Please don't go," he pleaded.

"No, really, I—"

"Please?"

She stopped. She looked up at him, her features soft in the early evening light.

After spending the day with a whiny half-man, Josiah craved intelligent conversation. He didn't realize how much he craved it until this opportunity presented itself.

"I've just come from the Pembertons," he said.

Mercy's eyes sparkled, anticipating good news. "Mary gave birth?"

"Twins."

"Praise God!" Her entire face lit up with joy in a remarkable way, confirming what Josiah had noticed about her before: Mercy was one of those unique individuals who knew pure joy from someone else's blessing.

"Boys," Josiah added.

"Mary was hoping for a girl."

"Was she? She seemed happy to have boys. Once the shock of having two babies at once wore off."

Mercy laughed. A heavenly sound. Perfectly at home in their surroundings.

"Now she has three boys to raise," Josiah quipped.

As soon as he said it, he regretted it. It was a comment unbefitting a pastor.

Mercy gave him a disapproving glance.

"Sorry," Josiah said. "I shouldn't have said that."

"No, you shouldn't have," Mercy agreed. "It's true, but you shouldn't have said it."

Both laughed.

When the laughter ended, they became acutely aware of the fact that they were standing an inch, maybe two inches, apart. Mercy blushed. Josiah took a step back, keeping the church door open.

"I was just coming to pray," he explained. "I've been coming here every day to pray for—"

"I know. Seven times around the building."

Josiah grinned. "You've heard."

"Aya."

"One more reason for the town to think their pastor's crazy."

"I think it's wise," Mercy said.

The way she said it made Josiah feel proud. He grinned self-consciously.

"The walls of pain and distrust in this town are at least as thick as Jericho's walls," she added. "It's going to take a lot of prayer, a lot of courage, and the hand of God to bring them down."

If only I had a hundred more like you in the congregation, Josiah thought. Then he realized that they were talking again, just like they used to talk on Wednesday nights over the dinner dishes while Grace knitted and dozed in the corner. It reminded him how much he missed those times.

"I pray for you daily," Mercy said softly.

It wasn't a boast, like some people would make to impress their pastor. And it wasn't a comment with as much sincerity of a "God bless you!" after a sneeze. It was a matter-of-fact, no-frills statement of such sincerity, that Josiah felt unworthy of her prayers.

He shrugged self-consciously and slipped his hands into his pockets. In the bottom of his pocket was a folded piece of paper. As his fingers brushed it, he gazed into the eyes of its author. He was certain of it now. He didn't know how she managed to deliver the notes, or when, but the moment she said she was praying for him, he felt ridiculous that he hadn't put Mercy and the notes together before now.

While making this discovery, the silence between them once again became uncomfortable.

"I . . . I should leave," Mercy said.

"Stay." There was no thought behind the request. It popped out so abruptly it surprised Josiah as much as it did Mercy.

"I'm sure you have things to do," she replied.

"I came into the sanctuary to pray. Stay and pray with me."

Mercy blushed. She stared at the ground and shuffled her feet. "I really should get home. Grace will wonder what's happened to me."

"Just for a while. We've talked a lot, but we really haven't prayed together. It would mean a lot to me if you stayed and prayed with me for the revival services."

Slowly, Mercy lifted her head until their eyes met.

Josiah found himself staring into the most sincere blue eyes he'd ever seen. What was the phrase Jesus used of Nathaniel? Had He met Mercy, He would have said it of her too. "Behold, a woman with no guile."

"Maybe for a little while," she at last agreed.

Holding the door open, Josiah stepped back to allow her to enter. At that moment he looked up and met the gaze of Goodwife Hibbard and Eunice Parkhurst walking arm in arm in front of the church. They wore identical shocked and disapproving expressions.

Josiah gave them a cordial nod and closed the door.

Mercy had her back to them and didn't see them. For that, Josiah was grateful. He considered telling her, but what then? Mercy would be embarrassed and would insist on leaving immediately. Her hasty departure would put a stamp of authentication of what the two women were undoubtedly thinking.

So he said nothing. He could only hope that, for once in their lives, the women would do the sensible thing and keep their mouths shut.

Unaware that anything was going on, Mercy had made her way into the boxed-in area of the pew in which she and Grace sat every Sabbath. Arranging her dress, she got down on her knees facing the front of the church.

Josiah stepped into the box and prepared to get down on his knees beside her.

"What are you doing?" she cried, looking shocked that he had stepped into her pew.

"I . . . I was going to join you. To pray."

"Where do you normally pray?" Her tone was defensive.

"At the pulpit. I usually kneel behind the pulpit and pray there."

"Then I suggest that's where you pray today."

It was more than a suggestion, though, Josiah realized. "All right." He stepped out of the pew. "I didn't mean to imply anything. I just thought . . ."

Mercy waited until he was all the way out of the pew, then bowed her head and began praying.

"I'll just pray up here, then." Josiah motioned in the direction of the pulpit.

But Mercy wasn't listening to him.

He made his way quietly to the front of the church and knelt to one side of the pulpit. He could see the top of Mercy's head bobbing up and down gently as she prayed.

He must have watched her for at least ten minutes. Never once did she look up, which was good, because if she did, he would have to hurriedly bow his head to keep her from catching him looking at her.

Finally, Josiah worked himself into a prayerful mood and bowed his head.

After several minutes a rustling interrupted him. He looked up.

Mercy was on her feet, preparing to leave. "I'm sorry," she apologized. "I didn't want to disturb you, but I need to get home."

Josiah got up. "Wait—I'll join you."

"That's not necessary."

But he was already halfway to her. "I'll walk you home. That is, if you don't mind."

Mercy smiled sweetly but guardedly. She apparently knew not to read too much into his offer. The expression in her eyes was that of someone who had learned from experience to be cautious.

"Thank you for praying with me." Josiah let her lead the way to the door. "And not just now. I want to thank you for praying for me daily."

"It's a church member's responsibility to pray for her pastor," Mercy explained.

"And your notes . . . I want to thank you for them too. They've been a source of strength to me."

She gave him a quizzical glance. "To what are you referring?"

It was the same expression Abigail had worn when he had mentioned the notes. And the same thought passed through Josiah's mind: Why would she deny sending the notes? Was there a reason for anonymity he didn't see?

Josiah produced the note from his pocket.

Mercy looked at it without any hint that she recognized it. "May I?"

He handed it to her.

After unfolding it and reading it, she said, "You think I wrote this?"

"Didn't you?"

"That's not my handwriting."

He studied her. Those sincere blue eyes, the ones that knew no guile, gazed back at him without blinking.

A sound from another room interrupted them. Loud. Like wood splitting.

Startled, Mercy stifled a cry. Josiah's head snapped in the direction of the sound.

"What was that?" she asked.

He shook his head. He couldn't identify it. At the moment all was quiet. Staring in the direction of the sound, they listened for several moments. Still nothing.

"Wait for me outside," Josiah said. "I'll take a look."

Mercy instinctively reached out and caught his arm.

Josiah smiled reassuringly. "Something probably just fell over. Wait for me? Please? It's getting dark. I want to walk you home."

He left her with her hand on the door latch. Crossing the sanctuary, his attention focusing beyond the back wall, he opened a door that led to the back of the church.

Curiosity drove him. And he wouldn't have been surprised had he searched all the rooms in the back of the church and found nothing. Buildings groaned and creaked. Doors shuddered. Things propped in corners for weeks and months suddenly and for no reason slipped and crashed to the floor. Most of the time these things went unnoticed when the building was in use. Or they occurred in the middle of the night when no one was around to hear them. He and Mercy just happened to be in the building this time. Other times, when he'd been in the building alone, he'd heard popping and groaning. But since the sound they'd heard was louder than those he normally heard, hence the investigation. Still, it was probably nothing.

He made his way down a hallway with an exterior wall to his right with a window halfway down the passageway. He checked the beams overhead and the floorboards as he walked and saw nothing unusual. Passing the window, he saw a dog outside rolling in the grass.

At the end of the hallway was a door that led outside. To the left another passage led to several small rooms. The back door was ajar. Josiah pulled it open and looked outside. He saw no one. Closing the door, he turned back into the church.

He caught movement out of the corner of his eye, then everything went black . . .

CHAPTER 34

Josiah's coughing roused him.

Throat raw, lungs burning, stomach convulsing, Josiah propped himself up on one arm. His free hand reached for the pain at the base of his neck and left shoulder. That's where the blow had landed, knocking him to the floor.

As his senses rallied, he realized he had a greater concern. His oven-testing arm felt a familiar heat. Only this time it was all around him.

As he hacked up smoke, Josiah's eyes fluttered and registered that he was sitting in the middle of a fire. The walls, the ceiling, the floor—all were in flames.

He managed to roll onto his knees. He looked for something to lean against or push against to get to his feet, for his legs were too shaky to stand without help.

The walls around him rippled with orange flame. He shielded his face against the heat.

His desperate coughing slammed shut his eyes, doubled him over into an immobile lump, and sapped his limited strength. Only seconds separated the spasms. If he couldn't get to his feet and escape the narrow walls of flame between convulsions, his goose was cooked.

Just then something chilly touched the back of his neck. He felt a breeze so cool he could have sworn it was liquid.

It came from the door, a few feet away, which was standing open about six inches. The opening was coated with fire, but beyond that were greens and blues.

Before he could move toward it, a spasm of coughing and retching folded him over at the waist. It felt as though he were being turned inside out.

Fighting to focus his mind beyond the cough, he maneuvered his feet under him and raised up to a crouching position. That was as straight as he was going to get. His eyes fixed on the door, Josiah commanded his feet to take him to it. All he managed was a stumble.

It was enough.

He leaned forward until his feet had no choice but to move just to keep him from diving face-first onto the crackling hardwood floor.

Josiah hit the door, diving into the outside air as though it were a stream, tumbling down the back steps and onto the grass.

Rolling onto his side, he sucked in grass-scented air, hacked it up, then sucked in some more. His lungs had been ravaged, but his arms and legs began to feel stronger, and his head—splitting with pain—began to clear.

Cries of alarm sounded from the village green.

For several minutes, Josiah lay with his head against the grass, able to do little other than gulp air and take in a sideways view of the flames as they reached for more and more of the church.

At least Mercy was safe. He remembered telling her to wait for him outside.

She would be worried about him. The thought gave him pleasure and pain. He liked the thought that she would worry about him, but he disliked the thought that he was causing her concern.

The longer he lay there, the more the thought of Mercy worrying about his safety caused him greater and greater discomfort. Enough so that he struggled to his feet and began making his way to the front of the church.

As he rounded the corner of the building, the first of the townspeople arrived. Those in front were empty-handed, simply drawn to the fire. But close behind them, men carried water buckets.

A couple of men approached him. "Reverend! Are you all right?"

"Get that fire out, boys!" Josiah managed to say.

By now a dozen men had arrived and were attacking the flames. Josiah turned and examined the building. The fire was restricted to the back of the church. They'd caught it soon enough. The back rooms would need to be rebuilt, but from the looks of it, the fire hadn't reached the sanctuary.

He stumbled to the front. People were running toward the church from every corner of town. Some of the men had stopped to gape. Josiah urged them toward the back of the building.

Eunice and Abigail hurried across the green. While Abigail continued toward him, Eunice stopped, hands on hips, to survey the building.

"Josiah! Are you all right?" Abigail cried.

Her hand was on his back. She leaned down to look at him. Until then Josiah hadn't realized he was still hunched over.

The feel of Abigail's hand on his back sent a wave of pleasure through him. He would have enjoyed it, had it not set him to coughing.

"I'm fine," he managed to say, looking up into her eyes.

Her face was close to his. Closer than it had been since . . .

Mercy!

Josiah straightened up and surveyed the front of the church. "Mercy," he said aloud.

Abigail appeared puzzled, as if she didn't know what he was talking about.

But Eunice heard him and came over. "When did you see her last?"

"Inside. I told her to wait for me out here."

Eunice looked around and shook her head.

Josiah scanned the area too. No Mercy. He turned back to the church.

"Josiah, where are you going?" Abigail asked.

There wasn't time to answer. His legs called upon a reserve of strength he didn't know he had.

Vaulting up the front steps, he flung open the door and lunged inside. Smoke curled in the rafters like a legion of malevolent spirits. He ducked down.

"Mercy!"

His shout was more of a croak.

"Mercy!"

He glanced inside each box as he ran past the pews, peering for a splash of pale yellow. Mercy had been wearing a pale yellow dress.

Josiah worked the length of the sanctuary and still saw no Mercy. He began to cough again, violent spasms that threatened to buckle his knees. At last he reached the door to the hallway.

Smoke curled under the door. Its dark, gray fingers reached for him, pulled him to the ground. Grabbing his throat and cutting off his air, they tried to suffocate him.

He yanked open the door.

Like an ogre, the smoke bounded out of the hallway, knocking him backward. Somehow he stayed on his feet.

Then, through the smoke, on the hardwood floor, he saw pale yellow.

Mercy.

At the far end of the hallway, he could hear the shouts of the men battling the fire, the clank of buckets, the sizzle of water hitting flame. White billows of smoke announced they were winning the battle.

Josiah tried to shout for help, but between the shouts of the men fighting the fire and the stranglehold the smoke had on his throat, no one heard him.

Dropping to his knees, he pulled Mercy into a sitting position.

She moaned.

He never knew where the strength came from, but he scooped her up, carried her the length of the sanctuary, and out the front door.

On the top step, Josiah teetered. He faintly heard Eunice Parkhurst's voice, ordering some men to help him.

By the time they reached him, not only did they have to carry Mercy down the steps, but Josiah too.

Alerted to the fire by the smoke, Philip Clapp arrived, driving his own carriage. Johnny Mott arrived at the same time on horseback.

Johnny ran to the back of the church to help fight the fire, but by now it was under control. Philip ran to Josiah and Mercy, who were stretched out beside each other on the common.

Josiah had rallied enough that he was sitting up. Abigail and Eunice attended to Mercy, who was coughing.

Philip surveyed the situation and took charge. He pointed to two men who were just standing around. "Get Dr. Wolcott. Have him meet us at the sisters' house." To another man, he said, "Help me get her into my carriage."

"No," Josiah insisted. "I'll do it."

"You're in no condition," Philip retorted. "This is no time to—"

But Josiah wasn't taking orders from Philip. He was on his feet and in position to lift Mercy into the carriage. Together he and Philip lifted Mercy into the open carriage. Abigail climbed into the back with her. Eunice began to get into the other side.

Josiah stepped in front of her. "I'll take her."

Eunice glared at him but stepped back.

Philip enlisted a man to drive the carriage. "I'll be there shortly," he told Josiah, "after I'm certain everything is under control here."

Josiah nodded.

It wasn't a long ride to the sisters' house, but it was an odd one. Josiah hadn't considered how odd it would be until they were underway, and he looked up and caught Abigail's eye.

Mercy sat back, her eyes closed. Her coughing spasms were easing.

With the danger passed, Josiah became uncomfortably aware that he was sharing a scrunched ride with the woman he loved while another woman—who had feelings for him—lay between them.

No words were spoken. But at one point, Mercy opened her eyes and caught Josiah and Abigail staring at each other. Then she doubled over with another coughing fit.

Grace was standing outside the house with a basket of eggs hooked on her arm when she saw the carriage coming. A flash of horror crossed her face when she saw Mercy in the back of the carriage. After that, she was all business.

Grace Smythe was one of those women who, in time of emergency, could detach herself emotionally and do whatever it took to meet the situation head-on. As instantly as the horror showed on her face, it was gone. She deftly set down the basket of eggs without breaking a single one of them.

"The fire?" she asked.

Evidently, she'd seen the pillar of smoke rising above the town common.

"She's not burned," Abigail explained. "She's just swallowed a lot of smoke."

Grace nodded. "Let's get her inside."

Josiah climbed out of the carriage and prepared to lift Mercy out of the back of the carriage.

Grace slid between him and the carriage, blocking him out. She ordered the driver to grab Mercy's shoulders.

Josiah stood by helplessly as the driver and the two women carried Mercy into the house. He followed.

The moment they cleared the threshold, Grace kicked the door, shutting Josiah out.

Twenty minutes later Dr. Wolcott appeared. Josiah gave him a brief report, considered following the doctor inside and challenging Grace to kick him out, then decided against it.

Instead, he remained outside and prayed.

Thirty minutes passed, during which time Grace came out once to go to the well and carry back a bucket of water. Josiah made a half-hearted attempt to offer to carry the water for her. Grace acted as though he wasn't there.

Finally, Philip and Johnny arrived. Philip had borrowed a horse from someone.

"How is she?" Philip asked, dismounting.

"I haven't heard," Josiah said lamely.

Philip lifted an eyebrow, then knocked at the door. Grace let Philip and Johnny in.

For another twenty minutes, Josiah paced outside the house alone.

The door opened. Philip, Johnny, Abigail, the stranger who drove the carriage, and Dr. Wolcott came out.

Philip instructed the stranger to drive Abigail home. She offered Josiah a weak smile and climbed into the back of the carriage.

"Thanks, Doc," Philip told Wolcott.

"She'll be all right?" Josiah asked.

Wolcott didn't answer. He scowled and walked past Josiah.

That left Josiah, Johnny, and Philip outside the sisters' house.

"Is someone going to tell me how Mercy is doing?" Josiah barked. His patience had run out. He'd been shut out long enough.

"She'll recover," Philip said.

Good news, except for the way Philip said it. He delivered the news solemnly. Josiah even thought he heard a nervous tremor in Philip's voice.

"She's suffered damage to her vocal chords," Philip added.

Josiah nodded. The way his throat felt, he wouldn't be surprised if it had suffered some damage of its own.

Philip walked a short distance from the house. Johnny followed him, avoiding Josiah's eyes. Something was wrong. They were keeping something from him.

"Tell me what happened," Philip demanded.

As clearly as he could, Josiah described what had happened—he and Mercy praying, the noise, telling Mercy to wait for him outside, going to investigate, the lights going out, escaping from the fire, realizing Mercy was still inside, carrying her out . . .

Throughout the narration, Philip listened. Johnny did, too, but with his back half-turned to Josiah.

"You act as though you don't believe me," Josiah said.

"You tell it different from what we heard," Philip claimed.

"Different? How different?"

Philip took a deep breath. "Eyewitnesses saw smoke and flames. When they came to investigate, they saw you running from the back of the church."

"Running! More like stumbling. I barely made it out alive!" Josiah exclaimed.

"They found the ashes of paper and tinder in the corner of a room where the fire was started."

So someone else was in the church! Until now Josiah couldn't have been sure. He knew something hit him on the back of the neck, but until this moment, he didn't know if it was intentional, or a beam falling down on him.

"Philip, I'm telling you, I didn't set that fire. Why would I do it? Why would I set fire to the church building?"

"Mercy was strangled," Philip said.

Josiah couldn't believe what he was hearing. He looked desperately at the two men he'd known longer than any others. Neither would meet his eyes.

"Did she tell you that I—"

"She said she waited for you, but when she smelled smoke, she went to investigate. Someone grabbed her from behind and strangled her until she passed out."

"Did she say it was me?" Josiah didn't know if he wanted to hear the answer to this question, but he had to ask it.

"She didn't get a good look at him, only that he was about your height and size."

Josiah began to pace. He felt panic's itchy fingers clawing at him and tried to shrug them off, but they were persistent. His breathing quickened, and he began to cough. The first cough set off the spasms again, bringing him to his knees.

Johnny retrieved a cup of water for him from the well. The cold liquid stung as it went down.

Sitting on the ground, Josiah stared dejectedly at Mercy's front door. He wanted to talk to her himself. To hear from her what happened. To console her. To apologize, though he didn't know for what—maybe for convincing her to stay? He wanted to hold her hand, look in her eyes, and chase any doubts she had from her mind that he didn't do this to her. But he knew he'd never get past Grace.

"So what happens now?" Josiah asked.

Philip gazed into the distance. "Life goes on," he said, not very convincingly. "We repair the church and go on."

From the ground Josiah squinted up at his friend.

"Do you need help getting home?" Philip questioned.

"No, I can manage on my own."

On his way home, Josiah took a shortcut through a patch of woods. Normally it was easier to take the road, the longer route, because there was no direct path through the woods. But for some reason, Josiah decided on the shorter route. Maybe because he could support himself against the trees every few steps.

He heard their voices before he saw them.

Philip and Johnny sat astride their horses, facing each other. Josiah couldn't make out what they were saying, but the tone of their voices and their gestures were that of a heated argument.

Josiah zig-zagged through the trees to get closer, but before he could make out what they were saying, the two men rode off in opposite directions.

CHAPTER 35

Tomorrow I preach my final sermon before revival services are scheduled to begin. Given the circumstances of this last week, I anticipate my message will receive a lukewarm reception at best. The encouraging spirit that had been building among the people was effectively quenched, ironically, by the fire at the church and the attack on Mercy. Despite my fervent protestations, a number of townspeople suspect me of both.

Nevertheless, I will preach from Second Chronicles 7:14:

> *If my people, which are called by my name, shall humble themselves, and pray, and seek my face, and turn from their wicked ways; then will I hear from heaven, and will forgive their sin, and will heal their land.*

And I will trust God to bless the message in spite of the messenger. I can only pray that God's Spirit will quench the flaming darts of the Evil One and that George Whitefield will be able to accomplish what I have been unable to do: to introduce this sin-sick town to the Cure, that He might heal them and revive their hearts.

All is not dark, however. Mercy—bless her heart—wrote me a long letter, which was reluctantly delivered by Grace, the grumpiest letter carrier I have ever seen. Mercy wanted to make it plain that she never suspected me of assaulting her or of setting the fire in the church. While she will be unable to attend this Sunday's services, she fully expects to be well enough to attend Mr. Whitefield's preaching. For that, I thank God.

Another bright note is Deacon Dunmore. He has attacked the damage to the rear portion of the church with the passion of a zealot. He has taken it upon himself to erase every evidence of a fire before revival services begin. I have never seen a man move with such conviction and sense of purpose.

And then there is the curious Johnny Mott. On several occasions now, he has gone out of his way to squeeze my arm, or shake my hand, or pat my back. He does this without verbal exchange, yet the message is clear: stay strong. May God bless him for his encouragement.

When we were young men, Johnny was always closer to Philip. It was as though the ties of our friendship passed through Philip—that if it weren't for Philip, Johnny and I wouldn't be friends at all. I believe that's changing. His recent actions are the foundation upon which lasting friendships are made.

Philip, on the other hand, is continuing down a dangerous path. As expected, word of the slave auction has begun filtering back to the town and can no longer be dismissed as rumor. He has stalled any discussion by feigning surprise and assuring the town that he has sent a letter to Lord Bellamont, demanding an explanation. With a three-month passage each direction, he can effectively delay the issue through the winter and right up to the time of the auction.

For my part, I have kept silent, as I have promised, even though I know Philip's tactic is a ruse. For this I wrestle with my conscience late at night. I had hoped the matter would not become public discussion until after the revival, when town opinion would be so evidently strong against a slave auction that it would be foolhardy to consider proceeding with the event. God willing, everything will soon be put right, and the town will no longer be deceived by the gods of this age, or as Edwards described them, "the river gods."

Until then, I am an anxious mother praying over her sick child until the fever breaks and good health returns.

The dawn of the Sabbath was but a promise in the sky. A faint blue line rimmed the eastern horizon as Josiah shrugged on his coat and stepped out the front door, Bible and sermon in hand.

"Reverend!?"

The speaker didn't seem to know if he was asking or calling. Nevertheless, his sudden appearance startled Josiah.

"You the reverend?"

Josiah didn't recognize the young man. He had a pile of unruly, curly blond hair that looked like a wig that had been slapped on top of his head. Apparently, however, it was real and attached, for when he moved, it didn't fall off.

After learning Josiah was indeed the reverend, the young man urged, "You'd better come. The wharf. It's bad. Really bad."

Josiah recalled a similar incident in which he'd been called to the docks. The result of that had been a fire and a run-in with Johnny Mott in one of his warehouses.

"I don't have time for wild-goose chases this morning," Josiah said firmly.

"No, this is somethin' bad, somethin' really bad. You better come."

Fear haunted the young man's eyes, but that emotion could have been planted there by the one sending him with a threat of what would happen if he failed to bring the intended target.

"Who do you work for?" Josiah snapped. "Who sent you?"

The boy's face screwed up with incredible anguish. His legs failed him, and he folded over in the dust. "O God, O God, O God," he moaned.

Josiah approached, concerned but still wary.

As it turned out, he didn't need to be. The young man was in no condition to harm anyone. From all appearances, he'd collapsed under the weight of his own grief.

Josiah could get nothing more from him. Nor could he prompt the boy's legs to unfold and support him.

Josiah had no choice but to go to the wharf and see for himself what could reduce a young man to such a state.

Bible tucked under his arm, Josiah half-walked, half-ran past Deacon Cranch's oak tree to High Street. With each step, the day grew lighter while a dark foreboding eclipsed his heart.

There was evil here. Josiah could feel it. It was as though someone were twisting a huge screw in his gut. The pain knocked him off balance so much that, had he passed anyone, they would have thought him drunk.

However, he didn't pass anyone. The morning air was still, and he was alone. No birds chirped. Nothing rustled in the dirt. The world's breath seemed to be caught in its throat, as if the very day itself was afraid to breathe for fear of what was to happen next.

Josiah approached the crossroads of High Street and Summit. The river and docks were to his left, shielded for the moment by trees and brush.

He looked for smoke.

The sky was crystal clear. So clear that Josiah knew, when he reached Summit, he'd get his first good view of the wharf and the harbor. Maybe he'd know more then.

Drawing in a ragged breath, Josiah pressed forward, remembering to pray. "Dear Lord, nothing surprises You, and there is nothing You cannot handle. Be this a prank or be it real, give us all strength for the coming day."

Stay strong. Those two words came to him the instant he reached the crossroads of High Street and Summit, the instant he turned toward the wharf. It was that instant he realized this was no prank. It was a black day, despite the dawn that backlit the harbor.

An animal wail leaped from Josiah's throat.

His Bible sprawled onto the road.

He sank to his knees.

And wept at what he saw.

There, in the harbor, dangling on the yardarm of a ship, was the body of Johnny Mott.

CHAPTER 36

Because of his size and the breadth of his shoulders, Johnny Mott had always been easy to spot in a crowd or from a distance. So when Josiah saw the body dangling at the end of a rope, there was never any question in his mind that it was Johnny.

A note stuffed in the dead man's pocket confirmed that his death was a suicide, and it pointed a finger at the person responsible for Johnny's fatal decision—his friend, Josiah Rush.

The note was a dead man's lamentation that the woman he had planned to marry would forever be loved by the minister of the church, and that she would always love him. It said he could no longer endure their exchange of longing glances every Sabbath.

Johnny Mott's death cast a long shadow over the town.

Shaken by his friend's suicide and beyond-the-grave accusation, Josiah preached that Sabbath as scheduled, though afterward he couldn't remember a word of it. What he remembered were the faces of the congregation staring up at him from the pews, and their hushed and somber voices before and after the service.

The suicide had stunned them. Like him, their minds were in a fog. But in time the fog would clear, and opinions would crystallize and be given voice. And Josiah would be called to respond to the charges that had been leveled at him.

How could he refute the testimony of a man who had been sealed with his death? How could he refute the charges when he knew them to be true?

Not the part about the exchange of longing gazes on the Sabbath. That wasn't true. At least he didn't think it was. But how could he be sure?

Did he still have feelings for Abigail Parkhurst?

He knew he did.

Had he gazed at her, at times even from the pulpit?

He knew he had.

Had he disguised his feelings so poorly?

And what of Abigail? How would she respond to these charges? How Josiah wished he could talk to her.

Abigail didn't attend the church services that morning. Her mother had stayed home with her. Following the services, a half-dozen women went to minister to her.

From the front of the church, Josiah gazed across the common at the Parkhurst house.

"That wouldn't be wise," Philip announced.

Josiah turned to see his friend. Philip was ashen-faced and somber, not himself at all. During the sermon he had sat in the deacons' pew, his back straight, his eyes fixed straight forward on nothing. At times he didn't appear to be breathing. When the sermon concluded, he'd failed to register the fact and had jumped when one of the deacons spoke to him.

Not unexpectedly, Philip had arrived at the church late. He had moved as though he were walking underwater. He would have stumbled into the wrong pew, had Anne not guided him before taking her own seat.

Now, in front of the church, he seemed to have regained a portion of his senses.

"Are you all right?" Josiah asked.

Philip stared at him as though that was the dumbest question he'd ever heard.

"Just asking," Josiah apologized.

"I'll handle the funeral arrangements," Philip said flatly, then walked off.

Johnny Mott was buried two days later, the day before revival services were scheduled to begin. The procession to the grave was the largest anyone could remember.

All the stores sold out of funeral rings and gloves.

Josiah prayed over the grave. As minister it was his duty, though several deacons openly questioned whether it was appropriate, considering the circumstances.

Philip settled the matter when he said, "It's his job. That's what we pay him for."

But that didn't stop the glares and whispers that circled the open grave and casket.

Philip stood at the head of the grave. He was the closest to family Johnny had. Abigail Parkhurst, the dead man's intended, stood next to Philip, with her mother next to her.

A long line—church members, business owners, dock workers, sailors—filed past the casket to pay their last respects. All business on the wharf had shut down for the funeral.

Finally, the only mourners remaining were Philip, Anne, and Josiah. For a long time, they stood in silence.

When Philip turned to go, he faltered and would have fallen, had Anne not caught him.

Josiah walked home alone. A note in now-familiar feminine handwriting was waiting for him, as usual, stuffed between the cracks of the clapboard siding. It consisted of two words, but those two words nearly knocked Josiah off his feet.

Stay strong.

Minutes later George Whitefield arrived.

Josiah was convinced that, had an angel of God appeared at that same moment, he would not have been able to distinguish between the angel and the evangelist.

After helping Whitefield carry his meager belongings into the house, Josiah felt compelled to inform him of the recent events in the town. The evangelist needed to know the size of the mountain he was being asked to climb.

Josiah put it to him bluntly. "Considering what has happened, no one would think less of you if, given the situation, you thought it best to cancel the services."

Seated at Josiah's table, Whitefield listened intently, at times wincing during Josiah's detailed description.

As Josiah spoke, the emotion of the last seven months, and particularly the last three days, at times nearly overwhelmed him. Twice his emotions affected his ability to speak; he had to pause to regain control.

When he was finished, Josiah fell silent. He'd presented the case as accurately as he could, even the evidence that condemned him—the part about his feelings for Abigail—and now waited for the verdict.

In the silence of the room, a few dying embers popped and crackled in the fireplace.

After an agonizing delay, Whitefield cleared his throat. "During my journey here, my thoughts kept returning to your journal, in which you recorded your spiritual evaluation of the town and concluded they were suffering from a condition you called Soul Sickness. Do you stand by that evaluation?"

Josiah sighed under the weight of the answer. "The spiritual condition of the town is worse than I've ever seen it. And I fear the town's esteem for their pastor is lower than it has ever been . . . worse even than when the fire seven years ago resulted in my exile to Boston."

Whitefield nodded. "Do you see any hope for your pastorate here?"

The question took Josiah farther down the road in his thoughts than he'd traveled to this point. Given Johnny's death and suicide note, did he have a future here?

"Since you've been using medical terminology," Whitefield said, "in medical terms, would you say your work here is critical? Or possibly beyond critical? Would you say your effectiveness as a pastor here is dead?"

Josiah winced. It was his idea to use medical terms, and it seemed a good idea when evaluating the town. But applied to himself and his current situation, it seemed harsh. Accurate, but harsh.

"Do you see any hope?" Whitefield pressed.

Josiah hung his head. "No, I don't see any hope."

"Then it's dead?"

Josiah swallowed hard. "Aya. I'd say it's dead."

Whitefield slapped the table so hard it made Josiah jump. "Good! Because raising the dead is what God does best! Come, we must pray."

After two hours on their knees, Whitefield sent Josiah to round up the deacons.

"Hogtie them and drag them here if you have to," Whitefield said. "Every Sabbath they sit in the deacons' pew and present themselves proudly as servants of the Lord. Tonight we're going to hold them to it. Tell them their Lord needs them."

Josiah nearly had to resort to hogtying a couple of them to get them to come, but ultimately he was able to assemble all of them, save one: Philip Clapp.

Philip's long-faced servant, acting under his master's orders, refused to let Josiah into the house.

"Master Clapp has retired for the evening. He is not to be disturbed under any circumstances."

Josiah could say nothing to sway Long-face from fulfilling his master's wishes. He'd let Josiah get by him once before, and Josiah could see by the servant's eyes that he wasn't going to let it happen again.

So Josiah tried a different approach.

He stood in front of Philip's house and shouted to him, telling him of Whitefield's request that the deacons join him in prayer, calling upon his sense of duty to God and church. He shouted until Long-face and two rather husky reinforcements ran him off.

When Josiah returned home, he found the deacons on their knees with the evangelist pacing, weaving in and out and around them, alternately praying and urging them to pray much as a coachman urges on a team of horses.

The deacons went home shortly after 2 a.m.

George Whitefield and Josiah Rush prayed the sun up.

CHAPTER 37

Bleary eyed from lack of sleep, Josiah sucked in air to clear his head. His lungs objected, not having fully recovered from the unhealthy dose of church smoke he'd ingested.

Whitefield glanced at him with concern.

They had stepped smartly from the house and were almost to Deacon Cranch's tree, where the road met up with High Street.

Josiah gave an "I'm fine" wave of his hand as he coughed and cleared his throat.

All along High Street, the sight of a steady stream of people bolstered Josiah's hopes. He glanced at the evangelist, wondering how much he was affected by the great numbers of people who flocked to hear him preach. Did the numbers rattle his nerves? Did he battle with pride every time he approached a pulpit?

Josiah saw evidence of neither on the face of the evangelist. He appeared serenely stoic. Distant. Preoccupied. Set apart from the tedium of this world, as though God had pulled him aside and was whispering in his ear what he should preach.

By the time they reached Summit Street, the crowd began to slow and thicken. By the time they reached Church Street at the common, the crowd was so dense, Josiah and Whitefield had to plow their way toward the church building with nonstop utterances of "Pardon me."

Josiah had never seen so many people in Havenhill. The common was filled, with the overflow spilling into every adjoining street.

"I can't even begin to guess how many people are here," Josiah told Whitefield.

The evangelist took a quick survey. "About two thousand."

Josiah didn't question the assessment. Whitefield had a lot more experience in these things. Besides, it was becoming readily apparent that Josiah had a more serious mathematical problem to solve—getting two more bodies up the steps of the church on which every square inch was occupied.

The front steps were packed so tightly there was no wiggle room, let alone enough space for grown men to pass.

Whitefield, too, assessed the situation. He cocked his head toward Josiah.

"Let's try the back," Josiah suggested.

Upon rounding the back corner of the church, Josiah had to give Deacon Dunmore his due. The man had worked a miracle on the building. Every evidence of a fire had indeed been erased. However, from the looks of things, a miracle of a different sort would be needed to get the evangelist through the back door and into the church. The back steps were as packed as the front steps, fanning out beyond the bottom step twenty, maybe thirty people deep.

Entering the edge of the fray, Josiah called for attention.

Whitefield tugged at his sleeve to stop him.

Josiah thought Whitefield was just being polite, not wanting to appear like royalty, expecting the people to part before him so he could pass. Josiah ignored him. As the host pastor, it was time to exert a little authority.

He announced himself and the guest of honor and explained his mission to get the speaker into the building.

The result proved counterproductive to the goal.

The two men were immediately set upon by a wave of people anxious to see the evangelist up close. Within seconds, Josiah and

Whitefield became as two bottles on the ocean, tossed this way and that at the whim of the current.

The only way to keep from being separated from Whitefield was to link arms. Desperate now, Josiah lowered his head, dug his toes into the turf, and began to plow his way forward, pulling the evangelist behind him.

"The window!" Whitefield shouted.

Josiah glanced up. The open portal appeared as an eddy beside a swiftly moving river. He swam toward it.

Countering the verbal abuse, jabs, and angry stares of those who had gathered by the window, hoping to hear the words of the evangelist, Josiah shouted that he was the pastor of the church and that he must get in. Some willingly stepped aside. Others, thinking he was lying just to get inside—which didn't make sense, did it? that someone would tell a lie to hear a religious sermon?—shoved back. Undaunted, Josiah pressed forward until they reached the window.

"Hold this," Whitefield said, handing Josiah his Bible. The evangelist lifted a leg expertly onto the sill, looked back at Josiah, and winked. "Not my first time," he quipped.

The next thing Josiah knew, the evangelist's hand was sticking out the window, asking for the return of his Bible. Josiah attempted to follow Whitefield. Hands pulled him back.

"I'm the pastor of the church," Josiah protested. "Really. This is my church."

No one was listening to him.

Just then Whitefield stuck his head out the window. "Good people, in the name of the Almighty God, let this man in. He speaks the truth. He is the pastor."

The hands released him, and Josiah climbed through the window, pulled by Whitefield from the inside.

Now the task was making it to the platform. There were people everywhere. In the pews. Lining the walls, two and three deep. Standing and sitting in the aisles.

Once again Josiah led the way, stepping over people, at times grabbing arms and shirtsleeves to keep from losing his balance, while repeatedly begging people's pardon.

They hadn't gone far when Josiah felt a hand tugging his arm. He turned.

Whitefield leaned close and whispered, "I smell the distinct odor of smoke in this sanctuary. Reverend Rush, have you been preaching fire and brimstone?"

The platform upon which the pulpit stood became their Promised Land. Josiah knew that if he could just get the evangelist to the Promised Land, they could begin enjoying the milk and honey of revival preaching.

Finally, after what seemed like years of wandering and wailing and tears—Josiah felt horrible, but stepping on the little girl's hand was an accident—they crossed the Jordan steps and ascended to the platform, only to find a familiar overcrowding problem.

In their eagerness to hear the great evangelist, the people had left him no place to stand. And even if somehow they managed to get Whitefield behind the pulpit, there wasn't enough room for him to raise his arms.

Relocation was the only possible solution. Whitefield concurred.

To the grumbles of those who arrived early enough to get seats in the pews, Josiah announced that Mr. Whitefield would be preaching from the church-house steps. He directed everyone to relocate to the common.

It took awhile to reverse the flow, but eventually the interior spilled out onto the lawn, and Mr. Whitefield stood on the top of the steps to preach.

Leaning against a tree, Josiah scanned the crowd. So many of the faces in attendance he'd never seen before. He looked for church members; he wanted to watch their reactions. Finally he located Mercy and Grace, sitting next to each other on the grass.

It was the first time he'd seen Mercy since the church fire. She looked wonderful. Her dress was fanned around her legs; her chin was lifted slightly as she clung to the evangelist's every word. It was clear Whitefield's sermon found in her an eager, receptive ear.

He located Philip and Anne about a third of the way back. Anne was listening. Philip seemed distracted.

Josiah also saw several of the deacons, Judith Usher, and her son, Edward.

Judith was holding what appeared to be a child's doll. She clutched it tightly to her bosom and occasionally buried her nose against it, as though she was sniffing its hair.

The two people he failed to locate were Abigail and Eunice. He hoped he was just overlooking them.

Whitefield was in rare form. Or did it just seem that way because Josiah was so much closer to the preacher than he was in Philadelphia and Boston?

There was no sign of fatigue in the evangelist after staying up all night to pray. His manner was vigorous. And, of course, his voice was as melodious as a sonnet.

A preacher himself, Josiah could appreciate Whitefield's delivery. Every gesture, every movement had purpose.

He had chosen for his text the burning bush passage from Exodus, where God spoke to Moses from a bush that was engulfed in flames but not consumed.

"It is a common saying," Whitefield said, "and common sayings are generally founded on fact, that it is always darkest before the break of day; and I am persuaded, that if we do justice to our own experience, as well as consider God's dealings with His people in preceding ages, we shall find that man's extremity has been God's opportunity. And I believe at the same time that however we may dream of a continued scene of prosperity in church or state, either in respect to our bodies, souls, or temporal affairs, we shall find this life to be chequered, that the clouds return after the rain, and the most prosperous state is attended with cloudy days, as may make even the people of God sometimes cry, 'all men are liars, and God has forgotten to be gracious!'"

Josiah nodded his approval. Whitefield had chosen a suitable topic for the occasion. In fact, maybe it was too direct. Josiah wondered if any of his church members would suspect him of collusion with the evangelist, of viewing Whitefield as a hired mercenary.

"I believe," Whitefield thundered, "we have often found that we are never less alone than when we are with God. We often want this and that companion, but happy are they that can say, 'Lord, Thy company is enough.'"

Josiah winced. That point stung. If Whitefield was aiming at the church, he'd just hit the preacher.

The evangelist elaborated for a time on the incident of the burning bush and inquired into its meaning. He concluded that the burning bush showed the fiery trials and afflictions of Christ's church in this world, trials that could not be avoided.

"I heard a person not long ago say, 'I have no enemies.' Bishop Latimer came to a house one day and the man of the house said he had not met with a cross in all his life. 'Give me my horse!' cried the good bishop. 'I am sure God is not here where no cross is!'"

Laughter and nods rippled across the common.

Then, deftly, Whitefield turned their laughter against them. "O, says one, I never felt the devil! I am sure thou mayst feel him now, for thou art dadda's own child! Thou art speaking the very language of the devil, and he is teaching you to deny your own Father! Therefore, graceless child of the devil, you never felt the devil's fiery darts, it is because the devil is sure of thee! He has got thee into a damnable slumber! May the God of love wake thee before real damnation comes!"

The listeners stirred uneasily. But they weren't going anywhere. The evangelist had hooked them, and now he would reel them in—Josiah with them.

"O poor, dear soul, you will never have such sweet words from God as when you are suffering the fiery trial; our suffering times will be our best times.

"I know we had more comfort in Moorfields, on Kennington Common, and especially when the rotten eggs, and cats and dogs were thrown upon me, and my gown was filled with clods of dirt that I could scarce move it. I have had more comfort in this burning bush than when I have been at ease. I remember when I was preaching at Exeter, a stone came and made my forehead bleed. I found at that very time the word came with double power to a laborer that was gazing at me, who was wounded at the same time by another stone. I felt for the lad more than for myself, went to a friend, and the lad came to me. 'Sir,' says he, 'the man gave me a wound, but Jesus healed me. I never had my bonds broke till I had my head broke!'

"I appeal to you whether you were not better when it was colder than now, because your nerves were braced up. You have a day like a dog day, now you are weak, and are obliged to fan yourselves. Thus it is prosperity that lulls the soul, and I fear Christians are spoiled by it."

Whitefield ridiculed those who would say that they did not know what to make of a bush that burned but was not consumed. That the mockers would someday be surrounded by millions of heavenly host, and then they would know everlasting burning.

"O you frighten me!" Whitefield cried. "Did you think I did not intend to frighten you? Would to God I might frighten you enough! I believe it will be no harm for you to be frightened out of hell, to be frightened out of an unconverted state. O go and tell your companions that the madman said that wicked men are as firebrands of hell! May God pluck you as brands out of that burning!"

Whitefield was weeping openly now.

"Blessed be God, that there is a day of grace. O that this might prove the accepted time! O angel of the everlasting covenant, come down, thou blessed comforter, have mercy, mercy, mercy upon the unconverted, upon our unconverted friends, upon the unconverted part of this auditory. Speak, and it shall be done. Command, O Lord, and it shall come to pass! Turn the burning bushes of the devil into burning bushes of the Son of God! Who knows but God may hear our prayer. Who knows but God may hear this cry, 'I have seen, I have seen the afflictions of My people; the cry of the children of Israel is come up to Me, and I am come down to deliver them!' God grant this may be His word to you under all your trouble. God grant that He may be your comforter.

"The Lord awaken you that are dead in sin, and though on the precipice of hell, God keep you from tumbling in! And you that are God's burning bushes, God help you stand to keep this coat of arms, to say when you go home, 'Blessed be God! The bush is burning, but not consumed!'

"Amen! Even so, Lord Jesus. Amen!"

CHAPTER 38

For five days Josiah reveled in exhilarating emotions as everything he had hoped for, worked for, prayed for came to pass within a couple of days.

Revival had come to Havenhill.

George Whitefield preached eight times—two times a day on Wednesday, Thursday, Saturday, and Sunday. The size of the crowds increased every day. Hundreds of people were saved. Everywhere Josiah walked, he saw clusters of people laughing, singing hymns, or circled in prayer or Bible study.

His own heart sang when he awoke and rejoiced when he went to bed. He told Whitefield, "I'm so filled with the Spirit, I have to backslide at night to get to sleep."

And his gut, which God had seen fit to turn into a spiritual barometer, rested easy, with only occasional minor discomfort.

The hours he spent with George Whitefield were beyond value. He listened with sympathy as the evangelist described the tears shed by believers in England as they labored to revive their dying nation; of the progress of the orphanage in Georgia; of the innumerable works of God he'd witnessed here in the Colonies. The two men reminisced with fondness and laughter the time spent with their mutual acquaintances, Ben Franklin in Philadelphia and Jonathan and Sarah Edwards in Northampton.

Once again Whitefield commented on how impressed he was by Sarah, and how meeting her had renewed his longing for a godly wife.

Josiah thought of Abigail, and the twist of circumstances that now made it possible for them to wed.

He rejected the accusation that came unbidden to his mind: that he had indirectly prayed for Johnny Mott's death and that God had answered his prayer for a wife by killing his friend. He also rejected the barbed thought that Johnny's suicide would result in his own joy.

He was innocent of the events that had brought them to this point. Yet here they were, and the way was now clear for him to court Abigail Parkhurst. Naturally, there would be a time of mourning. A year would be sufficient. But for the first time since returning to Havenhill, Josiah felt hope when he thought of Abigail.

And when it comes to the prospects of love, there is an eternity of difference between a year and never.

Following the final service on Sunday, Whitefield prepared to depart for Virginia. He thanked Josiah for the offering that had been taken for his orphanage, a generous amount.

"It is I who need to be thanking you," Josiah said. "What you take with you is mere money. What you have given us is hope and spiritual healing, for which we will always be in your debt."

"The battle is far from over," Whitefield told him. "Edwards warned you to beware of the river gods. Heed his advice. Wicked men such as Lord Bellamont, who have thrust England into spiritual night, would cast their wicked shadow across the Atlantic to the Colonies. You must resist their evil. Do not let them do to the Colonies what they have done to England."

Josiah nodded."We were once in darkness, but you have brought us the light. If we live in the light, we need not fear the darkness."

Whitefield placed a hand on Josiah's head and prayed God's blessing upon him. Then, along with a few straggling visitors from neighboring towns, the revivalist rode off.

Josiah retired that night, anxious for the coming day. As the town returned to normal, he would better be able to judge the results of the revival services.

Reality hit swiftly and with force on Monday morning.

Revival may have come to Havenhill, but it had left with the last of the town's guests.

Before dawn Deacon Dunmore was on Josiah's doorstep to present a long list of damages done to the church building by the herd of people who tramped through it during his revival services.

At least a half-dozen church members stopped him in the streets to complain about how they had been displaced and inconvenienced at their own church by the throngs of people invading the town.

"I've been coming to that church for forty-three years," one man complained, "and have sat in the same pew every Sabbath. Do you know how embarrassing it was to me and my guests to find strangers sitting in our pew? And when we asked them to leave, they refused! They were quite rude about it too."

Goodwife Hibbard informed him that Eunice Parkhurst and Abigail had not attended any of the services because they were in mourning, and for Josiah to hold church services on the common in front of their house demonstrated a total lack of Christian compassion for their pain.

The town selectmen announced there would be a meeting to assess the damages done to the common and to tally the bill for cleaning up the trash left by the hundreds of people who had turned it into a cheap tavern during their stay. A bill of repair would be presented to the church.

Josiah was informed by courier that the deacons would be holding a meeting to investigate the charge made by Johnny Mott in his suicide note that the pastor of the church had made repeated, unwanted advances to a woman pledged to Mr. Mott in marriage. The note instructed Josiah to come prepared to defend himself against these serious allegations. Should his defense prove unsatisfactory, Josiah could anticipate a motion of dismissal.

Josiah also received a summons from Philip for the next day. Hand delivered by one of Philip's servant boys, the note stated he wished to discuss Josiah's fulfillment of their agreement.

In other words, Philip wanted to make sure that Josiah would keep his part of the deal—that he would remain silent while the river gods strengthened their grip on the jugular of colonial shipping.

With one broadside after another hitting him, Josiah's hopes for a changed, revitalized Havenhill were taking on water faster than his faith could bail.

His mind couldn't grasp what was happening. Had he been the only person in town to be affected by the revival services? How could an entire town witness what had happened over the last five days and come away unchanged?

What went wrong?

Whitefield had been brilliant.

The Spirit had moved.

Evidence of His visitation had been everywhere.

The cure was here, of that Josiah was certain. How was it possible for an entire town to be immune to it?

Bruised, weary, discouraged, and defeated, Josiah dragged himself back to his house that night. If ever he needed a note of encouragement waiting for him between the clapboard slats, it was tonight.

But there was nothing but slats. No note.

Dining on three-day-old cornbread and warmed-over stew, Josiah slumped in his chair to the empty sounds of a man who lives alone. He had just dozed off and escaped the troublesome hounds in his mind when a tap, tap, tap on the door woke him.

Eunice Parkhurst's servant girl appeared when he opened the door. She handed Josiah a note.

"Who needs a visit tonight?" Josiah asked the girl.

She shrugged and ran away.

Carrying the note back to the table with him, he tossed it unread onto the table of breadcrumbs. He didn't feel like going out tonight, and he didn't want to wrestle with his pastoral sense of duty and try to convince it that whoever needed visiting could wait until morning.

He delayed the struggle by making himself some coffee.

Not until the cup was half-emptied did he reach for the note and unfold it.

We need to meet.
Abigail

Josiah could barely contain his emotion. Four words, and everything was different. Four words. They might well have been some kind of magical incantation. Once read, and poof! All the negative emotions he'd collected throughout the day were gone. Vanished. In their place was the sweet, warm excitement of anticipation. He would see Abigail. Free-to-marry Abigail. He hadn't seen that Abigail in seven years.

Moments earlier he had sought the forgetfulness of slumber; now he was too excited to sleep.

Taking a candle and the note, he went to the back room, to his writing table, where he would compose a reply and inquire where and when they would meet.

His heart skipped as he walked.

Not until he placed the candle on the desk did he notice something was missing.

His journal.

He always kept it in the same place—the upper left-hand corner of the desk, next to his books. It fit perfectly there. Out of the way when not in use, easy to reach when he was ready for it.

But it wasn't there.

That place on the desk was striking for its emptiness.

He checked the floor.

It hadn't fallen off the edge.

He searched in the drawer, among the books, on his bed, under his bed. He went back out to the front room and looked there too. The journal wasn't to be found.

The only other person in the house had been George Whitefield. To think that he would take Josiah's journal was ridiculous. Even if it was a mistake. And how would a person accidentally reach across another man's desk, pick up his journal, and not know it?

Besides, Josiah remembered writing in it last night following the Sunday service, shortly after Whitefield departed.

Josiah stared at the desk again. The journal wasn't there. With no other explanation than someone had come into his house while he was gone, the obvious question was, why would anyone take his journal?

It couldn't be sold for much. Who would want to buy a preacher's journal?

CHAPTER 39

The crunching of leaves announced Abigail's arrival. As Josiah watched her approach, his pulse quickened. Would it still skip like this after they'd been married ten years? Why wouldn't it? It had raced every time he caught sight of her since their school days.

The morning air was crisp. Enough to color one's cheeks, but not enough to penetrate one's clothes.

Abigail moved with grace through the same patch of woods Josiah had cut through the last time he saw Johnny Mott alive, arguing with Philip. He didn't tell Abigail about that incident when she suggested they meet here. The patch of woods was simply a good choice, not too far off the road, but far enough to afford them privacy.

She wore a blue dress trimmed in white with matching coat and hood. It was one of his favorite dresses. Had she somehow sensed this and chosen it with him in mind?

Her petticoat rustled from side to side as she zig-zagged toward him through the trees. She kept her head down as she picked her way around the underbrush. Her gaze remained lowered when she reached him.

"Mother thinks I'm at Judith Usher's house." She glanced nervously side to side. "I didn't lie to her. I'll go directly there from here."

A whiff of her perfume sent Josiah's head reeling. There was something about a woman's fragrance in the musty woods that compounded its femininity exponentially. Josiah found it irresistible.

"I want you to know," he said softly, "that I'm content to wait. It won't be easy. Every fiber of my being longs for you. But for your sake, it's best if we wait. And I just wanted you to know that however long you need . . ."

Abigail clamped her eyes in an unsuccessful attempt to stop the tears. Pulling a handkerchief from her cuff, she dabbed the little renegades.

"Nabby." Josiah put a hand on her arm.

She pulled away.

"I'm sorry," Josiah said. "I know I just told you I'd wait, and then I do something like that. It's just that it's hard for me. I'm sorry."

As he waited for her to compose herself, he fought wave after wave of urges to pull her to him, to cradle her head against his chest. He longed to hold her until she stopped trembling, until she knew she need never be frightened or alone again.

"Johnny Mott was killed," Abigail said.

The turn in thought was so sudden that it took Josiah a moment to catch up.

Abigail helped him. "It wasn't a suicide," she insisted. "He was murdered."

Josiah blinked repeatedly, not knowing how to respond. When he had left the house, he'd outfitted his mind for romance, not a murder mystery.

"But . . . the note," he said finally. "The note—"

"That's how I know Johnny didn't kill himself. He didn't write that note."

"But how can you be certain? I was told only a few people have seen the note. Philip verified that it was Johnny Mott's handwriting."

The mention of Philip's name seemed to unsettle her. "I didn't have to see the handwriting to know Johnny didn't write it."

"How—?"

Her words came with difficulty. "The note said that he killed himself because he knew that you still loved me."

Josiah nodded. Philip had told him Johnny suspected as much and was defensive about it. Josiah himself had witnessed on many occasions how uneasy Johnny had become whenever he was around.

Abigail continued, "It also said he knew I still loved you. And that was why he killed himself." She bit her lower lip. "Only . . ." She paused. "Only I don't love you. And Johnny knew that."

The double blast hit Josiah hard in the chest. He didn't know which one to deal with first.

"You . . . don't . . ." He couldn't finish the sentence. He didn't need to.

Abigail shook her head.

It was one of those moments when reality doused a dream. This particular dream had lived a long and healthy life and didn't want to go easily. But the coolness in Abigail's gaze, the finality of her tone was too much for even a healthy dream. And though he didn't want to admit it, even his heart knew what she said was true.

"You don't love me," Josiah said. "How . . ." He took a deep breath. "How long have you known?"

"Do you remember when you left for Boston? We stood on the steps in front of my house."

Josiah winced. "You've known that long?"

"I remember feeling guilty because I was glad you were leaving and that I wouldn't have to tell you."

A hollow feeling settled over Josiah. It was not surprising, considering the fact that Abigail had just sliced out a significant portion of his life.

"I'm sorry, Josiah," Abigail said. "I don't mean to hurt you, but I couldn't think of any other way."

Josiah's ego came back with any number of retorts, none of them flattering and none of them true. He clenched his jaw and swallowed them.

"And under the circumstances, with Johnny's death . . ."

Johnny knew Abigail didn't love him. All this time, Johnny knew. So why was Johnny always defensive whenever Josiah was around?

"He liked you. You know that, don't you? He admired you."

"We're talking about Johnny Mott?"

"He told me once that he'd never known another man as strong as you . . . inside, he meant. He said any other man never would have come back after what happened." Her eyes focused on the remembered conversation. "I remember him saying that you deserved better. He never spoke about that night. The night of the fire. He had nightmares about it, more frequently after you returned." Tears came to her eyes. "I think he would have done anything for you. He would even not have married me if you'd asked him."

"He loved you?"

Tears flowed as she nodded. "Very much."

"And you loved him."

He could see it now. His own love had blinded him to the possibility that Abigail might love Johnny Mott. Now it seemed so obvious.

"But if he didn't commit suicide . . ." Josiah couldn't bring himself to complete the sentence. Not yet, because it meant that if someone killed Johnny Mott, somehow Philip Clapp was tied into it.

Abigail shivered, but not from the October wind. It was obvious she was frightened.

"You've spoken about this to your mother?"

Abigail nodded, fighting back a fresh round of tears.

"She's not going to do anything reckless, is she?"

Abigail laughed. Josiah knew Eunice Parkhurst all too well. "She's scared, too. Mostly for me."

"What you just told me? Don't tell anyone else. Do you understand?"

"Yes," she replied with a certain amount of relief. She'd handed the problem to him and seemed content to let him take it from here. "What are you going to do?"

Josiah took a deep breath and exhaled all of it. "Pray a lot," he said glibly.

That got her to laugh. "Oh! I almost forgot." She opened her purse and extracted a sheaf of papers. Yellowed. Worn. With handwriting on both sides.

Josiah examined them. He recognized the handwriting, though he hadn't seen it in years.

"Father's last sermon," Abigail said. "He never preached it."

She didn't have to explain. Josiah knew Reverend Parkhurst had never preached it, because he had died before he'd had a chance to preach it, in a fire Josiah had caused.

"It's a loan. In fact, I have to have it back before tonight. Mother keeps it in the back of her Bible."

And reads it frequently if the wear of the pages is any indication, Josiah told himself.

"I'll send Sissy to pick it up."

Josiah was fascinated by what he was reading. Reverend Parkhurst's final sermon was a warning about encroaching evil from England and a prayer that God would fend it off with His Spirit in a great spiritual renewal movement.

"He loved you," Abigail said. "You know that, don't you? He was so proud of you."

Light dawned. "That's why you never broke it off with me."

Abigail shrugged. "He was so happy you were going to be his son-in-law. Mother was too."

Josiah looked up.

Abigail smiled sweetly and flew into his arms, but there was no romance in her gesture. In one way, it was a hug between friends. In another, it was good-bye.

CHAPTER 40

To be rejected by the woman you've dreamed about and loved for nearly a decade was not the best way to start the day. However, if anyone could counsel a wounded heart and put things in perspective, Reverend Parkhurst could, even when his counsel came from beyond the grave.

Back at his desk, Josiah temporarily forgot his pain as he read Parkhurst's sermon. Then he read it a second time. Though Josiah hadn't spoken to the man for nearly eight years, he could hear Parkhurst's voice and inflection in every word.

The third time, Josiah copied the sermon. Under normal circumstances, he would have copied the sermon in his journal. However, since he didn't know where his journal was, loose sheets of paper would have to do.

Copying Parkhurst's words seemed to connect Josiah with his mentor in a way that sent shivers through him, as though Parkhurst were guiding his hand, drawing his attention to key points, or at times withdrawing his hand and instructing him to meditate for a while on what he'd just written before continuing.

By the time he finished, it was midmorning. His heart resonated with the truth of the message. He knew now how the ancient prophet felt after recording the word of the Lord: "Write the vision, and make it plain upon tablets, that he may run that readeth it."

Josiah rose from his chair and took a brisk walk.

Solvitur ambulando.

And when he returned, he knew what he had to do. Reverend Parkhurst's sermon had given him a clarity of vision he had not had before. He knew what he must do. And he knew that he alone could do it. That it was God, not Philip Clapp, who had brought him back to Havenhill. And that he had been brought back for a purpose. That everything that had happened to this point—Reverend Parkhurst's death, Josiah's exile, even Abigail's rejection this morning—had been necessary to bring him to this point in time.

Most importantly, he knew why he had been chosen. It was because he had nothing to lose. And a man who has nothing to lose is a dangerous adversary.

Josiah pounded on the door.

As he waited for it to open, he told himself that one way or the other he was going to get inside this house and say what he had come to say. Nothing and no one was going to stop him.

The door opened.

Grace Smythe scowled when she saw it was him. "Go away."

"I wish to speak to Mercy."

"She's not receiving guests at present."

"Please let her know I've come to call on her."

Grace gave him an exasperated look. "Did your mother drop you on your head when you were a baby?"

Mercy's voice came from inside the house. "Grace? Who is it?"

"She sounds up to receiving visitors to me," Josiah said.

"She's not dressed."

Josiah took a step forward.

Grace blocked his way by bracing her arm against the doorjamb.

Josiah muttered, "Are you going to tell Mercy I've come calling, or do I have to—"

Grace narrowed her eyes. "To what? Hit me? Overpower me and force your way in?"

She appeared up to the challenge.

Josiah shouted past her, "Mercy, it's—" He hesitated, not knowing what to say. Was he Josiah, or Reverend Rush?

Grace seemed amused by his hesitation. "You don't even know who you are! You're confused. All you do is go around stirring things up. You're not good enough for Mercy."

"At least we agree on one thing," Josiah stated. "I'm not good enough for her." Then, shouting again, "Mercy, it's me."

Grace cocked an ear into the house. When no answer was immediately forthcoming, she said, "See? She doesn't want to talk to you."

"Mercy," Josiah called again, "I only want a couple minutes of your time."

"Look, Reverend . . . ," Grace began.

Mercy stepped out of the darkness of the house. She was wearing her hat and was pulling on gloves. "Let's take a walk."

Grace's arm remained rigid. "Are you out of your mind?"

Mercy rose up on her toes, gave Grace a peck on the cheek, then ducked under her arm. "I won't be long."

Josiah and Mercy strolled down the road with a respectable distance between them.

"She's only trying to protect me," Mercy said.

"You don't strike me as a woman who needs to be protected," Josiah replied. "Certainly not from me. And unless I miss my guess, I would think you can hold your own in a skirmish."

"Is that a compliment?" Mercy asked. "It resembled a compliment, but somehow it's not the kind of thing a gentleman would say to a lady, is it?"

"Sorry. I was presuming on our friendship. It was a compliment. I mean, it was meant to be a compliment. At least I think there was a compliment in there someplace. Buried, maybe. Deep. But definitely a compliment."

Mercy smiled. "Then, sir, I will take it as one. However, I believe you misrepresent Grace's intentions."

"On the contrary, I think her intentions are clear. She wants to keep me as far away from you as possible."

"She is protecting me," Mercy claimed. "She's protecting me from myself."

Josiah didn't quite know how to interpret that last remark. He looked to her for clarification. Mercy didn't offer any. She walked with eyes straight forward.

Several silent moments passed.

"This morning Abigail told me she doesn't love me," Josiah announced.

Mercy stopped abruptly. She cocked her head. This time she was studying him. Then, matter-of-factly, she said, "I know."

"You know? How could you know? She just told me."

Mercy continued down the path.

Josiah sighed. "All right. How long have you known?"

"Since school days," Mercy replied flatly. Then, pivoting swiftly toward him, she became animated. "Is this what this conversation is all about, Reverend Rush? A woman has cast you off, so you come running to me? And just what do you expect from me, Reverend Rush? To swoon and swear my undying love for you? To launch myself into your arms and tell you that I adore you madly? That I've had feelings for you since we were children? That I believe God created me for you? Or maybe that we can make good mincemeat together? Is that what you want to hear, Reverend Rush?" Her face was flushed with anger.

"Actually, I told you that because in Johnny Mott's suicide note he said that she loved me and he knew she didn't."

Mercy stared at him, her face crimson now for a different reason. "Oh." She swung around and began walking again at a much quicker pace.

Josiah had to hurry to catch up with her. "We need to talk."

"No we don't."

"Mercy." He touched her arm to slow her.

She shrugged it off.

"Mercy, please . . ." This time he took her arm gently.

She stopped but refused to look at him. "See?" she murmured. "Grace is right. I do need someone to protect me from myself."

"You've had feelings for me since our school days?" Josiah asked.

Fighting back tears, Mercy said, "I don't want to talk about this now."

"You're right. And I'm sorry I gave you the impression I came to see you just because Abigail tossed me aside."

It must have been the right thing for him to say, because she looked up. "Why did you come to see me?"

"Because you're the one person in town who doesn't seem to want to crucify me. And you're the one person in town whose prayers I covet. I don't know anyone more godly than you, Mercy Litchfield. And right now, the way things are developing, I need someone to pray for me. Someone who has God's ear."

"I have been praying for you," she said softly.

"Thank you."

They stood opposite each other in silence for a time.

"And then, after this is over," he suggested, "maybe we should talk about us."

"One thing at a time, Reverend Rush." She regained her composure. "You said Johnny was aware Abigail didn't love you, yet that's what he wrote in his suicide note. So if he knew that, why . . . oh! Oh! He didn't kill himself! Which means . . ."

Josiah nodded.

They walked, and he told her what he planned to do.

CHAPTER 41

Finding himself on familiar ground—in front of another door—Josiah raised a fist. The door opened before he struck it.

A startled Anne Myles stepped back. "Josiah! You frightened me!"

She looked striking, as always, and fragile in a feminine way. A lavender dress complemented her pale skin. Her hat was trimmed in lace. She pulled on traveling gloves. Josiah wondered how much Anne knew of Philip's dealings with her uncle, Lord Bellamont. Or, for that matter, how much she knew about Lord Bellamont himself.

"I assume you've come to see Philip," she said. Without waiting for an answer, she called to an unseen servant to announce Reverend Josiah Rush.

Josiah thought she was calling to Long-face, but just then he drove up with a carriage.

"A woman must attend to her shopping," Anne announced breezily, passing in front of Josiah and stepping into the carriage. "We must have you over for dinner soon, Josiah." A hand flew to her mouth. "Excuse me, Reverend Rush. I forget, us having grown up together."

Then, reminded by her own words of the spiritual nature of his office, lest he misinterpret her presence here, she added, "Silly Philip forgot to give me shopping money yesterday, forcing me to ride all this way out here so early in the morning to get it!"

Josiah nodded and smiled.

With a flick of the reins, the carriage took off. Anne fluttered her fingers at Josiah.

She was still the carefree, self-possessed Anne Myles he remembered from school days. Josiah found it hard to believe she knew where the money came from for her shopping trips.

Philip's buoyant voice came from inside. "Josiah! What brings you out this way on this fine morning?"

Josiah hadn't noticed it until now, but he was always Josiah to Philip. The only time Philip used his title was at church, and only occasionally when they were alone, in mock respect.

"I know about Johnny," Josiah said.

The two friends faced off in Philip's study, which was the size of Josiah's house. The door was closed, though from the elevated volume of their voices, anyone within three rooms could have heard them.

"How can I take seriously your ridiculous allegation if you refuse to tell me upon what you are basing your allegations?" Philip shouted.

Josiah wasn't ready to surrender his advantage yet. Philip had recovered quickly to his opening salvo about Johnny. But the fact that he had to recover was disturbing.

"You actually saw the suicide note?" Josiah pressed.

"Yes, I saw it."

"And you're certain Johnny wrote it?"

It was obvious Philip didn't like to be interrogated. He indulged Josiah either out of friendship or because he needed to know what Josiah knew. Either way, it worked to Josiah's advantage.

"You worked with the man for nearly a decade," Josiah pressed. "You're familiar with his handwriting. Did the suicide note strike you as odd in any way? As though it might have been written by a hand other than Johnny's?"

"You know what you're suggesting?"

Josiah didn't respond. Philip had not yet answered his question.

Philip conceded the advantage to Josiah. For the moment. "I'm as reasonably certain as a man can be under the circumstances," Philip insisted. "But remember, you have to take into account the circumstances. A man writing a suicide note is not himself. It is not unreasonable to assume that the anxiety of what he is contemplating might alter his penmanship."

He paused to gauge Josiah's reaction.

"Is that what this is all about?" Philip asked. "Do you want to compare the note with a sample of Johnny's handwriting for yourself? I can arrange it. But you'll come to the same conclusion as I have. The similarities are such that reasonable minds would conclude it was written by Johnny Mott's hand."

"That won't be necessary."

"Then what the devil are you driving at?" Philip challenged. "What's this all about?"

Josiah paced a minute. Philip's offer allowing him to compare the note to handwriting samples was either a bluff of incredible arrogance, or proof he wasn't involved with Johnny's murder. He hoped the latter was true, but he had to be sure.

Josiah took the next step. "It's the content of the note that proves it's a forgery."

Philip studied the floor, as if attempting to recall the wording of the suicide note.

Josiah used the time to study his old friend. Despite the opulence of the room—polished dark wood bookcases, a library to rival any in Boston or Philadelphia, ornate French furniture . . . Despite the finery of Philip's clothing, which came from the best shops in England and France, not the inferior colonial fashions . . . And despite Philip realizing his fantasy of winning the heart and hand of the wealthy and beautiful Anne Myles . . . Philip Clapp was different. He appeared old. Haggard. For several months he'd been jumpy, startled by any sudden sound. His anger had flared at the smallest trifle. These were not characteristics anyone associated with Philip.

"If I recall," Philip said, "the note gave two reasons for driving Johnny to desperation. Your love for Abigail and her love for you."

"Precisely," Josiah answered.

Philip's brow furrowed. He was attempting to find the error but couldn't, Josiah realized. Apparently, in matters of the heart, Johnny hadn't confided in his business partner.

"If you'll recall," Philip continued, "I warned you that he saw you as a threat. How could he not? Everyone knows how you feel about Abigail."

"Please, Philip. Don't say any more."

Philip evidently mistook Josiah's comment for weakness. With a grin, he approached Josiah. "Don't tell me you came here to attempt to convince me that you don't have feelings for Abigail Parkhurst." He laughed derisively. "Josiah, it's me you're talking to. And if this is the defense you've chosen to convince everyone that you bear no guilt—albeit, indirectly—for Johnny Mott's death, well, I'd advise you to choose a different tactic. Because that dog won't hunt."

Josiah looked down. "I spoke to Abigail this morning."

Philip threw up his hands. "Of all the boneheaded moves! Did anyone see you? Does Eunice know? What a stupid thing to do, Josiah! You'd think at least you could control your passion for more than . . . what? How long has it been? A week? Has Johnny been in the ground a full week yet?"

Josiah let Philip think he went to see Abigail. He'd given a lot of thought about how he would reveal what he knew. It was imperative that he did it in such a way that Philip did not suspect Abigail of knowing about Johnny's murder. Philip had always liked his women dumb. Josiah was counting on the fact that Philip thought of all women that way. By letting Philip think Josiah went to her, it was conceivable she could have contributed a piece of the puzzle without knowing it.

"Abigail told me she doesn't love me," Josiah said softly. It still hurt to say it.

Philip stared at Josiah, obviously not knowing what to say, not believing it was true. "You're making that up. Of course she loves you. She's always loved you. If she told you she didn't, it was for a reason. Maybe, because . . ." He cursed. "I don't know! Maybe . . . yes, maybe she's keeping you at arms' length. To protect herself. In fact, I wouldn't be surprised if Eunice didn't put her up to it. To keep Abigail from embarrassing the family during the time of mourning. That's probably what it is, when you come to think of it. Appearances . . . and this way, after the acceptable time, you'll come after her. Court her. You know . . . all the usual courtship ritual. Women live for that kind of thing. And, naturally, she couldn't want you to think that she was yours by default. No woman wants to be handed down to another man, as though she was part of Johnny's estate. It makes sense, doesn't it? Women are all about manipulation. I'm telling you, there's a reason she would want you to believe she doesn't love you."

"Abigail hasn't loved me since before the fire," Josiah stated. "She couldn't bring herself to tell me back then because her parents liked me so much."

Philip started to say something but stopped. Then he asked, "She told you that? In those words? She actually told you that?"

"She said deep down she was glad when I moved to Boston. She never thought I'd come back again."

The truth was beginning to sink in. Josiah could see it on Philip's face. He was pacing furiously.

It was then that Josiah placed the final piece in the puzzle. "Johnny knew."

Philip came to a dead standstill.

"He knew that Abigail didn't love me."

Philip began shaking his head. "No, that's not possible. He didn't . . ."

"He did. Johnny knew Abigail didn't love me. That's how I know he never would have written that suicide note. And if he didn't write it, someone planted it on him. Probably the same person who killed him."

Philip's chest rose and fell in heaves, as though he'd just run a great distance.

Josiah closed the distance between them until they were face-to-face. "Now, are you going to tell me the truth?"

With a shrug of resignation, Philip motioned Josiah to a pair of matching chairs set at a conversational angle.

It took Philip several minutes to compose himself. When he could speak, he asked, "What do you plan on doing?"

"First step: talk to you."

"They're ruthless," Philip countered. "Let this go. You don't want to go up against them."

Josiah lifted his chin. "Lord Bellamont."

At the sound of the name, Philip's eyes grew hard. "What do you know of him? Other than what I've let you know."

"That he's an unscrupulous, powerful English merchant who wants to establish a slave-trading port in New England, one that will rival any Southern port."

Philip nodded. "I see your little trek for a revival preacher turned over a few stones. I knew letting you go was a mistake."

Josiah leaned forward. "Philip, please tell me you didn't have anything to do with Johnny's—"

"Of course I didn't!" Philip shouted, jumping to his feet. "How can you say that? Johnny was my friend!" Philip was trembling. In a voice barely audible, he said, "Johnny's death was a warning. To me."

Josiah closed his eyes and slumped back into his chair.

"The suicide note was meant to cover their tracks," Philip added.

"Then Johnny was murdered." Josiah knew it before now, but saying it aloud brought it out into the open.

Philip nodded.

"Say it," Josiah insisted.

"Say what?"

"Johnny Mott was murdered."

"I don't see what good that will—"

"Say it!"

"Josiah—"

"Say it!"

"All right! Johnny Mott was murdered! I said it!" Philip dropped his head in his hands. He rubbed his eyes. "You think I don't see him hanging at the end of that rope every night when I close my eyes?"

Josiah stood. He walked around the room, touching the silk fabric on the chairs, the smooth finish of the wood. "How much do you owe Bellamont?"

Philip hung his head. "It's worse than that."

Josiah cringed as he realized the truth. "Seven years ago you rebuilt the town with Lord Bellamont's money."

"At the time his plans were to establish a shipping center for pharmaceuticals, importing drugs and herbs and exotic plants from the Caribbean."

Josiah nodded. "Peter Hutton's warehouses. The ones destroyed by the fire. Hutton Apothecaries."

"In a way, this is all your fault," Philip said. "It was you who provided Lord Bellamont with the opportunity he needed to gain a foothold in the Colonies. Bellamont's plan was to use Hutton's setback to his advantage. The plan was to move in quickly and challenge Hutton for the New England market."

"What happened?"

Philip sighed. "A couple of things. Economic reversals. Ships sunk. Hutton recovered faster than anticipated. But it still could have worked."

"Bellamont spied a more lucrative trade."

"When it comes to making money, the man has a wandering eye. He saw that a couple of his cronies were making substantial profits in the slave trade. He saw New England as a largely untapped market. The man is convinced he can double, possibly triple, the number of slaves in the New England colonies."

"Unless someone stops him."

"Don't talk crazy."

"Philip, buying and selling human beings is immoral. We can't let him use Havenhill as a trading post to peddle human flesh!"

"And how do you propose we stop him?" Philip shouted. "He owns this town! He has the power and wealth to do whatever he wants, including influencing Parliament legislation for personal gain! He has friends in the court, advisors to the king! How are we going to stop someone that powerful? Any attempt would be—"

"Suicide?" Josiah shouted back. "Do you really want to use that word, Philip?"

"I'm warning you, Josiah. Don't meddle in things you can't change."

"And I'm warning you: you're going to have to choose whose side you're really on."

"All right, Don Quixote. But mark my words: if you start tilting at English windmills, you might very well succeed in hurting this town more than you did seven years ago when you nearly destroyed it!"

Josiah headed toward the door.

Philip grabbed his arm. "It's me, isn't it? You're jealous of me. You always have been. After nearly burning down the town, you scurry off to Boston like a dog with his tail between his legs, leaving me to figure out a way to rebuild the town. And I did it!"

"By putting the town into debt to evil incarnate."

"Bellamont's a businessman! I'm a businessman. I made a business decision! And ever since then, you haven't been able to live with the fact that I am now the town's favorite son. So now you think you can just come in here, stumble into a victory, and ride off with Dulcinea. Well, let me tell you, if you play the role of the woeful knight-errant here in Havenhill, you're going to get us all killed!"

"You think this is about you and me?" Josiah asked defiantly. "It's about right and wrong. It's about what's moral and immoral."

"England and men like Lord Bellamont have the wealth, Josiah. They make the rules. They determine what's right and what's wrong. We can't afford to cling to a bunch of archaic first-century morals."

"You're afraid of Lord Bellamont," Josiah accused.

"Of course I'm afraid," Philip exclaimed. "Look what they did to Johnny!"

Josiah stared his friend in the eye. "There are worse things to fear than Lord Bellamont. 'Fear not them which kill the body, but are not able to kill the soul: but rather fear him which is able to destroy both soul and body in hell.'"

Philip waved his hands in disgust. "Great! Quoting Scripture. That's going to do a lot of good now, isn't it? Let's see how effective your Scripture quoting is when Lord Bellamont sets his bloodhounds on you."

Josiah gazed sadly at his friend. "We're on opposite sides of this battle, aren't we?"

"Don't fight me on this, Josiah. You can't win. And I won't be responsible for what happens if you choose to line up against me," Philip warned.

His heart heavy, Josiah turned his back on Philip Clapp.

It had been a rough morning. He'd lost the love of his life and turned his best friend into an enemy.

And it wasn't yet noon.

CHAPTER 42

On Tuesday, after the exchange of warnings with Philip, Josiah felt like an untested soldier poised at the edge of a great battlefield, waiting for the trumpet to sound the charge. By Friday he found himself still standing there. Still waiting. The trumpet never sounded. All was quiet. The kind of quiet that makes a person's muscles twitch with anticipation.

It was night. His Bible open, Josiah hunched over Sunday's sermon. From the book of Joshua—

> Now therefore fear the LORD, and serve him in sincerity and in truth: and put away the gods which your fathers served on the other side of the flood, and in Egypt; and serve ye the LORD. And if it seem evil unto you to serve the LORD, choose you this day whom ye will serve; whether the gods which your fathers served that were on the other side of the flood, or the gods of the Amorites, in whose land ye dwell: but as for me and my house, we will serve the LORD.

A call to arms. It had come to that. It was time to state the issue clearly. Bellamont had wealth. Philip had position and authority. But Josiah was not without weapons. He had the sword of God.

Josiah stared at the Israelite response to their leader's challenge:

> And the people answered and said, God forbid that we should forsake the LORD, to serve other gods.

He prayed that the people of Havenhill had enough spirituality left in them to respond in a similar manner. But he knew the allure of the river gods was great. He had seen the kingdom of the river gods growing in Boston and Philadelphia, and read about it in the middle and Southern colonies. To a people weary of the struggle of life in a wilderness country, the glitter of the river gods was hard to walk away from. But behind the allure of gold were the Lord Bellamonts of England who, without guilt, would knowingly enslave both Africans and Americans for profit.

Josiah wrote that down in his notes. *There was more than one way to enslave a man*, he thought.

A single candle illuminated the top of the desk, enveloping the Bible, the sermon, and Josiah in a comfortable bubble of light.

Atop the desk was his copy of Reverend Parkhurst's sermon. Josiah picked it up and read portions of it again. Abigail had, as promised, sent the little servant girl to retrieve the original.

Josiah couldn't help but wonder if things would be different if Reverend Parkhurst were still the pastor of the church. The people had loved him. They'd listened to him. If Parkhurst were still alive, the people of Havenhill never would have become entangled with the likes of Lord Bellamont in the first place.

Slumping back in his chair, Josiah let out a disgusted snort. What was he thinking? Of course they wouldn't. If Reverend Parkhurst were alive, they wouldn't have needed Lord Bellamont's money because their town would still be standing.

Philip was right. This was all Josiah's fault.

One careless night—and look what it had cost them. All of them.

Weary of the fight, Josiah placed his sermon notes in the Bible and closed it. At least he had a chance to make things right. God had brought him back to Havenhill for a reason. And as God was his witness, Josiah would fight to save the town—even if it was from themselves—until he had no strength left.

The battle was at hand. This was no time for timidity. Sunday he would draw a line. There were two sides. And it was time the people of Havenhill decided once and for all whose side they were on.

Josiah was ready—more than ready. He was eager. In that sense the week's inactivity had been maddening.

At first Philip's tactics had confused Josiah. Now he thought he understood.

Unexpectedly, the two planned skirmishes for that week had been postponed. The town meeting to address the issue of reparations for damages done by the revival crowds had been put off indefinitely. The deacon meeting to investigate Johnny's suicide accusations against Josiah had been delayed a week. Philip was behind both decisions.

Open meetings were risky. And Josiah concluded that Philip couldn't risk an investigation into the suicide note. Not after their little chat in his library.

And while Philip couldn't very well postpone worship services, it was a safer venue. He could gamble that Josiah would have enough respect for the sanctity of the Sabbath not to do anything foolish. And the sermon would give Philip a chance to gauge Josiah's intentions.

It was a shrewd move.

Which meant that Josiah would have to make the most of the one opportunity left to him. Sunday's sermon might very well be the most important sermon of his life.

Bone tired, Josiah cupped the candle flame and extinguished it. The bubble of light collapsed. Darkness covered him.

The snout of the serpent broke the surface of the water. Green scales slipped effortlessly upward as the beast rose to an enormous height over the town. Its roar shook the earth and could be heard several townships away. On the docks, on the streets, in the taverns, the shops, the townspeople went about their business, oblivious to the threat the beast posed. Josiah could do nothing to make them see the danger.

He grabbed them by the arms and shook them.

He shouted and pointed.

The townspeople ignored him.

Then a distant *clang* caught Josiah's attention. The roar of the beast almost drowned it out. He also heard faraway cries. He turned. There, on an auction block, slaves were chained in a line. But not slaves. Eunice Parkhurst. Johnny Mott. Abigail. Mercy and Grace. Young Edward Usher, whose sisters were killed in the fire. Their wails were drowned out by the beast. And as they walked, the chains clanged in rhythm with their steps.

By now the beast had risen to full height, revealing hundreds of arms with claws that began ripping at the town, tearing the roofs off buildings, snatching people from the street. And still there was no alarm, except for the people who cried because they were chained and about to be auctioned. The townspeople went about their business.

A whirlpool formed around the beast, spitting foam and fire. The beast lifted its head with an ungodly scream. Red eyes flashed. Its claws tore at the town, ripping it as though it were made of paper.

Then, with a roar of alarm, surprised by the grip the vortex had on him, the beast began to be sucked into the whirlpool. He could do nothing to stop it, though he tried by frantically clawing at the streets and docks. He only succeeded in pulling the entire town down into the vortex with him.

Helplessly, Josiah watched as the shops and streets, the auction block with the slaves, the docks, the church, the common—everything—was drawn into the swirling void with the beast. Josiah himself had to reach and grab at poles and buildings to keep from being pulled down.

The whole scene began to stretch out of shape. Josiah felt himself elongating as he grabbed the trunk of Deacon Cranch's old oak tree. His legs and arms stretched to three times their length; his forehead and nose and chin distorted.

Josiah woke with a start.

His chest heaving, his face a mask of perspiration, he blinked his eyes awake, searching for some recognizable shape, and saw only the darkness of a vortex. He thought he knew where he was, but he could still hear the clanging of the slaves' chains and their distant cries.

After several deep breaths and more blinking, faint shapes appeared. He was in his room. In his bed.

The clanging and the cries continued.

Throwing back the bed sheets, Josiah's feet hit the floor. The cold boards shocked his senses to full alert. Grabbing his coat and shoes, he ran to the door and plunged into the night air.

Bright shades of orange lit the eastern sky beyond the trees. Had it been evening and west, Josiah would have marveled at the beautiful sunset. Only it was night. And east. Only one thing could create such a display.

Fire!

Minutes later, fully dressed, Josiah's lungs were burning as he ran as fast as his legs could carry him toward the conflagration.

CHAPTER 43

Reaching Summit Street, Josiah got his first good look at the fire. What he saw nearly brought him to his knees. He stumbled to a tree to steady himself.

The entire wharf was ablaze. Every warehouse. Every pier. And somehow the fire had even jumped the water, setting a ship ablaze. Its stern was surrounded by orange flames, and more flames climbed the mast.

"O God . . . O God . . . O God . . ."

The words erupted from Josiah's heart. A litany consisting of two words. But Josiah had never prayed a more sincere prayer.

His eyes were hypnotized by the enormity of the blaze. Forcing himself to release the tree, Josiah let his weight start him down Summit Street. After a half-dozen steps, his feet slapped the road in a full run.

He approached three men coming up the street. Two of them flanked a third, who had difficulty walking. They were covered with black soot, their features obscured. As Josiah got closer, he saw that the clothes of the man in the middle had been burned off his body on one side.

As Josiah passed them, the man closest to him looked up. Their eyes locked for an instant. Josiah broke the gaze.

The other man's head swiveled, tracking Josiah. "Hey!" he called.

Josiah glanced over his shoulder. When he realized the man was addressing him, he slowed to a stop.

"What do you think you're doing?" the man shouted.

Josiah stared at the man. He tried to see past the soot in search of some recognizable feature. He found none.

The man passed the full weight of the injured man to his friend.

"Can I help you?" Josiah asked.

The man came toward him. His eyes were narrowed in a menacing fashion. His chin led the charge. "Where do you think you're going?"

"Do I know you?"

The man kept coming closer, but Josiah still didn't recognize him. Had the man mistaken him for someone else?

"Haven't you done enough?"

A lump of dread rose in Josiah's throat. "I don't know what you're—"

The rest of Josiah's sentence was shoved back into his face with a fist. With the impact came a white flash, then pain. Josiah's arms arced in circles as he stumbled backward, trying to keep his balance.

His tailbone hit the ground with a *thud*. The momentum of the hit slammed his head against the ground. Eyes clenched, Josiah cringed at the pain that filled his head. When he opened his eyes, he saw the stars.

But not for long.

The next thing Josiah knew, the body of his attacker was eclipsing the heavens. The man landed with force on Josiah's stomach, shoving the breath out of him with such pressure that Josiah's eyes bulged.

Knuckles hammered one side of Josiah's face, then the other. A blow caught his right ribs, then his left.

From somewhere beyond the blows, Josiah heard:

"My pal's burned bad 'cause of you!"

The news was delivered with a few more blows.

Josiah turned his head and lifted his arms in a futile attempt to block the blows.

"Mickey! Mickey! Git offa him!"

Mercifully, the rain of heavy fists let up. Then the great weight was lifted off his chest.

Josiah dared to open his eyes. His attacker was being pulled off him. But the man didn't go willingly, and Josiah prayed his friend was strong enough to hold him.

"He's not worth it, Mickey! He's not worth it!"

Mickey, however, didn't appear to be convinced.

"You stay away from the docks, understand? If me or my pals ever catch you near the docks, you won't be so lucky. You got that?"

When Mickey released him, Josiah propped himself up on one arm. The attacker glared at Josiah and made a motion that made him flinch. Then Mickey turned his back deliberately on Josiah. The two men picked up their injured friend and continued on their way.

Josiah didn't move until they were gone.

He tasted blood. His head was pounding. He couldn't take a deep breath. A couple of teeth felt loose. And his cheeks burned.

Pulling his knees to his chest and steadying himself with a hand on the ground, Josiah managed to stand. It was an effort in stages. One knee. Then the second knee. A foot. Pushing with his hand and leg, he managed to get the other foot beneath him and straightened up.

He didn't fully understand the reason for the attack, but even with his recently rattled brain, he was able to piece together enough to know that for some reason good 'ol quick-with-his-fists Mickey suspected Josiah had something to do with the fire that was blazing as strongly, if not more so, than when he'd been attacked.

After a couple of test steps, Josiah concluded he could still walk. He continued down the slope toward the fire.

What had once been a row of warehouses was now a wall of flame, its heat and light so intense, it was impossible to look at it directly for any length of time. Nothing could be done to save the buildings.

The docks, too, were gone. The ship in the harbor was listing to starboard. Sailors were scrambling to get off.

The effort now was to save the town. Bucket lines stretched from the river to the houses closest to the fire. In one line Josiah saw a woman and a little girl. The girl was faltering, and the interruption in the line was slowing the delivery of water to a house just as embers were sparking on its roof.

Josiah stepped into the spot. The little girl collapsed at his feet, her arms as limp as a rag doll's.

Soon his own arms were burning from the effort. Every bucket was heavier than the last, and they kept coming. His breathing was labored. And his head felt as though it would burst.

He wondered how the others managed to keep going. They'd been here longer than he. But somehow they found the strength to keep going, and so must he.

He tried not to think about it.

If they stopped, they could lose the entire town. It was that simple. They had to keep passing buckets, so they did.

Weary beyond exhaustion, Josiah surveyed the damage by morning's early light. Charred pillars and beams jutted heavenward, looking like the devil himself was trying to claw his way out of hell.

An acrid smell, so strong he could taste it, mixed with the moist air off the river. Smoke curled and rose from the ruins, as though the town had given up the ghost. In the harbor the bow of the ship jutted out of the water, refusing to surrender to the shallow waters.

For Josiah it seemed that the worst day of his life had risen from its grave to haunt him.

A handful of scavengers picked at the edges of the rubble, the only places cool enough to touch. Now that the town was no longer in danger, most people had gone home to collapse into their beds, which was exactly what Josiah planned to do.

As he approached Summit Street and was wishing there was a way up the hill without having to walk it, he recognized a carriage that had pulled off to the side of the road. Its door was open. A short distance away, four men stood talking, pointing at the ruins.

One of the men was Philip Clapp.

When Josiah approached, they fell silent.

With a quick word to the others, Philip separated himself from the others and intercepted Josiah. "It's worse than seven years ago, wouldn't you agree?" Then, as Philip drew closer, he exclaimed, "You look horrible! What happened to you?"

Josiah touched his cheek and winced. It was swollen. "It appears it's been a bad night for both of us."

Philip glanced at the three men who were huddled together and speaking in hushed tones. "The assessors tell me it's a complete loss."

But Philip didn't appear too shaken by the news, Josiah thought. In fact, Philip looked rested.

"I'm sorry for your loss, Philip."

"Of course, the assessors won't make their final report until after the investigation," Philip added.

Josiah glanced longingly at the carriage. He wondered if Philip would spare it and the driver just long enough to take him home, or at least to get him up the hill.

"They've already started," Philip said. "Taking reports. Interviewing witnesses."

Something in Philip's eyes sent shivers through Josiah's body, a painful thing for a weary man who has scrapes and bruises.

"It seems your name has surfaced," Philip noted casually.

"I was in bed!" Josiah snapped.

Philip smiled.

"You wouldn't do this," Josiah said, trying to convince himself. "I can't believe you'd do this. We've been friends too long."

"Go home and get some sleep, old friend," Philip replied. He turned to leave.

"Philip! Don't do this!"

Philip stopped. He pivoted, approached Josiah, leaned close, and whispered, "I warned you not to go against me."

The climb up Summit Street nearly did Josiah in. By the time he reached his house, he could barely put one foot in front of the other.

A folded white paper awaited him.

With hands so weary they shook, he opened the note.

Stay strong. Please, stay strong!

"Who are you?" Josiah cried.

CHAPTER 44

Saturday was a day of glances: some askance, others direct and hateful. Having snatched a couple of hours of fitful sleep, Josiah had returned to the docks to assist in any way he could. He stayed less than an hour, being more of a distraction than a help.

The seeds Philip had sown had already taken root. Everyone suspected Josiah of starting the fire.

One good thing came from the effort. Josiah learned that there were no deaths in the fire. Some who fought the fire were burned—a painful bit of knowledge Josiah had picked up during an intimate encounter with one victim's friend's fist—but none of the burns were life-threatening, for which he was grateful.

Trudging up Summit Street, he decided to spend the morning in prayer at the church and the afternoon finishing tomorrow's sermon. It was probably the last sermon he would preach in Havenhill, and quite possibly the last sermon he'd preach anywhere. For what other church would call him once they contacted his Havenhill pastorate?

At the corner of High and Church Streets, he heard his name. Turning, he saw Mercy hurrying toward him with Grace a few steps behind. Grace seemed in no hurry to catch him.

Mercy's face expressed sympathetic pain. She reached up and touched his cheekbone.

"Ow!"

"Did you get that from the fire?" she asked.

"It's fire-related."

"You poor dear. It's awful, isn't it? The entire wharf. What are we going to do?"

"We? Apparently you haven't heard."

"We've heard," Grace said, catching up with them.

"Hateful rumors—that's all we've heard, Grace. This is nothing like the previous fire."

Defensive and weary of the battle, Josiah felt an unintended barb in Mercy's protest. What he heard was, Josiah didn't have anything to do with this fire, unlike the last one, which nearly destroyed the town and left it vulnerable for an unscrupulous vulture to enslave the town in debt and pull them all down to ruin.

"Josiah, are you all right?" Mercy asked. "You look tired. Hurt."

A sweet face with a milky complexion and innocent blue eyes gazed up at him with concern. She was right. He was tired, which probably explained why the innocence and faith that stood before him stirred emotions that threatened to spill over.

Other emotions stirred in him as well. Their strength surprised him. Never had Mercy looked more attractive and desirable as she did at this moment. He wanted to . . .

Another female voice interrupted them.

Abigail quickstepped across the common toward them. Behind her, striding with purpose toward the church, was her mother, Eunice.

Stepping between Josiah and Mercy, Abigail grabbed Josiah's arm.

"Ow!" he exclaimed.

Startled, she released it. "Are you hurt?"

Mercy stepped back. "We should go."

Grace said nothing. Her expression—eyes narrowed to slits, her mouth a thin, disgusted line—spoke for her.

Josiah lifted a hand to say something. Mercy didn't see it. Her eyes were downcast. Without another word, she and Grace continued toward the church. Josiah watched her go with longing.

"Your face!" Abigail cried. "Have you been in a fight?"

"What's going on at the church?" Josiah asked.

"Oh, that. The women are organizing food and rolling bandages for fire victims and workers," Abigail explained.

Mercy disappeared into the church.

Josiah turned to Abigail, who was intimately close to him. His pulse quickened. He looked away. She still held sway over him. The passion he'd nurtured for a decade wasn't going to die overnight.

"Josiah?"

"I'm all right," he assured her.

"Why won't you look at me?"

She sounded hurt. Josiah's heart stumbled. Didn't she realize how difficult this was for him?

Taking a deep breath without being obvious about it, Josiah met Abigail's gaze with as much dispassion as he could muster.

"What I told you the other day . . . ," Abigail said, "it's not going to change things between us, is it? We can still be friends. Close friends. Please?"

Her hand was on his arm again. She meant it as a tender gesture, apparently having forgotten his injury.

"I can't imagine losing both Johnny and you." Her voice trembled.

"We may not have much choice in the matter," Josiah said.

"Why? What do you mean?"

"The fire. Or haven't you heard that—"

She dismissed the suggestion with an airy wave of her hand. "We both know you didn't have anything to do with that fire."

"Does your mother share your opinion?"

Abigail gave an exasperated frown. "No. She's convinced you set the fire, just like you did seven . . . no, is it eight years ago?"

"Nearly eight."

"Well, she says the town is getting what it deserves for letting you come back to Havenhill. But that's just Mother."

No, it wasn't just Mother. Abigail may have been able to dismiss her mother's comments as idle chat, but Josiah couldn't. Eunice Parkhurst was and always had been a force in Havenhill. Either as a barometer of town opinion or a molder of town opinion he wasn't certain. Did it matter? Eunice Parkhurst was Havenhill. That much was certain. And Abigail's report of her mother's position confirmed what Josiah suspected.

He was doomed.

"I'd better go," Abigail said. "If I stay out here much longer, the ladies will start to gossip."

Start? When did they ever stop? Josiah wondered. He smiled weakly.

"Friends?" Abigail asked.

Josiah nodded.

Rising up on her toes, Abigail kissed him on the cheek.

It stung.

CHAPTER 45

Josiah didn't sleep the night before his final sermon. He didn't try. There would be plenty of time to sleep in the days ahead. He may not have a roof over his head, or a pillow, but he'd have all the time in the world. The rest of his life. Where, he didn't know. Doing what, he didn't know.

He'd considered returning to Boston. He knew people there. People from his days at Harvard. Dr. McCullough. He could call on some of the people he traveled with on the road from Philadelphia. Surely someone would take pity on a defrocked pastor who had a reputation for burning towns to the ground.

Northampton came to mind. He might go there. It had a peacefulness about it that was attractive to a man about to be thrown to the lions.

Josiah pulled on his heavy coat. An early November wind had howled all night, and the temperature had dropped dramatically.

He went to his writing desk. Two sermons lay side by side. One of them was not his.

Normally he preached two sermons on the Sabbath. A strong intuition warned him that he'd preach only one today, if that. Having written two sermons and being handed a third, he'd prayed and wrestled all night with the decision as to which sermon to preach. He'd narrowed it to two.

He looked down at them.

On the right was his sermon echoing Joshua's challenge: "Choose you this day whom ye will serve."

On the left was Reverend Parkhurst's sermon, the one he hadn't lived long enough to preach. The idea of preaching his mentor's final sermon seemed a bold stroke of genius. In effect, Parkhurst would be preaching to his congregation from beyond the grave.

Now, in the light of morning, it seemed more foolhardy than bold. There were risks. Since his death, Parkhurst had been elevated in people's minds to sainthood. And it wasn't wise to splash in the fountain of a town saint. Then there were Eunice and Abigail to consider.

Josiah stared at the two sermons, as undecided as he was eight hours ago.

The only resolution Josiah had come to in the middle of the night was that he would make the decision before leaving the house. He would take only one sermon with him. If he took both, he would be double-minded up to the time he stepped into the pulpit.

Of all mornings, this morning he had to be single-minded and decisive. Now was the time for clarity.

Two sermons lay before him.

Like an Old Testament priest and the Urim and Thummim, he could take only one.

"God . . . guide my hand," he prayed.

Josiah picked up one set of sermon notes, placed them in his Bible, and walked out the door.

There is a moment just before every worship service when a minister is prepared to assume his function as an intermediary between God and man. When he rises from his knees, having succeeded in setting aside all thoughts that would distract him from leading his people to the throne of God in holy worship.

It is at this moment, someone will confront him to register a complaint.

Today it was Deacon Dunmore blocking the door.

This wasn't the first time Deacon Dunmore had used this time to have a personal meeting with his pastor. It wasn't uncommon for the deacon to lie in wait just outside the door that led to the sanctuary. In a way, it made sense. Dunmore knew he could find the pastor here at this time every Sabbath.

From the set of his jaw and squint of his eyes, Dunmore had worked himself into quite a state. When he spoke, his yellow-stained teeth resembled a dog's mouth when bared in a growl. His breath smelled of onions. "You are the lowest form of life on God's green earth," Dunmore stated.

"Deacon Dunmore, now isn't the time—"

"You would do this to the man who stood up for you?"

Five seconds. Probably a record. In five seconds Dunmore had succeeded in driving every worshipful thought from Josiah's mind and heart.

"How can you . . . he's your friend! Do you know why the town meeting was called off? Philip Clapp personally assured the selectmen that he would see to it that the town would not have to be burdened for the damages done to property as a result of that revival of yours, even if he had to pay for it out of his own pocket!"

"Deacon Dunmore . . . ," Josiah tried to interject.

"And then he made a personal call to every deacon of this church and convinced them not to call a meeting to investigate the charges of infidelity against you!"

"There were no charges, only spec—"

"What kind of . . . is this how you treat your friends? You go after their women and burn down their warehouses?"

Dunmore was teetering on the verge of losing control. His hands were balled into fists. Josiah didn't know what invisible restraints were holding the deacon back; he only prayed they would hold. The last thing he needed this morning was to be pummeled by a deacon moments before the service.

It also angered him that Dunmore would choose this particular time for a confrontation. A hundred retorts came to Josiah's mind—most of them inappropriate for a man of the cloth.

Instead, he said, "In the name of God, step aside, sir. I have a worship service to conduct."

Dunmore growled. "After today you won't be able to hide behind God any longer. And then you'll get what's comin' to you."

He shoved Josiah against the wall to make his exit.

Gripping the arms of the sturdy wooden chair—the one Reverend Parkhurst used to sit in every Sabbath—Josiah pulled himself up to deliver the sermon.

The service had limped along to this point. The singing was forced and uninspired. The prayers were monotonous monologues. The reading of Scripture was tedious. And the pain in Josiah's gut, evil's heartbeat, throbbed steadily.

On normal Sabbath days, a preacher's first task was to gather the attention of the congregation, which by this time had wandered in various directions, like so many sheep. Today that wasn't necessary. The congregation was focused, and Josiah was the focal point.

Angry stares defied him to preach.

Josiah removed the sermon notes from his Bible. While he'd made a decision as to which sermon to preach, he wasn't comfortable with the decision he'd made. In a moment of panic, he considered attempting to reconstruct the other sermon from memory.

No. This was no time to panic. He'd asked God to guide his hand, and now he had to trust that God had answered that prayer. He would preach from the notes in front of him.

He cleared his throat. "The title for today's sermon is 'When the Fire Falls.'"

A murmur rumbled through the room. Several mouths dropped open at the audacity of such a title, considering the week's events. Eunice Parkhurst sat up with a start.

"Our text comes from God's Word as recorded in First Kings, chapter eighteen."

Josiah took a breath. The die was cast. There was no retreating now. God help him.

"A personal note is in order before I begin," he said. "Since this is most assuredly my final sermon from this pulpit . . ."

He glanced down at the row of stern faces on the deacons' bench, Philip's among them. No one was disagreeing with him. Nor was there any audible protest from the congregation.

". . . after much prayer, I have chosen not to deliver a sermon. At least not one that I have written. Instead, I have chosen to relay to you the final sermon of Reverend Nathaniel Parkhurst. The sermon he would have preached, had he not been taken from us so suddenly."

The beehive had been poked and poked hard. The congregation buzzed loudly. Josiah heard bits of sentences, including words like "bad taste" and "insolent" and "of all the nerve."

Eunice Parkhurst fumbled with the pages of her Bible. She found what she was looking for—the original of her husband's sermon. However, it didn't take but an instant to piece together what had happened. Her face crimson, she spat words at Abigail beside her. Abigail held up her hands, palm side up, defending herself. Eunice wasn't listening. She stormed out of the pew. Abigail stood helplessly. Casting a glance of betrayal at Josiah, she ran after her mother.

For several moments Josiah didn't know if he'd be given a chance to continue. First, because of the uproar, but also because no sooner had Eunice stepped out the front door than the jailer and his assistant stepped in. Neither of them were church attenders. And the way the jailer took up a position against the back wall, with folded arms and an intense stare, Josiah knew that his after-service plans had been made for him.

He wasn't sure what kept them from taking him now, or what kept the congregation in their pews. Maybe it was tradition. They'd never left church before without first hearing a sermon. Or maybe he'd piqued their interest, and they wanted to hear a dead man's unpreached sermon. Or maybe the Holy Spirit had His hand on their shoulders and wouldn't let them get up until Josiah had his say. Whatever the reason, the murmuring subsided to the point that Josiah could speak.

"In Reverend Parkhurst's words," he announced, "and I quote: 'For some time now, a disturbing spirit has overtaken my soul. At first, I thought it was indigestion from Eunice's cooking. You all know what a fine cook she is, and how I tend to eat more than I should.'"

Josiah glanced up. The congregation had stilled. Recognizing the voice of their former pastor, they listened, eager to hear what he had to say to them.

"'However, as my discomfort stretched over a period of months, I came to realize that the pain was much deeper than my stomach. Dear friends, I have a pain in my soul. And I am greatly troubled. I am troubled that as your pastor, I have lost my effectiveness.'"

"No!" someone shouted from the pews. "That's not true!"

Josiah continued. "'For I have watched with sadness as you have wandered away from your first love, and though I have called repeatedly from this pulpit for you to return, you no longer heed the voice of your shepherd.'"

"Don't listen to him!" Deacon Dunmore shouted. He was on his feet, pointing an accusatory finger at Josiah. "Have you forgotten? This is the man who killed Pastor Parkhurst!"

Josiah thought the sermon would end right then. To his amazement, the congregation shushed Dunmore and told him to sit down.

Reverend Parkhurst's intermediary continued.

"'Our hearts have grown cold to the gospel. That which once stirred us to action now merely tickles our fancy. We have grown at ease in Zion. I tell you with tears, there is a coldness here that resembles death. We need fire from the Lord, and we need it now!'"

At the mention of fire, the congregation erupted with shouts and swoons at the remembrance that their beloved pastor had perished in flames.

Josiah shouted them down.

Grabbing the sermon notes in his fist, he raised them over his head. "Listen to this! Listen! Reverend Parkhurst's greatest fear was that you'd stopped listening to him! Listen to him now!"

Dunmore was once again on his feet. "Lies! Lies! Nothing but deceit and lies!"

Josiah shouted back: "How many years was Reverend Parkhurst pastor of this church? Thirty?"

"Thirty-two," someone said.

"Thirty-two years," Josiah repeated. "Certainly you recognize his voice. When I first read the sermon, I heard my pastor preaching to me as plainly as I did when he stood behind this pulpit. These are his words! You know that!"

The objections died out. The people took their seats.

Josiah risked a glance at Philip. He appeared amused by the proceedings.

With nothing left to lose, Josiah pressed on.

At this point in the sermon, Parkhurst addressed the text. He described how the Israelites had turned from God, allowing themselves to be seduced by the ways of the wicked king Ahab and his queen, Jezebel, and how Jezebel had been killing off the prophets of God, and how Elijah retaliated by shutting up the heavens so it didn't rain.

He described the incident in which Elijah presented himself to Ahab and how the king greeted the prophet by saying, "Art thou he hat troubleth Israel?"

Then Parkhurst described how Elijah called for a showdown, in which he would stand against the 450 prophets of the pagan god Baal in a contest of deities upon the summit of Mount Carmel. The rules of the challenge were laid down. Two altars would be built—one to Baal and one to God. No fire would be used to ignite the offering. In turn, the prophets would call to their respective gods, and the deity who supplied fire for the offering would once and for all prove himself to be Israel's God.

The day for the contest arrived. And from morning to evening the 450 prophets of Baal danced and cried out and cut themselves, calling to their god. Only no one answered. No one paid attention.

Then Elijah prepared an altar to God. He placed an offering on it and ordered a trench dug around it. He commanded that four large jars of water be poured atop the offering, then insisted it be done a second time . . . and a third time, so the altar was drowned in water.

Elijah prayed, and fire fell. The sacrifice was consumed, and the water in the trench was licked up. All the people fell prostrate and cried, "The LORD, he is the God! The LORD, he is the God!"

Josiah read Parkhurst's conclusions. "'From this dramatic account, several things have become clear to me. First, like the people of Israel, we have followed after other gods and allowed a distant king and his prophets of wealth to seduce us from the things of God. Second, I have noticed that when we do call out to God, we more resemble the prophets of Baal than the prophet of God. We stir up the dust with activity and then congratulate ourselves on the show. But where is the fire? Where is the fire?

"'What will it take for the fire to fall? We need a troubler. Someone who will make us uncomfortable. Someone who will scoff at our pretense when we claim to be God's people but don't live like it. We need a John the Baptist. Someone who is not afraid to look at our smug righteousness and say, "O generation of vipers!" We need a prophet with the Spirit of Jesus. Someone who is not afraid to liken us to whitewashed tombs, pleasant to look at on the outside, but a rotting stench on the inside! We need a troubler. We need an Elijah. Someone willing to call us out and challenge us to our face: "How long will you go limping after other gods? How long will you serve the gods of mercantile wealth? How long will you worship the gods of ease and comfort? If the Lord be God, then follow him! But if Baal be god, then follow him all the way to hell!"

"'Have I stated the argument too strongly? Have I offended you? I fear I have not offended you enough. I fear that my greatest sin as your pastor is that I have at times cared more what you think of me than what

God thinks of me. God in heaven, send us a troubler!

"'Not only do we need a troubler, we need dousers. Why did Elijah order the altar to be drenched? So that no one could accuse him of starting the fire. So that when the fire fell, there would be no doubt who sent it. Look at the record. Was there any doubt? No! When the fire fell, they all fell prostrate, their faces to the ground in awe and fear, shouting, "The LORD, he is the God! The LORD, he is the God!"

"'This is my prayer for Havenhill. I pray that God's holy fire will fall upon this town. And while I wish I were the prophet for this time, I know I am not. I am not a troubler. I am your father, quick to forgive. I am not a douser. I am your friend. And so, as I preach this, my final sermon as your pastor—'"

The congregation gasped collectively, caught completely off guard that Reverend Parkhurst had intended to resign.

"'I pray that God will send you a troubler. That God will raise up dousers. And that God, blessed be His name, in His time will send the fire of truth, the fire of cleansing, the fire of righteousness; so that all that does not matter will be stripped away and we will see the Lamb, pure and spotless, and lifted up. And when the fires falls, we will all cry out with one voice, "The Lord, he is the God! The Lord, he is the God!"'"

Having reached the end of Parkhurst's notes, Josiah looked up. "And now, from me. After reading Reverend Parkhurst's sermon, I knew he would want you to hear it. And I feel privileged to be able to make that happen. While you may not believe this because of all that has happened, I miss him as much as you do. He was my pastor.

"And having followed him in this pulpit, I share his desire for you, so it seems fitting that his last sermon would also be my last sermon. I know how he felt. I feel I, too, have failed you. To use a different analogy, I fear there were times I was so busy playing doctor—analyzing your symptoms and seeking a cure—that I forgot my primary duty. And that is to take you by the hand and lead you to the Great Physician. Only He can heal you. Only He can send the fire. And He will do it in His good time.

"I likened myself to the ancient Olympic torch runner, renowned for bringing the fire that would start the games. I wanted to be that runner, to be the man who brought the fires of revival to Havenhill. I forgot that God alone determines where His Spirit will blow and when. Having been reminded of that, I will continue to pray for revival, confident that when it comes, it will be evident to all that God, and God alone, sent it."

With that, Josiah stepped down from behind the pulpit and was arrested, accused of setting the fire that destroyed Havenhill's wharf.

CHAPTER 46

Josiah slept better in jail than he had the last two nights in his own bed. Relief figured into it. He'd run his course, and there was nothing left for him to do—nothing he was allowed to do—but wait.

There was a familiar feel to the cell. This was the same cell George Mason had been in. They still hadn't changed the straw on the floor. At first the interminable smell made Josiah nauseous. Now he barely noticed it.

Mercy noticed it immediately. It knocked her back a step when she appeared.

"Sorry," Josiah said. "Had I known you were coming, I would have tidied up."

"Is he sayin' we stink?" one of Josiah's cellmates cried. Jimmy the Giant was probably five feet tall on his toes. He and four others had been thrown in jail for brawling. They complained when they learned that Josiah was a preacher. Jimmy argued that being locked up with a fire-starting preacher was injurious to their reputations. Their complaints fell on deaf ears.

The jailer unlocked the cell and let Mercy in. He stood in the open doorway. "Rules. Can't leave a lady unattended."

"He's afraid she'll violate us!" Jimmy laughed.

Mercy seemed to be holding her own, given the circumstances. "I brought you a sandwich."

There was nothing in her hands.

"Confiscated it," the jailer announced. "Have to make sure she didn't hide nothin' in it."

Which meant that Josiah would never see the sandwich. And he was hungry too.

He led Mercy a couple of steps to one side. "This is as much privacy as I can offer you."

Mercy looked around. Everyone was staring at them and listening.

Mercy lifted an eyebrow. "Maybe next time you're arrested, you can request a better jail."

"Hey!" the jailer complained. "There ain't nothin' wrong with this here jail."

"Thank you for coming," Josiah whispered to Mercy. "I'm surprised Grace isn't with you."

Mercy gave him one of those I-thought-you-were-smarter-than-that looks.

"Yeah, I guess it would be asking too much."

"Has anyone else been here to see you?"

Reading between the lines, Josiah inserted *Abigail* for *anyone*.

"No, you're the only one."

"Nobody's come to see us either," Jimmy quipped.

They fell silent for a time. Mercy picked at her fingernails. Their audience didn't seem to mind the lull in the action. At least they didn't complain. But then, it wasn't like they were in a hurry to go any place.

Mercy whispered in Josiah's ear, "How are you doing? Are you holding up?"

Josiah nodded. "Actually, it's been rather peaceful."

"Everyone's talking about the sermon."

"Are they? Good talk?"

"Mixed. It shocked a lot of people."

"Eunice?"

"I haven't heard anything."

Leaning this close to her, Josiah could smell her fragrance and feel the warmth of her cheek. The sensations staggered him with unexpected strength.

"What are they saying about the fire?" Josiah asked.

"Everyone is convinced you did it."

"I know I am," Jimmy said. "He did it. No doubt in my mind."

To the man, his buddies agreed.

"I think he did it too," added the jailer.

Josiah sighed. "And you?"

Mercy stepped back. "Josiah Rush! How can you ask such a question?"

"She thinks he did it too," Jimmy concluded.

Mercy frowned, offended.

Josiah regretted asking. "I'm sorry. It's just that . . . no, no excuse. I shouldn't have asked it."

"No, you shouldn't have," Mercy said

But apparently she forgave him, for she stepped close again.

"I really am sorry," he began.

"Shhh." Mercy put a finger on his lips, which agitated the audience. Blushing, she put her hand behind her back.

The audience wasn't nearly as excited as Josiah. He knew he would relive that moment a hundred times tonight.

"I should go," Mercy claimed.

"Aya." But Josiah didn't mean it.

She turned slowly to leave.

"One thing more," he said.

"Yes?"

"Philip."

Mercy nodded. "The town is turning to him."

"Just like they did eight years ago."

"He says he's secured backing to rebuild the wharf at no cost to the town."

"Lord Bellamont."

"Philip is being quite open about it. Lord Bellamont will rebuild the wharf at no cost to the town in exchange for port privileges."

"Slaves. Do people know that means importing and selling slaves?"

Mercy pursed her lips. What she was about to say was difficult for her. "No one has voiced any objections. They don't seem to mind."

Josiah hung his head. "Philip said he'd win them over to his side."

Mercy raised a hand tenderly to Josiah's cheek.

The audience let out a collective "Oooooooo!"

She hesitated, but her hand remained. "You did everything you could."

"Sometimes that's not enough."

"Don't give up hope."

Josiah offered a weak smile, which vanished the instant he saw Mercy's eyes. There was enough hope in them for two people, and she seemed more than eager to share with him.

Time slowed as their gazes intermingled, as soul touched soul. It was an intimacy as deep as it was exhilarating. Josiah was drawn toward her and she to him.

He felt her breath on his lips. Then their warmth. Less than an impulse separated them.

"Ah, ah, ah, ah!" a voice broke in.

Mercy was yanked away.

The jailer had her by the arm. "Against the rules."

The audience let out a disappointed moan. "Tell you what," Jimmy the Giant offered. "After she leaves, I'll kiss you!"

CHAPTER 47

Josiah was released from jail the next day.

"Not enough evidence to bring charges." The jailer sneered. "Them eyewitnesses? Now they say they saw a man what looks like you, but can't say it was you for sure. Me? I think someone bought 'em off."

Brushing the straw from his clothes, Josiah started to leave. He didn't know what game Philip was playing by letting him go. But all Josiah wanted was to get home, change clothes, and make something to eat.

"Oh, yeah," the jailer added. "I'm supposed to give you this."

He handed Josiah a slip of paper.

Called Church Meeting
Tuesday, Three o'clock
Subject:
To Consider Termination of Pastor Josiah Rush

An hour from now.

The jailer said, "The guy what told me to give you that said you're supposed to be there."

Philip wasn't wasting any time.

Josiah had just enough time to go home and change clothes. No time to eat.

He stepped outside into a windy, cold, overcast day.

FIRE

The scene that awaited Josiah when he approached his house was reminiscent of the day of his arrival. All the doors and windows were torn out and tossed aside. All of his belongings were scattered on the ground.

As he approached, a loose sheet of paper, looking as though it were trying to escape, hit his shoe just as he was taking a step. Peering down at it, he recognized his handwriting. It was a page from a sermon, the one he hadn't chosen to preach, the one that drew the line and challenged people to determine whose side they were on.

A numbness settled over him. A resolution to his fate. He supposed he should be surprised at seeing his house like this. He wasn't.

"At least it saves me from having to pack," he mumbled.

Grabbing something to eat was out of the question. So was changing clothes. His best shirt was doing somersaults in the tall grass. With nothing else to do, he decided to go inside and see if there was anything worth salvaging.

Next to the opening where the front door used to be, he noticed a piece of paper wedged in a familiar place. He reached for it but doubted there were words sufficient to lift his spirits right now.

"What's that?" A man appeared suddenly from inside the house, startling Josiah. He snatched the note from Josiah's hand.

A second man appeared.

Josiah had never seen either of them before. They had a rough look about them. Both were bearded. In their eyes was a dull sheen—the kind that often accompanied those who were well acquainted with the wicked nature of the world. They were both taller and heavier than Josiah; and they both had club handles protruding from the waistband of their pants.

The man in front—brown, scrawny hair, as opposed to the second man, whose black hair resembled algae covering a rock—unfolded the note, read it, showed it to his friend, shared a laugh, then crumpled the note and tossed it over his shoulder.

"Who are you men?" Josiah asked.

"We're your bodyguards," the man in front said.

"Bodyguards?"

"We're here to see that you make it to the meeting without getting lost along the way."

Philip had thought of everything.

The two men stepped out of the house.

"Shall we?" The lead man motioned to the road.

With nothing to stay for, Josiah started walking down the road toward the church.

The sky was dark and threatening. An angry wind whipped his clothing.

Best get on with it, Josiah thought.

He'd hesitated at the bottom step that led to the front door of the church. He'd arrived early. They'd encountered no one along the way. It appeared everyone was already there.

"Go on!" his escort cried. "It's cold out here!"

Josiah mounted the steps and swung open the door. Immediately the collective spirit of the congregation assaulted him, knocking him back a step. Thick. Black. Oppressive. Suffocating. It reached into his gut and gripped him with unbearable strength. It was all Josiah could do to step across the threshold and willingly surrender himself to such a sick feeling.

Every head in every pew swiveled toward him. What had been a room of restless activity became as still and quiet as a bedside deathwatch.

Deacon Dunmore stood behind the pulpit. Philip stood beside him.

Josiah was suddenly the center of a frozen universe. But what unnerved him most was the way the church members stared at him. He'd seen these expressions before. They were the ones people wore when they witnessed an execution.

"I won't say no more," Dunmore said, though he clearly wanted to say more. "But I will say this, and I don't care if he hears me. The parts Deacon Clapp read to us from his journal turned my stomach. Turned my stomach. To think that he was sitting there in saintly Deacon Cranch's place and writing those things about us, the very people he'd been called to serve . . . well, it turned my stomach. That's all I can say. It turned my stomach!"

After aiming one last shot of disgust at Josiah, Deacon Dunmore vacated the pulpit. Philip thanked him, commenting that he knew it was difficult for Deacon Dunmore to say such things about his minister.

As he spoke, Philip was holding Josiah's journal in his hand. He addressed Josiah directly. "You're early."

Josiah felt a shove in the back as his two escorts pushed their way inside and closed the door behind them.

"My schedule freed up suddenly," Josiah said.

"No matter," Philip replied. "I believe we're ready to proceed."

So it appeared. The church was full. Church members Josiah hadn't seen since he'd arrived were there. All the regulars were in their pews. Eunice Parkhurst sat straight-backed, staring straight forward, refusing to look at him. Abigail peeked around her mother.

Seated in the Parkhurst pew with them was Judith Usher—the woman whose daughters were killed in the original fire—and her son, Edward. Judith clutched a rag doll, holding it tightly to her chest, as she had at the revival.

The deacons were perched on the front pew like vultures on a fence, shoulder to shoulder, stiff as wax. Grim-faced all, they were an immovable force.

To the absence of human sound, Josiah made his way to the front of the church.

He passed the sisters' pew. Grace looked up at him with compassion. She hadn't always liked him, Josiah knew, but it was clear she wished him no ill will. Beside her, Mercy was trying to put on a brave face, but it was obvious she was teetering on the brink of tears.

The wind howled. Tree branches slapped and scraped the

windowpanes. While it was only midafternoon, outside it was dark as night.

Josiah stepped to the platform. Philip met his gaze, unafraid. It was as though Josiah were looking into the face of a stranger. He motioned for Josiah to sit in the pastor's chair.

Doing as instructed, Josiah sat. His skin felt clammy beneath his clothes. He took a breath to steady himself.

So it had come to this.

Returning to Havenhill had been a risk. Josiah had known that when he came. What he didn't know at the time were the stakes. They were much higher than he'd ever imagined. He'd waltzed into town thinking it was all about him. At the time, his primary goal was to get the townspeople to accept him. To like him. How could he have been so self-absorbed?

Look what his shortsightedness had cost them. Johnny Mott was dead. His best friend, Philip, was now his greatest adversary. And the town was on the verge of selling its soul to a corrupt English merchant who would turn a profit by auctioning off human beings as slaves.

Had Josiah known these things that day he stood on Fiedler's Knob, he would have . . . At this point he didn't know what he would have done. His head hurt just thinking about it.

The door opened. A half-dozen dockworkers sauntered in and joined the two who had escorted Josiah to the church. Crossing their arms, they leaned against the back wall, making no effort to conceal the wooden clubs tucked into their waistbands.

It didn't take much to figure out why they were there. Once the meeting was over, Josiah would need an escort out of town. And from the looks of them, the end of the journey would undoubtedly be punctuated with a few personal good-byes—just in case Josiah had any ideas of getting in the way of Philip or Bellamont again.

From the back the dockworkers smirked at Josiah. It was their way of letting him know they were going to enjoy earning their money.

Under ordinary circumstances, the anticipation of a beating would have unnerved Josiah. But at present he was too tired to be scared. He was tired of going head-to-head with Eunice Parkhurst. He was tired of battling his best friend. He was tired of preaching to a people who already knew how they should be living, but who daily chose to ignore what they knew to be right. He was tired of being a target for their bitterness.

In a way, he was glad it would soon be over. He glanced at the dock-workers with their muscled arms. He would mend. He would go to Boston or Northampton, get a job, and build a new life for himself among people who had never heard of the Havenhill fire.

Someone in the back of the room cleared his throat loudly. The room stirred. They seemed as anxious to get on with it as he was.

Philip Clapp officially called the meeting to order.

The room hushed.

Josiah whispered, "Lord, into your hands . . ."

"We all know why we're here," Philip said, "so let's have done with it."

Having set Josiah's journal aside, Philip wielded a rolled-up piece of paper like a club. With it, he tapped an open palm.

"This being a distasteful business," Philip continued, "I see no profit in further discussion." He eyed Deacon Dunmore.

A prearranged signal, Josiah thought.

Dunmore stood. "I call the question," he said, then sat back down.

Philip obviously wasn't going to give Josiah a chance to speak. What did it matter? Nothing he said now would make a difference.

"The question has been called for," Philip announced. "Pastor, will you please stand?"

The use of Josiah's title sounded blasphemous coming from Philip.

Josiah stood.

"As you have already been instructed, we are not a court of law. While Reverend Rush's involvement in the recent fire has not been proved, your deacons have found his actions and his personal life suspect and have, after careful review and prayer, recommended that the church remove him from office. Furthermore, as a gesture to the town, we recommend that Reverend Rush be expelled from Havenhill."

Josiah glanced out at the congregation. They'd been busy before he arrived.

"A Yea vote is a vote for dismissal from his pastoral duties and banishment from the town. A Nay vote clears Reverend Josiah Rush of all suspicions and reinstates him as the pastor of this church."

They were itching to vote. Josiah could see it in their eyes. They couldn't voice their condemnation soon enough.

Mercy's head was buried against Grace's shoulder. Her lips were moving in prayer.

Lord, bless her . . .

Abigail dabbed her eyes with a lace handkerchief. Beside her, Judith Usher rocked back and forth.

"All those in favor of dismissing Reverend Josiah Rush from his ministerial duties and banishing him from the town, say Aye."

"AYE!" The room reverberated with the sound.

"Those opposed?"

"Nay," Mercy said softly.

Philip turned to Josiah, looking very much the victor. "The motion passes."

Both men knew the vote had just been a formality. Philip had won when the town did not object to turning Havenhill into a slave port.

Josiah studied his former congregation with sadness. They'd been blinded by Soul Sickness. Their lives, this vote, all were affected by it.

He knew that, right now, they probably felt good about what they'd just done. But what they were feeling was relief that it was over, not happiness. It was difficult for sick people to be happy. In a day or two, they would again know the pain and hurt of the sickness, and they would wonder why no matter what they did, they were never content.

Lord, forgive them. Open their eyes, he prayed.

In the back of the room the dockworkers brandished their clubs in preparation of discharging their duty.

From the pulpit, Philip said, "In anticipation of the verdict, I have arranged for Reverend Rush to be escorted out of town. Our business is concluded. I declare this meeting—"

"Wait!"

The cry came so unexpectedly it took a minute to discern who voiced the objection. Not until she stood did most of the room identify the source.

Judith Usher fumbled with the latch on the Parkhurst pew. She seemed most insistent to get out.

Philip said, "Judith, if you have something to say, you can say it from there."

She wasn't listening. Having figured out how to open the pew door, she made her way to the platform. Her eyes were downcast. Propelled by determined steps, she clutched the rag doll tightly to her bosom.

Lit by the interior lights, the tree branches outside the windows grew agitated. With soft fists, wind buffeted the glass.

Philip stopped Judith at the bottom of the platform steps. She brushed past him and went straight for Josiah. She stood in front of him, her head bowed. All Josiah could see was the top of her white mobcap and a few wispy curls on her neck.

At first she didn't speak. She clutched and reclutched the rag doll.

Someone said none too quietly, "She wants her pound of flesh for her girls."

"Two dead daughters gives her the right."

Josiah spoke softly to her. "Judith?"

She didn't respond. He spoke her name again, and she raised her head. Teary eyes met his. Josiah's heart went out to her. He ached for her, knowing that this whole evening was making her relive the painful memories of—

In a mousy voice, she said to him, "Stay strong."

"You!"

That's when he felt it. Or, rather, didn't feel it. She seemed to be radiating healing and goodwill. Standing this close to her erased the pain in his gut.

"It's gone," she said with a smile.

Josiah nodded. "Yes, I feel it. It's gone."

She shook her head, signaling he hadn't heard her correctly. "It's gone!" she said again.

"I . . . I'm not sure I understand."

She lifted the doll. "It's gone. The odor of smoke. It's gone."

Josiah shook his head. "I still don't understand."

She began to weep and laugh. Lifting the doll to his face, she invited him to sniff it. "The smoke. You can't smell it anymore. It's been there since the fire. It was there just a little while ago. But it's not there now, it's gone!"

Josiah obliged her. He inhaled. The doll smelled of cloth. He could smell no smoke.

Judith laughed. "God took the smoke away!"

The wind outside grew insistent. It beat hard now against the windows, as though it were testing them, seeking a way to break into the room.

Out of the corner of his eye, Josiah saw Philip motion to Eunice Parkhurst to come get Judith. Coming to the front, she took Judith by the shoulders.

"Come with me, dear," Eunice commanded.

But Judith refused to move. To Josiah, she said, "Can you ever forgive us?"

A wave of emotion surged through Josiah. Of all the things she could have said to him, these were the last words he expected. At this time. At this place. They were so alien to this setting, his mind refused to believe he'd heard her correctly.

He'd killed this woman's daughters!

Eunice gripped Judith's shoulders more tightly. "Come, dear. Come back to the pew."

But Judith was rooted to the spot. "We've hurt you so badly . . ."

"You're distraught, dear," Eunice soothed. To Josiah: "She's distraught. She doesn't know what she's saying."

Judith turned to Eunice. "We were wrong, Eunice. God forgive us. We were wrong. All this time, we've been wrong."

"I shouldn't have let you come tonight. Let's go home, dear."

This time Judith allowed Eunice to turn her toward the pew. But that's as far as she would go. Facing the congregation now, she held the rag doll over her head and shouted, "The smell of smoke is gone! God took it away!"

Her outburst was met with pained expressions of sympathy and concern. It was obvious to them that she was distraught and, perhaps, had gone mad.

Judith persisted, "Don't you see? It's an answer to prayer. God took the smoke away."

Philip walked over to her. He placed a hand on her shoulder. "Judith, I think it would be best if you—"

"No!" She recoiled from his touch, as though it had burned her. "This is Mary's doll!" She wept openly. "It was with them in the fire. And because . . . because I can no longer hug my little girls, every day I would hug their rag doll and smell the smoke. It would remind me that I would never again hear their voices in their room or watch them play or see them grow up to be women. Lately, I've been missing them something horrible. I wanted them to be near me. When I hold their doll, I feel close to them. Just now, sitting down there, I was thinking of them and smelling the smoke in the doll, and then . . . it was gone. Just like that! The smoke is gone!"

The room was still.

The wind shook the doors, but no one seemed to notice.

Wiping her eyes with the back of her hand, Judith cried, "Because I was praying . . . I wanted to know that my girls were with God, that they were happy . . . and they are! I know they are, because God took the smoke away!"

Before anyone could stop her, Judith descended the platform steps and shoved the doll in the faces of each of the deacons. "Smell it!" she insisted. "Smell it! Smell it!"

They sat motionless, like statues. None of them sniffed the doll. They only stared at her with stony eyes.

Philip had had enough. He moved to intercept her.

But Judith saw him coming. She shoved the doll in his face, surprising him. "Smell it! Smell it!"

Philip made no attempt to oblige her. "Calm yourself, Judith."

She swung the doll toward Eunice Parkhurst. "Eunice, you believe me, don't you? I'm not mad. You know how it smelled of smoke. Tell them."

Eunice placed a gentle hand on the doll and lowered it. She gazed intently at Judith with that look of authority she had honed over the years. "Come, dear, I'll take you home."

The hand holding the doll dropped limply to Judith's side. Her shoulders slumped. Joy drained from her face.

Eunice placed a comforting but firm arm around Judith's shoulders and guided her back to the Parkhurst pew.

The congregation stirred uneasily. Their expressions revealed a mixture of pity for the distraught woman and a fresh dash of anger for the man who was responsible for her pain.

The wind beat angrily against the windowpanes.

Josiah thought he should say something. Apparently Philip anticipated he might and shot him a warning glance. Josiah held his tongue. Philip was right. Anything he said now would only appear to be self-serving and would only hurt Judith more.

If only he could talk to her privately. To thank her for the notes.

He watched as Eunice led her away. The good feeling he'd felt went with her, absorbed by the dark spirit of the congregation. Oh, how he wished he could speak to her. But six dockworkers would see to it that he spoke to no one following the meeting. He'd probably never see Judith Usher again.

The two women had reached the Parkhurst pew. Abigail stood to let them in.

"I'll smell the doll!" It was Mercy's voice. She had stepped into the aisle.

Judith turned to Mercy with questioning eyes.

"I believe you, Judith. I'd like to smell the doll."

Judith brightened considerably. She handed the doll to Mercy, right in front of Eunice Parkhurst's disapproving scowl.

Mercy pressed the doll to her nose. Once. Twice.

She looked up. "I smell no odor of smoke."

The room buzzed.

The wind rattled the church doors.

Eunice was incensed. "Mercy Litchfield, you're not helping! Judith is not herself. We need to get her home."

From the pew, Abigail said, "Judith, tell them about Stephen's mother."

"Abigail! What has gotten into you?" Eunice replied angrily.

"Tell them!" Abigail insisted.

"She'll do nothing of the kind," Eunice barked. "We've heard quite enough already. We've done what we've come to do. Now we're going home." She grabbed Judith's arm and proceeded toward the door.

At the front of the church, Philip said in a loud voice, "Eunice is right. This meeting is over. We are officially adjourned." With a flick of his fingers, he motioned for the dockworkers to perform their duty.

There was a moment's hesitation. Then people began gathering coats and scarves and bags and children, telling them to bundle up because it was windy out tonight.

Mercy and Abigail exchanged frantic glances. At the end of the aisle, Eunice and Judith were jostled discourteously by the dockworkers, who shoved past them to get to Josiah.

Then Mercy Litchfield did something she hadn't done since she was eight years old, when she'd received a spanking for it. But now she again stood up on the pew.

Grinning, Abigail stood on her pew, too, and shouted over the din. "The doll isn't the only revelation God has granted to Judith Usher!"

At the sight of two women standing on the pews and the sound of Abigail's voice, everyone stopped what they were doing, except for the dockworkers who had reached Josiah. They surrounded him on all sides. With clubs in hand, two of them grabbed Josiah by the arms.

Eunice was mortified. "Abigail Parkhurst, I don't know what's gotten into you. Step down from that pew this instant!" The way her eyes darted side to side, she was very much aware that everyone was watching them.

"Go home, folks," Philip ordered. "There's nothing more happening here tonight."

The people weren't convinced. For most of them, nothing at home promised to be more entertaining than what was going on inside the church meetinghouse.

"Tell them what you told me!" Abigail urged Judith.

Everyone's attention was focused on Judith Usher, who clutched the doll to her chest.

"When Reverend Rush first came—" Judith began.

"Louder!" someone shouted. "We can't hear you."

Judith Usher fidgeted and began again. "When Reverend Rush first came here, he preached about the apostle Paul at Jerusalem. Do you remember that sermon?"

Nods indicated that people remembered the sermon.

"And he told us how before that time Paul—I mean Saul, he was still Saul at that time, wasn't he?—how Saul was responsible for Stephen's death."

Fresh tears came to Judith Usher's eyes. Her voice was so choked with emotion that her words came with great difficulty.

"And do you remember he wondered what the apostle Paul said to Stephen's mother when he saw her at the church in Jerusalem, since he had, after all, been responsible for killing her son."

Judith walked up the aisle. Eunice Parkhurst made no attempt to stop her.

"Well, it got me thinking about Stephen's mother. What it must have been like for her to see this man—the man who killed her boy—come up to her and say that he was changed . . . because I know how she feels. To have the man who killed my girls"—Judith Usher wept openly now—"and I wondered what this woman, Stephen's mother, said to the apostle Paul when she saw that he was a changed man . . . a good man . . . a man God could use."

Within the four walls of the meetinghouse, everything was still, everyone silent. Outside the wind grew to fevered pitch.

Judith had reached Josiah. She clutched and reclutched the doll. "He took the smoke away," she whispered to him. "Pastor, can you ever forgive me?"

Josiah smiled.

"You're a good man, aren't you?" she said. "A godly man. You've proven that. It doesn't matter what you were. I've seen what you are. I see traits of God in you. And now I think I know what Stephen's mother said to the apostle."

The room hushed.

Judith placed her hand on Josiah's chest. "She said, 'Stay strong. And go with God.'"

Before Josiah could answer, the door to the church flew open with a rush of wind and a thunderous crack. The sudden change of atmosphere in the room took everyone's breath away. They stood wide-eyed, with gaping mouths. Some were frightened; some confused. But all were amazed.

Judith was the first to feel the Spirit. She gasped. Her hands flew to her chest. The doll she was holding fell silently to the floor. Her eyes focused on something distant, as though she could see something that was hidden to everyone else.

She sank to her knees, her face contorted with both fear and wonder. She raised an unsteady hand toward whatever it was she saw that so captivated her.

"I see the Lord," she called, "seated on high!"

The walls of the meeting house shuddered, the joints creaked.

Judith tried to speak again, but the wind swept the words from her lips as though what she saw, what she was about to describe, was too fearful for human ears.

She tried again. Her words found a voice. She repeated them over and over with great lamentation: "Our sin . . . our sin . . . our sin . . ."

Then a terrible heaviness entered the room, a great invisible weight that pressed down upon them. People dropped to their knees, clutching their chests as though they would suffocate. In the aisle Eunice was on her knees, her face lifted heavenward in fear. Her mouth moved, but she was unable to speak. Abigail held her chest with one hand; with the other she clung to the pew. Without exception, the deacons slid from the pews onto their knees. On the platform, Philip was down on his hands and knees. His face was a portrait of surprise and terror.

Beside him Josiah heard the clubs fall to the floor. Soon afterward the terrified dockworkers dropped to their knees on the wooden platform. No one was left standing. No one, except Josiah.

A chorus of moans filled the room as the people cried out to God.

"Oh Jesus, sweet Jesus . . . I've sinned . . . I've sinned!"

"What a wretch I am. How could I have acted this way? And in front of my children! Oh dear God, I hit my wife in front of my children!"

"The stain runs deep, Lord, deep . . ."

"I stole it. And blamed William. How can I ever face him again?"

"I'm slipping, Lord Jesus, slipping . . ."

"God, rip these lustful thoughts from my mind. I can bear them no more."

"I was so careful in covering my tracks, I thought no one knew. But You know, Lord, You know."

"My anger—that beast within me—I can't control it, Lord."

"For years I've coveted his land."

"Black, black, dear God, my soul is black."

Abigail was slumped in the corner of the family pew. She wept softly. Eunice went to her. Judith Usher joined them. The three women embraced one another and wept bitterly.

Everywhere Josiah looked, he saw humbled, contrite lives. He felt their anguish as though it were his own. It grew to such intensity, he felt his chest would burst under the pressure. Then, just when he thought he'd surely die, it eased, and a new wind came.

A refreshing wind.

And with it came forgiveness.

Joy.

Laughter and hilarity.

At last revival had come to Havenhill.

CHAPTER 48

People huddled in groups everywhere. Couples. Families. Friends. The interior of the church was a field of clustered heads as the roar of the wind left sobs and laughter in its wake.

On the platform Philip slumped against the side of the pulpit with a tearful Anne on the floor next to him, her arms around his neck. Her eyes sparkled with tears. He whispered something to her. She laughed and kissed him tenderly on the cheek.

"Pastor, may we speak with you?"

Someone called him "Pastor." The voice was familiar, but he had never heard—nor did he ever imagine he'd hear—that word coming from this person's lips.

He turned to see Eunice Parkhurst.

She was flanked by Abigail and Judith. The faces of all three women were a mess of tears. They looked beautiful.

Eunice stepped forward.

She knelt at his feet.

"No! No . . . no . . . no . . . ," Josiah cried.

But she wouldn't stand. So he knelt with her.

She placed her arms on his shoulders. Her forehead against his forehead. "I'm so ashamed. I've acted so foolishly. You must hate me."

"That's all behind us now," Josiah said.

"Forgive me? I know I could never make it up to you. But I would like the chance. Will you stay? And let me learn from you?"

Josiah wanted to pull away. His eyes needed convincing that this was the woman he thought it was. Was this really *Eunice Parkhurst*?

She pulled back.

Still his eyes blinked, unable to comprehend what they were seeing.

"Pastor," she continued, "I know someone in our church who needs a visit—me. Will you come by the house?"

"It would be my pleasure."

With difficulty, Eunice tried to stand. Josiah jumped to his feet to assist her.

As soon as Eunice was up, Abigail threw her arms around Josiah's neck. She whispered into his ear. "I was furious with you for using Papa's sermon. But God used it for good, didn't he?"

She stepped back, and Judith approached him shyly with the doll in both hands in front of her.

Before she could speak, Josiah said, "Thank you."

She shook her head. "I didn't . . ."

"The notes. They meant so much to me."

She shrugged. "Edward delivered them. All I did was write them."

"But I have to ask—" Josiah hesitated, then plunged in. "Stay strong. Just before he . . . died, that's exactly what—"

"Johnny Mott," Judith said.

"Yes!"

"He would stop by once a week to see Edward. He said it was important for a boy to have a man in his life. He was real good to Edward."

"I didn't know that."

Judith nodded. "Every time, just as he was leaving, he'd look at Edward and say . . ."

"Stay strong." They said it together.

Judith stepped closer. "For years I hated you."

"That was my fault, dear," Eunice added.

"I was against the church calling you back, and I wasn't going to come to church ever again. But Eunice—"

Eunice was shaking her head. "No, my intentions were not good. I thought that if enough of us . . ."

Josiah placed a hand on Eunice's shoulder. "You meant it for evil. God meant it for good."

"And then I wasn't going to listen when you preached," Judith continued. "But you spoke of Stephen. And Paul. And Stephen's mother. How could I not listen? You made me wonder. And God used that. He used you. I figured, well, if God would use you, like He used the apostle, then He must have forgiven you. And if God had forgiven you, was I more righteous than God?"

"You're a wise woman, Judith Usher," Josiah said.

The sun came up before the first persons left the church meetinghouse. Sunlight burst suddenly through the windows.

The dockworkers were the first to leave. They had the morning shift, and there was a lot of work to do to rebuild the docks and warehouses. Before they left, however, they filed past Josiah with smiles.

"First time we've ever been outmuscled," one of them said.

To the man, they promised they'd start attending church services.

Then, one by one, clusters of people got up and left, but not without first standing in a long line to ask Josiah's forgiveness and plead with him to stay on as their pastor.

Josiah wished he could have had more time with some of them. Philip and Anne left before he could talk with them privately. Philip shook Josiah's hand hard and murmured, "We need to talk."

Josiah agreed.

Mercy tearfully kissed him on the cheek, as did Grace. Josiah wished he could spend more time with the sisters, too, but others were waiting. When they left, Goodwife Hibbard had him by the hand. She was going on and on about how in all her years she had never seen such a thing, and how she couldn't wait to get home to write to her sister in Deerfield, and her brother in Little Harbor, and her two cousins in Worcester, and her best friend, Martha, in Norwich, whom she'd known since they were knee-high to a rabbit, and who used to . . .

By midmorning Josiah stood alone in the church. He walked slowly up and down the aisles, going pew to pew, reliving the night's events.

Here, old Henry Wheelock and James Maury settled a two-decade grudge. Here, Peter Blair promised his family he'd be a better father and husband. Here, Grace and Mercy led Sara Greven to the Lord.

What a night it had been. Broken hearts. Mended lives. Singing. Laughter. Tears. Joy.

The room was silent now, except for the scuffing of Josiah's shoes on the wooden floor.

What a difference a night had made. Yesterday afternoon he had expected to be lying bloodied and bruised in a ditch beside the postal road . . .

Josiah made his way to the door. Squinting against the morning light, standing on the top step of the church, he inhaled the crisp air.

For the first time since his arrival, Josiah stood in the center of town and his gut didn't ache.

He'd dreamed of this day, hadn't he? Worked for it. Prayed for it. Finally it had arrived, and in ways, it was so much greater than he'd imagined it could be. To his dying day, he'd never forget what had happened here.

Shoving his hands into his pockets, he descended the steps.

He told himself that this was just the start. The best was yet to come. God had given him and the town a clean slate. God had given him a renewed congregation. Responsive. Supportive.

God had given him everything he'd asked for. Wasn't that enough?

So why did he have this empty feeling inside? Why wasn't he happy?

Hunching his shoulders against the morning chill, Josiah walked toward home.

CHAPTER 49

Josiah had no sooner reached the corner of the common when he saw Sissy, the Parkhursts' servant, running toward him. She was insistent that Josiah come with her to the Parkhurst house.

Eunice greeted him the moment he stepped in the door. "You poor boy!" She cradled his head in her hands.

Could she tell? Was it that obvious?

"Philip told us what they did to your house," she said.

"Oh, that."

"Well, you must join us for breakfast," she insisted. "Philip assures me that he'll have enough workers there today so that by tonight, everything will be back in place."

As Eunice tugged him toward the dining area, the aroma of bacon and fried eggs and cakes caused quite a sensation in his empty stomach. He realized he hadn't eaten in nearly a day, and his ration then had been prison bread.

Abigail appeared, carrying a hot bowl of porridge. Exactly how he'd pictured she would when they were married. She greeted him with a dazzling smile. Josiah returned the greeting but not as heartily, afraid that she would see in his eyes what he was thinking.

In his mind he'd come to terms with the fact that Abigail didn't love him. However, little scenes like this one still had the power to prick his passions to life. He wondered how long it would take before he could look at her as only a friend.

Once they sat down and said grace and started eating, Josiah's appetite claimed center stage, and he ate hungrily.

Josiah was having a difficult time holding on to the present. His mind kept darting here and there with complete disregard for time.

Eunice Parkhurst sat next to him on the sofa. She'd insisted on being alone with him. Abigail had gone upstairs.

As soon as they sat down, she'd taken both of Josiah's hands in hers. That's what had set off the avalanche of Eunice memories.

Two were prominent. Conflicting.

One recent.

The other years ago.

The recent memory was negative. Painful. Rage had twisted her face; double-edged hatred had flashed in her eyes. Every word had been laced with venom.

Josiah had stopped by the Usher house to make a call on Edward, who had the pox. He had never reached the boy. Eunice, who had been helping Judith, had driven him away, flinging cruelties in his face.

The next instant he remembered a kind, motherly Eunice. Younger. With fewer wrinkles. She was sitting opposite him much as she was now.

When Reverend Parkhurst was still alive, the days were carefree. As Josiah thought of them, his limbs and mind surged with the vitality of a young man . . .

It was a Sunday afternoon. Reverend Parkhurst had just finished preaching. He dabbed perspiration from his forehead. He'd pressed home the final point of his sermon with unusual exuberance.

"Who will go for me?" Parkhurst had thundered. "It is the Lord who asks the question. And it is the Lord to whom we must give an answer.

Who will go for me? Who will go?" He pointed to individuals in the congregation. "Will you? Will you?" The preacher's long, thin finger targeted Josiah. "Will you?" He paused. "The Lord Almighty awaits your answer."

It was a spiritually defining moment in Josiah's life.

Following the service, Abigail asked him if anything was bothering him. He seemed uncharacteristically subdued.

Josiah confided in her. "I want to go for the Lord, but . . ."

"But what?" Abigail asked.

"But I don't know where to go."

"Father will know."

Only Reverend Parkhurst wasn't immediately available. A few men in the church had pulled him aside to show him the damage on the church roof caused by a recent hailstorm. At first Josiah was relieved, since he wasn't sure he could put what he was feeling into words.

But Abigail was insistent he talk to someone. She took Josiah to her mother and announced, "God's calling Josiah, and he doesn't know how to answer."

Josiah's face reddened. "I always thought I'd be a doctor."

Eunice Parkhurst took him by the hands and told him, "The Lord needs godly doctors as well as preachers. Place your life in His hands, Josiah. God isn't shy about revealing His will to people who are ready to listen."

But a couple of months later, Reverend Parkhurst was dead, and Josiah was hoofing it to Boston.

Josiah had thought back on Eunice Parkhurst's advice many times. A part of him wondered if Eunice had said what she'd said because she preferred having a doctor over a preacher for a son-in-law . . .

Eunice squeezed Josiah's hands, bringing him back to the present. "This must be difficult for you."

Josiah flinched. It *was* difficult. He pulled away involuntarily; she held on tight.

"I'm to blame for that," she admitted. "And I am truly sorry. I have worked against you from the beginning—and in a most cowardly way, for which I am deeply ashamed."

Her confession made him uncomfortable. But it was obvious she needed to get everything out into the open.

"Every Saturday night for the past year," she said, "I've followed a ritual. I'd put a kettle on the fire to make myself some tea and sit in my rocking chair beside the fire and read Reverend Parkhurst's sermon."

The one Josiah had preached last Sabbath.

"I drew strength from it."

Josiah nodded. "It was one of his best sermons."

"Only that's not why I read it." Her face grew sad. "I read it because it fueled my resolve. It renewed my determination to block you at every turn. Because every time I took it from the back of my Bible, I was reminded that the people of the church never got to hear that sermon. And it was all your fault."

Which explained why she so quickly left the church on the day he preached it, Josiah realized.

"A shameful legacy to leave my husband, wouldn't you agree?" Eunice asked.

Josiah didn't reply. He just listened.

"I justified my Saturday night ritual by telling myself that mine was a righteous anger. That it should be Reverend Parkhurst standing in the pulpit on Sabbath, not you." She wiped away a tear. "Amazing, isn't it? All this time I've been reading it without once understanding it. And then, after last Sabbath, when friends commented on it, a veil was lifted. I feel such the fool."

Eunice Parkhurst wept softly.

"He was quite the prophet, my husband, wasn't he?" she added. "All that time, and he was talking about . . . I'm the douser—or at least *one* of them. I was determined that Mr. Whitefield's presence in Havenhill would be for naught. I undermined. Gossiped. Did everything I could to squelch anything remotely good coming out of those services."

"I knew you didn't approve of me," Josiah said. "But I had no idea—"

"That I was that bitter? That determined to destroy you?" She sighed. "In many ways you're still such an innocent. And you . . ."

Josiah fidgeted.

"Nathaniel prophesied you, too, didn't he?"

It was the first time Josiah had heard Eunice refer to her husband by his first name. She'd always been quite formal about the way she addressed him.

"He prayed for a troubler. God sent you."

"So that when revival came, no one could mistake its origin," he stated. "That it came from God."

"Quite a lesson, aren't we? For if God can bring revival to a town in spite of you and me . . ."

Josiah finished her sentence. "He can bring revival to anyone."

Eunice laughed. It was a good sound. "We're not unlike Euodias and Syntyche. Remember them?"

"Paul's letter to the Philippians."

"Nathaniel was fond of pointing out from the text that the women were so contentious that when Paul addressed them, he had to give them separate verbs."

Josiah laughed.

"Nathaniel was severely depressed the last days of his life, did you know that?"

"Why?" Josiah asked. "Everyone revered him."

"That's what disturbed him. The people depended more on him than they depended on God. Such trust and expectations are a burdensome weight for a man to bear."

"I didn't know."

"He kept it hidden. And while he tried to point people to the Lord, they'd grown so accustomed to having a physical savior in their midst—I know that's sacrilegious, but that's the way they'd come to look upon him—what need did they have for a spiritual Savior?"

Her eyes brimmed with fresh tears. "He knew he had to leave Havenhill. At the same time, he knew how rooted Abigail and I were here. Our whole lives were here. And he couldn't ask us to leave."

"Do you think he knew he was going to die?"

Eunice looked down at their hands. "I think it gave him the courage to run into a burning warehouse to save two little girls."

Josiah's heart went out to this woman, who so obviously missed her husband. For the first time, he understood how difficult it had been for her all these years.

"Now you," she said brightly.

"Now me, what?"

"All morning you've been moping when, of all men, you should be higher than a kite."

So he had been that obvious.

He shrugged. "I'm happy. Of course, I'm happy. Who wouldn't be? One minute I'm about to be run out of town. The next minute God answers my prayers in ways I haven't even begun to digest."

"And yet . . ." Her gaze was steady. Earnest.

Josiah produced a half-grin. "Not that I'm comparing myself to Elijah, or what happened here to Mount Carmel, but if I remember correctly, following the contest with the prophets of Baal, Elijah experienced something of a letdown. Didn't he sit under a juniper tree and pray that he might die?"

"Understandable, since Queen Jezebel had just promised to kill him. Remember, son, you're talking to a preacher's wife."

Josiah eyed the woman sitting next to him. His one-time future mother-in-law, his mentor's wife, his former adversary. He didn't know if he was ready to confide in her.

But she was waiting. Arching his shoulders as though he needed to stretch, he tried to pull his hands away. Again she held tight.

"It's nothing," Josiah said.

"Lying is unbecoming a minister of God."

This was the Eunice Parkhurst he'd always known—straightforward, hard-hitting. But she was right. He wasn't being truthful with her.

He shifted uneasily. "Last night, when the Spirit came . . ."

Her gaze was piercing. He could tell she was concentrating on his every word.

". . . when everyone felt the unmistakable presence of the Lord . . ."

She sat back and looked at him.

And he at her. He could see in her eyes that she'd guessed his secret.

"The Spirit passed you over," she said.

Josiah lowered his eyes. He spoke with a detached tone. "I was elated, of course, over what was happening with everyone else, but inside . . ." He took a deep breath. "When I lived in Boston, God gave me a spiritual gift with a physical manifestation. I have been able to feel people's spiritual condition."

"All this time? All the time you've been in Havenhill you've been in pain?"

Josiah nodded. "So, last night, when everyone was confessing their sins, and God was forgiving them, I knew. I could feel it. Layers of pain were lifted, one by one, until nothing was left."

"And now? Are you able to feel the joy of the people who are right with God?"

"I used to be able to feel the joy as well as the anguish. Until last night . . . When God took the pain away, He took my gift away too."

"You feel . . ."

"Nothing. Empty."

Eunice wore the expression of a woman attempting to solve a puzzle. There was more. She seemed to sense it. She prompted him. "And what hurts even more is . . ."

". . . is that apparently I was the only one passed over by the Spirit last night. It was as if I were outside, looking in, pressing my nose up against the window of this incredible party, watching everyone being given these incredible gifts of joy and peace and happiness, and . . ."

". . . and you weren't invited."

"Aya. And . . ." Josiah swallowed the next sentence.

"Go ahead," Eunice urged him. "You feel hurt because, of everyone in that room, you were the one who did the most to promote revival. You worked the hardest. You prayed the hardest. You endured the pain. Of all people, you deserved it most."

"I try not to think of it that way. I know I shouldn't."

"But you do. You can't help it."

"Aya."

Tears fell on her cheeks. Tears for him. She closed her eyes, and the next thing Josiah knew, Eunice Parkhurst was praying for him.

"Almighty Father, we do not pretend to fathom the mind of an all-wise God. And yet one of Your own is hurting. Questioning Your love for him. It would be impertinent of us to question Your will or to demand an explanation. So we pray for patience for Josiah. That he will trust You to reveal everything according to Your good and perfect will. We hurt for him. He has done so much for us, endured so much, that we want the best for him. We know that our desire is but a pale imitation of Your desire for him. And so we wait in anxious anticipation to see what You will do next in Josiah's life."

CHAPTER 50

Philip Clapp sent word to Josiah at the Parkhurst house that he and Anne would like to have him over for dinner that evening while his men completed work on Josiah's house. Josiah sent his compliments and said he would attend. He and Philip had a lot to talk about.

But first, Josiah had a call to make . . .

Edward Usher answered his knock and invited him in. Judith greeted him warmly. She looked radiant, happier, and healthier than Josiah had ever seen her.

They invited him into their sitting room, which was a small corner of a larger room that doubled as a dining area. Both mother and son seemed thrilled he'd stopped by.

At thirteen years of age, Edward was beginning the awkward and always embarrassing transition from boyhood to manhood. His jowls had fuzz on them. His face sported blemishes. His voice occasionally cracked when he talked. He seemed a good-natured boy and talked excitedly about what had happened at the church the night before.

Taking a seat, Josiah said to Judith, "I just wanted to stop by and thank you again for your encouraging notes. And thanks to you, too, Edward. I understand you're the one who delivered them."

"It was fun," the boy replied. "Ma wanted it to be a secret. So I would hide out in that patch of woods near your house and wait for a good time."

"Why a secret?" Josiah asked Judith.

Judith picked at a fingernail. "It seems silly now, doesn't it? But I didn't think you liked me. Because of what happened, well, we were supposed to be enemies. Mostly, though, I didn't want Eunice to find out. I was afraid she'd be real mad if she knew."

Josiah smiled warmly. "Now the notes mean even more to me, knowing that you were taking a risk to send them."

"I almost stopped once. I got nervous."

"Oh? What convinced you to continue?"

"Mr. Mott. He and Edward were the only two who knew I was sending them to you. Mr. Mott said it was a good idea and that I should keep doing it."

A wave of anguish swept over Josiah. How he had misjudged Johnny! Hearing that Johnny knew about the notes made sense.

"That's the other reason I wanted to stop by," Josiah said. He turned to Edward. "Your ma told me last night that Johnny—Mr. Mott—used to visit you once a week."

Edward nodded. "Mr. Mott was real kind to me."

"Aya. He was a good man, wasn't he? Anyway, I thought . . . well, no one could ever fill Mr. Mott's shoes . . ."

Edward laughed. "That's the truth! He had big feet! Did you ever see him with his shoes off? They were huge!"

"Hundreds of times!" Josiah laughed too. "You have to remember, we grew up together. Went swimming every summer. Anyway, I thought, if it's all right with you, maybe I could stop by once a week, and we could do things together. Like you and Mr. Mott used to do."

"Will you let me climb a ship's mast all the way to the top?"

Judith gasped. "Edward! Did Mr. Mott let you do that?"

"No. But he promised I could when I was older."

Josiah grinned. "Well, we'll see what we can do about that. With your mother's permission, of course."

"We'll talk about it," Judith said, which in mother language meant "not in my lifetime," Josiah knew.

And from the expression on Edward's face, he knew it too.

Judith touched her son's arm. "I'm not saying no," she insisted.

Edward's eyes turned in wonder toward her.

"Ever since the fire," Judith told Josiah, "I've been protective of Edward. Too much sometimes. It's just that, having lost two girls . . ."

Josiah hung his head. The sudden change of direction in the conversation made him uneasy. While he was glad the relationship between him and Judith Usher had been mended, the stupidity of that one senseless night would forever haunt him. She had forgiven him, and he believed her. But he still had to live with the consequences of what he'd done. He'd killed this woman's two little girls. And nothing would ever change that.

Judith didn't seem to see his anguish. She completed her sentence. ". . . because they were playing where they shouldn't have been playing. I feel I need to know where Edward is at all times, and what he's doing."

This was the first time Josiah had heard this part of the story. He had never questioned what the girls were doing in the warehouse, only that they were in the wrong place at the wrong time.

"Isn't that right, Edward?" Judith asked.

Josiah sat up. This, too, was a revelation. "You were on the docks the night of the fire?"

Edward cringed. "We weren't supposed to be. Ma warned us not to play there. She was afraid we'd fall in the river."

Judith added, "My sister lived in one of those little houses at the time—shacks, really—on Keystone Street. That little boardwalk that runs parallel to the docks."

Josiah nodded. He was familiar with the street.

"Susanna's husband had the night watch on the *Brighton*, and her baby . . ."

"John Jacob," Edward inserted.

". . . had colic." Judith thought back a moment. "That boy had a pair of lungs like . . . well, like a preacher . . . like Reverend Whitefield. He would keep my sister up all night long. So I would go over there a couple of times a week and take care of the baby for a few hours so she could sleep."

"And my sisters and me would play hide-and-seek," Edward said.

Judith frowned. "Where they weren't supposed to be."

"It was Katy's idea!" Edward protested. "And she was the oldest."

Judith nodded. "That girl could talk her sister and brother into anything! I swear, if she told them to jump off the end of the pier, they'd do it."

"There weren't any good places to hide outside the house," Edward said. "And the docks had all sorts of good hiding places. One time Katy and me climbed into the middle of this big coil of rope and pulled some of it over the top of us. Mary never did find us."

Josiah could see everything in his mind. Three children playing hide-and-seek at one end of the warehouse. Him, Philip, and Johnny passing liquor through a window at the other end. Neither group knowing the other was there.

"I hid when I saw Mr. Mott," Edward continued.

"That's enough, Edward," his mother said, eyeing Josiah. "We're making Pastor Rush uncomfortable."

"No," Josiah insisted, "unless this is hard for you, Judith."

She shook her head.

"You saw Mr. Mott?" Josiah asked Edward. "When?"

Edward looked at his mother.

She nodded for him to continue.

"They scared me," Edward explained. "Mr. Mott and Mr. Clapp came climbing out of a window. I was afraid if they saw me, they'd tell

Ma and we'd get in trouble. Katy and Mary were hiding. I didn't know where they were."

That fit. Philip and Johnny had left Josiah alone for a while, just as he was slipping in and out of conscious thought.

"Mr. Mott was real mad. He was yelling at Mr. Clapp and kept grabbing him by the arm. Mr. Clapp would shake him off. I think he was trying to get Mr. Clapp to go back inside, and Mr. Clapp didn't want to go back in. Then my sisters started screaming. Some men with torches came running to put out the fire. Smoke and flames came out the cracks in the sides of the warehouse. The windows started to explode, shooting glass everywhere, and people ran toward the warehouse, yelling. I saw one man jump out of a window. His whole back was on fire. I was real scared and ran back to Auntie Susanna's house."

Josiah listened intently. "Did you see Mr. Clapp and Mr. Mott pull me out of the warehouse?"

"No."

"Did you see Reverend Parkhurst go into the warehouse?"

"No. I don't remember seeing any of that."

"We don't know how the girls got inside the warehouse," Judith said. "They must have found a loose board or something."

After praying with Judith and Edward, and arranging to meet with Edward the following Wednesday, Josiah set out for Philip's house.

His chest felt as if it had a weight on it, like it did every time he remembered the night of the fire. Reliving that night was always emotional for him. It always took time to recover afterwards.

Only this time was different. After hearing Edward's account of that night, there were two weights on his chest. One was regret. The other, anger. And with each step, the second weight grew heavier as part of Edward's story played repeatedly in his mind.

"Mr. Mott was real mad. He was yelling at Mr. Clapp and kept grabbing him by the arm. Mr. Clapp would shake him off. I think he was trying to get Mr. Clapp to go back inside . . ."

Why was Johnny so insistent that Philip go back inside? They'd left him to do their business. What was there to fight about? Why didn't Philip want to go back inside?

"Then my sisters started screaming. Some men with torches came running to put out the fire."

How old was Edward at the time? He was thirteen now. That would make him five at the time of the fire. To hear his sisters screaming like that, and to see a fire like that. No five-year-old should ever have to experience those things. Naturally, he was scared. Confused. Maybe enough to get the sequence of events mixed up.

"Then my sisters started screaming. Some men with torches came running to put out the fire."

Or was it?

"Some men with torches came running. Then my sisters started screaming."

Josiah's breathing was labored, and it wasn't from walking. He had some questions of his own for Philip Clapp. Such as: What were he and Johnny arguing about? Why was Johnny so insistent about going back in? And why did *Philip* not want to go back inside that warehouse?

But most importantly, he wanted to ask Mr. Philip Clapp, "Why would men bring torches with them to fight a warehouse fire?"

CHAPTER 51

Anne Myles's beauty disarmed Josiah.

He was expecting Long-face, the servant, to answer the door. Instead, he was greeted by the future lady of the house herself. Her hair was done up fashionably and adorned with pearls. She wore a red silk dress that flattered an already flawless figure. Her eyes sparkled. Her smile, framed by girlish dimples, was genuine.

"The man of the hour!" she exclaimed upon seeing him.

Philip was right behind her. Anne stepped aside so the two old friends could greet each other. On his way to Philip's, Josiah had worked himself into such a state that he'd envisioned greeting Philip with a fist. With Anne standing there, looking all beautiful, Josiah offered a hand.

Philip stepped past the hand and embraced Josiah with a rib-rattling hug. "Wasn't last night amazing? I never knew," he said with wonder, "that it could be so powerful. God literally knocked me off my feet! It was . . . well, we have all night to talk about it. But you knew, didn't you? All along, you knew this could happen. And I have to hand it to you. You never gave up! Despite—"

"Philip." Anne touched his arm.

He gazed at her with obvious affection. "You're right, dear. First we feast! Then we talk."

Dinner was an ordeal. The room was brightly lit. The host and hostess were all smiles, at times tittering over each other like lovebirds. The food was plentiful and displayed attractively. But Josiah couldn't vouch for the flavor. He swallowed, yet tasted nothing. Even the servants reflected the new spirit in the house.

It made Josiah sick. All he wanted was to finish the meal and get on with the questions.

Finally, Anne signaled to a servant, who pulled her chair out for her. She stood.

The men stood.

"I imagine the two of you have a lot to talk about," she said. "So I will excuse myself."

Philip ordered a servant to summon her coach.

Approaching Josiah, she offered her hand. "Reverend Rush, you have truly opened our eyes. Even when we were treating you shamefully, you never gave up on us. I have never met another man who so genuinely has the stamp of the Savior on him."

Josiah must have mumbled something, because she smiled and left. He was glad when she was gone. Not only because he could now confront Philip, but because it was difficult for Josiah to maintain his anger in her presence. Difficult, but not impossible.

Minutes later the two men were alone in the parlor. Philip gave instructions that they were not to be disturbed, then closed the massive cherry wood doors.

Josiah fought the urge to pounce. He wanted to grab Philip by the throat and squeeze the truth out of him.

"You should hate me," Philip said.

He led Josiah to a sitting area, where three large leather chairs were arranged around a small table. On the table was a silver tray with two glasses and a bottle of something Josiah didn't recognize.

Philip offered Josiah a seat and sat down himself.

Josiah thought he showed great restraint in taking it.

The man seated across from Josiah was a humbler version of the Philip Clapp who had nearly orchestrated his ouster from First Church. He leaned forward, arms resting on his legs, the fingers of his hands intertwined. The very picture of contrition.

"You've probably pieced everything together by now, haven't you?" Philip asked. "Bellamont's men set the fire. Of course, someone had to take the blame. You'd been set up all along with a series of small fires, including the one at the church. Of course, it was made to appear that I'd lost everything. He promised to double the value of my holdings."

It took Josiah a moment to realize Philip was talking about the recent fire.

Philip let out a heavy sigh. "With the town already in debt to him, naturally he could have come in and demanded payment, thus forcing his way into the town. But what good is a town full of people who hate you? So he came up with this idea. He said he needed a lightning rod. If you don't know what a lightning rod is—"

Josiah interrupted. "I met the man who invented it when I was in Philadelphia. Franklin is his name."

"Really?" Philip looked impressed. "Anyway, we needed someone who would attract the town anger away from Bellamont and me."

"And who better than someone the town had a history of hating? That's why you sought me out in Boston. From the start, it was never out of friendship. It wasn't to give me a second chance."

Philip opened his arms, pleading. "Josiah, I wasn't my own man."

"It is better that one man die than the whole town perish."

Philip cocked his head. "Scripture?"

"It seems you and Caiaphas, the high priest who turned Jesus over to Pilate, think a lot alike. Only he hadn't counted on Jesus rising from the dead."

Instead of being insulted, Philip nodded. "And we didn't count on a stubborn troubler prophet named Josiah, calling fire from heaven."

"Let's make one thing clear," Josiah proclaimed firmly. "God, and God alone, sent revival to Havenhill. And only now am I beginning to see what a tremendous example of grace that was."

Philip sat back. All good humor drained from his face. "I didn't realize you'd still be this angry. Josiah, you won! But we still have Bellamont to address. The wharf is in ruins. We don't have the money ourselves to rebuild it. And there's the matter of the credit he's extended on the properties to rebuild the houses from the first fire. It's worse than I led you to believe before. The interest rate is so high, the amount of principle that's been paid on the loans is negligible."

Josiah said nothing.

"Look, I'm sorry," Philip said. "And I'll tell the entire town everything I just told you. If they want to throw me in jail, fine. If they want to banish me, fine. I was hoping that maybe together we could figure a way out of this mess, a way that can save the town and bring honor to God."

Josiah didn't move.

Exasperated, Philip stood. He yanked open a drawer and from it took Josiah's journal. He held it out.

Josiah made no attempt to take it.

"I'm a wretch!" Philip yelled. "A sinner. I betrayed my best friend, and I am responsible for getting my other friend killed! I made some bad decisions early and have sold out the town! But I've confessed these things to God, and He's forgiven me. Now I'm trying to make things right. That's what you're supposed to do, isn't it? And maybe I was wrong, but I thought my best friend, the godliest man I know, would at least show a little support!"

The journal hovered between them.

Philip let it fall to the table. He threw up his hands. "What will it take to convince you that I'm a changed man? That I'm repentant? That I want to make things right?"

"The truth," Josiah demanded.

Philip rolled his eyes in exasperation. "I told you the truth!"

"The *whole* truth."

Flapping his arms like a wounded duck, Philip cried, "What more can I tell you? I set you up! From the moment you stepped foot in this town, you were set up for failure! What more is there?"

Josiah stared at him. Sweat beaded on Philip's forehead and ran down his temples.

"I think it goes back further than that," Joseph replied.

Philip gave another exasperated arm-flap and sprawled into his chair.

Josiah stood. "You're sincere about being ready to tell the truth?"

Philip groaned. "Anything you want to know."

"In the presence of God?"

"In the presence of God and all the holy angels!" Philip replied.

Josiah nodded. "Then you can begin by telling me what you and Johnny were arguing about outside the warehouse the night of the fire."

Philip's eyes narrowed to slits. He sat forward.

"You remember, don't you?" Josiah prodded. "I was passed out on the floor. You and Johnny left to answer nature's call. The next thing I know, you're pulling at my arms, and fire's all around me. Outside. You and Johnny fought. What were you fighting about?"

"What did Johnny tell you?" Philip asked. Suspicion showed on his face.

Josiah shook his head. "Johnny Mott was a good friend, apparently to both of us. Loyal to the end. Neither of us deserved the loyalty he showed us."

"Then how do you know we fought? You were passed out."

"Someone saw you," Josiah said.

Philip accepted that. "We were . . . we were . . . Johnny wanted to . . ."

"In the presence of God and his holy angels," Josiah reminded him.

Philip swallowed hard. "You're making this up. No one saw us out there."

"Edward Usher did."

"Edward?"

"He and his sisters were playing hide-and-seek. That's what the girls were doing inside the warehouse. Hiding. He saw you and Johnny climb out the window and argue."

Philip shook his head. "All this time? He never said anything. Judith never said anything."

"Edward was five years old. He was so scared, he doesn't realize what he saw. But he saw enough to make me realize more about what happened that night."

"A fight between friends? We were always arguing over something. You know how it was. That's the way we were. I'd be willing to bet you can't remember everything we fought over."

Josiah reached down for his journal and turned to leave.

Philip bolted out of his chair. "What? That's it? You're walking out because I can't remember an argument that took place eight years ago?"

Josiah turned back. "Why would men bring torches to fight a warehouse fire?"

"What? What are you talking about?"

"Edward Usher saw men with torches. Men with torches don't fight warehouse fires. They *start* them!"

It was Josiah's best punch, and it hit its mark with force.

Philip stumbled backward and dropped to the edge of his chair, then slid to the floor. He looked up dumbly as Josiah loomed over him, feeling no pity.

"Johnny got scared that night," Philip mumbled. "I reminded him of how rich we were going to be. I told him you were the town's golden boy. They'd forgive you. Besides, you were going off to school to be a doctor."

"All these years," Josiah said, trembling, barely able to control himself, "you let me think I killed those girls."

"Nobody was supposed to be in there!" Philip yelled. "How could we have known? Apothecary shipments. That's all it was supposed to be. All those boxes we stacked and moved and loaded and unloaded. Boxes, not girls. And certainly not—"

"Reverend Parkhurst."

Philip began to weep.

"And the men. Bellamont. Even back then," Josiah guessed.

"It was our chance to make something of ourselves, Johnny and me. So Hutton would lose some inventory. What was that to us? We didn't even know who Peter Hutton was, only that his name was on all those boxes."

"All these years . . ."

"Johnny was going to tell you," Philip admitted. "I made the mistake of telling Coytmore. I thought he'd just relay the information to Bellamont."

"Coytmore—the captain who disciplined George Mason to death."

"It was his men who killed Johnny." Philip looked up at Josiah. "You met some of them last night."

"All this time," Josiah repeated. "Do you know how many nights I woke up in a cold sweat, hearing those screams? Hearing Reverend Parkhurst screaming in pain, begging God to take the three of them home?"

"You don't think I have the same dreams?" Philip shouted.

Josiah drew within inches of Philip's face. "But the difference between us is that you deserve to have them. I don't!"

CHAPTER 52

Winter struck with a vengeance this week. The first hard snow of the season. Snowdrifts are four feet high on the north side of the house. This morning I had to dig a path to get out the front door.

With the storm came an illness. I awoke this morning with a raw throat. Every swallow is painful. My muscles are achy. On days like today, it's hard to move far from the fire. But Goodwife Hibbard is feeling poorly, and if I don't get over to see her, she'll feel abused.

Yesterday marked the fourth week since revival came to Havenhill. As I walked the streets, I was reminded of Franklin's comment about how revival affected his Philadelphia. It was his observation that it seemed the whole world had suddenly become religious, that he couldn't walk through the town without hearing psalms being sung in various houses. Such is life in Havenhill now that revival has come.

From that first night in church, holiness has spread through the town faster than the smallpox epidemic. Everywhere I go, people are cheerful and friendly, eager to help one another, optimistic, quick to overlook slights, and quicker still to forgive.

This latter grace is an indictment to me. In this regard, the revival has worked to my detriment. I still have not forgiven Philip Clapp for eight years of torture. I haven't spoken to him since the truth about the fire came out. And every time I see a confession followed by forgiveness, I know what I should do. But, God help me, I can't bring myself to forgive him.

Philip confessed his sin to the church. Naturally, they were deeply shocked. Hurt. Angry. There were a lot of tears. Philip submitted himself to the church for discipline and requested that a body of elders be appointed to recommend and oversee a spiritual plan that would eventually restore him to fellowship. As pastor, I was consulted. My first thought was, send the man into exile for eight years, then maybe he can begin to appreciate the pain behind what he has done. Whatever happened to the good old days when an eye for an eye was the law of the land? However, in a rare moment of good sense, I let my duty override my vengeance, and Philip is now under the instruction and watchful care of two godly men.

Healing has already begun. Judith, bless her heart, led the way again. She forgave Philip. So did Eunice, but not without difficulty. It took Abigail longer. She loved her father deeply and still misses him. Then, yesterday, during Sabbath, she publicly forgave Philip.

I bit my tongue. I've found myself doing that a lot—in fact, every time someone forgives Philip Clapp. When it comes to Philip, every act of forgiveness is a betrayal to me. God help me, but that's how I feel. I cannot forgive the man who knowingly let me suffer in the stewpots of self-loathing and guilt for eight years while he grew rich on my pain. And cannot understand how others can be so quick to shrug off the sin of a man who would willingly torture another man and at the same time wear masks of friendship, deacon, and public leader.

Maybe in eight years I'll feel differently.

Mercy insists my refusal to forgive merely extends the torture Philip started. Her theory is that since I've lived with the pain for eight years, I don't know how to live without it.

We don't discuss the topic often. It always ends in an argument, with Mercy getting that hurt and disappointed look in her eyes.

Doesn't anybody understand what I feel? Can't they see that I have a right to feel as I do?

My unwillingness to forgive Philip is the one thing that mars an otherwise exhilarating relationship. I find it hard to think that I've known Mercy all this time and have never seen how attractive she is. Certainly, her complexion and idyllic eyes and the toss of hair are beautiful. But so is the woman within—the way laughter and playfulness originate from her soul.

It's different from the way I felt with Abigail. On reflection, better. Deeper. More satisfying. The kind of love a marriage can be built on.

I've not said any of this to her. It's too soon. However, we have reinstituted our cooking night on Wednesdays. Mercy and I flirt and play and throw foods at each other and somehow manage to come up with some rather tasty creations. As before, Grace sits in the corner and knits. She is our chaperone. Only now she is fulfilling that role in the true sense of the word. She has taken to liking me again.

Meanwhile the debt to Lord Bellamont hangs over the town like a thunderous cloud. I'm sure by now word has been sent to him about the revival. He will, of course, implement some sort of counter tactic. We must wait to see what that will be.

Come spring, Bellamont will expect to hold a slave auction in Havenhill. In the meantime we have been forming a strategy of our own. It was actually Eunice Parkhurst's idea. She got the idea while reading the Gospel of Luke. The woman has a devious side to her that is quite creative. Fortunately for me, Lord Bellamont is now on the receiving end of it.

We will implement the first stage of her plan during these winter months. A team of women meets every day at the church to write letters. We dispatch them weekly in batches on wings of prayer.

Whether by the directive of Lord Bellamont or by Captain Coytmore's own initiative, the forces arrayed against us have taken a more visible presence in the town. Bands of thugs have taken to roaming the streets. Mostly they have contented themselves with general mischief—harassing people on their way to church, vandalizing businesses, and disrupting Sabbath services with drums and other loud noises. Last Sabbath they released a dozen wild cats in the church while I was preaching.

Their actions only serve to strengthen our resolve. Since the earliest days of Christianity, believers have been targets of attack by the evil forces of the prince of this world. We consider it an honor to be counted among the faithful and have redoubled our efforts to deliver a blow for Christianity this spring.

In an ironic twist, the very men who were so eager to escort me out of town were redeemed the night the Spirit fell upon us. Now they have become my daily bodyguards, lest Bellamont's men get any ideas.

CHAPTER 53

The sky was a cloudless blue. A sweet, salty breeze ambled off the ocean. The sun's rays warmed clothing and skin just enough to make a person forget winter, but not enough to make them dread the approaching dog days of summer. It was a perfect spring day. Too nice to be ruined by peddling human flesh on the auction block.

However, the word had circulated, and a sizeable number of New England buyers had found their way to Havenhill. It was one year and one month to the day that Josiah took the same road into the town from Boston to assume the pastorate at First Church.

Josiah couldn't help but study the people who had traveled all this way to buy another human being. Some had come from a great distance; he'd already met one man from Norridgewock, Maine. The buyers came in all sizes and shapes. They looked like decent enough people. None of them had horns or forked tails or walked hunched over and spit sulfur when they talked. They didn't look evil, but they'd been touched by evil, hadn't they? They'd been deceived. It seemed incomprehensible to Josiah that some believed there was a race of people, created by God, destined to be the slaves of other men.

Indentured servants were one thing. Eunice Parkhurst's Sissy, for example, was part of a poor family that was willing to trade a couple of years of their lives in order to get established in the Colonies. But these African slaves were another matter entirely. Captured and transported against their will, they were destined to live and work the rest of their lives on the same level as someone's horse or cow or pig.

As he watched the buyers walk the streets of Havenhill, another thought occurred to him. Maybe, like him, they knew what they were doing was wrong. But they did it anyway.

Josiah still had not found it within himself to put the past behind him and make amends with Philip Clapp. And there was a price to be paid for his obstinacy. As he had told Eunice, the night the Spirit visited Havenhill, it was as though he were watching a party from the outside, with his nose pressed against the window. He still felt that way. All winter he had walked as a dead man among the living. Among them, but never one of them.

Yet, despite the hollowness he felt inside, he was happy for them. He awoke every Sabbath eager to go to church. The spirit of the place was unmatched by any place he'd been. Every Sabbath was a holiday. Every church member was family. Each week there was something new to rejoice over.

"Do you think we can pull this off?"

Josiah turned toward the voice. It was Mercy, clutching her purse tightly. Grace was beside her. They both looked nervous.

"God willing," Josiah replied.

When Grace patted Mercy's hand and smiled, Mercy relaxed a little.

The auction was about to start. The slaves were lined up on a platform, chained in a line. Men. Women. Boys. Girls. They stared wide-eyed at the assembled crowd. Most of them in fright. Some in anger. All morning long they'd been manhandled and inspected by prospective buyers.

Men with whips patrolled the line, should any of the slaves get any ideas.

Josiah wondered if any of the people on the platform knew what a beautiful day it was today.

The platform upon which the slaves stood had been recently constructed as part of Lord Bellamont's dock rebuilding program. It was a small addition. There weren't that many slaves to accommodate. Josiah had heard that they were just a portion of a larger shipment bound for Virginia plantations. Apparently Lord Bellamont was hedging his investment. Testing the waters, so to speak, to see what kind of return he could expect from New England slave buyers.

The auctioneer stepped to the podium.

Buyers migrated closer to the platform in anticipation of the first sale. Josiah surveyed the crowd. His people all seemed to be in their places. He spotted Abigail and Eunice. Deacon Dunmore. Philip and Anne. Judith and Edward. To him, they stood out. They looked out of place. He wondered if it was that obvious to everyone else.

The first slave was put on the auction block. A young man who appeared to be in his early twenties. His shoulders were hunched. Jittery eyes darted side to side at every sound.

Josiah and Eunice exchanged glances. It was agreed she would be the first. It was her plan. They'd been praying for this moment for five months. They had blanketed New England with letters and were encouraged by the response. But would it be enough?

The auctioneer began the bidding.

A man with a full gray beard led off. His bid was quickly raised by another bidder. And then again by another. The speed with which the bidding was escalating was not surprising. The man on the block was young and strong.

Josiah glanced over at Eunice. She glanced back nervously. He gave her an assuring nod. *Be patient*, his eyes said.

The bidding continued to escalate.

After a time, the pause between bids began to lengthen. It appeared three men remained in the contest. The auctioneer pointed to one. He shook his head. He was out.

Josiah nodded to Eunice.

It was time.

With a clear voice, Eunice Parkhurst raised the bid.

Her entrance into the contest caused a ripple of surprise among the crowd and raised the eyebrows of the auctioneer. Another man dropped out. Now it was down to two: Gray Beard and Eunice.

Gray Beard held his ground. He seemed determined.

Eunice quickly responded to each raise. Beside her, Abigail clung tenaciously to her mother's arm.

Gray Beard was taking longer between bids, seemingly unnerved by the quickness with which Eunice raised each of his bids.

Finally he waved a hand of surrender.

The auctioneer's gavel sounded.

Eunice Parkhurst had bought herself a slave.

After getting a hug from Abigail, she went forward to claim her purchase. Josiah wandered close to the platform, making himself available should he be needed.

Eunice opened her draw purse, extracted a large wad of bills, and carefully counted out the exact sum with her slave watching.

Next to him was a burly man with a whip. "You need help loadin' him, ma'am?"

Eunice straightened. "I am perfectly capable of handling my own slaves, thank you very much."

The young African was unshackled.

Eunice approached the slave with a disarming smile, assuring him that everything would be all right. She did this until the young man risked a smile.

Then she took him by the hand and led him away, talking to him in a soothing voice. "I don't know if you can understand me. But in the name of Jesus Christ, I redeem you and set you free."

She led him away from the auctioneer's block.

Mercy was next. She bought a fourteen-year-old African girl.

Deacon Dunmore bought a man who appeared to be in his mid-thirties.

Goodwife Hibbard bought a mother.

Grace bought the woman's daughter.

They paid for both purchases at the same time and led them away together. As they came near, Josiah could hear Goodwife Hibbard telling the African woman that her rheumatism had been worse than usual lately.

Josiah smiled. So far, Eunice's plan was working. While Abigail bid on the next slave, Josiah quoted to himself the Scripture that inspired the plan:

> "The Spirit of the Lord is upon me, because he hath anointed me to preach the gospel to the poor; he hath sent me to heal the brokenhearted, to preach deliverance to the captives, and recovering of sight to the blind, to set at liberty them that are bruised."

All winter long they'd sent letters to congregations throughout New England describing the situation—Lord Bellamont's deception, the recent revival, the upcoming auction. They described Eunice's plan: redeem the slaves by purchasing them, then set them free. Philip had arranged with a Christian merchant in Boston to ship the slaves back to Africa.

The response was overwhelming.

It was Grace who put it in perspective. "Mr. Whitefield has his orphans; Havenhill has its slaves."

Once again the gavel sounded. Only this time they lost one. Gray Beard was the highest bidder.

John Tibbs and Dr. Wolcott were in animated discussion. Josiah made eye contact with Wolcott and signaled, *What happened?*

Wolcott rolled his eyes and mouthed something. Josiah didn't catch it.

Chagrined, he watched as Gray Beard purchased his slave and led him away. They'd been hoping to get all of the slaves. Watching one being led away didn't sit well. Not at all.

Moments later Philip rode off.

Josiah turned his attention to the next person on the block. It was George Buckman's turn to bid. He was on it.

In short order, the congregation of First Church, Havenhill, purchased the last two slaves. They'd managed to get all but one.

The crowd broke up, unaware of what had just happened. All they knew was that they'd been outbid by people with more money.

Inspired by the psalmist, Josiah said, "Wealth and riches are in His house, and His righteousness endures forever."

Just then Philip rode up with Gray Beard's slave. He didn't say how he got the slave, just, "I believe that's the last of them."

That night First Church played host to the Africans, feeding them and providing for their needs. Dr. Wolcott made his way among them, tending to bruises and cuts and illnesses as needed. The Africans were given blankets and pillows. They slept on the floor.

The next morning they boarded the *Hartwell* for their journey back to Africa. Not a shackle was in sight. The entire town assembled at the docks to see them off. It was such a festive day: school was dismissed, and businesses were closed. Everyone was too busy celebrating to work.

The next week volunteers began writing letters to the churches that had made the plan possible, thanking them for contributing to the liberation of the captives.

Soon all of New England heard how Havenhill had rallied the countryside to rescue a band of slaves. The account was written up in nearly every newspaper. Everyone delighted in the ingenuity of a small group of New Englanders who had thwarted the mercenary plans of the well-known, wealthy Lord Bellamont.

By the time the story reached England, all of colonial America was laughing at Bellamont's expense.

Havenhill awaited Lord Bellamont's response. They didn't have long to wait. Word reached Philip through his Boston contact that Bellamont was furious. What came next was hard to believe to anyone who didn't know Lord Bellamont.

According to the report, Bellamont had gone to the king and wove a story of a colony that had defaulted on their loans and threatened those sent to collect payment. With the king's permission, Bellamont was sailing to New England to take possession of his property by whatever force necessary. He had a boatload of his own men—mostly street thugs—and an order from the king granting him authority over a detachment of British regulars. He also had an arrest warrant for Philip Clapp, who was named as the leader of the insurrection.

CHAPTER 54

As the ladies arrived, Eunice Parkhurst sat stoically on her sitting-room sofa. She greeted each woman solemnly, offering them seats in chairs that had been formed in a circle. Reflecting the mood of their hostess, the women spoke in hushed whispers, inquiring into the nature of the meeting. No one seemed to know, and Eunice wasn't speaking other than to greet new arrivals.

Grace and Mercy were the last to arrive. With all the seats filled, there were a dozen women in all. For a time, they sat staring at one another with funereal expressions. The only thing missing seemed to be a table in the center of the room and a dead body. Abigail closed the double doors, shutting them in.

In a grave, urgent tone, Eunice Parkhurst announced, "Ladies, we must pray."

"Dear God, what is it, Eunice?" Judith Usher asked. "What's happened?"

"We must pray as we've never prayed before," Eunice replied. "Tonight our pastor sorely needs our help. We must lift him up with our prayers."

Mercy gasped, evidently unaware of any danger to Josiah.

Eunice refused to give further explanation. "Let's get to it, ladies. Time is crucial."

FIRE

Reverend Josiah Rush gripped the knife in his hand. The only light was behind him, a single flickering flame in the fireplace that cast long, jittery shadows that stretched into darkness.

With a sharp thrust, Josiah attacked the carrot, lopping off an orange checker-size piece. It rolled off the cutting board onto the floor. With a disgusted grunt, Josiah kicked it into the fire.

Another grunt.

Grabbing the poker, he jabbed the embers beneath the black iron kettle and tossed on a couple of pieces of wood. Three forked tongues of flame curled around the bulbous sides of the pot. Inside the kettle, circles of surface oils floated atop a brownish broth.

Turning to the cutting board, Josiah returned his attention to the carrot. His knife moved in practiced motion. *Whack, whack, whack, whack, whack, whack, whack.* He reached for another carrot. *Whack, whack, whack, whack, whack, whack, whack.* Dropping the knife, he scooped the carrots and tossed them into the kettle. Broth sloshed over the lip, streamed down the bulge, and hissed when it hit the fire.

Josiah next attacked an onion. Cutting off both ends, he peeled the skin with knife and thumb.

"I've lived all my life without it," he said to the darkness. "And I'm not the only one. Hundreds of people have lived their lives without it. Millions. What does the book of Hebrews say? 'Not having received the promise, but having seen them afar off.' Well, that's me. I'm one of them. Good company, eh? From afar. That's good enough. I can live with that."

The blade of the knife cut through the heart of the onion. *WHACK!*

"Besides, what am I complaining about? I got what I prayed for, didn't I? And more! And in one short year.

"One year ago I came here, wanting people to forgive me and give me a second chance. Done. Prayer answered.

"One year ago I came here, hoping to find love. Well, it's a different girl than I thought it would be, but who's quibbling? I got what I wanted, didn't I? Prayer answered.

"One year ago, I prayed that my burden of guilt over Reverend Parkhurst's death would one day be lifted. Done and more. Not only has the guilt been lifted, I've been completely exonerated! Prayer answered!"

WHACK! WHACK! He sliced the onion halves in half.

Scooping up the pieces, he turned to the kettle.

With an animal yell, he threw the onion at the pot. Another yell sent the knife across the room. Still another yell, and the cutting board crashed against the wall.

Josiah stood with clenched fists, his chest heaving. One side of him was clothed with light from the fire; the other side was clothed in darkness.

"Why can't I let this go?" he seethed.

Wind rattled the shutters of the sitting room. A couple of bowed heads popped up.

"Pray, ladies! Pray!" Eunice cried.

The women had huddled in groups of two and three. Some were on their knees. A soft feminine buzz filled the room, punctuated by an occasional plea.

"Lord Jesus, help him . . ."

". . . give our pastor a clear mind, purify his soul . . ."

". . . take away his pain and give him peace . . ."

"He never gave up on us. Far be it for us to give up on him."

". . . a good man, with a good heart . . ."

Outside the wind muscled through the tree limbs, sounding like bone striking bone.

"For eight years I've served you faithfully!" Josiah shouted at the rafters. "I gave up a medical career for the ministry. And all this time, not only have I lived a righteous life, but I've borne a burden of guilt that was not mine!"

He paced angrily.

The rafters absorbed his words. When he wasn't shouting, the only sounds in the room were the bubbling of soup in the kettle and his own labored breathing.

"And what of them?" he shouted, motioning in the direction of the town. "They conspired and schemed against me. They allowed themselves to be seduced by evil and were ready to enter a pact with the devil to traffic in human flesh. And for nearly a year I suffered the pain, the physical pain of *their* sin! Yet you bless them with an overflowing measure of the Spirit and pass me by! You bless the sinners and curse the saint. What kind of a message do you think that sends to the faithful?"

He spied a wedge of onion on the floor and kicked it.

"I suppose you'll quote to me from Isaiah: 'My thoughts are not your thoughts, neither are your ways my ways.' Or possibly Habakkuk: 'The just shall live by his faith.' Well, that's all fine and good. But didn't you also say, 'If my people, which are called by my name, shall humble themselves, and pray, and seek my face, and turn from their wicked ways; then I will hear from heaven, and will forgive their sin, and will heal their land.' Well . . ."

Josiah stopped midstride. Conciliatory wrinkles framed his eyes.

"All right. I'll grant You that one. You did that. You forgave the town's sin, You healed our . . ."

Josiah's eyes blankly searched the ground. His limbs shook.

"Why did you pass me by?" he shouted.

Eunice Parkhurst rose, breaking from one group of ladies to join a trio of supplicants on the sofa. She sat next to Abigail, draping an arm over her daughter's shoulder.

Abigail prayed, "Lord, I see so much of my father in him."

"Yes," Eunice prayed. "Oh yes."

". . . give him strength to be the man he needs to be," Abigail continued. "And give Mercy the wisdom she will need to be his helpmate."

Mercy opened her eyes.

The two younger women exchanged glances, then smiles.

"Oh, amen to that!" Grace prayed.

Suddenly, the sitting-room floor rippled under their feet, taking on the characteristic of an ocean swell. On the walls pictures shook. Lamps shuddered.

Heads snapped up.

Several women gasped.

"No . . . no . . . no!" Eunice cried. "Don't let the devil distract you! Pray ladies! Pray!"

When the room could no longer contain the enormity of Josiah's rage, he fled outside, stepping into the crisp night air without a coat. It stung his exposed arms and cheeks.

For the last week, winter had tried to make a comeback. While the days were clear, the temperature had taken a nosedive, plunging to icy depths at night. The ground had yet to recover from winter's white blanket. It was hard and cold.

Overhead the stars were arrayed in force. The wooded area near the house stretched from dark to darker as beyond it the river slithered silently toward the sea.

Josiah filled his lungs with air from the stiff wind. Shaking a fist at the heavens, he cried, "Why? Can You at least tell me that? Why?"

The earth moved beneath his feet, painfully felling him to his knees.

Then he thought he heard a voice. It seemed to come from the distant treetops. But all he could see were naked limbs waving frantically in the wind.

He placed a hand on the ground and positioned himself to stand.

The earth moved again, knocking him to his backside.

Again he heard something that sounded like a voice coming from the treetops. Or was it to his left? Or maybe the right? He looked both directions. No one. The wind roughed up his hair and pulled at his clothes.

Then he heard it clearly.

Brace yourself like a man. I will speak, and you will answer Me if you can.

It came from all directions at once. Or was it merely inside his head? But it sounded real. And close.

His memory flashed. He recognized the words.

The situation was similar.

From the book of Job.

Hurt and alone, Job had challenged God.

Josiah knew the passage. He'd read it. But he'd never memorized it. Yet how was it that now he could remember the words with such clarity? It was as though something had snagged them from the recesses of his mind and dragged them to the forefront.

With authority.

Every word reverberated in his head.

Josiah waited for more. Was that it? He listened and heard only the wind. He began to shiver.

Finally, on wobbly legs, with a groan, Josiah got to his feet. He braced himself against the wind.The wind took this as a challenge, blowing harder, knocking him half a step to one side.

Do you command the wind? Can you hold it captive in the mountain crags, then release it at will? Answer Me, if you can.

Josiah opened his mouth. A gust of wind stole the breath from his mouth.

Tell Me, have you ever given orders to the morning? Or determined the length of the night? Can you clothe the hills with color? Or quilt the sky with clouds? Can you create a single drop of rain? Answer Me, if you can!

Ancient words assaulted him. Josiah couldn't explain it. He couldn't ignore it.

Then why do you presume to contend with the Almighty? Why do you discredit the God who made you? Would you condemn the One who breathes life into your lungs, who daily keeps your heart beating? Are you so powerful that you could adorn yourself with stars?

His own lips were shaping the words. Yet the voice was not his. Oh no, not his. Neither was the terrible weight he sensed of a Presence so great, so holy, so powerful, that human strength was nothing compared to it.

Josiah dropped to his knees, his face to the ground.

As Eunice rose from the sofa to join another group of praying ladies, suddenly her heart seized. It was as though an invisible hand had reached inside her chest and clutched it, not allowing it to beat.

With a strangled cry, she collapsed.

"Mother!"

Abigail dropped to her knees and took her mother's hand. Eunice opened her eyes to an arena of frightened and worried faces looking down on her.

She attempted to speak but managed only a wheeze.

"Please don't try to speak, Mother," Abigail pleaded. "We'll send for Dr. Wolcott."

Mustering all her strength just to force a little air past her lips, Eunice managed to whisper, "No! Pray! Pray!"

"But, Mother—"

"Pray!" Eunice squeezed her daughter's hand.

With tears, Abigail nodded. "Ladies, attend to your prayers. I'll stay with Mother."

Slowly, reluctantly, the ladies returned to where they had been praying.

Looking up at her daughter, Eunice managed to say, "Pray with me."

Abigail clutched her mother's hand to her chest. "Of course, Mother." As she closed her eyes, two tears squeezed out. "God of mercy, attend my mother—"

"No!" Eunice wheezed. "Josiah. Pray for Josiah."

Currents of wind stronger than any Josiah had felt in any river washed over him, polishing him as water polishes stone, removing the jagged edges of Josiah's rage.

He'd played the fool. He'd behaved like an arrogant schoolboy, spouting nonsense to the schoolmaster and thinking himself wise. He felt ashamed.

The earth chilled him. Cold seeped to the marrow of his bones. Having been knocked flat, he couldn't get up. The wind wouldn't let him.

He lay there, his cheek against moist ground, his breathing labored. He was shaking all over. His lips alternated between confessions of unworthiness and utterances of praise.

And then, suddenly, the wind was gone, leaving Josiah panting on the ground.

He blinked. All was silent.

He saw his house sideways, the door standing open, flickering firelight inside.

He took inventory of his condition. All four limbs seemed to be intact. He was cold, but there was no pain. He lifted his head. Bits of dirt and rock stuck to his cheek.

With a groan, he placed one palm to the ground, then the other. He pushed himself up to a sitting position and glanced around. The last of the wind played among the treetops.

His stomach growled. Inside his house, soup and a fire were waiting for him.

Josiah got to his feet and dusted himself off.

Had what just happened been what he thought it was? To say that nothing like that had happened to him before seemed a ridiculous understatement. Is this how the people in church felt the night of revival? Somehow it was different from what he'd imagined it would be. He felt more chastened than revived.

But he wasn't complaining! Good Lord, no, he wasn't complaining.

On stiff joints, Josiah hobbled toward the house. He felt better. The nasty load of anger he'd carried all winter was gone. He felt like himself again.

Of course he'd have to see Philip in the morning. Apologize. In the back of his mind, he'd always known he'd have to do it someday. Even now the thought of asking Philip's forgiveness didn't sit well. But he'd do it.

"I've learned my lesson," Josiah told the stars.

The invisible hand tightened its grip on Eunice's heart. She let out a cry.

"Mother!" Abigail wailed.

The praying ladies glanced worriedly at her, their mouths continuing to utter prayers lest she rebuke them again.

Except Judith Usher. She rushed to Eunice's side and clutched her free hand. "I don't care what you say, Eunice, I'm going to get Dr. Wolcott."

Eunice tried to say something. Couldn't.

Judith released the hand, but the hand didn't release her. Eunice Parkhurst may have been unable to speak, but her strength was that of a farmhand. She held Abigail in place with one hand and Judith with the other. Her eyes pleaded.

"Mother, you're hurting me," Abigail whispered.

"Pray, Abigail," Judith urged. "She wants us to pray."

Josiah Rush was a few steps from his door when the Spirit of God fell upon him. His knees buckled. He fell backwards, sprawling helplessly on the ground, and stared up at the night sky.

It was a crushing weight. He couldn't breathe.

Like Gideon, he felt he would die.

Like Daniel, his anguish was unbearable.

Like Mary, he was gripped with fear.

Like Isaiah, he felt undone and unworthy.

Holiness covered him. The stench of his own sin was suffocating.

A Presence surrounded him. Penetrated him. Linking him to eternity.

Josiah saw himself for what he was. A speck of dust in an infinite universe. Insignificant. Inconsequential. Small. Low. Menial. Utterly dependent. If God ceased to think about him for but a moment, Josiah would cease to exist. His atoms would fly apart and disperse.

He wept bitterly. He felt his heart would burst for sorrow over his sin. "Lord, depart from me, for I am not worthy!"

Then, lest despair overwhelm him, beauty appeared.

The glory of God.

As simple as a flower opening at dawn.

As large as a starry expanse.

Powerful.

It became so dazzling, so alluring, so intense that it was painful.

Josiah lifted his hand to shield his eyes.

The beauty of the glory of God filled him, and he gasped. It felt wrong. His chest was not a suitable vessel for such wonder. Immeasurable elegance did not belong in a jar of clay. And yet it came. Unable to contain such riches, Josiah's mouth formed the overflow and became a fountain of praise.

He stretched his arms wide in adoration. His mind swam in glory. He laughed, unhindered.

Rise, Josiah. Stand before Me.

A more tender voice Josiah had never heard.

Every instinct argued that he had no right to stand before such power, before such beauty.

The tone of the voice overcame his reluctance.

How he did it, he didn't know, but somehow Josiah managed to get to his feet.

The wind returned. Stronger than ever. But Josiah didn't seem to have any trouble standing in it. The trees waved their hands at the majesty of it all.

"L . . . Lord, I . . . I," Josiah stammered.

Be healed.

A rush of wind swept through him. And he was free. Free from doubt. Free from guilt. Free from sin—oh, that was the best feeling of all! For he knew he no longer caused God pain.

Josiah laughed gloriously, and then . . .

Be filled.

A sharp intake of breath staggered Josiah.

And God entered him.

Josiah had never felt so alive. He saw more clearly. Felt more deeply. He had more courage, more fortitude, more determination, and less fear than was humanly possible.

He looked around him. It was as though the walls that separated the created order from the spiritual realm had thinned, and he stood at the boundary of Paradise, looking in. No words could describe the landscape that stretched before him.

He knew he didn't belong there. Not yet. It wasn't his time. For the moment, he was content to look.

The next instant he was standing a few feet away from the open door of his house. It was night. The stars were positioned exactly where they were supposed to be.

Josiah knew what had to be done. And he wasn't afraid.

"Mother, come back! Don't leave me!"

Eunice's arms were limp. All was dark.

"Eunice? Eunice?"

Judith. Eunice recognized Judith's voice. *Dear Judith.* Her friend was alarmed. She needn't be.

Eunice didn't yet have the strength to open her eyes. But she did manage a smile and a few words. "Tell the ladies they can go home. The battle's won."

CHAPTER 55

This morning Philip and I returned from our trip to news that Lord Bellamont had landed in Boston and, after a meeting with the governor, had been assigned a detachment of regulars. We anticipate his arrival in Havenhill within a fortnight.

Accordingly, we will send out dispatches notifying the surrounding towns of his impending arrival.

Inspired by Eunice Parkhurst's concerted prayer effort on my behalf, and having felt its effects directly, we decided to utilize the same strategy against Bellamont, only on a larger scale. Concluding that prayer is our greatest weapon, Philip and I rode up the Connecticut Valley and then circled around by way of the postal road, calling upon pastors and churches to pray for us. It also gave us an opportunity to share the remarkable events of revival God has visited upon us.

I couldn't get Paul and Barnabas out of my mind as we traveled from church to church. Isn't this how they sowed the seeds that conquered the mighty Roman Empire? Could it be that similar actions on our part would likewise be blessed by God in ways we cannot now foresee?

We were encouraged by the response of the churches. It amazes me how such a ragtag group of scattered colonies has now, for the first time in our history, been united, and that by a spiritual movement.

Now that we know the time of Bellamont's coming, we will alert the churches so they can be in prayer the very hour he is here.

Maybe we are fools, but we are not afraid. United by prayer as we are with our brothers throughout New England, we feel it is we who have the advantage.

All that is left is to wait and watch the events unfold.

May God be with us.

The sight of redcoats on the village green was impressive. The military detachment entered Havenhill with precision to the sound of drumbeats and stood at attention, muskets shouldered, bayonets fixed.

Behind them Lord Bellamont rode into town, leading an ungodly array of men, at least a hundred in number. Attracted by the commotion of their arrival, another hundred men on his payroll came up from the docks.

Josiah watched from the top step of the church.

He stood alone.

Bellamont approached him. From atop a magnificent steed, he asked, "Are you the town parson?"

The question was devoid of any respect for the ecclesiastical office. A similar tone might have been used to ask, "Are you the town drunk?"

"I am the pastor of First Church," Josiah said firmly.

"Good. Then you know the whereabouts of one Philip Clapp."

"I do."

Bellamont was older than Josiah thought he'd be. The man's face was incredibly wrinkled. He had serpent eyes. The finery of his clothes indicated immense wealth. Beneath a black hat trimmed in gold, his dark gray wig fell past his shoulders.

Josiah was struck by the fact that the reputation was bigger than the man. However, it would be a mistake to underestimate him.

"Well? Speak! Where is the scoundrel?" Bellamont demanded.

Apparently, the man was not accustomed to waiting.

"He is here," Josiah said calmly.

The church door opened. Philip stepped out and stood beside Josiah.

Bellamont appeared surprised. "Philip! I would have thought you would have run away and hidden in the woods, possibly wearing skins and eating berries and nuts with the native savages. A part of me is disappointed. I was looking forward to hunting you down."

"I have nothing to run from," Philip replied, "now that I am no longer controlled by you."

Before Bellamont could answer, Anne stepped out the door.

Bellamont's eyebrows arched at the sight of his niece. "My task keeps getting easier and easier. Is that your strategy, Philip? Relinquish everything with abject contrition and throw yourself at my feet? I fear it is too late for that. Having soiled my niece's reputation and forcing me to travel all this way, I would be remiss not to have my pound of flesh."

Anne lifted her chin. "You're mistaken, Uncle. Philip has been a gentleman."

Bellamont sneered. "Gentleman? Mr. Clapp lacks the breeding. Anne, you're with me." He called her to him with his hand.

Anne inched closer to Philip. She clasped his hand.

With a disgruntled sigh, Bellamont motioned to a man close to him, who immediately started up the steps to retrieve Anne.

"Wait!" Josiah blocked his way.

The man produced a saber. He waved it in front of Josiah in a threatening manner.

It was working. Josiah felt threatened. But he didn't step aside. He spoke directly to Lord Bellamont. "Let's sit down and discuss this. There seems to be a misunderstanding. The town concedes that it is in debt to you. However, we dispute the fact that we have defaulted on that debt."

"You have defaulted because I say you have defaulted. There is no misunderstanding. And unless you are so feeble of sight that you cannot see as far as your own village green, I will say this once and only once: I am prepared to take what is mine by force." Reaching into his vest, Bellamont pulled out a piece of paper. "By the authority of King George of England, I hereby declare this town to be my personal property, and I will occupy and administer it by force if necessary."

Josiah stared at the piece of paper. He'd never seen a document signed by the king of England.

Philip stepped forward. "Lord Bellamont, take me. I offer myself in exchange for clemency to this town. Reinstate the original agreement with them, and I will go with you peacefully."

Bellamont laughed. "Yes, indeed, you will go with me. Clemency denied."

Josiah pulled Philip back. "That's not what we planned," he hissed. "Bellamont! You come in the name of the king of England. We stand here in the name of the King of kings, the Lord Jesus Christ. In His name, I appeal to you. Be reasonable. Let's sit down as Christians and negotiate."

Bellamont was unmoved. "The only way you can convince me that the Lord Jesus cares for a second about this town or, for that matter, this entire wretched country is if you can produce a legion of angels to back up what you say. Do that, and I will bow to the superior force."

Josiah opened the church door. Out stepped Eunice Parkhurst, Abigail, Mercy, Grace, Judith Usher, and the several other ladies.

"This is your legion of angels?" Bellamont scoffed.

"I wouldn't trifle with them, sir," Josiah said. "You don't want to align yourself against a band of praying women. Trust me."

"You're wasting my time," Bellamont scoffed.

"I just wanted you to see the faces of the people you have enslaved with debt," Josiah replied. "I wanted you to take a good look at the people who have so frightened you that you feel you have to come here with troops and armed thugs. Look at them! They are no threat to you. All they want is to live peaceably in this land, to raise their children to fear God, and to prosper. Your heavy-handed tactics have no place here.

In the name of God, disburse your men. Let's settle this as Englishmen. As Christians."

It had been a simple plan from the start. Pray with concerted effort that at least one of Josiah's words would penetrate Lord Bellamont's heart and make him see that he'd overreacted—that what he'd come to do was a great injustice.

Bellamont studied his opponent.

The longer the man stared at him, the more Josiah dared hope that he'd been able to make some kind of progress.

"Lord, open his eyes," Josiah prayed softly.

Lord Bellamont peered down at one of his lieutenants who stood beside his horse. "Do I look stupid to you?" he asked the man.

Bellamont's lieutenant knew better than to answer.

Straightening up in his saddle, Bellamont shouted, "This is all you've got? A mealy mouthed parson appealing to my Christianity?"

His thugs laughed and readied their weapons.

"You had better start praying, Parson," Bellamont vowed, "because you're about to get a taste of my kind of religion."

Like dogs on a leash, his thugs awaited the command that would release them.

A voice interrupted them. "Havenhill does not stand alone!"

The voice carried across the village green from the direction of the postal road. All heads turned to see an armed militia marching into town.

"In the name of God, Middletown stands with her!"

"Havenhill does not stand alone!" another voice cried from another direction.

Coming down High Street was another armed militia.

"In the name of God, Norwich stands with her!"

Behind them, another militia.

"And Kingston!"

From the postal road behind Middleton. "And Windsor!"

Coming down Summit Street. "And Brookfield!"

"Worcester comes in the name of God!"

"As does Hatfield!"

"And Deerfield!"

Men were coming from every direction. Some were armed with rifles. Some with pitchforks and axes.

"And Dedham!"

"And Pawtucket!"

Numbers of men grew steadily on every side, each militia announcing its arrival.

Saybrook. Huntington. Setauket. Reading. Londonderry. Exeter. Piscataqua. Yarmouth. Little Compton. Stonington. Bridgeport. Northfield.

Two thousand had come to hear George Whitefield preach. There were at least twice that many here now.

Josiah turned to Philip. "Not exactly a legion of angels, but they'll do."

Lord Bellamont and his men were surrounded. Outnumbered. His thugs grew nervous. A couple of them broke and ran. The militiamen let them run.

Once the leak started, there was no stopping it. Bellamont's hired army soon drained away to nothing.

The militiamen closed in on the regulars.

Their leader looked nervous.

"Lieutenant!" Bellamont shouted. "Perform your duty! Secure this town."

To their credit, the regulars never broke rank. To the man, their eyes were as wide as saucers, awaiting their lieutenant's command.

"Well?" Bellamont shouted. "I'm betting a single volley is all that will be needed. Give them a taste of lead, and they'll scurry back to the hovels from which they crawled!"

The lieutenant squared his shoulders. He glared at Bellamont, then barked his orders.

The column of regulars turned and marched off the common.

Bellamont was left alone.

Surrounded by thousands of cheering colonists.

"I warned you not to align yourself against a band of praying women," Josiah told him.

Bellamont tried to spur his horse through the crowd. One man caught the reins. Lord Bellamont wasn't going anywhere.

The leader from Middletown stepped forward. "What should we do with him?" he asked Josiah.

Philip answered. "I'll take care of him."

Bellamont's eyes were struck with terror.

"I can arrange to have him shipped discreetly back to England," Philip said.

"You won't get rid of me that easily, Clapp!" Bellamont sneered. "I'll come back with even greater force."

"It had better be the whole English army," the man from Middleton warned. "You attack one of us, you attack all of us."

Bellamont was led away by Philip to cheers from all two thousand militiamen.

Josiah approached the Middleton leader and learned his name was Spener, a schoolmaster by trade.

"We prayed, as you requested," Spener said. "And something told us that this was the kind of prayer that needed feet. So we sent a rider and . . ." He motioned to the men who filled the village common.

Josiah thanked them all.

They cheered.

Then they all got on their knees

Josiah led them in a prayer that, by their example, God would unite and bless the Colonies.

CHAPTER 56

Philip and Anne have left for Boston this morning, escorting Lord Bellamont to a ship that is bound for England. Anne is still holding out hope that she will be able to reason with her uncle. The ladies' prayer group here in Havenhill has taken him on as a special challenge.

Bellamont doesn't stand a chance.

Before the militias returned home, Philip and I met with representatives from each of the Colonies. We are not the only town that has nearly been brought to ruin by the unscrupulous practice and greed of an English merchant or consortium of merchants.

It has been decided that as soon as possible, Philip and I will sail to England and present a petition to the king on behalf of all the Colonies, addressing our grievances.

The mood in the town is encouraging. It will take longer to rebuild the docks, but we are optimistic that we can establish a competitive trade, possibly lumber.

Talk of rebuilding is not limited to economics. Some of our members are making plans to head west and take the gospel to the frontier. Here at home we will make renewed efforts to teach our young. One of the ancillary products of the revival is a renewed appreciation for the vision of our forefathers when they separated from

England to found colonies that were based on the Bible. Our prayer is that we will be as faithful in our generation as they were in theirs, and that we will pass on these truths to the next generation.

As I write this—this being Wednesday—I expect Mercy and Grace at any moment. Tonight we're going to be daring—Battalia Pie. I'm providing the chicken and pigeons. They're bringing the rabbit and oysters.

It should be interesting.

I thank God for these two women who befriended me during the early days in Havenhill, and especially for Mercy, whom I have come to love and whom I hope to marry.

Over a year ago, I came back to Havenhill searching for mercy.

And with God's help, I found her.

AUTHORS' NOTES

The town of Havenhill and the major characters in this story are fictional, though they have been created after extensive research to represent similar towns and people in the colonial New England area. While the characters—Josiah Rush, Philip Clapp, Johnny Mott, Abigail and Eunice Parkhurst, Mercy Litchfield and Grace Smythe, and Judith Usher—are not real, it is our hope they accurately reflect the lives of those who, with a heart for God, forged our country out of a wilderness.

The revival accounts as portrayed in the letters of Esther Garrick of Hadley, Massachusetts, are based on actual events. Many of the accounts are far more exciting than the fictional story we have written.

Several historical persons make an appearance in this story, including: Jonathan Edwards, Congregational minister in Northampton, and his wife, Sarah; George Whitefield, itinerant evangelist; and Benjamin Franklin, inventor and one of the future founding fathers of our nation. Each of their real-life stories is an account worth telling and retelling. For the serious student of Christianity in America, a study of Edwards and Whitefield is essential in order to understand the forces that shaped our country just prior to the Revolutionary War.

The accounts of George Whitefield's revival preaching in Philadelphia and Boston are based on actual events. And the story of his visit to the home of Jonathan and Sarah Edwards, including his comments about Edwards's godly wife, was taken from Whitefield's journal.

Jonathan Edwards's *Faithful Narrative of the Surprising Work of God* and sermon "Sinners in the Hands of an Angry God" are historical documents that are still readily accessible and worth reading. The involvement of well-known hymn composer Isaac Watts in getting the book published is a matter of record.

Finally, while the revival at Havenhill is fiction, we can't stress enough that the events portrayed in this account cannot compare to the reality of what God did among the American colonists just prior to the Revolutionary War. This movement of the Spirit of God, in a very real way, united the disjointed Colonies and was one of the foundation stones upon which America was built.

For more information about The Great Awakening and this series, please go online to www.thegreatawakenings.org.

READ THE SNEAK PREVIEW

OF THE EXCITING THIRD BOOK

IN THE

GREAT AWAKENINGS SERIES

STORM

1798–1800

BY

BILL BRIGHT & JACK CAVANAUGH

CHAPTER 1

The plan was simplicity itself.

Get up.

Say what you have to say.

Sit down and live to see another day.

But now that his time had come, his lesser goal seemed lofty and unattainable, and Asa would have sold his birthright just to be able to take a deep breath.

"Courage, Citizen Rush," said the tutor from the back of the room. "This is a disputation, not an execution. You have the appearance of a man mounting a scaffold to madam guillotine!"

The class laughed. Asa laughed with them. Not a real laugh, mind you, but some alien sound he didn't recognize that gurgled in his throat.

"Cooper, get up there with him," the tutor said. "Show him how it's done."

His opponent in this dispute, Eli Cooper, slipped out of his seat and strode to the front of the class with smooth, easy strides, his second-year camblet gown rustling with each step. A native of Kentucky, Eli Cooper was tall, broad-shouldered, with cheeks that creased handsomely when he smiled, which was often. Asa, a robeless first year student, had seen Cooper on campus. Had not yet met him. But the Kentuckian appeared to be someone Asa would like to have as a friend.

In his science class Asa had learned that physical bodies attract one another, a thought that happened to come to mind at this moment because it was the only way to explain how he found himself in front of the class. The body of Eli Cooper must have pulled him there.

From the back of the room, tutor Jacob Benson addressed the class. "The question for dispute is this: Whether the religious revivals of this century were of God or of men. Asa Rush has been assigned to defend the position they were of God; Eli Cooper, the position they were of men. As usual, each man will make a statement, after which the dispute will begin. Rush will go first."

Asa pulled at his shirt as though it didn't fit. He licked his lips, which had suddenly become two parched desert mounds. He summoned his opening thoughts to present themselves for duty, but cowards that they were, they remained in hiding within some dark corner of his mind.

But he had to say something.

His training came into play. Restate the question of the dispute. It would give him extra time to coax his thoughts out into the open.

Just as Asa opened his mouth to utter his first sound, a student he didn't know leaned over to another student sitting next to him and said in a voice too loud, "Poor devil. Whose mother did he murder to draw such a god-awful position to defend?"

The class laughed.

"Whittier, wait your turn," said the tutor, but from his grin, he clearly appreciated the humor as much as anyone.

The attitude behind the comment did not surprise Asa. He knew his Christian beliefs would be challenged at Yale. Having been founded by ministers, the institution had forsaken its spiritual roots. When Asa arrived on campus, he understood he would be one of four men at Yale who held to traditional Christian beliefs.

"Like Daniel walking into the lion's den," someone at church warned him.

"Not so," countered Dr. Dwight. "It's much worse than that. Lions are brute beasts. Asa will be facing an adversary far more crafty and just as deadly; a better analogy would be the magicians Jannes and Jambres in Pharaoh's court, who could charm snakes and win the Pharaoh's ear and enslave a nation."

Dr. Timothy Dwight was the reason Asa had applied to Yale. The new college president, a conservative preacher, made no secret of the fact he was looking to recapture the spiritual ground that had been lost at the institution. To do so, he needed soldiers. Asa enlisted.

Contrary to what the classroom wag had just said, Asa had welcomed the challenge to defend the acts of God in colonial history. What they didn't know was that he had a secret weapon for this dispute. If only he didn't have to stand in front of so many eyes when he used it.

He cleared his throat.

"Events of . . . um . . . the events of the decades . . . um, no. Wait."

Asa squeezed shut his eyes. Why was it that the same mind that hummed like a well-oiled machine alone in his room, chugged and started fitfully under public scrutiny?

"Take . . . take . . . um, taking up the subject on general grounds," he said, ". . . um, I . . . I mean, we ask, Whether the religious revivals of this . . . of this present century were of God or . . . or man. It . . . it is clear, once all the facts are assembled, that . . . um, that it is not only reasonable, but . . . um, prudent to conclude that the revival was from, . . . um, was from God."

Asa's opening statement was painful for both speaker and listener. Yet somehow he managed to assemble the facts of his argument—that in response to the influence of the declining morals of England, God raised up men of courage to call the colonies back to God. Men like Cotton Mather, Solomon Stoddard, Jonathan Edwards, George Whitefield, and Gilbert Tennent. As a result, God blessed their efforts with the unmistakable outpouring of the Holy Spirit.

"So . . . um, so while human agency played a part—for that, that is how God chooses to work in this . . . this world—the accounts of the day, both the written record and verbal accounts that . . . that, um, have been passed down to us . . . um, without blush or um, shame . . . um, shame, declares the events in question to be uniquiv . . . um, unquivic . . ." Asa cleared his throat. "Undeniably, from God."

Taking a half-step back, he exhaled, letting his knotted shoulders slump.

Silence followed.

He looked at the other students. Many of them were occupied by their own thoughts. Some scribbled on paper or in the margins of their books. A few looked at him, apparently expecting him to continue.

"Um . . . that's all," he said.

To Asa's left, Eli Cooper stood facing him, his arms folded, with his chin resting in his hand. Saying nothing, he stared at Asa. Not moving. Not blinking.

Asa nodded at him to indicate he was finished.

Eli stared.

Asa motioned with a hand.

Eli stared.

Asa said, "I'm . . . um, done. Your turn."

Finally, Eli Cooper turned to address his peers. He said, "Do not be swayed by my opponent's eloquence. God had little if anything to do with the events of the so-called revivals of the 1730s and '40s."

The classroom nearly came apart at the seams with laughter. Asa's face burned.

With a strong voice, Cooper continued: "The events of those decades are a shameful smudge on our nation's colonial history, the calculated invention of a band of unscrupulous New England ministers in an attempt to revive not the people but a dying Puritan religion that had been their bread and butter for nearly a century.

"Facts? My worthy opponent dares to call his offering facts? I'll give you facts:

"Fact. Upon careful scrutiny, the so-called Great Awakening was not that great and failed to awaken much of New England. The geography of recorded revival events is checkered at best. While enthusiasm ran high in the Connecticut Valley, it was barely visible along the Hudson River Valley. In fact, one minister wrote following the preaching of

George Whitefield that he could observe no further influence upon his people than a general thoughtfulness about religion. Had God shunned them?

"Fact. The so-called fires of revival spread where promoters of revival set them. The celebrated Mr. Whitefield followed a carefully planned preach-and-print strategy. He employed a man by the name of Seward who was a skilled and aggressive publicist, a stockjobber in London whose advertisements bore the same hyperbolic stamp as those he later placed for Whitefield. New England was fairly papered with Mr. Whitefield's sermons. I suppose Mr. Rush would have us believe that the very printing presses Mr. Whitefield used were possessed by the Holy Spirit!"

Laughter.

"Fact. In a popular handbook on how to promote revival through preaching, Isaac Watts stresses style and substance while using the art of oratory. Watt encourages would-be revival preachers to exert power over men's fancies and imagination. He urges them to practice his prescribed methods until they can rouse and awaken the cold, the stupid, and the sleepy race of sinners. I ask you, Why would an all-powerful God need to stoop to rhetorical tricks to spark the fires of revival, when in the Bible He managed to communicate well enough through the mouth of an ass? Or is it possible that during the time in question, God used the same method as He did with Balaam?

"Fact. While the revivalist historians are fond of portraying the revivals as unifying in nature, they were nothing of the kind, as the battle between Old Lights and New Lights attests. Indeed, the revival drove a wedge between churches and between members and clergy within churches. Moreover, in that day anyone who dared call attention to the harmful side of the revivals was singled out, harassed, humiliated, and vilified. This, by so-called renewed and refreshed souls within the revival movement.

"No, gentlemen. The revival was not of God. Generated by men, its fruit resembles nothing to what Mr. Rush and others would have you believe. Every aspect of the so-called fire from God can be explained away in natural and economic terms. It was nothing more than a combination of events, such as the increasing population of the colonies, the growing number of printing presses, the increasing circulation of newspapers, and the rhetorical theatrics of a handful of men who were attempting to breathe new life into a dead religion. That, gentlemen, is the true history of the 1730s and '40s.

"As for the Holy Spirit? All I can say is that there was little holy and nothing spiritual about those days."

Eli Cooper stepped back and folded his hands behind him, signifying he was finished.

The other students in the room stared with slack jaws. Not a one of them was dozing or staring out the window. No one was scribbling mindlessly in the margins of their books. To the man, they leaned forward, eager to hear more.

Which was fine with Asa. He intended on giving them more. He, too, had been impressed with Eli Cooper's rendition. The rendition, not the facts. Cooper's interpretation of events had goaded Asa to action. It was time to bring out his secret weapon.

The tutor cued him. "Citizen Rush, care to respond?"

But he didn't mean it. A half-grin on the tutor's face warned Asa that he'd be a fool to take this any further. The tutor—probably because this was Asa's first disputation—was being generous, providing a way of escape. Asa would be a fool not to take it.

With a half-nod and a sigh, Asa returned to his chair, the same chair that had been his secure island of anonymity only moments before. Only he didn't sit down. Reaching under the chair, he pulled an old leather-bound volume from his haversack.

Returning to the front, where a grinning Eli Cooper awaited him, Asa said, "I . . . I . . . um, have in my possession, a journal. A first-hand account of revival events on the dates in question."

He opened the journal to reveal page after page of elegant old-school penmanship. At that moment something happened. Just holding the book seemed to calm him. Seeing the carefully penned words on the pages gave him courage. It was as though the spirit of the journal's author had come to his aid. Asa was not alone.

He said, "This journal describes in detail the spiritual condition of the town of Havenhill, before and after revival." To his amazement, he was speaking calmly and without stuttering. "The author of the account, Josiah Rush, my grandfather, describes the people he had grown up with as a once happy and productive town. However, having become infected with a spiritual malady, which he termed soul-sickness, they became unhappy and unproductive. They'd lost the joy of living, the joy of relationships. Josiah Rush prayed for them, and after much prayer he records how the Great Physician cured the entire town. He relates that the change in them was so swift, so remarkable, that there could be no other explanation than God did it. God, gentlemen. For no man can in a single meeting transform the hearts of an entire town so dramatically and so completely."

"Nonsense," Eli Cooper said. "It's an old preacher's trick, perfected by Solomon Stoddard and passed down to his grandson, Jonathan Edwards, who freely published it among the colonies. It's a simple method. First, you prepare the people by telling them the signs of revival, so that they will recognize the visitation of God when it comes. According to Stoddard, these signs are threefold: the quickening of the saints, sinners converted in an extraordinary way, and the unconverted grow more religious. Notice how general these signs are, gentlemen.

"Then, having set the stage, you warn the people to be ever vigilant for these signs, and to alert others immediately to them if you should happen to see them, for no one should miss out on proclaiming the Acceptable Year of the Lord! Now, what do you suppose happens after that? The dear saints, ever eager for a visitation of God, primed and vigilant, will see signs of revival everywhere! And if they don't see them, they'll fabricate them! I dare say a people so primed and eager could look under their beds and see revival among the dust balls!"

Laughter ripped through the room.

"You weren't there!" Asa shouted at Eli Cooper. "You couldn't know.

How easy it is to malign something about which you did not see, nor could you comprehend!" He held up the journal. "This is the faithful record of an eyewitness to history!"

"Voltaire," Eli said.

"What?" said Asa, not understand what a French philosopher had to do with anything. "My grandfather . . ."

"Voltaire," Eli said again.

Asa waited for him to continue.

Eli just looked at him.

So Asa continued. "This record of revival is penned by an educated man; a man without guile; a man who . . ."

"Voltaire."

Asa waited for more. All he got from Eli Cooper was a grin.

"My grandfather, Reverend Josiah . . ."

"Voltaire."

Asa stared.

Eli stared back.

"If you have something to say," Asa said, "say it!"

Eli bowed slightly. "Thank you for asking." Turning to the assembled students, he said, "Let me tell you about Reverend Josiah Rush, something that his grandson would not want you to know. He was an arsonist. Preaching by day, setting fires by night."

Asa recoiled as though slapped. "He was not! Those charges . . ."

"There used to be a saying in Havenhill: 'Where there's smoke, there's Josiah Rush.'"

Laughter.

Asa was nearly beside himself. The dispute had gotten personal. His family honor was at stake. "My grandfather . . ."

"Voltaire!"

Hands on hips, Asa cried, "My grandfather . . ."

"Voltaire!"

Asa had had enough. Would you be so kind as to . . ."

"I put it to you, citizens!" Eli Cooper shouted. "Given two testimonies, who would you believe? That of a preaching arsonist or the great Voltaire, who said: 'Indeed, history is nothing more than a tableau of crimes and misfortunes.' Gentlemen, if ever there was a history of crimes and misfortunes it is the history which we have been led to believe was a Great Awakening!"

Asa opened his mouth to reply, but he was out-voiced by a roomful of students who were on their feet shouting:

Voltaire!

Voltaire!

Voltaire!

The dispute was clearly over. And there was no doubt as to who the popular winner was. Some of the students were standing on their chairs. Even tutor Jacob Benson had unfolded his long legs and was on his feet, caught up in the chaos, his fist pumping the air, his voice one with the masses.

Asa stood alone.

Then, as if his victory was not yet complete, Eli shouted over the din, "And what do we do to those who perpetuate the evils of our past?"

"Off with their heads!" someone shouted.

Everyone took up the chant.

"Off with their heads!"

"Off with their heads!"

"Off with their heads!"

Asa knew they didn't mean him. They were just giving voice to the popular sentiment of the day to all things French. At least, he hoped that's what they were doing.

But as the chanting continued, the faces of the men in the room changed as though a dark cloud had overshadowed them. Their voices sharpened to an edge, the kind that turns a crowd into a mob, as though evil was egging them on, looking for the slightest excuse to let loose the dogs of destruction.

It was at that moment that Asa Rush knew his days at Yale College would be more perilous than he ever dreamed they'd be.

ABOUT THE AUTHORS

Bill Bright passed away in 2003, but his enduring legacy continues. He was heavily involved in the development of this series with his team from Bright Media and Jack Cavanaugh.

Known worldwide for his love of Jesus Christ and dedication to sharing the message of God's grace in everything he did, Bill Bright founded Campus Crusade for Christ International. From a small beginning in 1951, the organization he began had, in 2002, more than 25,000 full-time staff and over 553,000 trained volunteer staff in 196 countries in areas representing 99.6 percent of the world's population. What began as a campus ministry now covers almost every segment of society, with more than seventy special ministries and projects that reach out to students, inner cities, governments, prisons, families, the military, executives, musicians, athletes, and many others.

Each ministry is designed to help fulfill the Great Commission, Christ's command to carry the gospel to the entire world. The film *Jesus,* which Bright conceived and funded through Campus Crusade for Christ, is the most widely viewed film ever produced. It has been translated into more than 730 languages and viewed by more than 4.5 billion people in 234 countries, with 300 additional languages currently being translated. More than 148 million people have indicated making salvation decisions for Christ after viewing it live. Additional tens of millions are believed to have made similar decisions through television and radio versions of the *Jesus* film.

Dr. Bright held six honorary doctorate degrees: a Doctor of Laws from the Jeonbug National University of Korea, a Doctor of Divinity from John Brown University, a Doctor of Letters from Houghton University, a Doctor of Divinity from the Los Angeles Bible College and Seminary, a Doctor of Divinity from Montreat-Anderson College, and a Doctor of Laws from Pepperdine University. In 1971 he was named outstanding alumnus of his alma mater, Northeastern State University. He was listed in Who's Who in Religion and Who's Who in Community Service (England) and received numerous other recognitions. In 1973 Dr. Bright received a special award from Religious Heritage of America for his work with youth, and in 1982 received the Golden Angel Award as International Churchman of the Year.

Together with his wife, Vonette, he received the Jubilate Christian Achievement Award, 1982–1983, for outstanding leadership and dedication in furthering the gospel through the work of Campus Crusade and the Great Commission Prayer Crusade. In addition to having many other responsibilities, Bright served as chairman of the Year of the Bible Foundation, and he also chaired the National Committee for the National Year of the Bible in 1983, with President Ronald Reagan serving as honorary chairman. When Bright was named the 1996 recipient of the one-million-dollar Templeton Prize for Progress in Religion, he dedicated all of the proceeds of the award toward training Christians internationally in the spiritual benefits of fasting and prayer, and for the fulfillment of the Great Commission. Bright was also inducted into the Oklahoma Hall of Fame in November 1996.

In the last two years of his life, Bright received the first Lifetime Achievement Award from his alma mater, Northeastern State University. He was also a corecipient, with his wife, of the Lifetime Inspiration

Award from Religious Heritage of America Foundation. In addition, he received the Lifetime Achievement Award from both the National Association of Evangelicals and the Evangelical Christian Publishers Association, which also bestowed on him the Chairman's Award. He was inducted into the National Religious Broadcasters Hall of Fame in 2002. Dr. Bright authored more than one hundred books and booklets, as well as thousands of articles and pamphlets that have been distributed by the millions in most major languages.

Bill Bright celebrated being married to Vonette Zachary Bright for fifty-four years. They have two married sons, Zac and Brad, who are both actively involved in ministry today, and four grandchildren.

Jack Cavanaugh is an award-winning, full-time author who has published sixteen books to date, mostly historical fiction. His eight-volume American Family Portrait series spans the history of our nation from the arrival of the Puritans to the Vietnam War. He has also written novels about South Africa, the English versions of the Bible, and German Christians who resisted Hitler. He has published with Victor/Chariot-Victor, Moody, Zondervan, Bethany House, and Fleming H. Revell. His books have been translated into six languages.

The Puritans was a Gold Medallion finalist in 1995. It received the San Diego Book Award for Best Historical in 1994, and the Best Book of the Year Award in 1995 by the San Diego Christian Writers' Guild.

The Patriots won the San Diego Christian Writers' Guild Best Fiction award in 1996.

Glimpses of Truth was a Christy Award finalist in International Fiction in 2000.

While Mortals Sleep won the Christy Award for International Fiction in 2002; the Gold Medal in *ForeWord* magazine's Book of the

Year contest in 2001; and the Excellence in Media's Silver Angel Award in 2002.

His Watchful Eye was a Christy Award winner in International Fiction in 2003.

Beyond the Sacred Page was a Christy Award finalist in Historical Fiction in 2004.

Jack has been writing full-time since 1993. A student of the novel for nearly a quarter of a century, he takes his craft seriously, continuing to study and teach at Christian writers' conferences. He is the former pastor of three Southern Baptist churches in San Diego county. He draws upon his theological background for the spiritual elements of his books. Jack has three grown children. He and his wife live in Southern California.

LOOK FOR STORM

THE THIRD BOOK IN THE GREAT AWAKENINGS SERIES, IN SPRING 2006

The Great Awakenings was an incredible era of national spiritual revival and controversy and one of the greatest periods of American religious history. Award-winning authors Bill Bright and Jack Cavanaugh explore these days of revival in their four-book Great Awakening series that shows the personal and spiritual upheaval that occurs when the Holy Spirit stirs the waters of our souls.

Drawing from historical references of the Second Great Awakening, *Proof*—the first book in the series—portrays the dynamic personal role of the Holy Spirit. When his daughter experiences a life-changing conversion to Christianity, a celebrated New York attorney takes the Holy Spirit to court in this dramatic courtroom thriller.

Set during the French Revolution, *Storm*—the third book in the series—portrays how prayer and revival on the campus of Yale College defeated the enemies of the early republic and reclaimed the nation for God.

"The Great Awakenings series will have readers waiting with Left Behind–like anticipation for the next episode."
—*Christian Music Planet* magazine

Available Wherever Fine Books Are Sold

Enjoyment Guarantee

If you are not totally satisfied with this book, simply return it to us along with your receip a statement of what you didn't like about the book, and your name and address within 6 days of purchase to Howard Publishing, 3117 North 7th Street, West Monroe, LA 7129 2227, and we will gladly reimburse you for the cost of the book.